The Crossing at Farrenhall

Andrew Wood

Dreamsphere Books
Winnipeg, Canada

Published 2024 by Dreamsphere Books, an imprint of Story Perfect Inc.

Dreamsphere Books
PO Box 51053 Tyndall Park
Winnipeg, Manitoba R2X 3B0
Canada

Visit http://www.dreamspherebooks.com to find out more.

The Crossing at Farrenhall

Prologue
A Taste of Winter

The Winterwood was always cold, but this would be a season colder than most. The Wolf trudged slowly through knee-high snow, crouched low against the howling wind. From a grim, unmoving blanket of gray that smothered the sky, flurries of snow billowed past, plastering the bare, skeletal trees of the forest and forcing them to dance. They groaned like wounded beasts as the storm painted them white, the slow rumble of quiet winter thunder like a warning growl.

The Wolf kept moving. Westward, away from the heart of the Winterwood. There was nothing left for him there, nor for his pack mates. They followed him now, their footfalls soft in the heavy snow, their scents masked by the stale air. Instinct older than the scent of the forest told him how wrong this quiet was. The woods had always cared for the wolves. The smell of flowers and pines, the taste of hot meat and blood, the howls of his pack mates, these were the hallmarks of home, the same as it had been for his forebears, and all the wolves who'd come before.

But now the heart of the forest was silent. The food was gone, driven west, and the Wolf's nose chased a distant scent, so faint he wasn't even sure what it was. His growling stomach urged him to follow and follow quickly. He hadn't eaten in three weeks.

He could feel his bones pressing up through his skin, his shaggy, gray fur almost useless against the biting cold. What *was* that smell? Why did it make his hackles rise?

He pressed on, as did his pack mates. There were only three of them left, a she and a he who'd sired pups together, and another she. The others had passed into the Long Sleep. The pups had been first. Each morning, the Wolf expected to awaken to find the rest gone, too. Or maybe it would be his turn to enter the Long Sleep. His stomach gnawed at him.

He didn't realize he'd stopped until one of the shes nudged his hindquarters. He looked back to see her questioning yellow eyes. There was hope in that gaze, still. And hunger too. They trusted him. He had to keep moving, chasing that scent.

Twilight descended over the Winterwood as they trekked through the snow. The trees around them grew dark and twisted, like the sallow, flesh-less remains of forgotten prey. There was a desolation to this place. This was a cold winter. Colder than living memory. Colder, maybe, than what would ever be remembered.

The silence only deepened with nightfall. No chattering birds, no angry squirrels, or foraging rabbits. No gentle stirring of the snow beneath tiny feet. Nothing at all, save the wolves and the crying wind. Most unsettling of it all, to the Wolf, was the absence of scents. There was one, still, that distant one that led them on, but scents were supposed to be hard to find, like a single thread buried beneath endless tangles. This one stood alone and naked. Too obvious, like a trap designed by Man. One scent. It made no sense to the Wolf. Where had the others gone? Maybe prey were hiding in their dens. Maybe they'd simply moved west themselves. But…there was no trace of them. It was like they'd never been at all.

They would be the next to disappear if they did not find

meat soon. As the shadows lengthened, the Wolf urged his tired body into a trot, determined to gain as much ground as he could before they were forced to take shelter. One of the shes howled, but there was no answering call. There hadn't been in weeks.

The Wolf could feel the end approaching. Could feel it in his marrow. Could smell it on his own breath. His body was weakening, the need for meat overwhelming. Why was this happening? Winters were always difficult, food always scarce, but this was beyond anything he or his pack mates had ever experienced before. The haunting emptiness of the deep, dark woods, the tepid staleness in the air, as if nothing had walked through it in a hundred seasons. Something terrible had happened to the Winterwood, but the Wolf was incapable of understanding further than that. He wasn't sure he'd want to, even if he could.

The Wolf stopped again. His pack mates nudged him, but this time he knew he'd go no further. He shut his eyes. It took effort to even remain on his feet. The wind assailed him like a rolling river, trying to take him. The exhaustion, the hunger, it was too much. Every instinct screamed at him to fight, demanded him to push forward, but... *The Long Sleep comes.*

And then there was something. The Wolf's eyes snapped open. His pack mates turned in perfect unison, sensing it too. For a moment, the smell they'd been trying to follow had been overlapped by another, shining clear as the moon, but the wind had ripped it away again. The Wolf turned, head tilted back as he searched. There! A phantom scent fighting valiantly against the drifting storm.

Meat! A swell of hope and hunger whirled with the snow, and he bounded after the scent, his pack mates loping to follow. The smell was an old one, but there was a freshness to it, too.

Something had fallen nearby. Catching the smell again, the Wolf adjusted his course, racing at full speed.

Yes, it was unmistakable now. His hunger was like a parasite gnawing at his insides, but he'd soon rip it free. This was it. This was all they needed. The carcass could keep them moving for days yet if it was large enough. Maybe they really could reach the edge of the Winterwood. Surely there would be warmth there, and new packmates and pups, and more food than they could ever hunt. Beyond the Winterwood. Beyond the stillness. There, they would find life again.

The body appeared in the heart of a small clearing. The Wolf slowed his gait, dropping into a crouch as he crept along its outskirts, careful to stay within the crooked shadows of the trees. The Wolf sniffed the air as his pack mates came alongside him, tongues lolling as they panted. The wind was stale, carrying with it only the whisper of death, and, more importantly, meat.

It was an elk, an adult buck, judging by its wicked antlers. The animal was lying prone on its side, back to them, hindquarters and legs submerged in the snow. The Wolf couldn't wait any longer. He stalked from the darkened ring of trees, advancing on the fallen elk. His stomach snarled, but instinct kept him in check while he circled the animal, sniffing the air cautiously. His pack mates followed; he could smell their impatience, their desperation.

The Wolf sniffed at the fallen beast's tawny fur, tail snapping back and forth, before nudging it gently with his muzzle. It did not stir. His lips peeled back, no longer able to resist the thunderous roar of his stomach. His fangs sank into cold flesh, and he began to tug.

Blinding pain. An explosion of snow and blood. The Wolf tried to howl, his mouth full of fur and flesh, as he was wrenched to one side. The elk ripped the antler free from his throat and staggered upright, its legs buckling under itself as it rose. The Wolf fell, panting and whining, but he was no longer able to rise. His pack mates snarled, leaping for their prey in unison.

The elk came at them like a wolf itself, antlers slashing, hooves hammering. The Wolf lay in the snow, feeling his own lifeblood pump from his throat, as one by one he watched his exhausted pack mates fall before the relentless assault. He could feel the shadow of the Long Sleep passing over him.

The once-fallen elk stood triumphantly over his slain pack mates, antlers smeared with red. It turned its head to stare at him. The right half of its face was gone, stripped to bare bone. Blackened, ice-edged flesh framed teeth still clamped over a pale tongue. A sightless eye rolled loosely in its socket before slipping out, landing softly beside the elk's hoof.

Then it turned, head wobbling precariously over a bloodless wound the Wolf had failed to notice, and lumbered into the line of trees, where it was lost to the swirling snow and the darkness of dusk.

The Wolf struggled to rise. That thing...it lived, but there had been no scent other than the faint smell of meat. Old meat. He whimpered for his pack mates, but they didn't stir. He was so hungry. The meat was gone, walking when it shouldn't walk, smelling of death though it hadn't been hunted. The Wolf didn't know what to make of it, but like the silence of the Winterwood, he wanted to run from it as far as he could. He couldn't run any longer. At least, with blood seeping down his throat, he felt warm again, if only for a moment.

The journey was over.

Chapter One
Whispers of the Wood

Haegar left his axe embedded in the tree and stepped back. He planted one hand against his aching back and stretched, groaning softly to himself as he tried to assuage pains that he could never manage to fully banish anymore. With his hand still on his back, he turned to frown up at the sun. It had begun its westerly descent, drifting toward the sapphire edge of the flat horizon. To the east lay the heart of the Winterwood, an endless sea of stocky, solid trees, all with empty branches and obsidian bark that stretched into deep shadow beneath heavy clouds. Under those same branches, the grunts of working men and the whickers of horses played out alongside the rhythmic chopping of axes. As familiar a sound to the Winterwood as any birdsong.

"The first storm of winter," Haza said from beside him. He leaned against the tree with arms crossed, a languid expression on his narrow face. He was a thin, bespectacled man, tall and knobby like a Winterwood tree. His long, shaggy hair was closer to a dusty brown rather than true Ruthborne red. "Do you think it'll reach us tonight?"

Haeger glowered up at the storm. "Just our luck," he murmured. "It's bloodied early." Two weeks early, in fact. They might not be able to reach the season's quota, if they didn't hasten. He wiped his brow with a handkerchief before shoving it back into the pocket of his gray overcoat. He reached down with gloved hands and seized the handle of his axe, nudging Haza aside before ripping it free from the flesh of the wood. "A good reason for you to start pulling your weight, aye?" It wasn't much—his brother's heavy coat probably weighed as much as he did. He chuckled once before swinging his axe, driving it back into the tree with a steady *chop*.

Haza glanced at him, a frown seeping across his face. "I'm not too keen on working through a storm, Haegar. It's much too cold already, if you ask me."

"I didn't." He didn't look up. He continued to hack at the tree, his axe swinging back and forth with heavy *whooshes*. It was joined by a chorus of other blades as forty Vruskmen continued their evening work, a crescendo that climaxed with shouts of, "Falling!" and the groaning crashes of lumber. Men with saws would then cut the branches from the trees, turning them into knobby logs.

As his own tree gave away with a splintering crack, Haegar relished the sound of it all. It was hard work. Good work. Every day, he led the men of his village, Palvast, into the Winterwood to cut down timber. Then, it would be taken to the Tagalfr, the River of Rushing Ice, and sent northward on a quest to the lumberyards. The world of Razzador was a large place, but everyone knew the best lumber came from Vrusk, and the best lumber in Vrusk came from the Winterwood. But with the wood perched on the easternmost edges of Razzador's maps, it made it all the more coveted. It would be sold to build palaces all the way in Havasa, to fuel the shipyards of Joromor, and to all the lands beyond. As his father had been, and his grandfather before, Haegar was proud to be a man of the Winterwood. It was hard work, but work the world needed.

"Perhaps we should head back?" Haza murmured, his eyes still on that distant line of shadow. "If it's going to storm through the harvest festival, we should help the village prepare."

"We are helping," Haegar spat. "By working. Grab an axe, Haza."

Haza sighed and sat against the tree he'd just felled. As he slung his axe over his shoulder, Haegar glowered at his brother. "What do you think you're doing? Stop loafing. We've got a good hour of sunlight left."

Though two years Haegar's senior, Haza had always looked the younger of the Ruthborne brothers. His eyes were blue as the sky, his nose hooked, and his beard trimmed short, almost in a mockery of his otherwise long hair. There was expectation in that stare, an unspoken demand. It had always been there. "Haven't we done enough for tonight?" he complained. "It's dark enough, and my fingers feel ready to break off. We should be back in Palvast before that storm arrives. Think of poor Makin." Haza nodded across the vale, toward the tiny figure taking practice swings with a crooked stick, swinging it through the air with such force he nearly toppled over.

Haegar couldn't help but smile at the sight of his son. Makin had only nine winters, but he was already eager to prove himself a man. The boy had dropped his stick and was watching in wide-eyed fascination as the men of Palvast moved around him. He stared intently as Torvust, a giant of a man with a mane of wild black hair and shoulders wide enough to carry an entire log, demonstrated the technique of his axe swings. When the boy noticed Haegar looking, he waved eagerly.

"You shouldn't have brought him out here," Haza muttered, crossing his arms and drawing his fur coat tighter about him. "It's much too cold, and there are too many sharp things. It's no place for a young boy."

Haegar blew out a long-suffering cloud that quickly evaporated. He raised a hand and brushed snow from his long, curling crimson beard. "He's as old as I was when Father brought us here for the first time, aye? The boy needs to see what real Vruskmen must do to survive in this place."

Haza plucked his spectacles from the bridge of his nose and wiped the lenses with a gloved thumb. "Father had a very poor sense of what was right for a boy. I used to think you were as miserable out here as I was, you know. Seems you grow more like him with each passing season. Hewn from the same unyielding oak."

Haegar made no reply, not knowing if Haza meant it as insult or not. He wasn't sure what his brother thought of old Kazzin Ruthborne, now that the man was gone. *Probably not an ounce of gratitude behind that thick skull of his.* With another derisive snort, he made his way to the next tree, not waiting to see if his brother would follow.

"Papa!" came Makin's shout. The boy came scurrying up, his eyes wide. "Let me cut down the next one! I can do it!"

Haegar swept up his son in one arm, bringing him to his shoulder, where the boy sat giggling opposite his axehead. "Oh, you think you're big enough, aye?" He nodded up at the great, leafless giant that towered over them. The tree was like an ancient fortress, its branches walkways and parapets that had suffered no defeats, piercing the sky defiantly more than fifty paces overhead. "These trees have stood for a hundred years or more!" He fixed the boy with a serious frown. "Can the mighty Makin Ruthborne cut them down?"

"Yes!" Makin declared, his tiny face fixed with the stern seriousness of a starving wolf. Much like his father, Makin had inherited a mane of wild red hair. His skin was pale and dusted with freckles, but he had his mother's dark, studious eyes.

"Let's find one suitable for you, then," Haegar said, turning to survey the lumber camp. They'd been working to fell the Westwound Nook for the better part of the year, and Haegar was confident they'd have the valley cleared by the end of spring. Vruskmen were working along the outer ring of trees, chopping and sawing. The mules then dragged the logs to the nearby spring which would carry them westward. Eventually, a several day's march from where they now stood, the water would join with the Tagalfr and carry the lumber into the arms of waiting merchants. It was a proud and noble work, no matter how difficult or dangerous. Despite Haza's misgivings, Haegar knew his son would learn the importance of their duty, as he would no doubt teach his own sons one day.

Haza followed behind him as they walked through the field of stumps, a worried expression still clinging to his face like a patchy beard. "Do you remember when Father tossed you in that stream for arguing with him? I remember how long it took the color to return to your lips. I can think of a hundred better teachers than Father. And that's in Vrusk alone."

"Only things in life worth teaching are right here," Haegar growled, barely able to keep the bite from his tongue. "This, Haza. Solid work. Real work. That's what our father taught us. You can read all the books in Razzador, but not one will show you how to light a fire or skin an elk." He sighted a young, knee-high sapling standing in the dark shadow of a towering oak. He placed Makin on the ground and held out his axe for the boy. "Here. See if you can topple this monster, aye?"

Makin grinned as he haphazardly holstered the heavy handle of the axe, wobbling with the effort. It stood nearly as tall as he did. While Haza looked on in disapproval, Haegar helped the boy steady himself and made sure that the razor-sharp axehead was well away from his face. "Hold it here, boy," he said, adjusting his son's hands to better grip the handle. "When you swing it, swing it good, aye? Mean it, or else the tree will turn you away. Trees don't bow to men who don't mean it. Right at the base. There you go."

"Aye, Papa," Makin muttered, his face scrunching with exaggerated concentration as he sized up the sapling. Nearby, the other workers paused in their efforts, some leaning against their axes and chuckling as they watched the display.

Haegar took a step back, nudging Haza with his elbow. He was staring at his nephew as if Makin had just been sent into the next Holy War. "It's just a sapling," Haegar growled. "One swing will be more than enough, even for a boy his size."

"Children shouldn't be playing with axes."

"I think old Haza's more scared of the blade than the boy," laughed Corvil, a lanky lad who barely had six winters on Makin.

"It's not 'play,'" Haegar said, nodding to Makin. "It's work. Do it, lad."

Makin clumsily raised the axe, chest swelling with a deep breath. Then he swung, a wild, heavy blow. He went too high, missing the base, and instead lopped off a few flimsy branches, before the axe slipped from his pudgy hands and tumbled to the ground. The Vruskmen assembled around him cheered uproariously.

The boy turned, grinning triumphantly. "I did it, Papa!"

Pride swelled in his chest as he swept Makin back onto his shoulders. He seized the fallen branches and passed them to the boy, who held his prize aloft for all to see. "Aye," Haegar boomed. "Not the first mighty Winterwood to be felled by a Ruthborne, and certainly not the last."

"Unless you're Haza Ruthborne, aye," gibed Corvil, a look of disdain still hovering on his face. From behind, Torvust cuffed him, but some of the others snickered. Haza only flushed, clutching his arms tighter about his chest.

A frown appeared on Makin's face as he motioned to be let down. He scurried forward to retrieve the axe, lugging it upright with some difficulty. He held it out toward Haza with both hands. "Here, uncle, you try next. It's not scary, I promise."

Maybe it was the sincerity on the boy's face, or maybe it was the red climbing Haza's pale face, but Haegar found himself taken by a gale of laughter. Haza flashed him an indignant look, but Haegar had already turned to find the next tree. "Back to work, you mangy scavengers," he barked. "The trees won't hew themselves."

As he went to work, he heard Makin behind him. "Uncle, did I say something wrong?"

Haza sighed. "No, of course not. Some men are meant to be woodsmen, Makin. Others are meant to be fishermen and hunters. All work that needs your hands. But others, like me, are readers and wanderers, preferring a pair of sturdy boots to an axe. Being an explorer is a noble pursuit."

Haegar's good humor was quick to desert him. He set to the tree, speaking between the rhythmic *chops* of his swings. "Is that what you were, Haza? An explorer?"

"Among other things," the man admitted quietly. He stepped into view, watching him swing. Makin looked between them, frowning inquisitively. "Not that you've ever bothered to ask."

"Is there something to ask? Some hidden talent you're saving in your pocket?" Haegar tried to focus on his work. It was an old argument; one they'd been having even before Haza had run away. Even as a boy, Haza had always been obsessed with seeing Razzador, from the western reaches of Vrusk, to the distant kingdoms of Havasa and Joromor. Haegar had never seen any appeal. The Winterwood was all he needed, and the wood needed him. He'd never been across the Tagalfr, much less seen the Grey Hinterlands or Vrusk's capital, Savisdale. Haza's obsession with the world beyond the other side of the river had never made any sense.

"Hardly any world left to explore, aye?" boomed Torvust, who stared skyward with narrowed eyes as another tree fell before him. "Nothing beyond the western maps but endless ocean. And nothing east of the Winterwood but more Winterwood. Unless you fancy going that way, Haza, but no one whose gone beyond the Forest Heart has ever come back."

Haza grimaced. "Most scholars agree that the forest has to end, eventually, and that it likely just ends with more sea. I'm not interested in becoming food for bears—the west has bastions of culture and history. Monuments to kings and kingdoms past. Libraries filled with knowledge from times long lost. That's what I want to see."

"You wasted half your life in the west," Haegar grunted as he beat the tree. His axe had bitten halfway through its trunk. "Why not go east? Into the forest, beyond the maps. That's where true adventure lies, aye? What are you waiting for, explorer?"

"Don't be ridiculous," Haza spat. He glanced down at Makin, then leveled his tone. "There's nothing out there but trees and dust. If the cold doesn't kill me first, the wolves certainly would. No one should go that way."

"We appreciate the warning," chuckled Torvust good-naturedly.

"What would we do without you, Haza?" laughed another worker. "We'd probably leave Palvast without our coats."

"What'll he warn us about next?" Corvil asked excitedly, eager to add his own taunt. "A timely warning about ear-snatchers and wood-spirits? Next, he'll tell us to pray to the God of the Highest Paths, or tell more tales about Malice."

A hush fell over the clearing, silent save for hollow chopping. The air of merriment was swept away by the wind leaving in its wake the shadow of unease. Anger closed a molten fist in Haegar's chest. His next axe blow fell with more force than he'd intended, flinging shards of wood in every direction.

"I won't have you speak such nonsense," he said, turning to face the young woodsman. "This is the Winterwood. Such stories are not welcome."

Corvil withered. The boy was not a true Vruskman. His dark skin and hair marked him of Joromori blood. But he'd been welcomed by Palvast, as the Winterwood welcomed all who came to shelter beneath its boughs. Despite the forest's isolation from the greater Vrusk, some traditions still prevailed.

But as quickly as the boy was cowed, his resolve reignited. "What's there to fear from stories, Haegar? Real or not, what does it matter?"

"Best not to speak of wicked magic," Haza said. His face had paled. "It's bad luck. Stories or no. Keep the Malice off your tongue."

"*You* would believe it," Corvil scoffed. "But don't tell me you really believe in any of that shit, Haegar." His incredulity only grew as he found the other Vruskmen watching him quietly. "You really are as superstitious as they say in the Summerlands, aren't you?" He shook his head. "Look at you, mighty men of the Winterwood, scared of talking beasts and hungry shadows."

"No self-respecting Vruskman believes in any of that," Haegar grunted, casting a derisive glance toward his brother. "The only thing I have faith in is the strength of my arm and the sharpness of my axe."

Torvust shrugged and resumed swinging at the next tree.

"Strange things happen in the woods, sometimes. Doesn't mean it's monsters and ghosts. Men go crazy when in the shadow of the trees for too long. Still, don't tempt fate, aye?"

"Falling!" Haegar bellowed as the tree lost its life. He watched it descend slowly, gaining momentum once its weight shifted and snapped through the remaining threads of wood that kept it alive. As it crashed, he didn't feel the usual relief that labor brought him. "There's too many whispers if you ask me," he growled. It had started months ago and had only grown more intense as winter crept closer. Merchants and peddlers coming from villages deeper in the Winterwood brought strange tales with their wares. Wolves and elk approaching villages in broad daylight, men gaping at the moon, unable to remember themselves when called. A talking cat. An old man in a gray coat who disappeared when you looked at him. More troubling to Haegar were grim truths. People who drew too close to the Winterwood's heart disappeared. He could count on two hands the number of men who'd vanished through his fifty years of life. In the last month, that number had doubled.

"People are afraid of winter, is all," Haegar muttered as he moved on to the next tree. He could feel all eyes upon him, but he didn't care. He began to swing. He felt like he was digging at a sore, and the pain only made his anger grow. "Frightened of hard labor and short food. Whispering stories to make excuses to go over the river until spring. It's pathetic." Life in the Winterwood was hard. It devoured the weak. Leaving his axe embedded in the tree, he rounded on the workers. "We're men of the Winterwood. Strange things happen here, aye, but does that end the work that needs doing? Will you go crawling across the river like bristling cats because of a few stories?" He pointedly did not glance at Haza, but he could feel his brother's stare intensify. Haegar didn't care. "I won't abandon the home my grandfathers built in the face of an early winter. We'll weather it, as we always have. That's what makes us the true Vruskmen, aye?"

"Aye!" The men of Palvast raised their axes as one, but behind them, the reach of the storm had lengthened. Darkness fell over the forest, and the heavy blanket of its shadow covered the Seventeen Stars with a smothering hand. A cold wind swept through the clearing, banishing the cheer as quickly as it had come. Makin whimpered softly.

Haza put a hand on the boy's shoulder and drew him close. "Truth or superstition, at least let us agree not to speak of such frightening things in front of children, yes? Light is falling. I think our work is done for tonight."

Haegar wrenched his axe free and met Makin's frightened eyes. He sighed and begrudgingly agreed with Haza. "Pack camp," he ordered. "If we leave now we'll reach Palvast just after nightfall." The decision irked him. He'd planned to have his men camp out here in the grove, which would have given them some time in the morning for a few more hours of work and still be home in time to prepare for the harvest festival. If there was daylight for more work, he was always of the opinion that he should be doing it. He looked up at the darkening sky and felt the faintest shiver of the cold. He scowled and adjusted his coat. "Light the torches. Keep them burning. We move quick." It was going to be a cold night.

Chapter Two
A Familiar Sort of Cold

Haegar watched the logs drift along the surface of the stream. For a moment, the procession of mounted men around him faded away. There was only the dark surface of the water, the golden lights reflected on its face bobbing and undulating as the lumber was carried along. The stream was merely a small sliver of the Tagalfr, like a single vein of the Rushing Ice's furious, pumping heart. The Tagalfr, the greatest river in the world, that which brought life to Vrusk. It felt good to see his own work carried along by the water, soon to be bought and sold across the entire kingdom. What he did was important.

But the stream ran slower than the horses, especially when they raced against night's descent. As the logs were left behind, Haegar turned his attention to the road ahead. It ran westward, alongside the stream. The Winterwood enveloped them, thick even alongside the paved thoroughfare. Though without their summer emerald coats, the trees were still tall and imposing. Patches of snow painted them gray and white, their silvery bark glinting faintly as the torches swept past. A trail of embers followed the horsemen, illuminating the flecks of snow slowly drifting from a veiled sky.

All was quiet save for the *tap, tap* of hooves on old,

weathered cobblestones buried in a fine layer of snow, and the creaking wheels of the carts that the mules pulled. Haegar raised his torch and watched his breath materialize before him in soft puffs. With his other hand, he gently stroked Heartwood's mane, muttering praise for the stalwart horse. Though the old stallion had carried him along this path countless times, Haegar had never once lost his appreciation for the serenity of the journey.

The pristine silence was abruptly shattered by Haza's voice. "Do you think there's any credence to it?"

Haegar blinked, startled as he was snapped back into reality. He glanced at his brother, who'd brought his own horse up alongside him. A worried, wide-eyed stare hovered on Haza's pale face. "Credence to what?" he asked in a hushed voice.

"The rumors?" Haza replied earnestly, his voice a hissing whisper. "Any of them. We've been hearing about this for weeks now, and they're not fading. More and more people pass through Palvast every day. They are leaving the Winterwood."

There was no assuaging Haza when the man latched onto something. He'd always been overly interested in the old religions. Haegar shook his head. "Ghosts among the trees. The Malice driving animals mad. Vengeful gods walking night-drenched paths." He shook his head. "You sound like Mother. She was always scared of the woods."

"With reason," Haza muttered.

Haegar's fingers tightened around Heartwood's reins. "And yet, she never left. There's no truth to any of it, Haza. The Winterwood breaks men that aren't strong enough for it. Cold winters and long nights, that's the hallmark of our home. These nonsense stories are the excuses of those who cannot stay." He leaned over Heartwood and spat into the water. These rumormongers who came to Palvast, if Haegar managed to get his hands on any of them, he'd show them a real monster of the forest.

Haza's eyes narrowed, but his head swiveled to face the road ahead of them. A creeping pool of gold and red slowly revealed the path, rolling back the darkness on the surrounding trees only moments before they passed. "Perhaps you should think of your children, Haegar. Even if there is no truth to these nonsense stories, as you call them, the winters here are too harsh. What harm would there be in crossing the Tagalfr for a season? There will be plenty of trees to cut come spring."

A younger Haegar might've shouted at his brother. Might've even struck him, had he been drinking. But Haegar didn't drink any more. *And I am not Father, no matter what Haza might think.* He made himself exhale slowly. "We've had this discussion too many times, haven't we? If you want to leave Palvast, you're welcome to it. Stop using my children as an excuse, Haza. They're Vruskmen of the Winterwood, and here is where they'll stay." He glanced over his shoulder. Makin was dozing behind him, his cheek pressed against Haegar's back, breaths escaping in tiny, gentle puffs.

"So they can die here?" Haza demanded in a soft growl. "Like our parents did? Like you will?"

The man was pushing him. Haegar forgot to measure his breaths. "There's no shame in dying, Haza. We all must, eventually. Not even the gods of Joromor could keep you alive forever. I live an honest and hard life, and I do my work well. What more could I want for my children? I wish you'd given Father's life a try. You're built for it. You're a Ruthborne, just like me." *As hard as that is to believe, sometimes.*

Haza shook his head. "None of you understood me. Not even Mother."

"We knew you were stubborn," he muttered. He shut his

eyes for a moment and tilted his head back, letting the quiet of the forest descend once more. The creak of the wagon wheels, the snorting and shuffling of the horses. The sound of his own breaths. How could a Vruskman wish to be anywhere else?

"What's wrong, Makin?" Haza asked quietly.

He looked back with a frown as Makin raised his head. The boy rubbed one eye sleepily and stared uncertainly up at the sky overhead. The light of the stars had vanished, now, as the storm crept slowly in their wake, the wind ushering it to swallow the sky. "It's dark," the boy murmured.

Haegar opened his mouth to offer comfort, but it was Haza who spoke first. "I know of another boy who hated the dark. Have you ever heard of Kama'Thrail, before?"

As his son shook his head, Haegar turned his eyes back on the road. "Kama'Thrail hated the dark," his brother continued, "and where he lived, it was dark all the time, except for the stars. There weren't always just seventeen, you know."

"Really?" Makin's voice was breathless.

"There were eighteen," Haza said. The man had a strange thrill in his voice. He'd always been far too absorbed in stories, even as a boy himself. "Eighteen Stars to light the sky. Kama'Thrail always thought that was far too few—it was always dark where they lived. Never morning, never evening, just an endless night. His mother would trip on her way back from the well, spilling their water down the hill. Over and over she'd try to climb, and, as a boy, Kama'Thrail would watch.

"Then, one day, after his mother broke her leg trying to climb, Kama'Thrail had to go up to fetch the water himself. As he fumbled through the dark, he grew furious with the stars and cursed them for their feeble light. In return, they mocked him, for they were far overhead, safe from his wrath. But while the stars laughed, Kama'Thrail went to the stable and wove a rope from the hair of their horses. With it, he crept to the top of the hill and hid behind the well so the stars would not see him. After he'd tied a loop in the rope, he suddenly sprang out from hiding and threw it around one of the stars. It fought him and pulled back, but Kama'Thrail had grown strong carrying the water, and he wrenched the star from its throne in the dark.

"Using all his strength, he pulled it to Razzador and tied it to the earth. It was so massive that it lit the day, and we know it now as the sun. Every evening, the sun tries to sneak back to rejoin the Seventeen Stars, but Kama'Thrail pulls it back every morning. He'd become a tall and valiant god, who—"

"Enough," Haegar snarled. He twisted his head toward Haza, and a glimpse of Makin's enraptured face only stoked his ire. "Bad enough you fill his head with stories, but now you're talking about gods?"

"It's just a parable, Haegar," Haza murmured.

"There are no gods," Haegar said, talking now to his son, who stared back at him wide-eyed. "Never was such a thing, never will be. We forge our own paths through life, aye? Sometimes it gets dark, but the light always comes back again. You must be strong, and not be afraid." He looked forward. "There's nothing else to it."

Haza went quiet. When Haegar turned again, he found his brother had steered his horse to the back of the procession. He shook his head. Haza was a lost cause, even if neither of them could admit it.

He'd left the Winterwood after only his eighteenth winter, crossing the Tagalfr at Farrenhall and forging a path west. Haegar had never cared to learn where he'd gone or what he'd been doing in the intervening twenty years; he'd been too busy raising his own family and caring for their parents. He'd buried his mother beneath the old tree they'd played in as boys. The letters Haegar had sent for his brother to tell him of her death had gone unanswered. But then, after two decades of silence, Haza had returned. Destitute. Broken. He'd begged their father to let him return and work as a woodsman. Haegar had immediately wanted to turn Haza back to wherever he'd crawled from, and he'd been so certain his father would say the same. But old Kazzin Ruthborne had done something Haegar had never seen him do before, not even when his wife passed. He'd wept. Wept for the son who'd abandoned him. And then he'd let him stay. Less than a season later, they'd buried Kazzin alongside their mother.

For five years, Haegar had carried out his father's final, unspoken wish and let Haza stay in household, eat his food, and live alongside his wife and children. His brother had never shown any gratitude, not to their father, not to Haegar. He seemed to want nothing more than to leave the Winterwood again, but this time take his family with him. As if he suddenly cared about what happened to his family.

Calm, Haegar told himself. His deep breathing was starting to prove ineffective. He watched frosty air rise before him and fade against the black sky. *Be calm. This is not a fight worth having again.*

If Haza chose to leave the Winterwood, Haegar would not welcome him back again. Haza could live an honest life alongside Haegar's family, or he could go west and do whatever selfish thing caught his eye. Haegar didn't care anymore. He would just enjoy the silence of the wood, the gentle serenity of his home.

Silence.

Haegar opened his eyes again, his heart fluttering with a sudden unease. He hadn't noticed it at first, but now that he was listening, the absence became more notable. Where were the animals? Night in the Winterwood was always a raucous affair.

Moose and elk would sing to each other as they crashed through the forest, while howling wolves would track their paths. Swarms of chittering bats and chattering squirrels, the skittering of rats and possums and foxes were ceaseless. But now he heard nothing. Only a deep and unmoving stiffness, like that of a corpse.

The storm rumbled behind them. Haegar glanced back, wondering if he could catch a glimpse of the lightning. And he did see a flicker, only it was bright crimson. He frowned. Crimson? Was that what he'd seen…? There it was again. A flash of red, but low to the ground, bleeding through the intertwining branches of the trees. He frowned as it flickered a third time. He'd never seen anything like that before. What was it?

"Finally," Torvust boomed, causing him to start. "I need my bed like I need a frosted ale."

Haegar looked forward again and found that the end of their journey had appeared. Palvast was visible long before they reached it, like a cluster of the Seventeen Stars fallen to kindle the forest floor. The lights of the town seemed to finally banish the air of unease that had been following the Vruskmen since nightfall, and it was now laughter and raucous shouts that trailed Haegar as he led them up to the tall, wooden walls that encircled the town. He felt better already, freed from that strange uncertainty that had taken hold. *I'm spending too much time around Haza.*

"Hail!" called a man from atop the wall, raising a torch above the sealed wooden gate. Much like the walls around it, it was composed of large, formidable gray stakes, standing twice as tall as any man. "Who's there?" the guard demanded, hefting his torch higher as the procession slowed before the gate. "Trespassers? Thieves?"

"Get on with it, Sorvak, you eyeless goat," bellowed Torvust as he cupped his hands to his mouth. "You know full well who it is."

Sorvak huffed indignantly and stroked his long gray beard with his free hand. With his thick brown coat hanging heavy over his shoulders, spectacles gleaming in the torchlight, he resembled a bearded turtle poking its head hesitantly into the night. "Maybe I do, maybe I don't," he croaked. "Can't be too careful of strangers these days, aye?"

Torvust laughed. "You'll have to be careful of my axe if you make us stand in the cold a moment longer."

"Maybe you *are* Torvust," the old man scowled, "or maybe you're some foul spirit who's mastered his bitter temperament. I'd best hear some manners before I can let you in."

While the other men laughed, Haegar nudged Heartwood closer to the gate. "Sorvak," he called sharply, "we've got a boy here who's cold enough already. Save your banter for the tavern."

Sorvak bobbed his head and withdrew. The groaning of old rope and wood followed, and a puff of snow rose steadily as the town's gate swung inward, revealing pools of light beyond. Haegar sighed as he spurred Heartwood into motion and led his men home. Once the wagons cleared the gate, Sorvak closed it behind them, shutting off the night and the Winterwood.

Haegar reached over and pulled Makin into his lap before he dismounted. He smiled as he held his sleeping son against his shoulder. The exhausted woodsmen began to strip down their horses and lead them to their stables, speaking softly as they trudged through nearly five inches of snow.

Haegar looked across Palvast as his own fatigue settled over him like a smothering, too-heavy cloak. The town was slumbering; quiet save for the returning workers and Sorvak, who had settled back into his perch on the walkway along the wall, his eyes on the night. Tall buildings, all fashioned from broad logs, lined the snow-buried street. Lampposts of solid iron lit the way through the town, and the flames flickering timidly in their heads revealed the gentle veil of snow falling slowly, quietly, to dust the town. The thatched roofs of Palvast were now turned white, save for the soft glow of the lamps.

The stream filtered beneath the wall, which had a gap at its base large enough to let its water bound cargo pass under it. The stream would cut out the other side of Palvast to travel another five miles through the Winterwood before finally reaching the Tagalfr. Other than the work of men, its gentle burble was the only true noise.

Haegar's smile faded. He looked up at the black sky and the tops of a few trees silhouetted against it. Their bare peaks reaching over the wall like the claws of wretched men, reaching for aid that would never come. *It's still so quiet*, he thought. His shudder had nothing to do with the cold. "Haza," he called to his brother. The man was struggling with his saddle straps. "Take Makin inside and put him to bed. I'll be right behind you after I put away the horses."

Haza frowned as he accepted his slumbering nephew in both arms. "Is something wrong?"

"No." Haegar readjusted his coat. "It's just a cold night, is all." Haza regarded him for a moment, then nodded and departed without protest, shuffling across the pale pools of torchlight that led deeper into Palvast.

Haegar turned and watched his men, who were unloading the last of their supplies from the wagons. "Torvust," he said, stepping closer to the tall, dark-haired man. "Put another guard up there with Sorvak tonight. Keep an eye on the road until dawn, aye?"

Torvust's heavy brow rose in surprise. "Don't tell me the rumors have *you* on edge, too?"

He glowered. "It's just to put my brother's fears to rest. Just for one night. We have many cold nights ahead of us through the winter. I can't have us be anything other than confident in our own safety. We have to fulfill those work orders for old Varkoth. If we must bend a little with the wind, so be it."

With a heavy hand, Torvust reached out and clasped his shoulder, a soft smile pulling apart the frenzied mane of his beard. "You're doing a fine job, Haegar. When we're through to spring, we'll have this lot shaped into a fine crop of woodsmen. Your father would be proud."

Haegar had to force a smile. "Let's see what comes of this winter, aye?" With cowards bringing wild stories into Palvast from the east, and Haza with his fantasies of the west, what little hope he had was fast depleting. But the work would continue. It was the only thing that mattered.

Haza trudged slowly through the snow, his precious burden clutched tightly to his chest. Exhaustion clung to him like a bundle of chains, weighing down his shoulders and knees. Most days, he refused to admit he was getting old. But tonight...old blood help him, but he could feel it.

That frightened him. Fifty years was a long time to walk Razzador, but he felt like he'd seen less than a tenth of what the world had to show him. He'd seen more than enough of the Winterwood. He didn't like the cold—it was like a set of freezing jaws, gnawing incessantly on his bones. The dark was no better, either, and there was plenty of both to be found here.

He was getting old. He was running out of time to explore the world. *So why am I still here? What am I waiting for?*

The house the Ruthborne family shared sat in a dark corner of Palvast, near the western gate that would lead on to Farrenhall and the river, if one followed the road long enough. It was no different than any of the other dwellings; sturdy and tough, built by the hands of Haza's long-dead forefathers. The first pilgrims to step warily into the Winterwood had become expert craftsmen, wresting for themselves a life within the harsh forest.

Frost covered the single window that stood beside the wooden door, and the path that normally led up to the porch was buried beneath the snow. As the wind crawled across his back, Haza pushed the door open to find darkness on the other side. He closed it just as thunder rumbled. Shivering, he crept silently forward, all too aware of every creak of the floorboards beneath him.

He lit a candle and moved down the hall, past the room that Haegar shared with his wife, Tayja, and then past the one that had become his own domain. The last room at the end of the hall was where he found Rala, five years younger than her brother, already asleep. She was curled up in a ball, nestled in a veritable mountain of heavy fur blankets, her long dark hair fanned about her freckle-dusted face. Haza lifted the blankets and gently placed Makin beside her, resting his head against the pillow. He hummed to himself as he tucked them both back in, careful not to disturb their slumber. Then he stepped back, and for a moment, he watched his niece and nephew beneath the flickering candlelight.

Had he ever had a similar peace with his own brother? Haegar had always been fierce and stubborn, even as a boy. Haza could remember quivering before him, stepping lightly so as to not bring his brother's wrath upon himself. He wondered if little Makin would grow to treat his sister the same way, one day.

Haza turned to creep back the way he'd come, but a soft voice made him stop in the doorway. "Papa? Is that you?" He turned to see Makin sitting up, his eyes still squeezed shut.

"No, it's your Uncle Haza," he said. "We're back home now. You're with your sister."

Makin frowned. His voice was groggy. "Is it morning yet?"

"Not quite." Haza raised a finger to his lips. "Everyone is sleeping now. Go back to sleep."

"Uncle, were you really scared of the axe?" Makin's eyes were still sealed shut against the candlelight, but his lip was wobbling.

Haza swallowed a sigh. "Sometimes it's all right to be scared, Makin. There's no shame in it."

The boy nodded. "I'm sorry they laughed at you."

"Ah…" Haza blinked, taken aback. "It- it's all right, Makin. Get some rest now."

"Goodnight, Uncle." Makin flopped back into his blankets and snuggled against his sister.

"Goodnight." Haza smiled as he turned, and he blew out the candle's flame with a soft puff. No, Makin was nothing like his father. And he never would be, if Haza had any say in the matter. He wouldn't let Haegar do to his own children what their own father had done to them. It wasn't right. Razzador was a harsh enough world on its own; there was no need for men to force it further.

Haza staggered into his own room, where he collapsed into bed and was swiftly swallowed by the darkness surrounding him. He dreamed of cold winds and distant storms, but their shadows never grew close enough to disturb his rest. Instead, when he opened his eyes, he felt refreshed. Light filtered through the window beside his bed, painting the flower-embroidered blankets with streaks of gold.

He groaned in protest of the morning, rolling over on his side to pursue sleep. But his wracking shivers were enough to banish it entirely. He grimaced and opened his eyes again. He couldn't get used to these cold mornings. The chill of the

Winterwood never left a man. It clung to his soul like icy spiderwebs.

He sat up, his stockinged feet slapping against wood that felt like ice, and he stood beside the window to dress himself in a vain attempt to capture more heat. The sun's light felt about as useless for warmth as the Seventeen Stars.

Haza shouldered the cold in bitter silence, but he wrapped himself in two woolen shirts before he donned his coat. He sat down on the edge of his bed to rub the last vestiges of sleep from his eyes before placing his spectacles on the bridge of his nose and blinking blearily at the room around him.

It was a small corner of the Ruthborne house, more closet than bedroom, and it felt as much like a home. Despite the presence of his every possession, he still felt like he was waking in a stranger's bed, and alone at that, as if he were some sneaking intruder. A set of bookshelves lined either wall alongside him, filled to overflowing with the books he'd collected over his travels. Some were as ancient as Vrusk itself, dating back to the elder years of Razzador, when the mighty kingdom had been little more than a cluster of villages and no one had ever dared cross the Tagalfr. Haza found himself with little time to read anymore, though. The work of a laborer was a demanding one, and what little free time was given to him was usually spent sleeping. He was simply too tired to consider doing anything else.

As his eyes traced the weathered, leather-bound spines of his collection, he felt that familiar itch again. *I need to travel.* Even admitting as much sent a trill of excitement through his stomach. His journeys had taken him to every major city in Vrusk, and then through much of Havasa as well. He'd flitted from place to place like a bird trying to outrun the changing seasons, never staying quite long enough for winter to catch him. There had simply been too much to see, and so little time, to stay in one place.

I'd like to see more of Joromor, he mused as he stood and started for his bedroom door. He could forget the cold and the ache in his bones as thoughts of adventure filled him. *I'd go further north, this time, I think. I'd like to see the Mountain of the Highest Path. And maybe cross the Blistering Sea.* There was too much of Razzador for any one man to see in his lifetime, but by his blood how he wanted to try. It had been near the Joromori border that the last of his fortune had run out, and with no other place to go, he'd gone home. Back to the Winterwood.

Before he reached the door, the smell of eggs and bacon reached him, and he forgot his melancholy and eagerly made his way down the hall and into the dining room.

"Morning, Haza," said Tayja without looking back at him. She was busy at the stove, maintaining a careful vigil over a half dozen pots. "Haegar said you lot managed to clear half the Westwound Nook yesterday. I think that's deserving of a proper breakfast, don't you?"

"Don't tempt me," Haza said, fighting a yawn as he approached the dining room table. "With the festival tomorrow night, I'm not sure where I'll have room for it." He had no intention of skipping a meal, of course, but it was polite to bemoan one's growling stomach while doing nothing to slow it.

"I'm sure you'll find it, in the end," Tayja chuckled.

He frowned at the table in front of him. Of its five seats, only his was now occupied. "Where are the children?"

Tayja, still engrossed in her work, didn't look back at him, but her voice was merry as she spoke. "Still sleeping. No need to rouse them before breakfast is ready, aye? Especially not poor Makin. How did he do yesterday?"

"He was excited. Eager to learn his father's craft. And Haegar couldn't have been prouder." Haza suspected his brother cared only to see his son following what he considered to be the proper path of a Vruskman.

"Good." Tayja turned, bearing a plate laden with eggs and bacon in either hand. She beamed at him, and Haza felt more at ease. Though he'd never met his bloodless-sister before she'd joined the Ruthborne family, Tayja was, in his opinion, a most welcome addition. She was a tall and fluid woman, as quick to laugh as she was to temper, and never taking either seriously. There was a gentle grace to the way she moved and spoke, putting her immediately, and noticeably, at odds with the stiff, heavyset people around her. That, coupled with her dark skin, hair, and eyes, marked her as Havasan—not of the Winterwood, nor of Vrusk, at all.

And Haegar thinks I spend too much time around foreigners. Haza smiled privately to himself. He felt a stab of jealousy, too. In the ten years she'd been here, Tayja seemed to have adapted easily to the harsh, icy hand of the Winterwood. After traveling the world, how could she be so content to stay in a place like this? Why had the people of Palvast accepted her so readily? Haza had never found even half as much acceptance in his own birthplace as this woman had.

He didn't voice any of his frustrations, instead smiling as she laid his plate before him. "Thank you, as always," he muttered. "I think Haegar would be content to feed us snow and bark, if not for you."

"He'd probably think it tastes better, too," Tayja laughed.

Haza quickly settled into breakfast, devouring the bacon in three bites as Tayja set out three additional plates and poured milk into waiting clay cups. "Where is Haegar?" he asked from around a mouthful of egg.

"Hunting," she answered. For a moment, her eyes narrowed, but only for a moment. "They're still after a prize buck for tomorrow's feast. They've been trying for the better part of a week, now. Game has been scarcer of late, apparently."

Haza shrugged. He knew nothing of hunting, having adamantly refused to participate with either his father or Haegar over the years. "Probably moving north to escape the winter," he said. He'd never liked venison anyway. If a buck couldn't be found in time, they'd slaughter one of the old cows. Either way, the feast was going to fill him so full that he wouldn't eat until spring.

Tayja left the room to fetch her children, leaving Haza alone with his steaming plate. He stared down at it for a moment before his eyes were inevitably pulled upward, as they always were when he sat at this table. A narrow doorway led off the kitchen, through which was the living room and the front door. He could see the leather couch beside the hearth, where the family spent their frigid evenings snuggled together. The solitary chair nearby was where Haza would sit, on the rare occasion he had time to find himself with a book.

It was the thing above the hearth that drew Haza's eye. The painting hadn't existed before Haza left Palvast, which meant Haegar had commissioned it sometime later. It depicted Kazzin and Raina Ruthborne—Haza's parents. In somber hues of yellow and gray, they stood together before a blazing fireplace, holding to each other. They looked old, older than Haza remembered them. It must be how Haegar remembered them.

Raina looked meek and tired, her blue eyes lowered and her face creased in a worried frown. It didn't look like the mother Haza recalled, a gentle and caring woman who tended to Palvast's sick and elderly, who'd always had a welcome shoulder for Haza to cry upon. This fragile painting was but a shadow compared to the real Raina, a half-formed recollection and nothing more.

Kazzin Ruthborne, however, had been captured with frightening reality. Kazzin towered over his wife, and his shadow seemed to fill the room. His face was broad and pale, and a flat nose sat beneath blazing, sapphire eyes. The hair on his head was white, but his beard was still streaked with pale red. The lines on his face made his expression seem sallow and tired, save for a scowl that was anything but. It was every bit as frightening here as it had been in life. Haza had often felt the sting of those eyes, the warning in that frown. It had been the herald to anything from a shouted tirade, a heavy strike, or simply a silent glower of disappointment.

From beyond the reach of life and time, those eyes still followed Haza. He could feel his father's anger trailing his every step. And every time he sat down to eat, that phantom stare only became more heightened. For years, he'd suffered his father's enduring anger. The only escape had been to abandon the Winterwood entirely.

So why, then, did that pristine image of his father clash so readily with the Kazzin Ruthborne that he'd found upon his return home? That man had wept to see him. That man had accepted him back into his home. That man had eyes wrought of guilt, rather than rage, but he'd slipped from Razzador before Haza had found the courage to ask him why. Why had his father, who'd hated him, let him come back?

Troubled, Haza gathered his dishes and moved around the table, putting his back to the painting. It was a little better. But before he could resume his breakfast, Tayja returned, leading his niece and nephew by their hands. "Uncle!" Rala squealed. She broke free of her mother's grasp and rushed around the table. Haza stood and spread his arms wide, and she leapt at him. He swept her up as she giggled and spun her around. "Again!" she cried as soon as he stopped.

"Maybe after you've had something to eat," Haza said as he

plopped her in the chair beside him. He nudged her stomach with his forefinger. "I can hear your tummy growling from here."

Rala frowned in suspicion and wrapped her tiny arms about her chest. She'd inherited her mother's dark skin and hair, but her eyes—a biting and frigid blue—were those of a true Ruthborne.

Makin, who sat himself stiffly in the chair beside his sister, stared studiously at his plate. Haza frowned. The boy's enthusiasm from the previous evening was gone, replaced by a source-less disappointment that clouded his face.

"You'd best eat," Haza remarked, pointing with his spoon. "You wouldn't want your Mama's excellent cooking to grow cold, would you?"

Makin ignored him, turning instead to his mother, who'd finally sat with her own plate beside him. "Did Papa go without me?"

Tayja's eyes narrowed slightly. She'd clearly been expecting this. "He did," she said after a moment's hesitation. "He wanted to get an early start, Makin. We've not much time before the harvest festival; he couldn't wait."

Makin's expression only darkened. "He promised he would take me with him."

Of course he did, Haza thought incredulously. To complement the axe he'd already shoved haphazardly into his son's hands, now it would be a bow with razor arrows strung across it. What could possibly be the harm?

"We were out all day in the cold yesterday, weren't we?" he pointed out. "Look forward to spending a day in the warmth of the village. Colder days are still to come, with winter almost here. Besides, your mother could use some help with the preparations."

Makin threw him a withering look while Rala drummed the

butt of her spoon against the tabletop. "Play in the snow, play in the snow!" she chanted merrily.

When Makin, a glower still on his face, failed to be stirred by the promise of snow and fun, Tayja sighed softly and shook her head. "You can take this up with your father when he gets home, if you wish. This was his promise, not mine."

"You should make him keep his promises," the boy muttered.

They sat together in silence for a time after that. Haza slowly and deliberately ate the rest of his breakfast, mulling over his nephew's foul mood. He couldn't imagine being so excited about a day spent shivering in ankle-deep snow, trying to be as quiet and still as possible for hours on end. It seemed the opposite of what a young boy should want to do. And yet... *Perhaps he just wishes to spend more time with his father.* Ill company, in Haza's opinion.

From across the room, the unblinking eyes of his father continued to frown.

"Makin," Tayja said as she stood and reached for his empty plate. "Why don't you take your sister to the stream for a while? Make snowmen to guard the walls, aye? Just don't go into the water, and stay on this side of the gates."

Makin's stare was full of the miserable reluctance that only a young boy could muster. "Mama, do I have to? I was going to stand on the wall and watch for Papa."

Haza chuckled and crossed his arms. "You'll know he's returned when you hear his voice booming through every corner of Palvast. Go on now. Mind your mama."

"Aye, uncle," Makin murmured sullenly. He stood and beckoned for his sister, then waited by the front door with a glower plastered on his face as Rala insisted on hugging both Haza and Tayja before she would follow him outside.

Haza clucked his tongue as the door slammed shut behind them. He reached into his coat pocket and pulled out his pipe. It was an old, weathered thing, of Havasi craftsmanship. He'd purchased it while visiting the dock at a port-city, and its clay sides were chiseled with the images of ships on frozen waves, their sails forever outstretched. "Your son will have his father's temper ere he's grown," he muttered as he lit his pipe.

Tayja dropped the dishes in the washbasin. She cast a glower over one shoulder as the first puffs of smoke began to rise. "Haven't I told you not to use that sun-blighted thing in my house?"

He frowned from around his pipe before taking another pull. Its heat filled his lungs as he breathed deeply. "It warms the soul, it does. 'Forgive a man his vices when the winter starts to cling to his bones.' Akarama said that, you know. The greatest of your philosophers."

"You could still do it outside."

Haza's eyebrows rose. "In the cold? That defeats the purpose. I'll be brief, on my blood." He adamantly kept the pipe clamped firmly between his teeth. Once a decision was made, one couldn't go back on it, right? That was how he'd always tried to live his life.

Tayja shook her head as she took to washing the dishes. "You two are more alike than either of you'd care to admit. Stubborn old men. And Makin too, if he's not quite so withered yet. He shares your old, stubborn soul."

Stubborn? Haza's puffing came more steadily, indignant. "What do you think of Haegar bringing young Makin to all these dangerous places? First it was trekking to the Tagalfr with the lumber, then to cutting down trees themselves. Now he's telling the boy he'll take him hunting? He's only seen nine winters, you know."

"I trust Haegar's instincts." Tayja shrugged. "If he says Makin's ready, and if Makin wants to go, then he will go. There's nowhere safer for him than by his father's side."

"Debatable," Haza muttered, continuing to puff on his pipe. He blew a ring of smoke from between his lips and watched it fizzle away. "I'm glad Makin will spend the day here, with his family. That's what this festival is supposed to be about, right?"

"And what will you be doing to help out?" Tayja asked. "Mayor Garvim was looking for volunteers to help set out the tables in the town square. He's says we should expect to see more than three hundred people from both sides of the wood."

Haza let his lip curl. Tugging heavy tables and chairs through the snow sounded only marginally less appealing than hunting with Haegar. "I thought I'd stay home and do some reading." It really had been too long. "Seems like a nice, quiet day for it."

"I wish I could join you," Tayja said as she began to store the cleaned dishes back in the cupboard. What was that side-eyed look for? "But I'm going to be cooking all day today and tomorrow. Anyone who fancies themselves good with the stove will be at it."

"Will there be a contest again?" he asked eagerly. "For the pie?"

Tayja glanced at him and smirked. "Aye."

"Not that there's ever much competition," he winked. "But even if you're the clear winner, it's still my solemn duty to taste every contender. Don't worry, though, you'll always have my fullest support."

"It's appreciated," she remarked, not slowing in her work.

Haza lowered his pipe and finally extinguished it before placing it back in his coat pocket. He steepled his hands on the tabletop and leaned forward, studying his gnarled knuckles with worried scrutiny. *Stubborn old man. Boil my blood, but when did I become that?* "Do you ever miss home, Tayja?"

"Hmm?" She paused, one hand on her hip as she regarded him with a raised brow. "I am home, Haza."

"I meant Havasa. You grew up in Sivilan, yes?" It was Havasa's capital and had been among the first places he'd traveled to during his pilgrimage across Razzador. It was a warm and splendid place, one of the richest, most modern cities in the world. "We were there at the same time, I believe, before you left for Vrusk. A pity we did not cross paths back then. Isn't that interesting, though? It makes the world feel so much smaller than it really is."

Tayja pulled out a chair and sat back down at the table. She frowned at him. "I do miss it, in a way. It *was* home, once, and I suppose it always will be, in some fashion, no matter where I might go." A grimace crossed her face. "I was forced to leave, Haza. It wasn't safe for a woman to walk those streets any longer, not with the rebellion turning from sparks to flame." A soft sigh escaped her lips. "Why? Do you miss it too?"

"It's not *my* home." Haza puffed. The riots had been intensifying when he'd left Sivilan. He'd been tempted to stay, to witness history as it unfolded. He wondered if there were any books written on the event, yet.

"You're allowed to miss it," Tayja said with a small smile. "It doesn't have to be the place of your birth to be your home. You're not happy here, Haza. You never have been."

Haza opened his mouth to protest, but instead he closed it again as he considered the steady, curious expression on the woman's face. "I've never considered my own happiness to be terribly important. That's why I'm here."

"Why did you come back, really?" Tayja asked. She met his eyes, and a shadow passed over her face. Haza's stomach twisted.

He recognized that look, that ever-so-faint displeasure. It was the air of unwelcome that permeated the whole of Palvast. That sense of truth, that he did not belong.

He could only bring himself to shrug. It was a decision he'd questioned many times, but a part of him was still certain it was the right one. "I…thought my parents might've needed me. So I came back to help them. And you."

"You didn't know I was here," she corrected sternly. "Me or the children. It was just Kazzin, and Haegar took care of him well enough. That's not why you came."

Haza narrowed his eyes. What little comfort breakfast and his pipe had brought him withered away. He could feel the cold again. "I offered what help I could. I knew what Haegar must've gone through while I was gone."

Tayja sniffed as she stood. "How could you? You were gone twenty years, Haza. We buried your mother without you. A month later, and we would've done the same for your father. You needed somewhere to go, aye? You didn't have any other choice."

"Maybe I didn't," Haza growled, crossing his arms over his chest as he glowered up at her. "But that didn't change that I missed my family. I wanted to see them again."

The woman turned back to her stove, putting a few more pots atop it. "And you were welcomed back, aye? A fine job you've done of repaying that kindness with your endless complaints every day for these last five, miserable years."

He felt like he'd been slapped. "Haegar never welcomed me back."

Tayja rounded on him. "What's wrong with you, Haza? My husband let you stay here even after Kazzin's passing. All he asks of you is to participate in our way of life. If you hate it here, why have you stayed? If you don't want to leave, why won't you carry your weight? Even the children work harder than you."

Haza stood slowly, his anger mounting like pipe smoke in his chest. "That's not fair, Tayja. I work just as hard as anyone here, and you know that. I'm not made for life in this place, but I do my best. I get enough shit thrown at me by your husband, don't I?"

"I'm not trying to hurt you, Haza," Tayja said, her voice as stern as her flashing eyes. "I just don't think you should complain about things you're unwilling to fix, aye? If you want to leave, nothing's stopping you. Cross Farrenhall and live further west. Go to Joromor. Go to Havasa. Or wherever else you could possibly want to go. But if you want to stay with us, you're welcome, Haza. But you must be a part of this family."

Haza clenched his jaw. Protesting was useless. Arguing was fruitless. They never cared to listen. Instead, he stalked past her, drawing his cloak around his shoulders, and leaving the kitchen behind. As he passed through the living room, the eyes of his father found him again, but he didn't acknowledge the old painting with even a glance. Instead, he passed through the front door and into the cold beyond.

Chapter Three
A Festival to Remember

Haegar had woken that morning feeling foolish. The storm had passed nearly as quickly as it had come, leaving nothing more than a light dusting in its wake. Gone with it were any apprehensions from the other night. In fact, Haegar looked back on his worries with shame. He'd been letting the mood of his brother get to him. The morning was young and beautiful, the Winterwood an inviting maiden clothed in white. It was a new day, and with it came limitless promise.

That said, the hunt did not go well. A day and a night spent stalking through the cold hills of the deep forest yielded nothing for the weary hunters of Palvast. When the village came back into view as the first pink and orange rays of morning crept across the sky, Haegar exhaled, a long stream of frost escaping from between his lips. The day of the harvest festival had come. "What a disappointment."

"Perhaps we should start holding the festival earlier in the year, aye?" suggested Torvust. The man shook his shaggy head as he looked back at their cart, which, instead of being laden with prize game, was instead filled with mundane supplies and weaponry, alongside a pair of rabbits that Haegar had managed to kill when they'd suddenly fled their burrow.

"Two rabbits," Haegar growled. He unslung his quiver and dumped it in the cart, before dropping his bow alongside it. "That's what a whole hunt has come to. Two blood-cursed, scrawny vermin. If my father could see this sorry lot…"

He flinched when Torvust's meaty hand clamped his shoulder. "That's the way of things, sometimes, my friend. No sense in torturing yourself, aye? We'll butcher one of the cows and have a fine feast this evening."

Haegar didn't protest, but only because there was nothing more he could do. What Torvust said about moving the festival worried him. It had never been like this before. Last year, they'd caught and prepared seven elk for the harvest, and the celebration had lasted three days, with hundreds of folk pouring in from across the Tagalfr, crossing the Gated Bridge for a yearly chance to visit the Winterwood and celebrate the true spirit of Vrusk. These visitors always spent enough coin to keep Palvast alive nearly the whole winter, and that was not to mention the other villages who would come from the east, all converging right here to celebrate.

In turn, this would be a miserable affair, and Haegar couldn't escape feeling that it was somehow his fault. He sighed as he watched the road ahead of them. Before long, guests would be arriving, no doubt well before it was proper to do so. No one would care, however, as the guests always brought their own contributions to the feast, the labor of a year's work, to be shared in solidarity with all Vruskmen.

The gates of Palvast slid inward with a slow grind, and once the passage had been opened, it would remain so until the following evening. The sun climbed ever higher, glinting off the white tops of the surrounding trees, and painting the sky with the ethereal shades of the morning, yellow and red against dark blue clouds.

Beyond the gate, Palvast was already gripped with the throes of preparation, as the townsfolk raced to complete their final tasks before the first guests arrived. Colorful streamers had been strung along the street, stretching from one rooftop to the next, and the children had constructed snowmen all along the path, like a vigil of guardsmen to protect and welcome weary travelers. Paper lanterns in hues of red, green, and blue had been placed over the lampposts, so that when they were lit at evening, Palvast would be transformed into a place of radiant color. A light wind was blowing gently across the town, proving no threat to the decorations, and the sky stood clear of clouds, save for those over a few dark mountains creeping along the eastern sky.

"Seems like it'll still be a grand festival even without a buck," Torvust said as he stepped up beside him.

"Your wife excelled with the decorations, as always," Haegar said.

Torvust grinned. "Magda's always had the eye for it. Though I'd gladly trade it for your Tayja's flair for cooking." He laughed loudly and clapped him on the shoulder.

Haegar smiled fondly as he smelled fine cooking on the wind. Ever since her arrival, Tayja had spearheaded the food preparations for the festival. Maybe it was some outlander trait she'd inherited from beyond Vrusk, or perhaps the people of Palvast were simply poor cooks, but Tayja always prepared a feast that could make the wood itself sing in envy.

He remembered the first time he'd seen her. It had been at Farrenhall, which was as far west as he'd ever gone, and as far as ever intended. Even going to the Gated Bridge was rare, but a problem with a lumber shipment had demanded his attention. Lord Varkoth, who ruled at Farrenhall, was a fickle old man who'd tried to swindle his men out of what they were due, but Haegar had forgotten any irritation when he'd first lain eyes on

Tayja. An outsider, a Havasan, standing alone amid a sea of Vruskmen. It had been like a light had shone directly upon her, signaling his attention. She'd been a refugee, running from troubles back home. He still wasn't entirely sure what had inspired him to invite her back to Palvast, nor why she'd agreed. Neither of them had left since.

The hunters dispersed, leaving Torvust and Haegar to walk down the center street alone. It had been cleared of the previous day's snow, leaving rough cobblestones exposed to the air above. Around them, children screamed and laughed as they chased each other through the alleys between houses, pursued by baying, shaggy dogs, safely corralled by the walls that enveloped the town. The women of Palvast came laden with dishes and tablecloths, all to be set out for the evening, while the men hauled tables and chairs about, and lugged untapped kegs of wine from out their cellars. The sweet smell of pie and roasting vegetables filled the cold air, and Haegar took a deep breath, reveling in it all.

At the heart of the town was a circular clearing, its perimeter now surrounded by several stands that had been set up by the townsfolk to sell their various wares to the travelers. Assortments of knitted clothing and blankets were stacked high alongside wooden dishes and painted carvings, and all manner of baubles that could be found and touted, especially to folk coming from the other side of the Tagalfr. Most Vruskmen from outside the Winterwood, Haegar had noted, were fascinated by it. They took any opportunity they could to get close to it, but never made the choice to move beyond the river permanently. It was, in his opinion, what separated true Vruskmen from the rest of the kingdom.

A stage was set in the center of the circle, and several instruments were already waiting upon it, though Palvast's resident musicians were nowhere to be seen. Haza had picked up a lute from somewhere along his journeys, and when he could be coaxed into playing, Haegar would begrudgingly admit he was good. A hundred long tables, each sporting at least a dozen chairs, were being set up throughout the circle in broad rings, to face the stage. A pathway was left along the outer ring, and one on the other side of the yard, to allow passage back onto the main street and out the western gate, which now stood open. Before long, hundreds of outsiders would be pouring through it, and as the sun began to sink toward its western berth, the harvest festival would begin. Without that centerpiece buck though, to spearhead the roasting, Haegar didn't think he'd truly be able to relax.

Excited and merry chatter filled the circle as Haegar and Torvust made their way toward the stage, upon which Mayor Garvim stood with his hands on his hips as he watched two young boys try to position a banner bearing the Royal Crest of Vrusk—a grey-scaled dragon on a field of white—to his liking.

"Further over," Garvim snapped, his finger extending like a whip to jab in the specified direction. "They all need to see it, aye? Where's your patriotic spirit, lads!"

One of the boys winced. "It can't face every direction at once, sir. We should get another banner."

"Well, we've only got the one, so move it!" Garvim crossed his arms over his broad chest as he glowered at his charges. He was a tall, dark-skinned man, and despite his cumbersome weight, there was an air of callousness to him that was well-suited to the toil of the Winterwood. His jowls quivered when he spoke, and his gray eyes seemed permanently narrowed. What little hair left on his head was white and formed a ring around its perimeter.

"A bit early to be panicking, aye, Garvim?" Haegar called as he approached the stage. "We haven't even seen our first guest yet."

Garvim didn't smile. Instead, he hopped down from the stage and glowered at the two of them. "This is a disaster already. Three of our tables were eaten through by termites. Three! And another was plastered with mold. Tell me you two have good news, aye?"

Haegar glanced at Torvust, who rolled his broad shoulders in a shrug. "Sorry, but no." The mountainous, black-haired man held up the pair of rabbits they'd caught by the ears. Boil his blood, but they looked even smaller in Torvust's hands. "We've got nothing but this to add to the rest. I'm afraid we'll have to cull our own cattle tonight."

"Blood be damned," Garvim cursed. He busied himself with readjusting the collar of his cloak, but it couldn't hide the scowl on his face. "The stormcrows fly in droves this day."

Haegar found himself frowning. He'd seldom seen the old mayor so furious. The festival was always a stressful time, as much as it was about the relief of a year's end, but there was a black anger in Garvim's eyes. Something more than the disappointment of a failed hunt. "All this for a few tables? What else is troubling you, Garvim? There's something more."

Garvim's eyes flicked up, but only briefly. He was still fighting with his collar. "A rider from Farrenhall came just before dawn, flying as if wolves were at his heels. He spoke his word and turned about again, vanishing as quickly as he'd come."

Something stirred in Haegar's stomach. He pushed away his unease. The wind wasn't suddenly colder; it was just a trick of his nerves. *Get it together, you superstitious summerman!* "What did he say? News from Lord Varkoth?"

"News from the Old King," Garvim spat, his voice grinding behind teeth clenched in thinly veiled rage. "There will be no visitors from the other side of the Tagalfr today. Something happened west of the Hinterlands; the Kingsmen have seized control of the roads. There's no passing through, not unless you're on His Majesty's business. The revelers can't even reach Farrenhall, much less cross in time."

It was the weight of disappointment, not anger, that settled over Haegar. He nodded slowly, while beside him, Torvust crossed his arms and grumbled, "Ill news, indeed."

Ill? It was closer to fatal. The Winterwood was vast, but its people were few, and many days of travel separated them. Palvast was always the host for the harvest festival, as it was the closest to the Tagalfr and the 'civilized' country beyond Farrenhall. This made it an ideal place for the Winterwood to converge, as foreigners would pour in from over the river, eager for a taste of Vrusk's harshest land. No foreigners meant no one to sell to, and with winter arriving so early, it was likely Palvast's neighbors would swiftly turnabout and head back the way they'd come. The festival had been dealt a death blow.

The three men stood silently beside the stage, while around them the townsfolk blissfully continued their preparations. When Haegar could stand the quiet no more, he coughed once and looked up. "What should we do?"

"Nothing," Torvust replied. He looked between them, his features dour. "We can't let this ruin the celebration, not after all we've put into it, aye? You'll have to make the announcement, mayor, but wait until closer to evening. Then, we'll have a smaller affair, just us folk of the Winterwood."

Garvim reached up and rubbed the bridge of his nose between thumb and forefinger. "Aye…you're right, Torvust. But still…who does that old goat think he is, impeding the likes of us? His good, hard-working subjects? Why couldn't he take his politics north, eh?"

Torvust smiled wryly. "I'd wager he thinks he's king, Mayor."

Haegar was not about to wager a guess as to what kings and lords thought. His business was with wood and game, not war or squabbles or whatever it was noble folk actually did. "The timing is poor, but there's no fighting it. No use getting upset, unless we want to destroy our festival entirely. Keep your spirits high, Garvim. For their sake." He nodded to the passersby.

The mayor seemed to deflate, growing noticeably shorter, as he exhaled his rage with a suffering sigh. "Of course. But blood be tainted, as if we needed this, on top of all else that's happened to us this season. If I believed in any gods, I would think they'd forsaken us."

"Gods are too smart to come to places like this," Torvust said with a chuckle.

When nothing more was said, Haegar bid them both farewell and turned back into the town proper. He shoved his hands into his pockets and balled them into fists, but he forced smiles and nods whenever the people around him greeted him. Inwardly, his thoughts swirled like a dark storm, rumbling with ill intent. The more he thought about it, the more the situation stirred his anger. Garvim was right; as if dwindling game and an early winter weren't wretched enough for Palvast, now their most profitable event had been smothered. And there could be no canceling or rescheduling the festival, especially not on such short notice. There was simply too much work to do in the coming weeks. An early winter meant less time to fulfill the work orders, and in his experience, early winters tended to run long, too.

He looked up at the distant treetops as he walked, their branches like lifeless bones, straining for the sky. He could sense a change on the wind, but he didn't know it for a good omen or ill. *I hardly recognize you anymore,* he thought at the forest. *What's happening? Are you changing, or am I?*

Haegar went home, eager to strip himself of sweaty clothes

and ill thoughts. The smell of baking pie, of sugar and pumpkin and apple, all came wafting out the open windows of his home, the home his grandsires had built for *him*. At the sight and smell of it, his uncertainties melted like afternoon snow. This was where he belonged. For a moment, all he could hear was his lovely wife, making their home ever more comfortable, all while accompanied by the laughter of his children.

"I thought you were going to be late to the festival," came Tayja's mocking voice from the kitchen as he stepped through the front door.

"Just trying to avoid your cooking," Haegar announced as he relieved himself of his coat. As he walked across the living room, he could feel the stares of his parents follow. Five years, and he still could not shake his father's disappointment. *He'd never let the wood reach such an uncertain state. He would've done something.* "You'll poison me yet, aye?" he teased playfully.

Tayja met him at the doorway of the kitchen. That familiar, knowing smile was on her face as she wrapped her arms around his waist and pulled him close. Their lips touched briefly—far too briefly, in his opinion—before she pulled away. She still held him, though. "If I was trying to poison you, my love," she whispered, her eyes flashing behind her kindly smile, "you'd have died quietly in the night, never knowing the danger."

As Haegar held to the fearsome, lovely woman in his arms, he wondered how anything in the world could be amiss. As long as he had the love of someone like her, what more could a man ever want? "You're as beautiful as the day I first met you," he said quietly.

Tayja snorted. "Flattery? That's not going to get you out of comparing my cooking to poison."

"I mean it, Tayja."

She grinned again, then kissed him. "Well, I'm glad someone thinks so. I still stand out here like a tree in a clearing."

He took one of her dark, slender hands in his own and brought it to his lips. "That just means of all the seeds planted, you were the only one strong enough to take root."

She gently pulled away from him and sauntered back into the kitchen. "You're certainly in a poetic mood this morning, aye?"

"It's an old proverb," Haegar said, raising a hand to scratch the back of his head. He spared a glance over his shoulder, toward the painting. Kazzin and Raina stood triumphantly over their own home, their eyes forever witness to the providence of the Ruthborne family. They'd held each other like that for so many years; all Haegar had ever wanted as a boy to find a love like theirs. "It was something my father used to always say about my mother. He said she could've been hidden amid a thousand trees, and he'd still know which one was her."

The clamor of pots and pans caused Haegar to turn back as Tayja resettled herself before the blazing stove. Already, three pies were resting on the open windowsill, with steam wafting gently from their golden-brown tops. She laughed as she stirred a pot. "Is it victory that makes you so poetic? How was your hunt?"

Haegar's good humor was swift to crumble before the crippling wind of reality. "Cold," he said. "And uneventful."

Tayja turned, concern in her deep, dark eyes. "No luck at all?"

"Nary a hoofprint," he muttered. He crossed his arms and leaned against the doorframe, lacing one booted foot behind the other. "It's like a great wind swept the game away. There was a pair of miserable rabbits Torvust and I managed to snag, but other than that, not so much as a whisper of life. The forest never really dies when winter comes; it just goes to sleep. But this season…" Blood forsake him, but he needed a nap. Or to throttle anyone repeating those worthless stories. It wasn't just Haza, much as he'd like to blame the man. Those travelers who passed through town, those craven men fleeing the Winterwood for the season, it was them and their dark tales. The Malice turning ordinary men into blood-thirsty monsters, wolves that stood on their hind-legs like men, entire groves of trees rotting right where they grew. Or just people going missing on safe roads. Rumor planted seeds of fear in superstitious men, and if he didn't stamp it out, it could take a fetid root. *Or maybe I should just find a stiff drink. It's not possible for an entire forest to die. Think rationally.*

"An early winter means an early spring, aye?" Tayja asked hopefully. Haegar gave her a thin, false smile as she continued. "The game will come back, Haegar, no need to worry."

He nodded. He was not the worrying sort. Leave that to Haza and other foolish folk. Leave that to their whispers and stories. Haegar was a man whose troubles had only physical ramifications, and that made him frown again. "There's more." He told her about the gutted festival, the troubles in the west.

Tayja paled. "Sunfire," she muttered, using a curse from her native Havasa, as she was oft to do when surprised. "They closed the Gated Bridge itself?"

Haegar grimaced. "Thank your sun, but no. I can't imagine something so bleak." Farrenhall was the only way to cross the Tagalfr—the river was simply too vast, too deep and swift, to allow any other fording. Without Farrenhall, there would be no passage in or out of the Winterwood, and without that, the lumber couldn't be inspected by the king's officials, who had to cross and examine the work before letting it flow north. That would ruin Palvast's entire season, much less the festival. "Just the roads west of the river. Our work will go on unimpeded, at least, but the festival itself… We won't be getting many visitors. Not this winter."

Tayja turned back to her cooking and leaned against the counter, bracing herself with both hands. She blew a long, frustrated sigh between her teeth. "What are we going to do?"

He stepped up and embraced her from behind, lowering his head to rest it on her shoulder. "What is there to do? The festival will continue as planned. Garvim will make an announcement when evening draws closer, to help preserve the mood. No one needs to know before then." He thought nothing of telling Tayja. She abhorred gossip nearly as much as she did burnt pie.

"Palvast needs those travelers," she murmured. "We really need that money."

"I know." Haegar straightened and set his jaw to one side. Trading in the Winterwood was rarely needed outside of winter. The excess wealth Palvast made off the festival had helped them endure many a difficult season. He gently began to massage his wife's upper back, moving his palms in slow circles. "We'll be all right. We've been through worse, aye?" *Haven't we?* How could he be certain? He supposed that, in every man's life, one winter *had* to be the worst one. Was this his? He held Tayja close. "We're all we've ever needed, you know."

Tayja sniffed and put her own hand over his. "The children will be so disappointed… Poor Rala's so been looking forward to this."

"She'll have her celebration and fun, I promise you that. There will still be music, dancing, and a fire tall enough for all the Winterwood to see. Not to mention the finest cooking you'll ever taste from the loveliest woman in all Razzador."

"I'd like to meet this woman you keep talking about," Tayja chuckled softly. "She sounds like quite the find."

"She is." He kissed her cheek before he turned away. "I'll be back later. I'll find the children after I wash, and then I have to meet Garvim again, to work out whatever it is we're changing for tonight."

Tayja nodded wordlessly as she stared down at her cooking, her face a dark mask of worry. Haegar hated to see her so tense, but the urgency of his business forced him on. Evening would arrive before he could blink, if he let it.

He retreated to their bedroom and hastily washed himself, then donned fresh boots, along with a heavy grey coat, a red scarf and long, brown pants. He said goodbye to Tayja before he left the house and made his way back out into the cold.

The sun had nearly reached its zenith now, and it hung over them like a single yellow diamond, set in a face of endless, clear blue. Though cold, at least the weather would hold until after the festival. He passed the center of town again, where Garvim was still standing with his assistants, who were now piling wood into the pit that would become the bonfire.

It was his children he sought currently. Following Tayja's directions, he found them near the eastern end of town, close to the gate, which stood open to face the white-coated expanse of the Winterwood. The stream still burbled merrily through the large gap in the wall, wholly unimpeded by the barrier. Makin and Rala were on its bank, starting work on a new snowman. They laughed together as they rolled mounds of muddy snow and small rocks and sticks into its head to form a makeshift, smiling face.

Haza was with them, his back to the stream. One hand was folded behind his back, while the other held a small book up to his face. He used his thumb to turn its pages, and occasionally his eye would glance at his young charges, but it would quickly slip back to whatever dreary story was waiting for him.

"Aren't you supposed to be watching them?" Haegar demanded.

From behind the frayed edges of his book, Haza fixed him with a glower. "I can multi-task, you know."

Rala poked her head from around the snowman, her face splitting in a broad grin. "Papa!" she rushed him like a bloodhound, bounding up the bank with dizzying speed. "Papa, you're home!"

Haegar dropped to one knee and spread his arms wide, and Rala collided with him, giggling. He swept her up and spun her about. "Rala, the wind of the forest!" he declared. "Have you behaved while I was gone? Your slice of pie depends on what you say, mind you."

Rala furiously nodded. "I was good, Papa. I promise!"

While he spun with her, Makin approached more bashfully, his eyes downcast. Haegar placed his daughter back on the ground and she scampered back to the snowman, shouting, "Papa, look what we built! The cold man for the festival, Papa!"

"You promised you'd take me with you, Papa," said Makin quietly.

But before Haegar could address either of his children, Haza sidled up to him. "I *was* watching them, you know," he said, sniffing as he pushed his glasses further up the bridge of his nose. "They've been out here for two days now, waiting for your return. They would've spent the night out here, if their mother had let them."

Haegar glanced down at the now-closed book in Haza's hand. One finger was jammed in between its pages, holding his place. "It looks to me like you were reading."

The older man's eyes narrowed. "Yes, I was doing that, too. You see, unlike you, I was born with the ability to make more than one thing the subject of my focus. I haven't heard any news of that young, prize buck you were seeking. Perhaps you would've found something if you hadn't been preoccupied with teaching your children how to swing sharp objects."

Haegar couldn't help his irritable laugh. That gnawing, needling tone in his brother's voice was what finally dissolved the last vestige of festive cheer he'd been harboring. He straightened, faced away from his children, and balled one fist at his side. Haza looked him up and down, hesitant, but not fearful. *Give me one reason,* Haegar thought. *Just one.* But then a voice cut through his anger.

"You promised, Papa." It was Makin.

Haegar blinked, taken aback. His mouth snapped shut as he remembered that he had, in fact, promised. He'd just forgotten. *It's probably better that he didn't come, miserable as it was.* Still, it would've done the boy good to experience the harsh disappointment that sometimes came from long, cold hunts. But he wasn't about to tell his son he'd forgotten him. *Blood be preserved, I feel like my mind is everywhere but where it needs to be, these days.*

"I'm sorry," he said, dropping to one knee to better face his son. "It was too cold, Makin, and the journey was too long. Here in Palvast is where you should be, helping your mother get ready for the festival. When the frost clears and the herds return, then we'll go hunting together. And that I truly promise."

Makin's scowl only deepened. "You *already* promised, Papa." Haegar winced. He didn't like lying to his son, but it was better than telling the boy a painful truth. There would be other hunts. Too many to count.

"Your father is right," said Haza, turning on his nephew, his book still clasped tightly in his hand. *Echoes of the Fallen Gods* was the title inscribed on its dark, leather cover in golden stitching. "He knows the Winterwood much better than you do, right? He knows when it's safe to go hunting, and when it's better for young boys to stay home. Trust your Papa's judgment. It's the best I know. For this place, at least." His brother cast him a sidelong, withering glance.

He frowned as his son nodded in mute understanding before turning to rejoin his sister in the snow. Haegar gave Haza a single, stiff nod of thanks. "He looks up to you," he growled softly. Strangely, the idea wasn't as insulting as he'd first imagined. It was good that Makin already knew the value of family, no matter what stress might be placed on the bonds of blood.

"He shouldn't," Haza said with a snort. "Not if he wants to be as strong as you, someday. I can teach him little more than how to read and write properly, but Tayja can do that already."

Haegar found himself studying the dull cover of the book. It seemed every day Haza had a new one dug out from that mountainous collection of his. "What is it you're reading that enraptures you so that you forget your own kin playing by a freezing river?"

Haza at least had the grace to flush. It was soon eclipsed by an excited look as he hefted the book for Haegar to better inspect. "It's a dissection of the various religious facades of Razzador," he said, tapping the book's title rapidly. "Some of those rumors we've been hearing piqued an old memory of mine, but I've yet to satisfy that particular itch. Most religion is defunct, you know. Havasa as a whole outlaws it."

"With good reason," Haegar said with a light chuckle. He crossed his arms and settled himself to watch his son and daughter play by the stream. They scooped balls of snow and hurled them at each other, laughing as they ducked around their snowman. "Vrusk and Joromor should do the same. I wonder how many prayers it took before our forefathers realized no one was there to hear."

Haza clucked his tongue, his laugh lighter and scornful, as if he'd just been privy to some marvelous secret jest. "Far too long, I'm afraid. It took three bloody campaigns for our ancestors to realize their God-Emperor wasn't going to conquer any kingdoms, no matter what their scripture predicted. The Holy Empire tried to consolidate power, unifying its territories to prepare for some apocalypse they named the 'Malice.' But when the prophesied day came and went without incident, faith as a whole was swift to crumble. It's funny you mentioned Joromor; it's the only real place in all Razzador where you can still find the devout. Though they don't worship the True God or Gurnam Helm-King or any of the old empirical religions. They serve older, primal gods."

Haegar scratched idly at his chin through his thick beard, his interest swiftly waning. "Is there a reason you're telling me all of this?"

Haza shrugged. "It's just curious, is all. People in Havasa hate religion and folk tales, just like you do. To them, it's worse than nonsense. A frivolous waste of time, at best, and a precedent for dangerous ideas, at worst. Vrusk seems uniquely poised between the ideologies of our neighbors, doesn't it? Neither wholly atheistic nor religious. This seems the sort of place where you'd expect the stories you hear to carry with them a seed of truth. It just feels more plausible, doesn't it?"

"That gods exist?" Haegar curled his lip at the thought. He had little love for any outsiders—excluding Tayja, of course—but they had one right idea; such stories were a waste of time. *Or else dangerous.* Fear did strange things to the mind of a rational man. It was why he always made himself stay calm around his men, no matter what he might feel or hear.

"That *something* might exist," Haza said eagerly. He opened his book again, thumbing through its pages as he cradled the spine in his other hand. "The Holy Wars were fought over something, yes?"

"Aye, power and wealth, just like everything else." Haegar turned his head and spat in the snow. "Let them and their gods rot in their graves." The Holy Wars were more than five hundred years gone, now, and the patron gods who'd supposedly started them hadn't spoken a word since. Why would they start now? Here?

Haza sighed, but he nodded. Boil his blood, but why did the man have to sound so disappointed? "It's more a study of the power of ideas," Haza shut the book again, "rather than a true evaluation of the validity of their beliefs." He squinted up at the clear blue sky and grunted scornfully. "We modern men, with our higher understanding, so much wiser than those who came before us."

"You sound dubious."

"A good word, brother," Haza chuckled. "Perhaps I just worry that all things past are doomed to come again, given enough time. Every history book I've read, they start and end the same way, like you could go right from one to the next. A cyclical tale, our story."

Haegar set his jaw. These stories were bothering Haza more than he let on. There was something in the way his brother shifted, in the shadow that lurked beneath his eyes. What was that fear he saw? "You're reading too much," he muttered and contented himself with watching his children play.

The sharp clang of a bell rang through Palvast, and Haegar looked up at the nearby watch post, standing over the open gate. Old Sorvak was on his feet as he paced back and forth on the rampart, jamming a finger eastward. "Riders approaching!" He struck the bell again before noticing Haegar. He turned, cupping one hand to his mouth as he shouted, "Looks like a caravan."

Finally. He made himself exhale and went to the gate, clasping one hand to the loop of his belt. "Let them through, aye? They're a might early, but I don't think anyone will mind." Even though most travelers didn't arrive until after midday, he'd had a faint, irrational fear that no one would show up at all. He was quite pleased to have that fear dashed. *Goes to show you what worrying gets you, aye?*

Makin and Rala came scurrying up behind him, and he put out his hands, cradling the back of their heads as he pulled them close to himself. Haza lurked behind like a second shadow, never stepping into the light. All the while, the familiar clatter of wheels and ropes, the trudging of hooves and boots through the snow, came closer.

Something was missing. The caravan came without chatter and laughter, without festive song or even the shouts of impatient wagon drivers. First came a haze of an immutable hush, which grew into the whispers of wary conversation, but even they lacked the good cheer he'd been expecting. A harsh journey, perhaps?

The first horseman passed through, and behind him rode two more, flanking a cart drawn by a mule. Sitting in the bed of the cart were five women and more than a dozen children, all sitting quietly in a huddle. The rider at the front was a tall, wiry man with a long mane of red hair hanging down his back in a long, plaited braid. His face was heavy-set and weary, his eyes like cold emerald pits.

The man dismounted in a flurry of brown and gray furs, and the eyes of his followers trailed him. From beyond the gate, more horses stamped and snorted. "Hail, brother," the rider said, raising a gloved hand in greeting. There was no cheer on his face, no life save the steady puff of frost pulsing from his mouth. "We seek passage through Palvast."

Haegar glanced up at Sorvak, who looked down from the battlements, and shrugged. The old man shrugged right back. "Of course," Haegar said, eyes dropping back to the stranger. "All Vruskmen are welcome in Palvast, especially on a day such as this. If you want to leave your horses in our stables, we'll show you to the festivities. You'll have to excuse us if everything isn't ready yet; we weren't expecting guests for another few hours."

The man blinked and scratched the back of his head, grimacing. "Festivities? Boil my blood, is the harvest festival today? These days pass so quickly." He chuckled, but it was a sound drained of all humor. "I'm sorry, brother, but we're not here for any festival. We only seek passage."

Haegar closed his mouth. A prickling of cold surprise skittered down his back. He appraised the stranger with a suspicious eye, and when he glanced across the women and children in the wagon, he saw fear on their pale faces. In the stranger's face, he saw a lurking apprehension. The still-mounted men shifted warily in their saddles, throwing uncertain glances back over their shoulders.

"Why?" Makin demanded, stepping forward. A furious redness clung to the boy's face as he glowered up at the tall stranger. "Why wouldn't you want to stay? Our festival is the best. You can see the fire from all the Winterwood!"

The man smiled faintly. "I'm sure you can, but we haven't any time for it, young'un. We must continue."

Haza moved up alongside Haegar, a frown on his face. "Where are you bound in such haste?"

"Farrenhall," the stranger said. He turned that cold, anxious stare on Haza, unblinking. "With any fortune, we'll cross the Gated Bridge before tomorrow night and see the end of this cursed place." He swung back toward Haegar. "If you want my advice, brother, you'll do the same. Don't wait. Take your children and get across the Tagalfr, ere too many nights pass."

Haza's face paled, and Haegar couldn't lie to himself—he felt the frigid touch of fear's finger, trailing lightly up his back. But the heat of rising anger was quick to burn it away. "You do a disservice to your homeland, Vruskman," he growled, not bothering to hide his scorn. "Why are you abandoning the Winterwood?"

The man stiffened, glancing back at the women in the cart. The one in the driver's seat, a portly woman with silver hair, slowly nodded. The rider cleared his throat. "You must've heard the stories by now, aye? Even as far as Palvast, you must know. Strange happenings. Things that come crawling only after dark. Tales I'd rather not utter in front of your children, brother."

"I'm not afraid of the forest," declared Makin, thumping his fist against his chest. Rala, however, sank bashfully behind Haegar's knee, clinging tightly to his pants with both hands.

"Another faithful fool for your books, Haza," Haegar sneered, arms crossed as he faced the stranger. "A believer in haunted trees and talking beasts. You bring shame to the Winterwood. You'd rather abandon it than face a harsh winter."

The stranger's eyes narrowed. "You presume much."

"I see what you show me," he snapped back.

"Laklin," hissed the silver-haired woman from the bed of the wagon. "We don't have time for this. We need to keeping moving."

The stranger glanced at her and nodded. Then he took a step forward. Haegar's hand dropped to the hilt of his knife, but the man did not reach for his own. Instead, he leaned forward, until his lips nearly brushed Haegar's ear. "It's not just us. Everything is running. The wolves, the elk, even the birds. And

I've seen them, brother. They're real. My mother, she was old…she went to sleep and didn't wake up. Except…" he lowered his eyes. "She got up again. Do you understand? She wasn't herself anymore. They're coming for us all. It's only a matter of time, now. You must leave."

Against all instinct and reason, Haegar found himself voicing his fear. "What…what are you talking about?"

The man leaned back, his emerald eyes wide. Horrified. "The dead." The stranger suddenly gripped his shoulder, dragging him closer. Makin and Rala shouted, but Haegar held his ground, meeting the man's stare. "My mother is one of them now," he rasped. "They changed her. She ripped my brother's jaw from his face, then he became like her, too. I saw it all. Take your children, take anyone you care for, and leave. Leave, before it is too late."

Laklin released him, straightened his coat, then turned to climb back onto his horse. He flashed the silver-haired woman a nervous smile as he gathered up the reins. "I'm sorry, brother," he said. "I wish you a swift and safe journey, to you and all Palvast."

He kicked his horse into motion and started down the road, and the other men were quick to follow. The silver-haired woman flicked a cane at the mule to start the wagon rolling again. Behind them, more passed through the gate. Some were riding on horses, all dressed in heavy coats, some with axes and long knifes worn openly at their belts. The rest rode in wagons and carts; the elderly, the sick, the women and children, with small flocks of sheep and goats coming too. More than a hundred, all told, their faces identical masks of quiet terror.

Haegar stood by, stunned, as the caravan trundled past quietly. No one spoke again. The only sound to mark their passing was the rumble of wagon wheels and the occasional nicker of an irritable horse.

"Papa, what happened?" Rala asked, stepping out from behind him. "Are we still having pie?"

Take a deep breath. Haegar exhaled. *Stay calm.* His fists trembled at his side, his eyes closed. *Focus on what's real. Their stories are nonsense. They're cowards, hiding behind pagan beliefs that should've died centuries ago. Winter drives false men from the wood, that's all.*

"Papa?" It was Makin's voice, now. "Are you sick?"

"Why don't you run home?" said Haza. "Go find your Mama, yes? She still needs help for tonight. Go now. I'll see to Papa."

Haegar opened his eyes, and his children were gone. There was only Haza, face pale as if he too had seen whatever had sent a hundred men fleeing west, and old Sorvak, who was still leaning against the top of the wall, frowning.

"What did he say to you?" Haza asked quietly.

"Mad things," Haegar replied with a soft growl. "The whole bloodied Winterwood has gone mad."

Haza shifted uncomfortably, glancing after the fleeing wagons. "What did he say, exactly?"

Haegar met his brother's eyes. The words escaped his lips before he could stop them. "The dead," came his whisper. "That they're coming."

Haza turned as pale as the snow beneath his boots. "Do you…think there's any credence? To what he's saying, I mean?"

"Haegar!" called Sorvak from above. "You're not gonna believe this; we've got more coming. Another caravan!"

"Boil my blood," Haegar snarled. He whirled about. He had to find Garvim and Torvust. He didn't mean to let this next caravan pass. If the smell of Tayja's cooking wasn't enough to entice them, maybe he'd take an axe to their wagon wheels. *You're overreacting,* he warned himself. *They're here for the festival. They must be.* But doubt had seized him and was busy chewing into his heart.

Haza hurried in his wake, clutching his book to his chest, as if it were a shield over his heart. "Perhaps…we should consider this warning, Haegar. If something bad is happening, maybe we could go over the river. Just until spring."

He stopped mid-stride and rounded on his brother. "You'd like that, wouldn't you, Haza?" He let fury burn wild through his veins. He was finished with Haza's sniveling, his not-so-subtle hints that they should go west. "To go to Havasa, or to Joromor where they worship pagan gods in the mountains. Go with them, if you'd like, but we're staying here. In Palvast. In our home."

"That's not why I'm saying this," Haza said, his face falling. "Think of your children, Haegar. The Winterwood is different of late; you've seen it, as have I. People are leaving for a reason. We should consider following them, else—"

"Else what?" Haegar demanded. Haza retreated a step, startled, but Haegar followed him. "Are we to be swept up in the madness and fear of these stories? Abandon our home? Never. Never, Haza! We are not weak, like you, like them." He thrust a finger toward the retreating backs of the caravan. Haza opened his mouth, but Haegar shouted over him again. "Do not speak of this to me again. Do what you will, but you do not make decisions for me and my family. Is that understood?"

Haza's face paled further, then turned sharply to a deep shade of red. But the man only nodded and clutched his book closer to his chest.

Haegar turned and left him there, trudging in the direction of the town's center. He had to find Torvust and whoever else remained. Palvast would stand where it was. The festival would continue as planned. The men of Vrusk, the true men of Vrusk, would never leave the Winterwood. Never.

Chapter Four
Fangs

That second caravan was not the last to pass through Palvast that day. Before the bonfire of the harvest festival was finally lit at dusk, more than five hundred Vruskmen had come to town. And not one had stayed. Despite the inviting smell of baked goods, the prospect of roasting meat, and the lively music of the townsfolk, the visitors from the Winterwood had only stared at the festivities with haunted, worried eyes as they passed. Even those that could be persuaded to take food hadn't stayed to enjoy it, retreating to their wagons and horses to eat as they resumed their journey west.

When the blaze of the bonfire faded to a despondent, sputtering pile of embers, a bleak and miserable harvest festival concluded. The music stopped, food was packed away, and the villagers of Palvast quietly retreated to their homes. A muted aura of apprehension lurked over the town; the passing of men had not gone unnoticed, nor had their tongues been silent. Everyone had heard the stories, now.

Haza sat on the darkened porch, reclining in his chair, which he'd dragged outside. He was still wrapped tightly in his coat, but had also found a heavy blanket to drape across his shoulders, and he did his best to read in the nearby light of the lamppost.

But try as he might, Haza found himself unable to focus on the book. He rested it in his lap and instead frowned at the street before him. The light of the lamp glinted palely off the snowflakes silently whirling down from overhead, falling atop the blanket of snow that already covered Palvast. He'd rather be inside, next to the hearth, but Haegar was in a black mood. Outside was better. He shivered, from more than just the cold and quiet night.

The exodus of the Winterwood had him on edge. Haza couldn't remember a time when he'd ever felt so tense, like a spring wound to the point of snapping. He still couldn't believe it. Hundreds of Vruskmen, all abandoning their homes, everything they'd built, without a backward glance. This was no ordinary case of what Haegar named cowardice that led a handful of men to flee the winter, this was a sickness of terror that had infected half the wood. But how? How could so many people be convinced of something that wasn't real? *Unless...?*

Another shiver made its way down his spine. The travelers had been anything but tight-lipped, and the elders of Palvast had done their best to discourage what they'd dubbed as 'worry mongering.' Still, Haza had heard more than enough whispers. Children who wandered out into the woods vanished, never to be seen again. Lone riders would disappear too, be they woman or man. To hear some say it, an entire town had gone dark, with nothing coming from beyond its closed gate but a cold, gusting wind. A silence was creeping out of the Winterwood's heart, and the Vruskmen were running before it could reach them.

Haza drummed his fingers against the cover of his book as the tempo of his breathing began to rise. Was this creeping strangeness in the Winterwood real? And if it wasn't, would it even be worth staying, if so many others were leaving? Who would Palvast have to trade with? How could they alone meet the lumber needs of the rest of the world? *Do we even dare to hope that it's not real?* The price they would pay if they were wrong...

He glanced to his side, where his longbow lay against the wall of the house. Beside it was propped a leather quiver, filled with arrows fletched with red feathers. He wasn't the best marksman, certainly not compared to his father or Haegar, but he could point it in the right direction, at least, if it came to that.

"Troubling," he muttered to himself, making an effort to open his book again. "Too troubling for a night like this."

Across the street, the stream burbled softly by, and Haza kept looking up when the lamplight glinted off its choppy surface, like flashes of stars gleaming through the boughs of thick trees. That silence, whatever it might be, was coming for them. Maybe it wouldn't come tonight. Maybe it was still too far away. But it *would* come if they waited long enough. They needed to leave. The stream almost seemed to whisper to him as he watched, its voice a chanting rustle, trailing just beyond his hearing. If he only leaned a little closer, maybe he could hear what it was saying.

"Uncle?"

Haza jerked at the sound, hissing through his teeth, as he whipped his head around to see Makin standing in the half-opened doorway, peering out at him uncertainly. Haza clamped a hand over his heart to try and still its frantic beating. *Gods be damned, but he nearly scared my last years away.*

He cleared his throat and set the book on his lap. "Makin? What are you doing up?"

"Can't sleep," the boy muttered, still standing in the shadows of the darkened house.

Haza grimaced. He hadn't even thought of how the sight of the refugees might've unsettled the children. "Is it the travelers? Are they what's bothering you?" In reply, the boy nodded, so

Haza waved his hand. "Come here, then, Makin. Sit on my lap, and we'll talk."

Haza set his book aside as his young nephew stepped hesitantly into the open, sliding the door shut behind him. Makin clambered up onto his knee, draping his legs to one side, while Haza wrapped his heavy blanket around them both. He nodded out toward the street. "What do you see out there, Makin?"

The boy squinted, a frown creasing his pale face. "I see...the lamppost."

"What else?"

"The snow," Makin replied.

"Anything more?"

"It's too dark."

Haza smiled and nodded. "When I was a boy like you, I was scared of the dark. My grandfather would yell at me for it. He didn't understand how I could be afraid of something that wasn't real."

"But the darkness is real," Makin said, looking up with a confused glance. "I can see it."

"Darkness is what you can't see," Haza replied. "But no matter how dark it is, everything is still in its proper place. Palvast is still there, even when the lights go out. Every building, every stake in the wall, it's all accounted for. The sun, the blue sky, all still there."

Makin glowered. "Why can't I see it, then?"

"Sometimes things just vanish for a while." He looked up at the night sky. The Seventeen Stars were there, glittering like tiny eyes upon a canvas of infinite black. They held off that darkness, no matter how feeble their light might seem, bastions against its smothering grip. They would stand until the sun could rise again and chase the night away. "But they always come back again. Remember that the next time darkness scares you. It doesn't last forever. The world around you, Razzador, our family, *that's* forever."

Makin looked down. He had such a studious expression. *So much like Mother.* "Are those travelers scared of the dark, then?"

Haza's blood grew cold, slowing to a creeping sludge in his veins. "Yes," he whispered. "That's why they're going away for a while. But they'll come back again, too. You have to believe that, yes? No matter what happens. The darkness will not stay forever."

They sat together for a while as the wind gusted softly through slumbering Palvast, while the stream whispered its silent promises, ever-present. *Do I really believe what I'm saying?* he wondered as he readjusted the blanket to better sit around his nephew's shoulders. *This darkness* is *real, I'm sure of it. We have no choice but to leave, don't we?* And there was no way to promise that they could ever come back. He felt a great and terrible fear, then, realizing that Haegar would never leave. If the darkness was real, Haegar would never escape it. He'd vanish with his home, interred forever into the silence of the Winterwood.

"I'm still scared, uncle," Makin whispered.

Haza wrapped one arm around the boy, the other reaching for his book. "Why don't I read to you, then? We'll keep going until you feel safe again, all right?"

Makin snuggled against his chest, settling down. "Thank you, uncle," he muttered, his eyes already fluttering shut.

Haza thumbed through the book back to its beginning, but as he drew a breath to begin his recitation, he stopped. There was a new sound. The stream…it was no longer whispering. Something was disturbing the water, sloshing through it. Haza peered into the darkness, his eyes settling on the gap in the wall that led to the outside world.

Something had slipped through, silent save for the water it disturbed, paddling down the stream. Haza tensed in his chair, a shout of warning to the watchmen dying on his tongue. There was something familiar about the dark shape now cutting through the water, and it was a marriage of terror and caution that kept his mouth firmly shut.

The shape turned and rose out of the water, climbing up the short bank and up into the snow that clogged the street. With water trailing from its sleek form, it made its way into the light. Haza's breath caught in his throat.

The wolf kept to the dark side of the street, leaving it veiled in half-shadows as it padded its way unhindered into Palvast. It took slow, stiff steps, as if it had a lame leg it was trying not to put weight on. Haza's heart was hammering in his throat as he glanced down at Makin, whose eyes were still shut.

The wolf was utterly quiet, its massive paws silent in the snow. Even the water dripping from its fur made no noise, and neither did the snowflakes that lighted on its back. Its mouth was agape, ears perched erect, but he couldn't see its eyes.

He dared not move an inch. He could immediately recognize odd behavior when he saw it, even in an animal as elusive as this. Wolves were rarely far from their packs, yet this one had come alone, and he could not remember hearing any howling before. This beast was on its own, likely outcast from its companions. It moved without fear, boldly entering Palvast, a place that all animals knew to avoid, even in the dark.

Is it rabid? The foaming sickness could drive animals mad. It stripped them of fear and hunger, replacing it with malice. Haza glanced at his bow. The wolf had stopped moving. It stood just beyond the light of a lamppost on the other side of the street, facing ahead. Not even its ears stirred. Something had caught its attention, something Haza couldn't see or smell. *The feast, maybe? Is that what's drawn it?*

He needed to warn the town. He had to tell someone. But

the moment he shouted, that thing would turn on him, on Makin. But if he did not act…if it slipped into the dark and he lost sight of it… A rabid wolf could not be left loose in Palvast. *What do I do? Blood be with me, what do I do?*

"Uncle?" Makin murmured. "What's wrong? Why are you not reading—?"

Haza clamped his hand around his nephew's mouth, causing the boy to squeak. He drew him closer to his chest and hissed, "Shh. Don't move. Don't speak." Ahead of them, the wolf had not moved. It stood as if made of snow, and the storm overhead was doing its best to bury it in white powder.

Makin's eyes found the wolf and widened. Haza could feel the boy stiffen in his grip. His mind was spinning, searching for a way out. He glanced at his bow again. *I'd only have one shot. I can't let this thing roam unchecked.*

"I'm going to set you down," Haza whispered, his eyes never leaving the beast. "Gently. Don't move."

"Uncle," Makin whimpered, "Don't. Don't leave me…"

"I won't. I promise. But I have to put you down." Slowly, as slow as melting ice, Haza lowered his nephew to the ground beside him. The wolf gave no sign that it had noticed them. Instead, it turned slightly, facing the stream again.

Once Haza was free of the boy, he slowly climbed to his feet. The chair creaked as he left it and he cringed, freezing in place. The wolf didn't stir. Haza exhaled slowly, looking to the bow once more. He had to be swift.

"When I tell you to run," Haza growled, "go inside and shut the door behind you. Wake your Papa and tell him that there's a rabid wolf. Be clear about that, Makin. It's rabid. But don't move until I tell you to, all right?"

"What about you, uncle?" The boy was trembling where he

stood, shivering so violently that Haza thought the wolf might be able to hear. They didn't have time for any of this.

"I'll be fine," he promised, hoping his voice did not betray his terror. "But you move when I tell you to. Only then. Get ready." He drew a deep breath, casting a glance up at the watch post, where the guardsman had yet to notice anything amiss. *I have to do this myself.* Haza swallowed his terror and braced himself. "Run!"

He threw himself at his bow, breath escaping his lungs in a furious rush. He heard the front door swing open, but paid it no heed. His hands closed around the haft of his bow and brought it spinning around, a crimson-fletched arrow coming up with it. Before he could even take his next breath, he'd drawn the arrow back and sighted on his quarry. Haza wasn't the greatest shot. In fact, he was quite certain he was terrible. Haegar could do it, if he were here. Haegar never missed. *I'm not Haegar. But I'll still protect this family. By my blood, I will!* As he trained the arrow on the wolf, arrow stretched back as far as he could pull, he knew he wouldn't miss.

The arrow split the night with a soft hiss, cutting through the gentle curtain of snow before pinning itself in the back of the wolf's head with a wet *thunk.* Haza whooped in excitement as the wolf stumbled forward, a feathered shaft protruding from between its ears. He spared a glance for the front door. Makin was gone, and he'd closed the way behind him. It was over. Palvast was safe. His family was safe.

Except, the wolf did not fall. It turned, still as quiet as the snow whirling through the air. Haza's heart went cold in his chest, and he stumbled back a step in horror. The wolf advanced fully into the light.

The arrowhead protruded from the center of its forehead, black even in the firelight. Blood matted the fur on its back, but it lacked any flesh on the right side of its body. From throat to waist, it had been ripped apart, stripped like a dress torn down its hem. Lifeless eyes glistened in the wolf's head, turned toward the ground, staring at nothing. But despite that dead, frozen stare, Haza knew the beast was looking at him.

Haza stared back, transfixed. Never before had he been held by so furious, so terrifying a gaze. He couldn't explain it, but he knew this thing hated him, hated him more than he'd hated any man. He tensed, fingers coiled around his bow, still raised in an attack position. While plumes of mist rose from out his own gaping mouth, nothing came from the wolf. It gave not a sniff, not a blink. Nothing. The horrific puncture wounds in its throat and chest, caked with dried blood, told him what he was looking at, but Haza still couldn't believe it.

Time slowed around him, the snow pausing in its downward spiral to float suspended in the still light of the lamppost. Haza's fingers inched backward, straining for another arrow. The wolf watched him without further motion.

And then the voice of someone overhead on the wall shattered it all. "Ho! Who's down there? What's the matter?"

The world exploded in a hail of white fury. Haza screamed, flinging himself backward, desperate to find purchase on a shaft. But the wolf had already reached him. He tried to swing his bow to bat its head aside, only to find himself toppling as a tremendous weight hurled itself against him. He found himself on his back, forced up against the wall of his house, and he threw up his forearm, futilely trying to drive away those flashing fangs.

The wolf seized his arm. Pain. Pain unlike anything he'd ever felt before latched onto him, biting to the bone. By his blood, was that screaming voice his own? It sounded inhuman, the cry of a dying animal. And that's what he was. Haza thrashed and wriggled like a fish on the end of a spear, kicking, hitting, doing anything he could think of as he tried to wrench his arm free of the wolf's maw. But the wolf began to pull in the opposite direction, dragging him from the wall. A rabid panic seized him, and he drove his booted foot into the beast's exposed ribcage, feeling it crack.

Triumph turned to blind agony as the wolf bit down harder in response. He couldn't scream any longer, only gasp breathlessly as he felt his own bones crunch beneath its jaws. The wolf was silent too, a distant part of him realized. No snarling, no growling, not even a grunting breath. His blood, warm and wet, spattered across his chest and speckled the wolf's face. It twisted his arm, one way first, then the other, and he could hear more of his flesh rip with every tug. Somewhere far away, someone was shouting. Sorvak? It felt like a dream. The wolf was all he could see, all he could hear. Its claws slammed into his chest every time he tried to wrest his way upright, pinning him. The wolf pulled his arm to its limit, then pulled further. Haza could only stare, a strange dizziness washing over him. There was blood everywhere. Red snow.

He met the wolf's eyes.

Those eyes. They were clouded, lifeless, long abandoned by the creature that had once dwelled behind them. Instead, there was something new in those empty eyes, something that did not belong. Like a parasite, darkness dwelled where light had once lived, a hungry and terrible darkness. Hateful darkness. It would devour him and make it like himself. It would not stop until it had ripped him to pieces, purged that which it hated so deeply. In that eye, flecked with blood and snow, Haza saw death.

A terrible ripping sensation radiated up and down his arm. His eyes rolled back in his head, but the pain kept him awake, kept him aware of what was about to happen. *Make it stop! Please, make it stop! I'll pray to whatever god makes itself known! I'll-* Even thought was swept away by the pain. Those malevolent eyes filled his vision, overwhelming all else. There was nothing now but that deep, creeping malice. That, and the blood.

The pressure gave way suddenly and Haza gasped like a man pulled to the surface of the water. He stared down at the wolf's fangs, still embedded in his arm. He saw fresh blood, and the axe blade buried through the nape of the wolf's neck. Time had frozen again, and in that ageless moment, cold, yet burning eyes rolled upward in the wolf's head, craning to fix its baleful stare on Haegar Ruthborne, who wrenched his axe free with a single pull.

Time moved.

The wolf leapt for Haegar's throat, but he was already swinging. The wolf's head toppled into Haza's lap, its body staggering off the porch and falling into the snow. As silently as it had come, the monster died, its black blood smearing Haegar's axe blade.

Haza found breath and screamed. He rolled away, tossing the head from his lap as he cradled his mangled arm to his chest. He pulled himself to his feet, turning to run into the dark, into the cold. If he could slip away, melt into the forest, he could escape the sight of that hateful eye. But he could feel it watching him still, chasing him. And when something strong and powerful seized him from behind, he screamed and writhed. He had to escape! He had to! He had to… Boil his blood, but it was cold. When had it grown so dark? He could feel himself falling, but he never hit the ground.

Chapter Five
The Heart of Farrenhall

This time, she had him. Kasara was sure of it. She drove her blade for his chest, but his sword batted hers away with a casual swipe. "Swing faster," came his sharp reprimand. "The wind can make the Cho'mori trees bend faster than you."

Kasara sneered and brought her sword up defiantly. She'd been slashing with as much strength and speed as she could muster. Sweat was bleeding down her chest and the undersides of her arm. Her hair felt slick against her scalp. How much harder did she have to push herself before she could prove him wrong? "All the books I've read," she panted, drawing gulps of air between her words, "compare swordplay to swaying trees. That should be a good thing, aye?"

Berethan did not so much as crack a smile. But then, he never did. He was a behemoth of a man, the tallest she'd ever seen, with shoulders near as broad as the gates of Farrenhall and a chest as large and round as a wagon wheel. He stood before her bereft of his usual armor, garbed only in dark trousers. His bronze Jormori skin glistened in the torchlight. As did his scars, which decorated him in such thick, overlapping lines that they seemed almost the work of a deliberate hand, a tapestry carved in flesh. "Those books you read know nothing about the art of the sword."

He had a harsh voice, sharp as the jagged peaks of the glaciers that crowned the Sunless Sea. It fit well with the rest of his features; his gray eyes were sunken, watched over by a hooded brow. His nose was flat and bent, clearly broken innumerable times. His gray hair was tied back in a topknot behind his head. Even with only a wooden sword held before him in one hand—the other wrapped behind his back—the Grand Crusader was an intimidating man. He radiated power much like a torch gave heat. "'Swordplay,' as you so indelicately put it, cannot be captured with written word. It must be experienced."

Kasara took a deep breath. She focused on the wooden training sword she held in both hands. Facing a giant like Berethan, she felt a child again, forced to face her own father. Of course, her father would never touch a sword, nor let his daughter get her hands around one. This small rebellion, as well as the thrill of combat, gave her renewed strength.

She took to her teacher's words and stepped forward to experience the sword. She threw herself at Berethan, swinging wildly. The books said the way to win a duel was to outmaneuver your opponent. Throw him out of balance, force him to make a mistake. Every swordsman had a weakness. Find it, exploit it, end it.

Except Berethan had no weakness, not that she could see. He fought her still one-handed, his feet planted firmly on the sand -swept floor of the sparring chamber. Every blow she threw at him, he turned aside with graceful flicks of his blade. It was like trying to drive her sword through water; the current pushed her aside each time. Berethan never counterattacked—he let her try everything she could to throw him off balance. That irked her, giving her the distinct impression that she was little more than a troublesome fly. He could swat her from the air easily if he really wanted to. For now, though, he was content to brush her aside.

Her blade never struck anything but wood—she might as well be hammering a wall.

"Anger does not win fights, little Lordling," Berethan chided. His voice showed no strain, only a distant, even more vexing amusement. "That power you feel in your blood is illusory. Rage blinds you, gives way to recklessness. Mistakes mean death on the battlefield."

But this was not a battlefield. This was a training hall meant for Farrenhall's garrison. There were no windows in the wide, spacious chamber, as it was enclosed deep in the heart of the Gated Bridge—the torches on walls of deep, dark green stone were the only source of illumination. It gave the room a suffocating feel, like she was trapped in a box. The whole of Farrenhall felt like that, of late. Heat from her own breath burned beneath her skin. Frustration. She tempered it like steel. Berethan thought rage was useless, did he? She threw himself at him with a roar, driving her blade for his throat, determined to carve her way through his defenses even if it meant grinding her practice sword to splinters. All she needed was more power, more speed, more—!

Her blade went flying from her hands. Kasara had only a heart's beat to register surprise before something struck her in the leg. Hard. She dropped to the ground with a yelp, clutching her throbbing knee as her eyes blinked back stinging tears. It was only through gritted teeth that she managed to keep from groaning.

Berethan's shadow fell over her. She made herself look up to see his disappointed frown. "Some lessons are only learned through pain," he grunted. He nodded to her fallen sword. "Pick it up and try again."

As she sat there amid a small cloud of dust stirred by their churning feet, Kasara struggled to swallow her temper. It burned like the afternoon sun, fueled, rather than dampened, by the humiliation she felt. "It's not a fair fight," she panted. "Look at you...you're barely human. And me? I..." She was short, scrawny, hardly the thick-armed Vruskwoman that were common in the Gray Hinterlands. Her twig-like appearance, complete with the gangly limbs of a boy in the throes of growing, would make her forever a stranger to the mysterious beauty women like her mother, who'd come from Havasa far to the east, wielded so easily. She felt trapped between two different faces, and stretching between them had resulted in...well, whatever this was. She just didn't have the strength necessary to beat a man like Berethan. Nor did she have his decades of experience.

Staring down at her like he might a cringing child, Berethan's eyes narrowed. "Perhaps we are finished with today's session, then." He turned and made his way toward the barrel by the door, which held an assortment of sparring swords and spears, all with their handles facing up.

A new kind of shame was finally able to swallow Kasara's anger. She scrambled for her sword, pulling herself upright, involuntarily brushing the dust from her blouse with one hand. "I'm ready," she said, still panting. Her leg twinged painfully, but she would not limp in front of him. She would not!

But the giant didn't even look back at her. He placed his weapon back among its fellows. "If you wish to learn the sword, there are two things you must understand before I can teach you how to swing a blade. First, there is no defeat. You fight until the fight is finished. Forget that and you will not be alive any longer to worry about it, yes? Fight because you *will* win."

Kasara stared uncertainly down the length of her sword. Was he telling her to fight even if she knew she would lose? *The stories say they all fight like that. Men who know they won't die.* "Can't we just go another round? I won't stop this time. By my blood, I swear it."

"No, Lordling," Berethan rumbled. "The second lesson is to learn to not enter fights you cannot win. It is time I saw to my other duties, anyway. We will try again tomorrow." He was already moving for his armor, which lay neatly arranged where he'd left it at the start of their bout. "Assist me."

Kasara obeyed, returning her own sword to the barrel as the man began donning the armor. Though Berethan was their Grand-Crusader, the Myrmidons all wore identical suits. It was work of plated steel, fitted to his form as if carved by the hand of a master sculptor, an unparalleled piece of art. The steel was crimson, marked with curling sigils of silver, spinning and overlapping to give the impression that the two colors intermingled, blood marbling with iron in a patchwork language that only the Myrmidons could understand.

She was getting faster at assembling armor. For the last three months, nearly every day, they'd come here to spar. She'd been half-joking when she'd asked him to teach her. He was here on business, after all. The Myrmidons had been hired by her father, Kalivaz Varkoth, to defend Farrenhall, and considering their storied dedication to duty, she'd been surprised when Berethan had agreed. Secretly, she felt a thrill as she helped tug his vambraces into place, then fastened the straps behind his breastplate. She'd always wondered what it might be like to squire for a mighty knight. This was probably the closest she'd ever get.

They were silent as they worked, but Kasara didn't mind silence, and neither did the Myrmidon. She dwelled on her failings as she worked. How did Berethan expect her to overcome him, when their physical and technical levels were so different? Did he really demand perfection from her already? Kasara knew that she loved swordplay; she'd already memorized every sword form—Berethan called them Ka'lori—that her father's old books could show her. But passion did not equal talent. *I must work harder.*

"You are frustrated," Berethan rumbled, distant, like a far-off storm. Kasara didn't reply. She was binding his leg armor back into place while he worked on his spaulders. "Make peace with failing," he continued. "You will not carry it with you when you return here tomorrow. Understood?"

"Yes, Grand-Crusader."

His sword—his real sword—came last. Like his armor, it was a work of wonder. Its scabbard continued the theme of silver over red, and housed a blade wide as two palms. Its hilt was gleaming silver, leather-wrapped and studded with rubies at the leaf-shaped crossguard and pommel. This Kasara could barely manage to lift between both hands, but Berethan hefted it easily and slung it across his back.

They left the room, stepping into the hall beyond. Outside the door, two Myrmidons were waiting. Like Berethan, they were large, towering men who wore crimson-and-silver steel that gleamed in the torchlight. Broadswords hung from their backs, and over top lay wide, circular crimson shields, which bore their sigil, a single mountain peak, in silver. Shorter swords—Kasara was sure she'd still have to use two hands to wield them—hung from their belts, as well. They inclined their heads to Berethan when he emerged, their faces veiled behind marbled helms with dark, cross-shaped visors.

As their escort fell in behind them, they made their way further down the hall. The walls were a deep green, so dark a shade they almost seemed gray. Only the periodic torches that they passed revealed their true color. Farrenhall had been built some five hundred years ago, during the Holy Wars, and it was said that it owed its strange color to being made from untainted stone; despite fearsome battle, the Gated Bridge's defenders had let not a single drop of blood cross the line. In truth, it was just built from the earth of the Winterwood.

She chuckled at that but kept her mirth to herself. She glanced up at Berethan, who walked beside her, armor clanking, and the twin Myrmidons who followed in his wake. She wouldn't voice her scorn for stories like that in front of religious men. For all she knew, they believed this place really was holy.

A shudder washed over her, and she suddenly felt quite small, flanked by three mountainous figures encased in steel. The Myrmidons were mercenaries. Their so-called god commanded them to offer their services to others without question, to fight for causes that were not their own, in order to garner their deity's favor. It was said that Myrmidons never disobeyed orders, no matter what they might be, so long as their buyer could afford their exorbitant price, of course. For now, their commander was her father, Kalivaz, who'd charged them to defend Farrenhall. They'd give their lives for the Gated Bridge, though they were not Vruskmen, nor was this their home, which was far away in the northern extremes of Joromor, where the mountains grew tall enough to kiss the sky.

The whole thing reeked like a barrel of fish, though Kasara couldn't quite say why. All she did know was that the Myrmidons, the most prestigious, efficient hireswords in Razzador, were completely unnecessary to defend a pile of stones like Farrenhall. To the west was Vrusk, with the entirety of the kingdom and the king's own army between them and any foes. To the east, of course, on the other side of the river, was just the Winterwood.

All around them, doorways led deeper into Farrenhall. On occasion, they'd pass stairs that led up or down. Servants hurried all about, ducking around doors, passing by with brooms in hand. Few went downward, as the bottommost level of Farrenhall was just the main road—the only part of the fortress-bridge that actually served as a passage. The upper two levels were a warren of hallways and chambers, dormitories and kitchens, the stockades and even a grand banquet hall fit for kings, though no kings had come here in a hundred years. Farrenhall was a veritable city perched upon the river, stretched long and serpent-like across the breast of the Tagalfr. Though its ancient purpose of defending bastions in the Winterwood from invasion had long since passed, the Varkoth family still proudly ruled over the bridge, devoted to its defense and maintenance.

Kasara snorted. *We proudly rule over a stack of rubble.*

They pivoted right and followed another hall. Kasara was bound for her own chambers, where a veritable mountain of paperwork was waiting for her. Her father insisted on her shouldering some of the responsibility of rule, to help her prepare for the day she'd inherit Farrenhall for herself. That was all well and good, but she suspected Kalivaz was purposefully depositing all of the most mundane, laborious work in her lap.

Most recent was this business with the harvest festival. Every year, the local village closest to Farrenhall put on a festival that managed to draw the whole of the Winterwood, as well as visitors and even the occasional dignitary from greater Vrusk. Kalivaz had long desired to hold the festival in Farrenhall, but his subjects seemed to prefer visiting the forest and celebrating around a great bonfire rather than a stuffy hall. Kasara couldn't blame them. Kalivaz refused to attend out of spite. But this year was already proving to be different than most. There was some trouble further west—she wasn't sure what it was about—that had led to several of the main roads closing. There would be no visitors for the Winterwood from over the river this year. No trade, either.

"Have you heard anything from the west of late, Berethan?"

she found herself asking idly. "The Old King has his breeches in a twist about something."

The Myrmidon glanced down at her, his stare as flat as his voice. "I concern myself only with my charge. That is the only way to climb the mountain to the Highest Path. You must always look forward, little Lordling, and tend to your own matters."

"Well, these are my matters," she snorted. "At least, adjacently. Trouble for Vrusk means trouble for Farrenhall. It just comes slower to these parts."

"My only concern is the defense of Farrenhall," Berethan replied.

"From what? The early winter?"

She searched her giant companion's face for any hint of mirth, any crack in that mask of icy fortitude he always wore. She found none. "That is not for me to question," he said. She was quite sure he meant it. He didn't care a damn about why he and fifty more of Razzador's best fighters had been brought to the loneliest corner of the world.

They emerged into one of the outer halls. Windows now lined the right wall, letting the gray light of a cloudy morning spill through square frames with rounded tops. Far below, the Tagalfr dominated the landscape. It spanned nearly across the breadth of her vision, stalled only by opposite shores studded with towering Winterwood trees and buried in banks of snow. The surface of the vast river rippled in the wind, while great shapes burst to the surface like whales breaching through the surf, sending plumes of frost to arc through the air. From this height, the ice floes looked like tiny flakes, but she'd stood on the Tagalfr's bank before and seen them carve through the water like floating hammers. Though the river itself never froze, there was a continuous stream of small glaciers that broke away from further south, pushed into the Tagalfr by the force of the Sunless

Sea. It only ever cleared out completely for a single month in mid-summer.

Kasara found herself pausing by the window. Her breath fogged the glass, but she could still see the river far below, seeping endlessly past. "Whatever reason brought you here, Berethan," she murmured, "at least, once it's finished, you can leave this place. Go back home."

Berethan had stepped past her, but he paused and looked back. The other two Myrmidons stared straight forward, faceless, watchful. "Home is wherever your duty lies," he said. "The God of the Highest Path expects you to meet your every calling with a full heart. Whether that is to the sword, or to this place. Your home is here."

Kasara's lips peeled back. She kept her face to the window. "I want to wear a sword. I want to see the world, like you."

Berethan chuckled, causing her to blink and turn around. The look on his face was strange. What was that expression, in his eyes? That fondness? "There are better ways to see Razzador than through eyes like mine," he said. "Wear the sword, if you wish it. And put your full heart into it. But, in the meantime, you will put your heart to this place too. Understood?"

She found herself nodding, unable to fight a small smile. "Yes, Grand-Crusader."

"Lady Kasara!" A voice rang from the hall behind them. She turned with a frown as she heard clanking footsteps following the sound of her name. Bjern hurried toward her, his pale eyes wide, his long blond hair bouncing around his shoulders. Kasara narrowed her eyes, her mood souring. He was the last bloodied man she wanted to see.

Compared to the Myrmidons, his gray plate looked drab as a pewter cup next to a crystalline wine glass. Even his sword seemed dull in its plain leather scabbard, its hilt naked of any gemstones or engravings, though, truthfully, she'd always been jealous of his sword, too. She'd give anything just to wear it. The garrison at Farrenhall only consisted of fifty men, and there were barely enough weapons and armor to supply them all. They guarded their equipment vigilantly.

Kasara looked Bjern up and down. They were of age, and she could remember a not-so-distant time when he'd managed to hit himself in the face the first time he'd picked up a training sword. He was a fool, and she'd hoped he'd learned by now to avoid her. Just the sight of him made her blood start to boil. Once, she thought she might've loved him, now she could only think about remarking again on how he needed to cut that tangle of hair perched on his head, but the look in his eyes forestalled her tongue. "What's wrong?"

"The Winterwood!" Bjern exclaimed, thrusting a finger back the way he'd come. "There's people. Hundreds of them! They're all pouring out of the forest, trying to get through, but the Myrmidons—" he choked off, looking up at Berethan, whose face was still flat. "You need to come help, Kasara—ah, my lady—before there's bloodshed."

"Bloodshed?" she blurted incredulously. She threw a startled glance back at the Myrmidons, but received nothing but empty stares in return. "Lead me, Bjern," she said, her petty displeasures forgotten.

He bobbed his head and raced away, waving frantically even as she sped to keep up with him. She didn't look back to see if Berethan was following. Somehow, she knew he always would.

Crack! Kasara jumped, spinning toward a window, but she only caught a glimpse of a dark shape plummeting away. Berethan turned too, one hand rising toward the hilt of his sword. His Myrmidons had moved with him, as if they were one fluid being, all acting at once.

Kasara frowned at the window. All she could now see were the distant waves of the Tagalfr, glinting in the pale light of the moon and the Seventeen Stars. They were so high above the river, what could have—? *Crack!* She jumped again with a squeak as something slammed against the glass, causing it to rattle. This time, she could distinctly see the small shape peel away, vanishing into the night.

She rounded on Berethan, who'd dropped his guard. He was staring out the window, face as unreadable as those of his helm-shrouded bodyguards. "What was that?" she demanded. "Did you see it?"

The Grand-Crusader's eyes narrowed, if only by a hair. "I believe…it was a bird."

Kasara scoffed incredulously. "A bird?" It had flown into the window? Why would—? She saw it again, out of the corner of her eye, and turned as a dark shape drove itself against the window. She gaped as the crow pulled back only a few feet, flapping above the dark expanse of the Tagalfr. She took a hesitant step closer, only for the bird to drive itself into the window again. The glass shook, but did not yield. The crow's head now hung from a crooked angle. "Curse my blood, why…?"

It was staring at her, wasn't it? Its black, beady eyes seemed to follow her as she slowly swayed before the window. It wasn't actually staring at her, right? She flinched when the crow struck again, and this time she saw its wing snap. It dropped as suddenly as it came and was swallowed by the darkness.

She stared into the night, unable to close her mouth. Far below, the Tagalfr still gleamed in the moonlight.

"Strange creatures you have here in the south," Berethan grunted. He'd turned from the window, already starting back down the hall, trailed as always by his silent armsmen. "I can't imagine how a creature with wings could miss seeing a place as large as this bridge."

Kasara was finally able to close her mouth as she made herself fall in beside him. "Well, windows are clear, you know," she said, chuckling. But as they walked, she found her eyes drawn back over her shoulder. What was this icy uncertainty she felt, as if eyes were tracking her every step? Why did she feel so strongly that that crow had wanted *her*?

She found herself longing for her coat. The corridors of Farrenhall were cold.

Chapter Six
Decision

"Help me get him inside!" Haegar bellowed as he cradled his brother's unconscious head. He knelt in the snow, gathering Haza up into his lap. He couldn't wrench his eyes away from the tattered, bloody mess that had become of his right arm. He could see white breaching through red like a jagged glacier. Haza's eyes were shut, and his face had gone as gray as ashes. Anger and fear warred in Haegar's chest, twin storms trying to smother the other. He lifted his brother with a grunt, the thrill of battle still pulsing through his veins. "Hurry, damn your blood! To the healer, swiftly!"

He shoved his brother off to Sorvak and Corvil, who hefted Haza and carried him down the street, followed by a small swarm of startled onlookers. More people were pouring out of their homes, awoken by the noise.

Haegar seized his axe from where he'd dropped it and swung it up and around so that it balanced on his shoulder. He paced back and forth, still panting, as the men watched him with startled, wary eyes.

He had no time for his brother, no time for the onlookers. He could already hear their worried questions rising on the wind. The greater problem had to come first. The wolf lay at his feet, still twitching. Feeble claws kept trying to find purchase in the snow, struggling to raise the headless corpse onto its feet. Haegar kicked it back down. The head lay nearby, on the porch, its murky eyes rolling about, jaws working in a chewing motion, dragging blood-drenched fangs up and down. It made no cry of pain, no yelp, gave not even a rattling breath.

Haegar stepped up, hefted his axe, and slammed it down into the wolf's skull with a furious roar, shearing the arrow that had already punched through its head. Those dead eyes stopped spinning. They were looking right at him now. An involuntary shudder crawled over him. He knew what a dead animal's eyes looked like, but blood be blackened, this thing was *looking* at him. Its jaws did not stop grinding, despite the axe cutting it nearly in two, and after a moment, its eyes started rolling again. The body had to be kicked down a second time.

Mutters of fears and disquiet rippled behind him as if his blow had been a rock thrown in a still pool. Haegar glanced back to see that the number of onlookers had swelled. The people of Palvast hung back in the shadows of their homes, whispering on their porches as more and more emerged groggily into the night, many still rubbing sleep from their eyes.

Haegar glanced at Torvust, who had his own axe at the ready, frowning uncertainly at the twitching corpse. "Drag it outside and bury it," he ordered. "Be swift now. Mind those jaws."

Torvust made no move to obey. His eyes were locked on those of the wolf, following its maddening stare. "What is it?" he asked softly.

Haegar stepped up to the man and seized him by the shoulder, dragging him forward. "Take it from here, before too many see it. Now!" Torvust met his eyes, then blinked, and seemed to come to himself again. Haegar released him.

After taking a deep breath, Torvust pounced on the severed head, forcing its jaws shut as he lifted it. Other men rushed forward and grabbed the wolf's flopping legs, and together they dragged the beast toward the gate, which now stood open for them.

Blood-matted snow dwelt where the beast had been a moment before. Haegar stared at it, axe still gripped in one hand, as shadows and snow danced before him in light flurries. For a moment, the storms in his mind were eclipsed by confusion. What...what *was* that thing? *Haza is dying. It killed him.* Fear returned, and it startled him how strongly he felt it. *Not my brother...*

"Haegar!" Mayor Garvim came hurrying out of the crowd, dressed in thin linens, followed by a score of young townsmen in varying states of dress. "Your brother is with the physician now."

Haegar could barely make himself meet the shorter man's eyes. "He...he'll live?"

Garvim's face was as bleak as the snow. "Conyr will cauterize the wounds," he said. "That'll stop the bleeding. What happens after that will be up to the winds of fate, aye?"

Haegar closed his eyes and took a deep breath. It didn't help. *Superstitious old fool. Ignorant-* He choked off that thought. It wouldn't do Haza any good. Conyr was the best healer in the Winterwood; if anyone could save his brother's life, it was him. But something had been loosened in Haegar, jarred by the mingled horror of waking to hear Makin shouting his name while Haza screamed in the distance, and the sight that followed. Haza, on his back, the wolf looming over him, jaws filled with blood. Haza's shrieks... That inhuman sound clung to his bones like a vile film. It was never something he'd expected to hear from his own flesh and blood. The sound of true fear.

Garvim sidled closer, his bulbous face red and slick with

sweat. His eyes darted back toward the crowd, which was looking on curiously, their anxious rumblings like a distant storm. "What was it?" the mayor asked.

"A wolf," he replied. Already, he knew that wasn't right.

"A...sick wolf? Foaming mouth?" Garvim's eyes widened with each word. "I...I saw it. It wouldn't die. I could see it kicking in the lamplight, even from across the road."

Haegar set his jaw to one side. He could feel every inch of his flesh prickling with denial, but he made himself say what he knew was true. "It was already dead before I attacked, Garvim."

Before the stupefied mayor could reply, Torvust came trudging back through the snow, followed by the men who'd helped him. They dispersed to stand quietly with the rest of the townsfolk, who shifted and muttered with quiet discomfort. Haegar couldn't let himself display that same restless helplessness. Someone needed to be strong. *Blood quench me, I can't stop shaking...*

"It's done," Torvust said with a soft grunt. "Still kicking, but we piled rocks over it before we laid earth and snow." He glanced back at the gate, which was sliding shut behind him. "How did it get in?"

"The stream, I think," said Sorvak. "The gates were shut, and I never took my eyes off that blood-cursed road. It must've swum through the gap."

"Dam it off," Haegar growled. He'd yet to wrench his eyes away from that bloody patch of snow. "Let the road outside flood, if you must, but I want it stopped off from both ends. I don't know if this...wolf had a pack, but we can't take that risk." If there were more things like that, more monsters creeping into Palvast...

"Yes, that's best," sputtered Garvim. "There can't be more of them. This was a fluke. A…a…" he trailed off, mouth working as he sought the proper words.

"We'll handle it, Mayor," said Torvust, giving the portly man a stiff nod. "Why don't you see to our townsfolk, aye? Assure them the danger has passed." Garvim stared at him for a moment, seeming to doubt that such assurances could be made. Torvust turned to depart for his task, followed by his workers.

The mayor, however, sank shakily onto the porch, his eyes as wide as the full face of the moon. He stared up at the sky, a cold and quiet look passing over his face. Disbelief. That was it. "Boil my blood, Haegar, what do we do about this?"

Haegar could only clench his jaw. He tried to steady his breathing again, but he'd sooner have tamed the wind. Haza's screams were still ringing in his ears. "Nothing," he finally growled. "Seal the entrances to Palvast, and post an additional watch, if it soothes you. Some sick beast got in. That's all. And it's gone now. There's no need to make this larger than it is."

"How can you be so certain, Haegar?" Garvim's voice sounded desperate.

"The dead!" came a strangled cry from somewhere nearby. The watching crowd shifted and murmured, searching for the voice. "The dead are coming for us, like the refugees said!" And like a spark to tinder, that was enough to set off more. Soon, panicked shouts filled the night air.

They were the words Haegar had dared not think. The men who'd passed through Palvast had wagging tongues; they'd corrupted the festival with dreadful rumor and whispers, pressing warnings to any who would listen. Instead of trying to convince them to stay, Haegar had found himself driving the travelers out of the town as quickly as possible. But his efforts hadn't been enough. Rumor had taken root in his home.

Dead beasts. Dead animals in the forest. Dead men, too.

The fallen, the hunted, rising with the moon to creep along the undersides of lengthening shadows. They were everywhere now, filling the Winterwood to bursting, scratching at the walls around their towns until they managed to push them down. It was the kind of madness one would hear a Joromori pagan rave about, or else read in one of Haza's stories. It had no business in the Winterwood, in the minds of solid, indomitable Vruskmen. *This cannot be happening. I must be dreaming.*

"That thing was dead before it attacked Haza, wasn't it?" someone demanded. "That's why it was still moving after you chopped its bloodied head off, aye?"

The crowd's rumblings only grew more heated, frantic, as voices argued and competed to be heard. "It can't possibly be true." "Dead beasts, hunting the living?" "You saw that thing thrashing same as I did, aye? It didn't have its bleeding head!" "The belief of pagan gods, it is." "But you saw it, didn't you? You heard what our own people said."

And then he heard the door creak open. Tayja was there, her face so pale she almost looked Vrusk. Makin and Rala both clung to her skirts, their faces twin mirrors of terror. "Enough!" he turned on the crowd, his voice like splintering ice. Silence was a falling cloud of mist, all eyes lighting upon him. He stepped forward and brandished his axe, thrusting it toward the stain of blood on the snow. "My own brother is attacked by a rabid beast, and here you stand, fantasizing about stories of walking corpses? Fools and cowards, all of you!"

"I saw what I saw," that first voice protested. It was the young Corvil, who stood with arms folded, fear and anger marbled on his face. "That thing had neither breath nor life, yet it walked."

"What would a young fool know, aye?" Haegar demanded, looking out at the rest of the crowd. He could feel Tayja's eyes on his back like twin needles, but that storm of anger had hold of him now, and it would not relent. "It's the cold. The darkness. The eyes play tricks. What nonsense is walking corpses? Have you ever heard of anything like it before? Have your fathers? What's happened to your senses, brothers?"

Garvim stood. "He's right. Something's happened in the Winterwood, that much is undeniable. But it can't be more than some strange sickness, aye? Makes beasts go wild. Insane, maybe. They ignore pain, ignore fear. That's why people are afraid. But is it something you'll abandon your homes over? One mad wolf? Will you follow them, Palvast, out of our homeland?"

The crowd began to murmur again, and now fear and anger were diminished by satisfaction and reassurance. Garvim looked to Haegar and nodded, convinced the battle was over. But Haegar knew what had just been unleashed would not be so easily put back again. The invisible terror that had been plaguing the Winterwood had just invaded Palvast and attacked one of their own. Like an open wound, if left untreated, it would soon fester. And what would come then, he dared not imagine.

"Go back to your homes," he commanded. "We're safe, now. We'll dam the stream and post more guards along the walls. Sick animals don't usually travel in packs, but we'll make certain, nonetheless. Go back home and don't worry any more. Nothing is wrong. Nothing is…" His thoughts fled from him. Haza's scream was still echoing through his mind. That dead wolf's eyes were an accusation.

"And don't let your minds be troubled by foolish stories," Garvim finished.

One by one, the Vruskmen began to disperse in silence, but the cold veneer of mistrust and doubt still lingered in the air. Men gathered their wives and children and whisked them away from the cold and the dark, retreating into the shadows of Palvast and to their own worried thoughts.

That left only a vigilant few, whom Garvim assigned to watch from the walls with Sorvak. Haegar went with them, axe still in hand, to watch the quiet, empty road that led up to the gates. Through long and dark hours, he saw nothing but the stillness of the Winterwood. He longed to rush to Haza's side, but a sense of duty kept him rooted in place. Even if it all was just nonsense, even if he couldn't get that angry voice that thought all this was ridiculous out of his head, he knew he had to keep watch. He had to keep his family safe.

Torvust, once he'd returned from successfully damming the stream, climbed to the ramparts and frowned at the first sliver of dawn creeping over the forest. He clapped a hand to Haegar's shoulders, who had yet to move. "You should go see your brother," he said quietly. "Get out of the cold for a while, at least."

"I should've been there to protect him," Haegar found himself murmuring. He couldn't get that sight out of his head. The wolf's thrashing. Haza's helpless screams. "My own brother, and I wasn't there. I wasn't fast enough."

Torvust's grip tightened. "You did all you could, aye? Haza is a Vruskman, same as us. Strong blood. He'll pull through."

Haegar made himself nod. *He has to.* He couldn't imagine losing his brother over something so random, so meaningless. He'd watched his parents succumb to death slowly, bent by age, broken by sickness. But they'd had countless years together, and they'd passed in peace, content and ready to depart Razzador. But Haza...Haza would be ripped away by chance. Gone without a word. Suddenly, all the anger and resentment Haegar held for his brother seemed silly. Foolish as any of his old stories.

He turned and left Torvust behind, descending back onto the road and hurrying past his home, past that bloodied snow.

He was running now, dashing up the street with the wind roaring in his ears, heedless of the snow that billowed up around him.

At the home of Conyr, Palvast's resident physician, lights were streaming through the windows, bathing the yard in front in bars of bleak yellow and orange. A sense of unease settled over him as he approached. Things seemed too quiet. Shouldn't he still hear screaming? Or else, Conyr shouting for his assistants? *Is Haza already dead?*

He hammered on the door, ready to break right through, but it was opened immediately by a wide-eyed Karra, Conyr's wife and assistant. She stared up at him with terror on her face. "Haegar?" she asked with a gasp. "What happened? Is the beast gone?"

"My brother," he growled, pushing the woman lightly aside as he barged into the house. "Take me to him. Now."

"He is resting," Karra replied. She was a wide woman with waist-length brown hair. The bags under her eyes seemed darker than when he'd last seen her. "Conyr recommends we don't disturb him... Hey! Haegar!"

But he didn't look back. He stormed ahead, straight past the living room and down the hall, shoving his head into each room he passed, but all were empty. Karra's shouts followed him, but his steps grew faster, spurred by panic. He needed to find Haza. He had to see him. He had to make certain- There!

In the last room at the end of the hall, he found his brother. Haza was laid out in a long bed, a heavy woolen blanket drawn up to his neck. His eyes were shut, his mouth slightly agape, as he lay on his back. Several candles had been placed on the various shelves and cabinets that lined the walls of the room. It made the dark patches that marred the blanket, stained the floor, unmistakable.

Haegar's eyes were drawn to the right side of the bed, where the blankets were partially tossed aside to expose his brother's mangled arm. Except there was no arm. Only a stump, sprouting from his shoulder and ending just above where his elbow had once been, remained. Red-soaked bandages veiled the wound from sight, and soaked towels were draped across his shoulder, neck, and forehead. Haza's skin was gray as a dead fire.

"He'll live, I think," said a voice from behind. "Hard to say, especially with the early cold, but he's got strong blood. I'm sorry, Haegar."

Haegar closed his eyes, but that did not stop the hot tear that slid down his cheek. Breathing came harder. He started to tremble, from anger's heat, not the cold. "What did you do to him, Conyr?" he asked in a quiet voice.

"There was no saving the arm," Conyr said as he stepped up beside him. The physician was an old, stooped man, back bent and skin gnarled by time. Yet his walk was still steady, and his hands never trembled as he approached the bedside and gently removed the towels from Haza, soaking them again in a steaming bucket before replacing them. "It had been partially severed already," he explained in a calm, business-like voice. "Nasty work, too. Nastier than I've seen in years. I had to cut above the wound—the damage was too severe to salvage, otherwise."

Haegar stumbled back a step and bumped into a nearby chair, which he slowly sank into. He didn't think he could've stayed standing a moment longer. "You said...he'll live, right, Conyr?"

The old man straightened and nodded. His leathery face was creased by a studious frown, and he wiped his brow beneath a bald scalp. "Aye, provided he survives these first few nights, and has enough time to rest. I'll keep him here until the risk of infection wanes, but even after, until that wound heals, I expect him to make regular visits. Rot kills more men than any sword, and I worry this may be beyond my skill to heal. It could be a close thing."

Haegar could only nod. "I'll make sure he comes to you. Thank you, Conyr."

Conyr set his jaw to one side. He glanced at Karra, who now stood in the doorway with a look of worry on her face, then back to Haza. "Tell me what happened, Haegar. What sort of wolf wanders willingly into Palvast?"

"I don't know," he whispered. His eyes were on Haza's stump. His own arm twinged painfully. He couldn't imagine the agony his brother would wake to. The idea alone filled him with anger and sorrow, but he didn't know which one to voice, so opted for silence instead.

"Our brothers were whispering of dark rumors all day," the physician said in a grave, flat voice. "The same stories I've been hearing all through autumn. If there's any credence to them, Haegar, we deserve to know. We have a right, ere we end up like your brother here. I heard you buried the wolf; I'd like you to show me the corpse."

Haegar closed his eyes again. "No need," he said softly. "I'll tell you what it was. Dead, Conyr. Dead before it ever entered the town. Its chest…it had been hollowed already. Haza put an arrow right through its head, and it didn't fall. Even after I'd decapitated it…" he looked up at Conyr, struggling to speak through a throat that felt strangled. "Have you ever heard of anything like that before?"

"Only in old stories," Conyr said, crossing his arms. "Ill remembered, and with good reason."

"But there can't be any truth to them." Haegar leaned forward, clasping his head in his hands. "It's all madness, isn't it? The religions died hundreds of years ago, because they were nothing but wind. All these stories are the same. Only fools believe in them."

"Even fools must have a reason to fear," Karra murmured from the doorway. "I heard the travelers speak of Malice. Lives in dead things. Hates us, it does. Hates all living things."

"I can't believe it," Haegar growled. He looked up at Haza. "I can't…but this will not happen again. I won't allow it. What if it had been one of my children in that thing's jaws tonight?"

The old healer shared another glance with his wife, both their faces dour. "They'd be dead, Haegar," he grunted. "I hate these stories as much as you, but what happened tonight was real. None of us can deny it now. And if it's true that dead things are wandering the wood, then perhaps our brothers are right to flee over the Tagalfr."

But Haegar shook his head, his every drop of blood revolting at the idea. "If we ran from every unexplained whistle in the night, every unknown shadow, we'd have abandoned the Winterwood centuries ago. What if we're overreacting? This Malice must be exaggerated."

"Is that what you would call this?" Conyr nodded toward Haza and the bloodied stump of his arm. "An exaggeration, aye? This and worse is what we risk if we ignore what we've seen and heard today."

Haegar put his face in his hands again, struggling to control his breaths. His fingers curled around thick, shaggy hair, pulling tight. "Stories are just stories…"

Conyr sighed as he stepped up to receive a new bucket of water from Karra. "That's what becomes of everything in the end, aye? What will this attack be tomorrow? Or three years from now in Joromor? Nothing but a story."

Haegar sat quietly as the physician and his wife continued to work. He watched Haza, but his brother didn't stir. It didn't even look like the man was still alive, so shrunken he seemed in that bed. So fragile. *Father, help us. How could things have twisted sideways so quickly? What went wrong? I should've been faster. My blood be damned, but I should've been...*

His forefathers had no answer for him, and Haegar realized, perhaps for the first time, there was no one left in his life who could make decisions for him, who could lend him advice or direction. He was alone. And he had a family to protect. Again, that gap between himself and his brother, once an impossible chasm, had diminished into something that seemed quite small. Was their constant bickering really worth it? What did it all matter if Haza died on this bed? *If he'd never come back, he'd still be whole. But a part of him wanted to be with his family. With me. And I shoved him aside.*

He leaned his head back again as another silent tear escaped down his cheek. He stayed there, eyes shut, and listened to his brother's quiet breaths. Yet for the stillness of the room, his mind was tormented by questions of fury and terror, and he had answers to none of them.

Haza woke with a startled gasp. He launched upright, swatting at the image of a twisted wolf hanging before his eyes, its fangs glistening red. Only one hand obeyed. In the other, there was pain. He cried out again, rolling to one side, reaching for the source of the wracking agony, only to find a bandage-wrapped stump. He stared for a moment, horror, revulsion, and confusion rolling over themselves like crashing waves. Haza groaned as the pain redoubled, pulsing unlike anything he'd ever suffered before. An iron rod blazed through his missing arm, as if his limb were still there, burning all over.

He forced himself to breathe as he fought to ride out the

storm of fire. All the while, groggy images of snow and blood flashed through his mind. He was alive. Haza could've laughed—how strange it was to realize that only now. The wolf had been killed. He could see Haegar's axe swinging, blade glinting in the light of the Seventeen Stars. He could feel the monster's teeth grinding on his bones.

Haza screamed as the pain intensified yet again. He was left panting, his clothing slick with sweat, as he tried gingerly to hold his stump with his other hand, but the searing intensity of even the lightest touch was enough to make him want to vomit, which he did, spilling the last night's feast into his lap. *Let it end,* he moaned. *Let it end, let it end!*

The sound of a creaking door brought a momentary distraction. He clenched his teeth to stay his tongue and drew a hissing breath. It was then that he was able to notice his surroundings. This was not his own room. Light was streaming through a nearby window, casting itself across lifeless candles. Metallic instruments were arranged neatly on a table, laid upon crimson blankets. Knives, needles, spools of thread, and a large, menacing saw greeted him as a man pushed open the nearby door.

"You're awake sooner than expected," said Conyr as he hobbled into the room.

Haza exhaled when he recognized the physician. *I'm still in Palvast.* He wasn't quite sure what else he'd been expecting, but there was a bizarre, nameless paranoia chewing at his heart. He knew where it came from. Those eyes. Those dead eyes. Those eyes had *hated* him, hated him more than he'd ever hated anything in his life. Not even his father. But the wolf was dead… why did terror still cling to him so tightly?

The pain struck him again. It was all he could do to keep

from screaming. "Wh-what happened t-to my arm?" he rasped breathlessly. "Where is it?"

"My apologies, but there was nothing else I could do. You're lucky to be alive at all, young one. Stay still. I need to change your bandages." The physician frowned at the puddle in Haza's lap. "And your sheets as well."

Haza stiffened, too agonized to feel shame, as he braced for the old man's touch to bring a new burst of agony. It was worse than he could've imagined. He writhed the moment contact was made, groaning, trying to grip the blanket with both hands. Only one obeyed. Only one *could* obey. *Boil my blood, I'm dying! This is what dying feels like.* His stomach turned as he watched Conyr unroll the blood-soaked bandages, and he caught a glimpse of glistening, red flesh beneath. Haza snapped his head to one side, struggling vainly to banish the image of his own mutilation. He blew out his breaths in panicked puffs. "Tell me...what happened..." he grunted, desperate for anything to distract him from the fire chewing his stump.

Conyr displayed no revulsion or hesitation as he took up a bucket of water and began to clean Haza's now-exposed wound. His voice was calm as a windless day. "The wolf tore the flesh of your arm nearly right off the bone. The attack was vicious, worse than I've ever seen. Amputation was the only way forward if you wanted to keep your life.

Haza looked down at his remaining hand, clenched into a fist at his side. Waves of shock still rolled over him, his body wracked with needle-like shudders. *It's gone...it's really gone.* How had this happened? He felt like he could still feel his missing hand, still close his fingers. *How could it just be...missing?* His memories were muddled, and though he was struggling to think, he suddenly remembered those hateful eyes again.

"The wolf," he rasped. "Something was wrong with it. It wasn't—"

"Alive?" Conyr paused in his work to cough. "Yes. The whole town knows, by now. They've been arguing all morning. Something bad is headed for Palvast."

Something bad. Haza found himself mouthing it wordlessly like a mantra. He needed no further proof. In those dead, unseeing eyes, he'd glimpsed a dark and terrible shadow lurking. A blistering, hungering darkness, one that would've consumed him utterly. "What are we going to do about it?" he asked softly.

Conyr rebound his stump in bandages, wrapping them with a tight, clean knot. Haza breathed through his teeth the whole time, and the waves of pain did not abate for the physician's hands finally releasing him. Conyr stood and wiped blood from his hands with a cloth. He also helped Haza change into a fresh set of linens, free from the stain of his stomach's contents. "That's not up to me, is it? They're talking out there, right now. They say dead things wander the Winterwood, and now they've come to Palvast. Malice, some are calling it. An old, old story. What would you want to do, Haza? You're the first among us to feel this malady's bite."

Haza worked his teeth. The grinding noise was distracting, but he still couldn't escape the sensation that his arm had been drenched in fire. It was everything he could do to keep from thrashing to put it out. "What of the wolf?" he made himself ask. *Breathe. Breathe. Blood be cursed, my arm! I must keep breathing. Keep breathing, Haza.* Dead things walking. It was the same warning the travelers had brought with them yesterday. "When my brother cut off its head, did it die?"

Conyr threw him a flat look over his shoulder, his face blank.

A hand seemed to close around his heart. "How can you fight an enemy that does not die?" he wondered aloud.

"I don't know," Conyr said. He paused in the doorway and tapped one finger against its wooden frame. "Most of our kin seem to believe you can't. That's why they flee west. And I think I'll be joining them."

Haza blinked, so startled he nearly forgot his pain. "Really? Where would you go? Savisdale?" Vrusk's capital might be able to use a skilled old physician like him, but the Winterwood would sorely miss his talent. *Without him, I'd likely already be dead.* His tongue crumbled to ashes in his mouth.

"At least to Farrenhall," Conyr said, his frown growing grim. "Even the dead cannot cross a river like the Tagalfr, aye? If you want my recommendation, convince that headstrong brother of yours to go too, along with everyone else in Palvast. The Winterwood isn't safe for us, anymore."

Haza nodded slowly. He made himself look at his freshly bandaged stump. "Am I...able to walk, Conyr?"

"Try not to move your arm," the physician grunted. "That wound will need to be monitored carefully if we're to prevent infection. It might be beyond my skill to tend. Yet another reason to come with me when I leave, aye? Unless you'd rather trust the healing to your brother."

The old man vanished from the room, leaving Haza alone with his throbbing arm and his spectral, missing fingers. He shut his eyes, but no motion he made, no muscle he tensed, helped assuage the pain. And in the darkness of his mind, he saw the wolf. Its fangs. Its terrible, hateful eyes. His heart began to race and his hair stood on end, but he forced himself to take a long, steadying breath, and after that was able to collect his thoughts. *We have to leave. Tonight. No, immediately.* They couldn't spend another minute in Palvast.

Slowly, he tried to rise from the bed. It was a laborious process, limited both by his single hand and the relentless burning. Inch by painstaking inch, Haza turned and lowered his legs over the side of his bed. He had more difficulty than he'd expected getting onto his feet; his legs were trembling, and he had to awkwardly push off the bed to manage it. He stood there for a moment, wobbling. *This can't be real, can it?* It all felt so ridiculous. Like he was caught in some horrific waking nightmare. This couldn't possibly be happening to him. He couldn't have possibly lost his arm, right?

If not for the pain, Haza wouldn't have any trouble believing he was dreaming. But the piercing wound was like an anchor, linking him solidly in the twisted new world in which he'd awoken. *How can I travel like this? Pull myself up on a horse? Hold my niece and nephew again...?*

That last thought was enough to break him. He collapsed into the nearby chair, nearly ramming his stump against the wall, and he clamped his remaining hand over his mouth to keep from sobbing. He gaped at the sunlit room around him, shaking silently as tears rolled down his face without restraint. This wasn't real. It couldn't be.

I'm wasting time. The dead were coming. Every second they remained in Palvast only brought a calamity closer to his family. His mind reeled with the horror of it all. The worries of yesterday, of festivals and restlessness and exhausting labor, were all dashed by this harsh new reality, vanishing like spring snow.

Haza forced himself to stand again. He stumbled forward, using his outstretched arm to grasp the walls and steer his trembling feet out the door. He soon emerged into the daylight and groaned as the sun of a clear morning found him. His hand snapped up to block the light, but the sudden motion made his vision swim. He stumbled, reaching out to steady himself, only to try with a hand that no longer existed.

He fell heavily, landing on his side in the thin layer of snow over the road. Haza cried out as the impact made bone grind against flesh. He staggered upright, mortified to see a faint blotch of red seeping through fresh linen. *I can't do this. I'm going to be sick.* More men died off the battlefield than on, the victims of infection and living rot. He was in grave danger.

So distracted was Haza by the pain that he nearly missed the activity unfolding around him. Palvast was aflame with motion, dozens of men and women rushing by. They didn't notice him, so fixated were they on their destinations. Many carried sacks or tugged wagons in their wake, all piled high with chests, crates, and barrels, stacks of blankets and bags of clothing. Food unsold in yesterday's festival was piled on haphazard pallets. Still more helped the elderly hobble forward, while mothers dragged quarreling children along by the hand and clutched wailing infants to their chests. The shouting and yelling, the crying, the confusion, all blended into a wordless drone.

Haza forced himself forward, his step uncertain. He couldn't believe what he was seeing. The milling crowd was slowly siphoning toward the heart of the town, and those who finally did catch sight of him only paled and pointed. Some shouted his name. All looked afraid.

Palvast has already reached the same conclusion that I have, Haza realized, and the thought both saddened and relieved him. They would abandon their homes. Go west. Escape those dead eyes.

He began to follow the crowd, but he soon found himself ushered forward by yelling men. They called his name. They saw his wound. They asked him what had happened. He didn't need to say a word; he was living justification of their terror. A beacon of warning before the coming darkness. He tried to cradle his chest, but he couldn't hold himself anymore. He felt strangely naked, a part of himself stripped away. Haza could feel the eyes, too. Everyone was watching.

He flushed with rage and embarrassment, but there was nothing he could do about it. He kept walking, accepting the sympathetic whispers, the endless tirade of questions. His attention was on a greater matter.

At Palvast's center, wagons and horses waited beneath the baleful eye of the mid-morning sun. Glistening snow blanketed the nearby rooftops and had buried the ashes of the previous night's fire in a smothering veil. Everyone had gathered. Nearly a hundred figures all clamoring to reach the center. Some swarmed the wagons, piling more of their possessions onto already precarious piles, while the rest stood apart in a small, separate group.

Heated arguments were brewing in the crowd, stirred like embers into flame. Only the dead fire and a small strip of ground separated them. "I don't need to see it," one man protested. "all I need is the word of another Vruskman, and that bloody snow, to know that I won't put my children at risk for another hour in this wretched wood."

"You have no courage! None of you!" Garvim barked. The bulbous man was stalking back and forth in front of the smaller group, his face dark and pinched. He jabbed an accusing finger at those gathered around the wagons, most of whom did not slow in their packing. "Our forefathers built this place from nothing! Do you think they feared wolves or bears or a too cold winter?"

"Maybe they feared dead wolves," called young Corvil, who stood atop one of the wagons with his arms crossed over his lanky chest. There was a sneer nestled behind his patchy, blonde beard, and his eyes were as cold as the sky overhead. "But if they had wits to match yours, mayor, I'd guess not."

"Aye, and what of you, Torvust?" came the shout from

Sorvak. The old man had stepped up alongside Garvim, his blotchy face gnarled further by his outrage. "You're one of the strongest men we've got. You've lived your whole life in this wood, same as I. And you'd abandon it now? Over the events of one night?"

Torvust stood stoically beside one of the wagons, Magda beside him. His pregnant wife bore naked fury on her pale face, one hand cradling her swollen stomach. As she took a step, Torvust placed a forestalling hand on her shoulder, his expression determined. It was not anger that made his eyes hard, his voice as steady as a mountain. "Maybe you didn't get close enough to that thing, Sorvak," he said. "Maybe you didn't see the way it kicked and snapped, even with its head cloven from its shoulders. You think men can fight against something like that?

Garvim blew out his whiskers indignantly. "Well, it's stopped moving now, aye? We dug it up this morning to discover a corpse. Nothing more. This was a sick animal, my friends, and it's dead, now. Who can really say there are more? You'd abandon your whole life on a whim. Everything we've worked so hard to build. I never knew you as a coward, Torvust."

The crowd murmured quietly on both sides, but Torvust only frowned in disapproval. "I'll take my chances in the Summerlands, regardless. I won't let what happened to poor Haza happen to anyone in my family."

"Look!" someone shouted. "Haza! There he is!"

All eyes swiveled toward him and the crowd drew back. Haza shuddered, shrinking before their stares. His absent arm flared in agony. Now that they could see him, the people of Palvast grew quiet. The fear on those gathered around the wagons grew sharper, more certain, while those who decried the danger grew pale.

"Haza?" It was Haegar's voice that broke the silence. He

stepped out from amid the dissenters, pausing alongside Garvim and Sorvak. Tayja was with him, her head wrapped in a pale blue scarf. Makin and Rala clung to her skirts, and twin expressions of worry passed over their faces when they saw him. Rala tried to break away, to run to him, but Tayja gripped her by the shoulder and held her back. Her face was an expressionless mask.

Meeting his brother's eyes, Haza could see that Haegar had come to the same realization; the time to leave was now. So why, by all the blood of their ancestors, did he and his family stand on the wrong side? Guilt, so quick that he was half-sure he'd imagined it, flickered in Haegar's eyes.

Haza made himself meet the mayor's stare instead. Garvim had grown pale as the snow at his feet, unable to hide his discomfort as he stared at Haza's stump. "Torvust is right," he said, and though his voice was soft, it was the only thing audible amid the hush that had taken hold of the town. Garvim finally met his eyes. "We need not go as far as the Summerlands and Havasa. If we cross at Farrenhall, we can seek Lord Varkoth's protection. The dead won't be able to ford the Tagalfr, they'd be swept away as surely as any living man. And the Gated Bridge has never been breached. The Old King, and our fellow Vruskmen, will defend us. But we cannot stay here. The Winterwood is not our home anymore; it's changed." He felt dizzy again. He stumbled, but Torvust was there, catching him by the good shoulder. He had to lean against the bigger man just to stay on his feet.

"You might as well be a foreigner," Sorvak sneered. He pounded a fist against his narrow chest. "What blood flows in your veins, Haza Ruthborne? What do you know about making this place your home, aye? You came crawling back here when there was nowhere else for you to go. Had your father not been so sick, he would've tossed you back into the river. Damn my blood, I'll help you do it right now, Haegar."

Haza faced his brother, whose eyes had dropped. "Haegar, look what it did to me." He pointed at his stump. "Look at it!"

The town held its breath as the younger Ruthborne brother hesitated. At his side, Tayja stiffened, and Rala began to cry softly into her skirt. Only Makin looked at Haza directly, eyes on his face. Not even a glance for his maimed arm. He felt a deep rush of love for his young nephew. *Not like his father at all. Not like any of us.*

And then Haegar looked up.

"All this for a wolf?" Garvim scoffed, cutting across whatever was about to be said. He rounded on Haegar, voice scathing as a dull razor. "You're a Ruthborne, aren't you? I see so much of your father in you, Haegar. He built this place for *you*, and your family."

"Aye," growled Torvust, "but did he mean for you to die in it?"

Tayja squeezed her husband's forearm, her voice a sharp, urgent hiss. "You know what we need to do."

Haegar' seemed to have lost the ability to blink. Haza had never seen his brother like this before. A man of such raw strength and resolve, confused and helpless as a blind man trying to find the road again. He was torn. Truly torn. And that made Haza quiver. He might really choose to stay.

"Leaving now doesn't mean we must leave forever," Haza pressed gently. "By winter's end, the Old King can have thousands of men marching through the Winterwood. They can put an end to whatever is causing this, yes? Then we can come back. Our home will still be waiting for us, no matter how many seasons pass. But we won't be, unless we leave right now, before more of those things find us. We cannot fight them. You know this."

Makin reached up and tugged on his father's sleeve, finally pulling Haegar's eyes away. The boy said something Haza couldn't hear, but the expression on his brother's face changed. It was…settled. A decision had been made. Haegar seemed to shrink beneath the stares of his kinsmen, becoming little more than a hollow-eyed man, resigned to his fate. Wordlessly, he hefted his children, taking one in each arm. Tayja came beside him, and together they stepped across the small clearing to stand beside Haza and the caravan.

"Coward!" bellowed Sorvak. Beside him, Garvim was shouting something, but it was swallowed in a furious roar. Both sides were shouting at each other, and the wailing of frightened children and the braying of mules rose over all.

While the chaos ignited, Haza rested his remaining hand on Haegar's shoulder and smiled at his brother. Haegar wore no smile. But he did nod, and that was all the understanding that needed to pass between them. Makin came to stand beside him, so he dropped his arm to rest it on his nephew's back. He stood with his family and watched the madness unfold, knowing that the consequences of their decision, whatever they might be, would soon be upon them.

Chapter Seven
Consequence

By midday, the caravan of Palvast was ready to depart. Haegar still couldn't believe it. *This isn't really happening. I never came back from that blood-cursed hunt, did I? I'm lying in the snow, dreaming my life away.* Except he wasn't dying. He wasn't even dreaming. He was tying casks of water to the back of a wagon alongside Tayja, securing them in place. He'd made the decision to abandon his home and flee west. *It's not too late,* a persistent voice was quick to interject. It must've been the hundredth time it had appeared since he'd sided with Haza. *You don't have to go. It's not too late. The Winterwood is the only home we've ever needed.*

But Haegar did not give voice to his thoughts, nor did he offer complaint. Instead, he spent the morning hours working with Tayja to help the other townsfolk finish their preparations. He glanced over at Haza, who sat nearby on the end of another wagon, entertaining Makin and Rala with one of his books. Haegar was tempted to chide him for whatever foolish stories he was filling their heads with, but he couldn't bring himself to do it. He'd never seen Haza look so weary before. Dark red was bleeding through the bandages around his stump.

He's right, Haegar told the voice. *Damn my blood, but he is. We don't have to leave for long. We'll go to Savisdale. The Old King must know how to fix this. He can give us answers and tell us when we can return.*

His stomach churned. Haegar couldn't remember ever feeling so dizzy, so sick. It wasn't right. He was his own man, he had his own life, and to uproot it over this, over a stray wolf… He made himself breathe out slowly. All he wanted to do was turn and walk back into his home, to sit in front of the cozy, stone hearth, or at the hand-carved table where they ate dinners every night. His parents were still in there. He'd opted to leave the painting behind, much as it pained him. He couldn't take them out of Palvast. He wouldn't do it. *They can watch over the Winterwood until we return.*

"Are you feeling all right?" Tayja asked in a soft voice. Her hand brushed lightly across his back before dropping to wrap about his waist. She leaned her head against his shoulder as she spoke.

"Yes." He made his breathing more regular. A pale cloud of white frost escaped through his clenched teeth. "What about you?"

"I'm not worried about me," Tayja replied. "I've been across the Tagalfr before, Haegar. I lived more years in Havasa than Vrusk. You've never even set foot beyond Farrenhall, have you?"

He closed his eyes. "No." He'd been to the Gated Bridge many times, of course, but only for the sake of business. The stream that cut through Palvast emptied its cargo of lumber into the Tagalfr just a mile from Farrenhall. It was more a fortress than a bridge, mighty and vast and guarded by the Varkoth family. Lord Kalivaz had ruled there Haegar's entire life, and, in truth, he was the true ruler of the Winterwood. But Vruskmen swore fealty to the Old King, not an old family, no matter what land they claimed to own.

"It's the greatest bridge in all Razzador," Tayja continued, her smile framed as comforting. "It's impregnable, Haegar. And it's what brought us together, if you recall."

Haegar snorted. "Our love united us, not some bridge."

She sighed softly. "Trust in it, Haegar. Not even the God-Emperors and their holy hosts could breach it. And once we're across, we'll still be in Vrusk. It's not like we're really leaving our home, aye? It might be good for the children to see more of their own kingdom. And you, as well."

Haegar snorted. "God-Emperors? You've been listening to Haza too much." His eyes found his brother again, who was still entertaining Makin and Rala. A frustrated look was on his face as he tried to juggle the book one-handed to turn the pages. Rala reached up to aid him and he tried to hide his relief. The man looked ready to keel over just from the effort of reading. He hadn't risen from that spot since sinking there after the greater crowd had dispersed, like he'd spent some last, hidden spring of energy to hobble into the square and speak. "At least Haza gets what he wants, aye?"

Tayja cuffed him on the shoulder. "At what cost? Hardly seems a fair price to pay for passage out of the Winterwood, aye? I wish he'd just left years ago, like he wanted."

"He's a stubborn man," Haegar said softly. He stiffened as a new blast of cold wind came up from behind him, weaving slender fingers unbidden across his flesh. "I…I don't know if he'll survive that wound." He'd spent the last hour talking to Conyr. The physician's confidence from the previous night had faded after watching Haza try to move. He wanted the man tied to a wagon and on the road to Savisdale, where healers of sufficient skill could see to him.

"He's Ruthborne," Tayja whispered. She held him, momentarily shielding him from the cruel touch of the wind. "Just like us. And we're all too stubborn to die, aye?"

"Aye."

The sound of a ringing bell marked midday. Activity around the wagons began to slow. The preparations had been completed. Women corralled their children into the waiting caravan while men saw to the mules, the dogs, the cattle, and sheep. Most of Palvast's animals would be coming, though the farmers had almost unanimously decided to abandon their holdings. Beneath a clear, empty sky, eighty-five Vruskmen and their possessions faced the western gate of Palvast, which stood open to reveal the open road and the endless, snow swept trees of the Winterwood.

As the first wagons of the caravan creaked into motion, Haegar's heart quickened. He watched the children help Haza climb into the wagon. The three lay down together, Haza with painstaking care while Makin and Rala piled blankets on him. "Are we making the right choice?" Haegar whispered. "Is this what we should be doing?" He looked beyond the caravan to where near fifty men and women were still gathered, many with their children, looking on in contempt as their fellow townsfolk abandoned their home.

As she followed his gaze, Tayja's hand fell away from him. "You tell me." She turned to look up at his face, her eyes seeking an answer. "You saw it, right? Is it as bad as everyone says? This threat, *is* it real? Haza might bear its marks, but it's your word I trust, my love. If you say we should stay, we'll stay. But only if you say it."

Staring into his wife's searching eyes, it was then that he realized she was just as frightened and confused as he was. His cheeks flushed with shame as he took Tayja gently by the shoulders and inclined his head. "I don't know. Damn my blood, but I don't. Maybe we're running from wind, or maybe… But I must protect you. All of you. I've already failed Haza. I can't promise that I won't fail you as well, if we stay."

Tayja nodded, like this was the answer she'd been expecting. "Then we should go."

"Aye."

They stepped toward their cart and climbed together onto the driving seat. Haegar gathered Heartwood's reins, and the horse looked over his shoulder and gave an irritable snort. Behind him, Makin and Rala bickered over a blanket, tugging it back and forth. Muted chatter rose all across Palvast as the crowd waited their turn to start forward.

Torvust, astride his own dapple horse, trotted up beside the Ruthborne wagon. "It warms my heart to see you still breathing, Haza," he said with a nod. Haza, who struggled to rise, smiled weakly, but Torvust's attention had already turned. The man's eyes were wary, and his long, heavy hood framed his face in harsh shadow. "I think Garvim means to try and stop us."

Haegar frowned. He searched for the old mayor among those who'd chosen to remain in Palvast. Unrest boiled among them, angry murmurs rising like a simmering steam, but there was no sign of the man. "By force?"

"I don't know," Torvust looked over his shoulder too. "But this is the right choice, Haegar. I'm proud that you could make it. Cling to that feeling in your belly." He looked to Haza again. "Forgive me, but if that thing hadn't gotten hold of you, I don't think I would've believed these stories. But I saw that thing with my own eyes. I'm sorry you had to suffer to show us the truth."

Haza chuckled, but his face was pained. "I wish I could say it was more of a pleasure, Torvust."

"You've never been outside the Winterwood either, have you?" asked Tayja.

The bearded man only nodded stoically. "This is the right choice. For our families." He smiled at Makin and Rala, who had ceased wrestling and were sitting together, watching with intense eyes. "For our children."

Haegar wished he had something to chop down, anything to keep his mind off the unbearable slowness of the caravan. He just wanted to be on the road already, as if the sooner they left, the sooner they might turn back around again. "When do you think we'll return?"

Torvust's face darkened. He flicked his reins, stirring his horse into motion. "Don't waver from this path, Haegar," he said as he passed. "Leave those worries for the warmth of spring, aye?"

The warmth of spring. It seemed a lifetime away. The wind was like a gentle, mocking laugh as it swept over Haegar, tickling the back of his neck with icy breath. Tayja's hand found his, and he made himself relax. *Remember why we're doing this. Remember. Not for you, not for Haza. For all of us.* The safety of his family was all that should matter.

They sat in silence for a moment, with nothing for company but the clanking of wheels and the groan of ropes, the braying of mules and the blustering of the wind. And then it was their turn. Tayja, who'd taken Heartwood's reins, gave them a snap, and the old horse harrumphed as he began to trot, following after the train of wagons and carts that went before them. Haegar closed his eyes, breathing sharp and cold breaths, as he was carried, without taking a step, away from his home. It was somehow easier, that way, like he was being taken away against his will. The longer he could pretend that, the more rest he'd find.

It was a grim and silent passage. No one in the caravan spoke, not even the brash Corvil. Instead, the newly christened refugees went quietly through the gates of Palvast and out onto the long, winding road that would take them to the edge of the Winterwood. There was no jeering either. Even with his eyes closed, Haegar could feel the stares of those who'd chosen to stay behind. Old Sorvak, with his furious scowl and disapproving glare. Mayor Garvim, his mouth no doubt still agape in surprise, as he watched his own people leave him. Others, hard and faithful Vruskmen, who'd served Palvast all their lives, all watching. As if waiting.

He knew he was abandoning them. Red shame crept up his face, but with it came a strange feeling of pride. He admired those with the courage to stand by their home, and he wished he was with them, watching in silence as the weak-willed abandoned the place their grandsires had built. *Just stories. Nothing but blood-cursed stories.* Every inch of him screamed to leap from the wagon bed, to drag his children and wife from the cart and tell them that they were staying, that there was nothing to fear, that the land that had always sheltered them would continue to do so, no matter how the beasts might howl or the storms might rage. This place was their home. Their only home.

It was only after Haegar was sure they'd passed out of sight of Palvast that he dared open his eyes. He turned to look over his shoulder, past his brother, who was sitting against the side of the cart with eyes shut, a look of pain on his face, and past his children, who sat quietly together amid the blankets. There, beyond the white-topped trees that marched alongside the road, before the pale blue sky that cradled them, Palvast stood somewhere framed between the wood and sky. Pointed roofs peered over the wall of stakes, painted in snow. He blinked, trying to capture that image forever. He feared it might be the last time he ever saw it.

Haegar sat back after that and said nothing even when Tayja asked him if he was well. How could he answer such a question? How could he tell her he wanted to turn the wagon around and ride right back the way they'd come? He listened to the trundling of the cart, the quiet conversations rising around him, and the burbling of the stream that ran alongside the road.

Haza resumed reading from his book again as the caravan pushed on. Makin was stoic as he listened but Rala giggled and demanded another story once he'd finished. Haegar ignored them, his whole body only growing more tense as they pushed further west. It was slow but steady going—the warm sun had left the road clear of snow, and the recent influx of travelers between Palvast and Farrenhall had kept the trail free of debris and branches. It seemed a mockery to him, somehow. There wouldn't be a single inconvenience to slow his departure. *It's still not too late to turn back,* that small voice whispered again.

It would be so easy. The sun had only just eclipsed its zenith. If he turned them around now, he could make it back by nightfall. His skin was crawling, his teeth clenched so tight he feared they might break. This was the hardest thing he'd ever done.

What if it's all just an overreaction?

He blinked. It was nightfall. Haegar blinked again, startled. When had so much time passed? The caravan had slowed to a crawl as darkness descended on the Winterwood, and now, as if of one mind, every wagon stopped. The Vruskmen lit fires along the shore of the stream and watered their animals beside it. Soon, the people of Palvast were gathered about their campfires, separated into family units, and an air of much-needed levity began to rise over the makeshift camp like smoke. Before long, laughter and song were thick overhead. They brought out the leftover food from the harvest festival, heaping generous portions of steak, pie and produce that had gone untouched the night before.

Makin and Rala laughed as they chased each other around the fire, seemingly oblivious that they'd been taken from the only home they'd ever known. Haegar, now seated on the ground with his back to their cart, watched them uncertainly. How could they not feel the same apprehension he did? Where had this jovial air come from? *We're abandoning our home! Can't you feel some proper reverence?*

Haza, despite his obvious pain, seemed in high spirits too, though he was still pale as a spirit from one of his books. He sat by the fire and turned his body so that his stump faced the darkness of the forest. A weathered smile flickered across his face as he gratefully accepted a plate from Tayja.

Haegar couldn't touch his food. He stared at it, ignoring a gentle reprimand from his wife that he was giving his children a poor example. He didn't care. They needed to see him like this. They needed to understand.

"Perhaps Papa just isn't hungry," Haza suggested when Rala asked why he wasn't eating. He coughed and pressed his remaining fist against his chest. "He'll eat later, won't he?" He shot Haegar a meaningful glance.

"Mama, can we go play by the stream?" Makin asked as he set his empty plate aside. "There's nothing to do here but sit and listen to boring songs."

Tayja threw a doubtful gaze at the stream, which crept along nearby, gleaming in the firelight while darkness shrouded its opposite shore. "No, I don't think so," she said. "It's too dark, and I want you to stay close."

"But Mama," Rala protested, scowling, "we wanna play in the snow!"

"Listen to your Mama," Haegar growled without looking up. He flexed and unflexed his fingers around the handle of his axe, which rested on his lap. They had the cart to their backs, facing the forest, and the stream on the other side, but he still felt exposed. Misgivings or no, the darkness was making him anxious. "It's dangerous in the wood tonight."

"They can accompany me, Tayja," Haza said as he rose unsteadily, his movements exaggerated as he staggered onto his feet. "I think I need to see Conyr. I…I'm feeling rather light-headed. We'll stay in the light, in the camp. They'll be safe, and…" he looked helplessly up at the sky, as if beseeching the Seventeen Stars for some answer, "and they can call for aid if I fall."

Haegar looked up at his brother, into his sincere, deathly-pallid face. "Keep them close to you, aye?"

"Of course," Haza said.

Makin immediately began to protest, but Tayja overrode him with a soft hiss. "Your uncle has offered you a kindness. You can go with him, or you can stay here for the rest of the night. It's up to you, aye?"

A shadow passed over Makin's studious face as he appraised his mother, and she stared back with a glare no less imperious. Finally, the boy wilted and wordlessly accompanied his uncle out of the cart, followed by his sister, who was skipping and laughing all the way.

The fire crackled as they faded from view. Haegar pushed his food around his plate. "I don't think they understand," he murmured. "All three of them." He nodded at Corvil as he rode past the wagon. He was one of thirty men, all armed with bows or axes, keeping a careful eye on the darkened forest. Haegar would have his own turn astride Heartwood in a few hours.

"They're children, Haegar," Tayja said with a soft chuckle. She shifted to scoot closer to him. "And Haza is Haza. They don't need to understand what's happening. A part of me hopes they won't. Not entirely, anyway. They don't deserve to have their lives shattered, like we must."

"This is important. They should realize what we're doing. The weight of it."

"They do," she placed her hand on his shoulder. "I promise you, they do, if not as fully as we do. You think they've missed Haza's injury? The way we've been speaking to each other? Had we tried a trip like this in any other season, you know they'd be complaining all the way to Savisdale."

Haegar nodded mutely. He'd noticed that they'd been more subdued than usual. Still, he couldn't help but put himself in their position. If his own father had suddenly announced that they'd be abandoning Palvast, he would've had non-stop questions. He never would've stopped pestering his father until the old man gave him an answer. No matter how frightening it might've been, he would've wanted to know.

"We must protect their innocence." For a moment, her hand tightened around his shoulder, fingers biting anxiously into his flesh. "Even if we get away from these creatures on the other side of the river, the Winterwood will never be the same after the Old King's men go tramping through it. We'll have to be ready for whatever is next, no matter how different our home becomes."

"Different?" Haegar didn't shrug out of her grasp. He met her eyes. "Different how?"

Tayja dropped her eyes, her face darkened by regret and apprehension. "You realize what this must mean, don't you? Those dead creatures will need to be hunted down. All of them. I imagine it will be a long and grueling task. The Winterwood will have to be scoured. They might set fire to the forest." Her voice dropped to a hush. "Even the dead cannot rise again if they're burnt to ashes."

Haegar looked up at the leafless trees towering over them, his heart racing. He could see it, suddenly. Fire. A great, terrible blaze, leaping from one dry, cold tree to the next. He'd seen forest fires before, but only from a distance. They came sometimes, especially in the heat of summer, when the armor-like bark of

Winterwood trees cracked and splintered, surrendering their vulnerable hearts to the merciless sun. All it would take was a summer storm's stray bolt of lightning, and suddenly one could see black clouds on the horizon, spanning for miles.

It was a natural part of life in the Winterwood, his father had told him. Fire razed the old and withered trees, and from their fertile ashes, saplings would grow anew, taller and stronger than before. Much like the work of a woodsman, it was purposeful, methodical, careful to not let destruction overwhelm the cycle of rebirth. The old had to be stripped away so that the new could grow. That was just the way it had always been.

But now Haegar was picturing a different sort of fire. The military of Vrusk unleashed on the Winterwood, their catapults and arrows falling among the trees like screaming, molten stars. They would be careless in their ravaging, hunting their quarry at any cost. They wouldn't stop until everything had been razed; both the living and the dead consumed by the wrath of men who did not, who could not, understand the delicate balance of the Winterwood.

Before long, Haza returned, Makin and Rala in tow, still looking dizzy. He sank back down beside the fire and thanked Tayja quietly when she wrapped a second coat around his shoulders. Makin and Rala both snuggled in their mother's lap, and as they sat there together, watching the embers flicker in the sky, their eyes slowly fluttered shut.

"Thank you," Haza said after a time. His eyes, turned amber by the firelight, almost seemed to glow as they flicked up. "Thank you for saving me."

Haegar shifted the handle of his axe in his lap. "Think nothing of it. Anyone would've done the same."

Slowly, Haza's eyes dropped back toward the fire. "Might've done you quite a service, though," he said quietly, "to finally be rid of your black-wool brother. Smother that blot on the family name. You could've let me die."

Haegar glanced at Tayja, but she was already looking at him, her eyes cool as the air around them. What did she expect him to say? What else could he say? Had it even been a conscious choice to leap in and save his brother? Had he acted before he'd even known who that wolf was killing? *So much blood.* He could still see it when he closed his eyes. Still hear Haza's desperate screams. "I thought you would die in that bed," he growled softly. "That blood…" He'd never seen anything like it. He wished he could pray that he never would again. "I wouldn't have made any other choice, Haza." The choice to protect. Yes, he was sure he would've made it, even if he'd known before he acted who the wolf had in its jaws. He didn't want to see his brother hurt. Damn his blood, but he didn't.

Haza nodded silently.

Corvil rode past again, and then it was Haegar's turn to take the watch. He kissed his wife and said a quiet goodbye to his brother, then mounted Heartwood and began his patrol. The camps had fallen silent by now, fires either put out or dwindling. In one hand he held a torch, Heartwood's reins in the other, and his axe hung from a loop on his belt.

The road was quiet, the night dark, but somewhere in the distance, he could hear the rustle of distant wings. *"Even the birds are running,"* he heard that coward, Laklin, say again. But this night was just like any other in the Winterwood. Their song made his blood boil. He found Torvust doing his own patrols on the other side of the camp, and as he turned his horse, Maple, about to go the other way, Haegar turned with him. "Do you hear that?" he demanded.

Torvust cocked his shaggy head to one side, a frown behind his beard. "Skylarks, it sounds like. Maybe a few wood-singers?"

"Aren't they have all supposed to have fled?" Haegar growled through his teeth. "Isn't that the whole reason we're running?"

"I think part of why we're fleeing is that we buried your brother's arm yesterday."

Haegar couldn't help but flush. "I feel like I'm going mad, Torvust," he said quietly. "Or maybe it's all of Razzador, instead. One sick wolf, and the whole of the Winterwood uproots itself and runs west. All for a rotten pile of stories. It doesn't make any sense."

"Sick wolf?" Torvust squinted at him. "You saw the same beast I did, aye? Those stories you scoff at, I think they're becoming all too real. Besides, stories or no, do you really need me to tell you why we're doing this again?" The man shook his head. "What more do you need to see? What are you looking for? A reason to turn around?"

Haegar tried to wet his lips, only to find that his tongue had gone dry too. "What if we reached Farrenhall...and I turned around then?"

"And leave your wife and children to cross alone?" Anger flickered across the bigger man's bushy face. "You're better than this, Haegar. Stronger."

Haegar looked down at his hands. They trembled like fresh saplings under summer rain. *Curdled blood, what would Father think of me now?* "No, I could never leave them," he said softly. "I just can't justify what I'm doing. I can't make it feel right in my head."

"Do you need to?"

"*Do* I?" He looked up, meeting his old friend's dark eyes. He found the answer there, but it brought him no comfort. "I don't know what to do."

"We move forward," Torvust grunted. "Even into the

unknown. Never stop moving until your family is safe. You understand that, aye? Never stop."

He nodded. "I'm sorry to despair."

"And I'm sorry we've lost our home," Torvust sighed.

They were approaching the back end of the caravan, with their torches now the only true source of illumination, save for small patches of smoldering red embers. The gentle song of the wind, the horses' hooves clopping on stone, the river passing softly through its slippery confines. On their other side, the Winterwood rose tall and dark, neither their torches nor the face of the full moon and the Seventeen Stars strong enough to penetrate it.

"Tayja says the Old King will send an army over the Tagalfr," Haegar growled as he turned Heartwood to start their patrol again. "To clear it out. What do you make of that?"

Torvust still rode beside him, back to the forest. "Seems unlikely." A silver horse was staring at them from the edge of the tree line, perfectly still. Haegar frowned at it. Had someone's mount come untethered and wandered away? Torvust hadn't noticed it. "Since when has the Old King cared about what lies east of—?"

Haegar launched himself from his saddle, colliding with the man, who cried out, and threw them both to the ground, just as a pair of hooves slammed into Maple's side. The animal screamed as they hit the road.

The silver horse reared again, this time driving its hooves into Maple's front leg, snapping the limb with an audible *crack*. The stallion writhed, still screaming, as the other horse began to trample its head. Heartwood reared too, only to turn and run, crying all the while.

Haegar cursed as he rolled onto his feet, ignoring the sting from half a dozen ripening bruises. He brought his axe up but hesitated in advancing. Torvust's mount had stopped thrashing, but Haegar could still see its chest rising and falling weakly. The attacking horse turned. It was a scrawny creature, slat-ribbed and seemingly frail. What he'd first thought was a silver coat was really blotchy gray hair, with large barren patches where it had simply fallen away. The skin on its face was shrunken, lips peeled back to expose flat teeth. Eyes, dead eyes, still hung sunken in their sockets. A wave of hatred rushed over him. But it wasn't his own.

Those eyes—they were the same as those of the wolf.

He hesitated, staring up at the beast, and it stared back at him. Hating him. Then Torvust rushed past with a bellow, axe raised. The cry snapped Haegar from his stupor, and he could hear more shouts from behind as movement stirred in the slumbering camp.

The dead horse reared again, legs lashing out at Torvust. He threw himself to one side, avoiding a crushing hoof by mere inches. In the same breath, Haegar charged, ducking under the flailing limbs and driving his axe into the animal's back leg. The horse didn't scream. Nor did it fall. Front legs down again, it rounded on him, mouth agape, seeking his throat. But Torvust swung his own blade into its remaining back leg.

That time it did fall, still without a sound. Haegar swung his axe for its head, connecting easily. But even as he felt the blade crash against the skull, the horse came at him, struggling to crawl with its front legs, neck strained as far as it could. Torvust rounded the beast, driving his axe into one of its forelegs from behind. The horse collapsed completely, jaws wide as its head still strained futilely to reach them.

Haegar and Torvust stood panting, weapons still raised, watching the crippled beast struggle to reach them. "Bloodied shit," Torvust cursed. He wiped a spatter of black blood from his face with his sleeve, wild eyes turning to Haegar. He seemed to be struggling to come up with something intelligent to say. "Bloodied shit!"

Haegar concurred. Cautiously, he moved around the beast, careful of its still-snapping teeth. He recovered his torch from where he'd dropped it in the snow, too caught up in the chaos to even notice its fall, and held it closer to one of its hooves. "Torvust, this thing is shod."

Torvust, still panting, glanced over his shoulder, where the shouts of startled townsfolk were growing louder. Fires were beginning to appear amid the darkened wagons. "Bloodied shit," he said again, now quietly. "We can't stay here."

But Haegar was already moving. He stepped around the corpse again, axe held in a white-knuckled grip. "We need to get everyone up and moving. We can't stop until we reach the river." Horses were rare in the Winterwood. Heartwood and Maple, along with the mayor's horse, were the only ones in Palvast. If that horse was from a stable, it meant it was from inside a town. He couldn't even bring himself to think about what that might mean.

"Torvust?" Haegar paused, half-stumbling, when he realized the other man wasn't following. Torvust was kneeling beside his horse, whose chest still rose in shallow swells. There were tears in Torvust's eyes as he stroked Maple's neck with one hand and raised the axe with the other. "Stop!"

The man looked up, startled.

"You can't do it," Haegar growled, rushing to his friend's side. "We have to leave, now."

Torvust gaped at him. "I…I can't just leave him suffering like this, Haegar."

"Use your head," he snapped, unable to hold a lid over that bubbling cauldron in his chest. "These things we're fighting—

they're dead, aren't they?" he pointed with his own axe at the hamstrung horse. "What if you kill him and he gets back up again? We'll have to cut him down all over again. And maybe next time we won't win." He feared the physical injuries now keeping Maple on the ground would matter little when that hatred settled itself behind his eyes. *Would* a fresh corpse get back up again? Were all dead animals afflicted by this madness, or only a select few? His thoughts strayed back to those stories from the caravan the day of the festival, the ones he'd so quickly dismissed. *"She went to sleep and never woke up,"* the man had said, of his mother. *"Except she got up again."* This madness…did it afflict everything that died? Were the graveyards overturning themselves, emptied as their charges stirred from their rest? A stray vision of his own mother crept into his mind, with sallow features and a slack jaw, her eyes gaping sightlessly.

No. He shook his head to rid himself of the visage. He had too many questions with no answers, and he did not dare learn them now. Whatever was causing this didn't matter, he needed to get his family over that bloodied river. He seized Torvust's shoulder. "We can't take any risks. I'm sorry, but we can't."

Torvust, his hand still on Maple's neck, bowed his head, putting it against him. "I'm so sorry," he sobbed. Then he stood, his eyes glistening, and together they rushed toward the now-milling camp. Haegar threw a glance over his shoulder as darkness swallowed the two horses, one thrashing silently, the other still breathing. For now.

"We need to keep moving," Haegar growled through huffing breaths. The thrill of the fight was beginning to fade, leaving his bones soaked with sudden weariness. "If we push hard, we can reach Farrenhall by midday. We don't know how many of those…things they are, or how close they might be. No risks. We move through the night."

Torvust stared straight ahead. "I'll gather the woodsmen. We need to wake the caravan and keep everyone from panicking. We must stay organized, stay together, even if it means a slower ride than we'd like. We'll double the guard until we're moving forward again."

"Keep it doubled until we're on the other side of the Tagalfr." Torvust was right—if the caravan was spurred into panic—especially in the middle of the night—it could end up scattering them all into the forest. "We can't tell them how imminent the danger is, but make it known that we *must* move."

As Torvust peeled away, leaving Haegar alone at the camp's rear, he suddenly thought of Palvast, of the men who'd chosen to stay with their homes. Twisted claws of dread crept up his spine. What if something got inside the wall again? What if someone on the inside died of illness or accident? Would they...? It was mostly old men who'd remained. Sorvak and Garvim, a few other families. Too proud. Too stubborn. *Our fathers built the walls of Palvast strong... If they keep the gates shut, the stream dammed, they'll be safe. Our harvest will last them through the winter; it's not going anywhere now.* But as he tried to convince himself all would be well, that they could outlast whatever was coming for them, he couldn't shake that single, horrified thought: *If we'd stayed, it would've been us.*

By the time he reached his own wagon, Tayja and Haza were both awake, staring up at him from above the sputtering fire they'd managed to coax back to life. "They're here," he said softly, noting his children still cuddled together beneath their blanket. His wife's eyes widened while Haza's face paled and he sank against the cart.

"We need to move," Haegar continued. He grabbed piles of bedding and clothes and threw them into the waiting cart bed.

"Haza, how are you feeling?" He couldn't avoid glancing at his brother's stump. Were those stains in his bandages larger?

"I've been better," Haza murmured, staring sightlessly ahead. "I've been less terrified, too. When do you think we'll reach the river?" He scooted to one side as Tayja joined in the mad scramble to replace all their belongings. Around them, shouts were growing louder. Other families rushed to tear down their camps. He could hear Torvust's booming voice from further down the stream bank. *So much for avoiding panic…*

Haegar stared at his children. They were still somehow slumbering peacefully, unaware of the terror that was building around them. He suddenly found himself longing for their innocence, for the irresponsibility of youth, the carelessness of the dangers of the world around them. They had to be protected.

"Haegar?" Haza's voice came through, insistent. "Did you hear me, Haegar?"

"Aye?" Haegar blinked, then shook his head. "Yes. The river. Midday, maybe. I'll feel safer with the dawn, though. At least then we'll be able to see whatever is following us."

Haza stared down at his lap, the fear on his face as plain as his wound. "Do you think we'll be safe, even after crossing the Tagalfr? Will the dead be able to follow us over?"

Haegar made himself breath normally. His body was still brimming with a strange electricity, the mingled horror and excitement of sudden battle. He'd never felt anything like it before. But with that energy came memories he couldn't banish. Maple, bloodied, left to die. The pain on Torvust's face. "The Tagalfr is a brutal river," he made himself say, "even in the heart of summer. By now, the ice will have come in earnest. Crushing glaciers above hidden currents. If the living cannot swim across it, I doubt the dead will, either."

"Besides, the king's men at Farrenhall will protect us," Tayja put in earnestly. She was cradling Rala in her arms now, moving her onto the makeshift mattress of blankets. She murmured groggily in her sleep but did not stir. "They'll have all the weapons and armor needed to drive back wolves or whatever else comes out of the woods."

Haza chewed his lip. "The garrison is small, isn't it? Lord Varkoth doesn't have anything more than a token guard. After all, there isn't anything east of Vrusk to fear. Or at least, there wasn't…"

From what Haegar knew of Farrenhall, the old fortress was impregnable. Even he knew of how the God-Emperor had broken his hosts on its stalwart defenses, while the last bastion of Vrusk had sheltered on the other side of the river. Farrenhall had held; no force could breach it. Once its gates were sealed, there could be no crossing. His chest swelled with pride for his long-dead kinsmen, who'd labored to build the Gated Bridge and connect the lands separated by the water. That same blood still flowed in his veins.

"We'll be safe," he promised. "Once we're across the river, we'll be safe."

As the wagons began to move again, Haegar found Heartwood standing at the edge of the stream, tensed as if ready to spring across. He was able to take his reins, but rather than tether him to their own cart, he left that to the mules and rode Heartwood at the back of the caravan, watching their flank.

The night passed slowly, the caravan now hushed as they made their way through the dark. An hour before dawn, Haegar suddenly realized he could hear crickets again. He hadn't even noticed that they'd stopped. And as the sun brought to light a fresh wave of gray clouds rolling from the north, Haegar could breathe normally without strain. No more corpses had appeared, and the sunlight road behind them was empty. They'd made it through the night.

While the sun slowly ascended over the Winterwood, the caravan of Palvast continued westward, following the road and the stream closer and closer to the forest's edge and the Grey Hinterlands beyond the river. To his own surprise, he could feel his fear trickling away as salvation approached. Once they were across the Tagalfr, his family would be safe.

From over the trees, a shape appeared on the horizon, framed against a sky melting from pink to pale blue. Haegar drew a sharp breath as the trees grew thin around him, then gave away entirely to a swathe of flat ground, painted white with snow and devoid of any visible life. They'd reached the edge of the Winterwood.

The stream continued forward, slipping down a short incline before winding across five hundred paces of barren shore where it finally met the Tagalfr, the River of Rushing Ice. The thunder of the distant water rose above the sound of wagons and horses, a steady rumble, like a storm without end.

It was a staggering sight. He could've easily mistaken the Tagalfr for a lake, if not for foreknowledge. Mist was rising across its entire length as the waters boiled and frothed like a great cauldron, surging toward the north. Great patches of ice swept across the surface of the river, demonstrating the Tagalfr's stomach-churning speed. He doubted even Heartwood could outrun those glaciers. The icy behemoths crashed against each other, wild as leaves spinning on the wind, and they sent plumes of glittering showers rising into the mist, and the sound of their groaning carried across the shores to the Winterwood. Across its breadth, the opposite shore was an indistinct mass of white on the horizon.

And above it all stood Farrenhall, the Gated Bridge, the only path across the maelstrom of the Tagalfr. It was immense, its sheer scale catching Haegar off-guard every time he saw it. It was so far away that even the road leading up to it seemed nothing but a fading forest trail as it drew near. Two great pillars rose from out of the heart of the Rushing Ice, holding Farrenhall aloft. Its underbelly was sleek, gray-green stone, perfectly uniform and ancient in craftsmanship. It gave the bridge a solid, militaristic appearance, absent of the trappings and distractions of decoration.

Above, pale brick gave way to dark, seamless stone, forming a straight-backed, almost spinal shape, like a tunnel through the sky. Hundreds of glass windows lined the length of Farrenhall, clearly marking out three different floors. Though Haegar had never been inside the Gated Bridge himself, he knew that first floor served as a central thoroughfare—the bridge part of the bridge—while the rest above was a complex of rooms and halls, of elegant domiciles befitting noblemen, alongside armories, stables and barracks for the garrison. Farrenhall was like a miniature city, set upon twin hands and held aloft over the world, from where the Varkoth family could reign.

The top of Farrenhall was where the simplistic architecture of ancient Vrusk stonemasons blurred with the tastes of the nobility. Polished wood, cut from the heart of the Winterwood, formed the spine of the bridge. It was a ridged design, pointed roofs like spikes on the back of a great beast, rising in an overlapping formation. Twin towers, parallel to the pillars far beneath, rose from the top of the bridge, and he had no doubt they rivaled any of the spires of Savisdale.

A bell sat in the top of the foremost tower, large enough to be seen even at this great distance. And above it, a banner was flying in the wind, matched by its twin on the bridge's other side. The gray-scaled, grinning dragon of Vrusk danced on a white field, its claws outstretched toward the south. Despite his fears, Haegar found himself relaxing in his saddle as he gazed up at the Gated Bridge. No force could get through something so mighty.

Ahead, the caravan began to slow atop a small rise right at the forest's edge, bunching up on itself as the riders were forced to pull up before men slowing suddenly ahead of them. Haegar frowned as confused mutters rose from the townsfolk.

Haegar turned his horse, riding around to reach the front of the halted caravan, gaining a better vantage of Farrenhall and the land waiting before it in the same breath. That breath then caught in his throat.

As he crested the rise and exposed the shore to view, he saw a massive crowd had gathered before the Gated Bridge. Hundreds, no, thousands, of figures were spread before the gates of Farrenhall, smothering the road, clogging the land. They had wagons with them. Mules and sheep and cattle, enough to feed half the kingdom. Why were there so many people waiting? Farrenhall could admit such a crowd in a day's time; it was built for a capacity that far exceeded the number of people who ever passed in a year. *Curdle my blood, what—?* Then his eyes found the front of the crowd, and confusion turned to terror.

The gates of Farrenhall were sealed shut.

Chapter Eight
The Duty of a Lord

Three days. The gates of Farrenhall had been closed for three days. Though she'd spent nearly all of her waking days within the dark-green walls of the bridge, Kasara felt like a cat trapped in a cage. She prowled the corridors, compelled by an unknown force to keep moving, as if her restless pacing could somehow banish the storm gathering on Farrenhall's doorsteps.

She could feel the rumblings of the unhappy crowd rising like mist from the river, clinging to her. She hurried along one of the bridge's outer corridors, with windows at her side overlooking the Tagalfr, but the familiar hallway now felt like the gullet of some great beast, stretching wide to swallow her. The roar of the river below was still audible, even from so high, a constant and steady hum that never faded. Most days, she never even noticed it, but now paired with the crowd waiting at the gates, the twin noises had joined into a warning growl.

She had to do something. Anything! Instead, she was pacing.

Three days. It had started slow, a few travelers hurrying out of the wood, when her father had suddenly commanded that the gates of Farrenhall be shut. Before the end of the day, it had turned into a flood. Vruskmen had started to pour out of the forest in hundreds, carrying with them carts and livestock and children, as if they'd uprooted their entire lives to bring them over the river. That was when Bjern had come running to find her. The crowd had swiftly grown restless and furious, and a large group had rushed the Bronze Gate, demanding entry. The Myrmidons, charged by their sacred duty to follow the orders of Lord Varkoth, threatened to drive them back with shield and spear.

Kasara had put herself between the two groups, addressing her people from the safety of the walltop. With Berethan at her side, she'd managed to quell the disquiet by promising them an audience with her father. Surely this was some misunderstanding. Surely the closing of the Gated Bridge was an overreaction. She hadn't been able to piece together much about what had brought the folk of the wood in such great numbers—something about dark magic and dead creatures. Whatever the source of these rumors, it had whipped the Vruskmen to near-rabid frenzy. Only the promises of the daughter of Lord Varkoth had managed to settle the flames back into glowing embers.

That had been three days ago, now, and Kasara had failed to even meet with her father, much less discuss those sputtering embers on their shore. The congestion was only getting worse as the crowd continued to swell, but for some reason beyond her imagination, her father allowed not one to cross.

Soon, her pacing led her to the eastern end of the Gated Bridge, where the many halls arced inward to coalesce into one grand room on the uppermost floor. Pillars of amber held aloft a flat, stone roof, and the torches that hung upon them banished the shadows more effectively than the gray sunlight filtering through the windows on the far side. Through them, she could see the tops of the Winterwood trees.

Berethan was standing before the windows, one hand

holding his helm, the other draped across the hilt of the sword at his waist. His broadsword was strapped to his back. His marbled silver-red armor glittered in the firelight. Kasara froze at the threshold of the chamber. Beside the giant warrior, the chain-wrapped wheel that controlled Farrenhall's inner gate, the Iron Gate, stood. Two other Myrmidons, faces veiled by plate, attended their Grand-Crusader.

"Lingering in darkness accomplishes nothing, little Lordling," rumbled Berethan. "Step forward, into the light, and speak."

Kasara obeyed, stepping swiftly past the colorful tapestries that lined the walls to take her place at the Myrmidon's side. In full plate, Berethan towered over her. With a glance, he could cow entire rooms—she'd seen it, a silence that followed him wherever he went. There was something unnatural about him, a regality that mortal men couldn't understand. It was almost enough to lend credence to his so-called God of the Highest Path. Almost.

She cleared her throat as she peered out the window. "Have they approached the wall again? Have they done anything at all?"

"Nothing of consequence," Berethan replied. "They remain where they stand, and shout beyond the range of spears. Perhaps they are wiser than I believe, and they will turn around and return home."

Kasara frowned. She couldn't see Farrenhall's inner gates, as they stood directly below her, but she could see the wall-wrapped outer courtyard where bridge met solid ground, and the second set of doors, the Bronze Gate, set into the wall. Sealed shut. Closed for the first time in her living memory. The courtyard's twin on Farrenhall's opposite shore had sealed both entrances too, though there wasn't a crowd marshaling in the west. Not that she knew of, anyway. More men in crimson-silver armor were patrolling the walls below, spears in hand.

Behind the walls, the crowd of Vruskmen had swelled overnight. A shiver of sourceless terror crawled up her back as she looked over it. Why had they come? Why were so many trying to get across? And, more confusing, why had the Gated Bridge been sealed to them?

"I don't understand," she murmured as she watched the crowd roil quietly among their wagons and tents. She could see the tiny shapes of children running between the legs of their elders. "Why would Father seal Farrenhall? Have these men done something to offend him?" It would be the first she'd heard of any such insult, though Kalivaz Varkoth was known to find slight in the way the wind blew. But he'd never ordered anything like this before.

The giant shifted, his features painted ashen by the gray morning. "It is not for me to question such things. We serve the God of the Highest Path, as should all. Tend to your own matters, young Lordling."

Kasara wrinkled her nose at that. Myrmidons never refused orders, she'd heard. Never. So long as they came from the one who'd hired their services, they treated their word as doctrine. *They* never *refuse orders.* She'd heard stories about just how far that ideal could go. "What was it, precisely, that my father instructed you to do, Berethan?"

The Grand-Crusader's expression didn't change, but she thought she saw the faintest flicker of suspicion in his eyes. "We have been commanded to deny passage through Farrenhall to all intruders, and to defend this place against any who might trespass."

Kasara made herself grin. "Well, those people down there are Vruskmen, same as me. They can't trespass on land they already own, aye? What harm could there be in opening the gates for our own people?" Surely Kalivaz hadn't meant to catch so many of his own subjects at the crossing. It had to be an unfortunate coincidence.

"My orders are not for interpretation," Berethan said flatly. "A word spoken cannot be unspoken. I will follow any command I am given until I am tasked otherwise, or until my service here ends. This is the only way to climb the steps of the Highest Path."

She made herself nod. She had no desire to grow closer to to the Myrmidons' god, or climb their holy mountain, or whatever else nonsense they believed in. They *were* fascinating soldiers to watch, though, far more so than any of Farrenhall's regular garrison, which was manned by youths who could barely lift their swords and old men who should've retired winters ago. "You've never questioned orders before, Grand-Crusader? Not even once?"

The man arched an eyebrow at her, taken aback. For a moment, he regarded her, his pale eyes seeming to glow beneath that hooded brow. Then he snorted, a slight smile appearing on leathery lips. "Perhaps when I was young, like you. And foolish. The Highest Path is a long and arduous climb, and every misstep sends you hurtling back toward the base of the mountain. Life is much too short to do anything but progress as far as you can, at whatever cost, Lordling."

"Has anyone ever reached its peak?" she asked. "That's where your god dwells, aye?"

The smile slipped away. "That is between God and the dead."

Kasara went back to watching the crowd. They milled like ants from an overturned hill, and she could feel their unrest bleeding into her through the glass of the window. There were no crows flying about this morning, which brought her relief. "It's strange though, isn't it?" she muttered. "Farrenhall has never been shut, not one day in my life. And these travelers...this is not a back-up of our usual visitors. There are too many of them. These are woodsmen and farmers. Do you know why that's strange, Berethan?"

He glanced at her. "Should I?"

"Men of the Winterwood don't leave the forest," she said quietly. "This is unprecedented. Something is driving them to flee." *But what?* The folk of the Winterwood were like the old trees they lived among; large, gnarled and with deep roots. Few ever left, and even then they never strayed far. To bring so many to the Gated Bridge now, it couldn't be happenstance. Something was happening, something that had unsettled Vrusk's most stalwart men.

"Their reasoning doesn't matter to me," Berethan rumbled. "If it is passage they seek they will not find it, so long as your Lord Father commands it. Now that they've seen the standard of the Myrmidons rise, they would do well to return to their homes, lest there be blood."

Kasara shivered again. Her fascination with the religious man came paired with a generous portion of revulsion, or maybe morbid curiosity. She glanced hesitantly up at the giant mercenary. "Would you really kill them if they attempted to breach the gates? Vruskmen, just like me?"

The Myrmidon's impassive gaze swept back toward the window, his eyes settling on the crowd, which was still growing by the moment. Another caravan of wagons and mules was trickling out of the forest and onto the shore. "Your Lord Father has commanded that no man from outside step foot in Farrenhall. If violence must be used to fulfill my command, then it will be done." His eyes flicked toward her. "If your Lord Father asked it of me, I would kill any man. Even the Old King. Even you."

The intensity in the man's eyes was like a cold blade pressed against her throat. It was all Kasara could do to keep from edging back warily, withering beneath the Grand-Crusader's stare. "You…you mean it, don't you? Why?"

"The God of the Highest Path commands it," Berethan replied, his voice without hesitation or doubt. "Lord Varkoth has paid our Faith Price until spring. We will serve his every order until then."

Kasara bit her lip. That Faith Price was a different matter of contention entirely. The Myrmidons were feared for their flawless record of service, as well as the exorbitant price they charged for their swords. The Varkoth family's wealth might not be legendary, but it was hardly a trifling, considering Winterwood lumber was coveted far beyond the borders of Vrusk. But even so, Kasara had seen the ledgers. The hiring of Berethan and his followers had cost House Varkoth half its treasury.

Kalivaz Varkoth was not a man known for his loose pockets. Something had scared the Lord of Farrenhall, friend and loyal vassal to the Old King, to seek out mercenary protection from beyond his own kingdom. And not some meager band of hireswords, either. No, he'd purchased the unquestioning, zealous loyalty of the Myrmidons. What terrified her the most was that she couldn't discern the danger, couldn't figure out what had frightened her father so. And now with the Gated Bridge sealed, her suspicions, and worries, were festering.

"It won't come to bloodshed," Kasara said with all the certainty she could conjure. Her breath lightly puffed against the window, briefly obscuring the crowd behind a veil of frost. "These are men of Vrusk. They will wait upon the command of their liege lord."

Berethan treated her to a dry chuckle. "The hearts of men are not so far from beasts, Lordling. Fear strikes a crowd, and they begin to beat in unison. That quiet camp out there will become a mob, desperate and clawing. The faces of individuals fade, and they will act as one. If they perceive true danger, they *will* attempt to take the bridge."

"You know this how?"

"I've seen it before," the Myrmidon said. "When hunger or fear takes a crowd and sets their minds aflame, there is only thing that can be done." His gauntleted fist tightened about the hilt of his sword, but his expression never changed.

Kasara stared out the window, uncertainty like a set of grinding teeth in the depths of her mind, worrying away at any solution she tried to muster. *Something has to be done about this. If Berethan is right, we must disperse the crowd before those embers turn to flame again.* But how could she be rid of them without starting a panic herself?

The simplest answer was the quickest to come to mind; Farrenhall should open its gates and let the crowd pass through. The men of the Winterwood were still men of Vrusk, after all. They had every right to cross over the Tagalfr at will. Once they were through, the Gated Bridge could be sealed again, if it eased her father's mind. *I need to talk with him. This is unacceptable.*

She'd only just turned on her heel, when Berethan called, "Lordling." She paused mid-step, turning back, but the Myrmidon was still staring ahead. "A word of advice for you, if you're of mind to take it."

She could only nod. As strange as the religious man was, she couldn't help the deep respect she felt for the disciplined, honor-bound mercenary. He'd already taught her more of swordplay than she'd ever managed to learn from her books or the piss-poor "swordsmanship" of the garrison men. Berethan had an air of wisdom about him. His mind might be addled by faith, but what he did know, he knew perfectly.

Berethan didn't wait for a reply. "Your Lord Father seems to me a man haunted by insight. He is not mad, not as I can tell. Farrenhall has been shut for a reason, and perhaps it would be best for you if you do not seek to learn why."

"Do you know?" she demanded. Would her father really tell this stranger over her? "Did you talk to him? He hasn't let me see him in almost a week now. I can't get through to him."

Berethan's eyes dropped, suddenly. "I…was not entirely truthful with you when you asked me if I'd ever questioned my faith. I have, once. Long ago. I betrayed my Faith Price."

"You did?" Ridiculous though his beliefs might be, she found it impossible to imagine that the mountain of a man before her could ever waver. "What could have made you doubt?"

The knight looked up at her, but it was only a flicker of the eyes. She saw something there, a look she'd never seen on the man's face before. Pain? "That is my burden to carry, Lordling. The only wisdom I can offer you is that some truths are not worth confronting."

Kasara set her jaw to one side. The blood-blighted man's face was unreadable. *Would* Kalivaz have told him over her? "I'm the heir to Farrenhall," she said, "and I'm a Vruskman, just like all those people down there. If we're going to turn them away, and if there's a chance it might turn into something like you fear, then I *will* know why it must be."

Berethan's armor clanked as he shifted from one foot to the other, his eyes still fixed to the glass before him. "The Highest Path is neither paved nor solid. There are many snares and traps that will send you down the side of the mountain, if you are not vigilant."

I'm not climbing to your vaunted peak, Berethan, she growled, but she kept her mouth shut and stepped back into the hall, leaving the gatehouse and the Myrmidons behind. But as she made her way back through the bridge, the Grand-Crusader's words followed her. *This place was sealed for a reason.*

Why? What could it be? Irritation became like an itching pest, crawling and clambering across her body unopposed. There had been no forewarning, no announcement of her father's intentions to close the bridge, only a sudden, sharp command three days ago. And now, with hundreds amassing on the shores of the Winterwood, Kasara needed no further convincing that something deeper than paranoia was at hand. But, thus far, Kalivaz had evaded all confrontation, vanishing into his chambers, protected by guardsmen who turned his own daughter away.

She'd had enough. Storming through Farrenhall, she swept past servants and garrison guards alike, heedless of the startled looks they gave her. Let them see her anger. Let them see her confusion. They said nothing to her, of course. The same questions clouding her own mind had also been boiling through the Gated Bridge. Everyone wanted to know why the gates had been shut, why a crowd beyond anything any harvest festival had ever mustered was now gathering outside. Whispers of uncertainty and confusion had been skittering through the keep for days now.

Kasara reached the third floor of the bridge and made her way into the innermost halls of Farrenhall, where the chambers of its most distinguished denizens stood high above the rest of the bridge. She passed her own room, standing alone at the end of a small offshoot of the hallway, where another guardsman stood watch. There were no windows here, so torches illuminated long stretches of stone, with a dark wooden roof overhead.

More guardsmen appeared ahead of her, soldiers in plate armor. Compared to the shining steel of the Myrmidons, the garrison equipment looked like unpolished stone. They wore blue tabards over their chainmail, embroidered with the dancing dragon of Vrusk. Over their hearts, a smaller symbol depicted the seal of House Varkoth, a silver fish with long, shimmering fins.

Behind them stood the door to her father's personal chambers. As Kasara approached, the five guardsmen exchanged wary looks. It was Bjern who stepped forward, his eyes downcast. He had pale features and a flat nose, and there was a patch of dark hair clinging to his chin, which he stubbornly refused to shave. "Kasara," he hesitated, glancing at his fellow soldiers, all little more than boys. It was still hard for her to remember they were of age. Did she still look so young? "Ah, my lady, your father has commanded that no one may disturb—"

"We're not doing this again, Bjern," Kasara growled impatiently. She couldn't help being angry with him, still. She counted him as a friend, and maybe more. Or else, she had, until she'd found him sharing spittle with a kitchen scullion. Even the sight of his face made heat prickle beneath her skin.

Bjern had the audacity to blink. "But, Kasara, I—"

"It's Lady Varkoth to you." She shoved past him and he stepped back with an indignant sputter. The other boys wisely retreated, too, allowing her to seize the door and thrust it inward. It was caught mid-swing by a man in crimson armor painted with swirls of silver. There was a look of bemusement on the red-bearded man's face. For a moment, they regarded each other, the Myrmidon with that blood-boiling smirk, Kasara with hesitation.

Her nerve wavered as she appraised the mercenary, a man who, though not as tall as his Grand-Crusader, certainly had strength to rival him, and the broadsword strapped to his back was wide as both her palms. "You will let me pass," she commanded. "I will speak to my father." She could see Bjern and the others clustered around her from the corner of her eye, uncertain how to react.

The Myrmidon did not release the door. "Your father has declared that none may enter," he said easily. "Turn away, child."

Kasara forced herself against the door, only to find herself pushing against an unyielding strength. "I won't be denied," she declared anyway. "Stand aside."

The last remnants of amusement crumbled from the Myrmidon's face, replaced by a dark shadow. His massive, armored hand fell heavily to the hilt of the shorter sword he wore at his side, the clank of metal on metal an unmistakable warning. "I have my orders, child. Turn away, or I'll send you myself. You will not like the manner I choose."

Kasara seized the hilt of her own sword, earning a startled squeak from Bjern and the others. Someone tried to grab her shoulder, but she shrugged away and bellowed, "Father!" She tried to peer around the Myrmidon to catch a glimpse of the room beyond. "Father, I know you can hear me. We need to talk. No more hiding!" Her voice boomed through the hall, and the Myrmidon's scowl deepened.

"Are you deaf, heathen?" he demanded. "Obey your father's orders. I will not command you again."

Kasara watched the door, waiting for a sign of movement. But there was nothing, and nothing to be heard from beyond. Her heart began to climb into her throat. She almost took a step back. *I can take him.* She could use Berethan's training against him. Hack around his armor, seek flesh beneath. *It won't be like last time. I won't lose.* She *had* to get to her father, at any cost. With a deep breath, she advanced again.

The Myrmidon stepped back, though her hope that he'd retreat was dashed when he dropped into a crouch, legs spread as his hulking armor was splayed to cover as much of the entryway as possible. The hand around his hilt drew his sword a quarter of its length, baring steel that glittered in the torchlight. "One more step and you'll never walk again," the man warned.

The man would really kill her. Kill her just for breaking her own father's orders. Kasara drew her sword, too, slipping it swiftly from its sheathe and holding it before her. *Curdle your blood, Father. Why are you doing this to me? Where are you?* She readied herself, standing as Berethan had instructed, her breaths coming in shallow gulps. She tried to fight her terror, but even as she succumbed, she made herself take another step. She wouldn't back down.

Steel plates clanked and groaned with warning as the Myrmidon wrenched his flashing blade from its sheathe, lurching forward. "Wait!" a voice bellowed from behind the armored man. "Hold! Not another step, Sir Joros!"

As swiftly as the Myrmidon had leapt into action, he withdrew, fluid and lithe as a serpent recoiling from its strike. His blade slammed back into its sheathe as Joros turned and stood aside, revealing the man standing in the open doorway.

"Father," Kasara gasped, half in relief, half in exasperation. She sheathed her own blade but kept one hand gripped to its hilt to hide the way she was trembling.

Kalivaz Varkoth frowned uncertainly, first at the Myrmidon, then down at his own daughter. He hardly looked the man she remembered as a girl; a tall and powerful figure, a commanding presence that brought awed hushes to every room he entered. He was still garbed in the trappings of a powerful man—majestic robes of red and white, trimmed with gold and silver in overlapping folds of silk. A golden chain hung around his neck, and the sigil hanging from it was their gem-encrusted family crest, its fins fanned around emerald scales. The illusion of the Lord of Farrenhall remained, but Kalivaz himself looked more shadow than man. Fear was in his every motion, in the frantic way he motioned with his hand, in the way his blue eye— only one; the other he'd lost in a hunting accident long ago and now wore a dark patch over the long-since healed wound— roamed ceaselessly, daring not to land on anything for too long. What little remained of his hair was a patchy mass of white and gray. His face was long and wrinkled, skin pale and blotchy, so thin that she could see it press against his skull.

It pained her to see her father as he was now, more ghost of memory than a living man. It had been a slow and terrible transformation, one she'd barely noticed until the beginning of autumn, when it had suddenly intensified. She'd found herself wondering of late, much to her own shame and fear, how many more years Kalivaz had left on Razzador. But even to contemplate her father's death felt unnatural, almost like a paradox— something that could simply never happen. Kalivaz had always been a part of her life, a natural constant of existence. How could it be that Razzador went on without him?

"Come on, then," Kalivaz growled. The fear lurking in his eye did not taint his tongue, which remained as scorching and spiteful as ever. "I know what you want, girl. If it's answers you seek, come along. I'm tired of hearing you skulk about Farrenhall like a rat." As he spoke, the nobleman turned and limped back into his chambers.

Kasara felt cold. She'd never heard him speak like this, not even in anger. His was a fiery sort of wrath, but there was a quiet chill about him now, as if her mere presence turned his stomach. Biting anger at her heels, Kasara followed, but she spared a glare for the Myrmidon as she passed. The knight did not give her so much as a glance, not a lingering look of anger, not a flicker of annoyance. It was as Berethan said; they never questioned their orders. From being ready to cripple his liege lord's daughter to standing calmly at attention, the Myrmidons seemed to flip like flickering flames. It was like they had no soul. Maybe they'd lost them on that mountaintop of theirs.

"Do I look like a man who has time to be pestered, girl?" came the demanding voice of Lord Varkoth, carrying through his chambers.

Kasara was quick to hurry after him into a smaller study, and she closed the door behind her, blocking the Myrmidon from view. Then she rounded on her father, who had already seated himself at his desk. This secondary room was as grand as one would expect the Lord of Farrenhall to occupy; a wide and spacious chamber that could've housed fifty men, if needed. An elaborate, sprawling bed, complete with silver-veil curtains, sat in one corner of the room, opposite a window that looked out over the heart of the Tagalfr. Numerous cabinets and shelves, all stacked high with books and scrolls in jars, alongside piles of loose paper, cluttered the sides of the room, all leading like arrows toward the massive Winterwood desk pressed up against the far wall, at which Kalivaz now sat, his back to her.

Kasara hesitated, remembering the countless hours she'd spent in this room as a girl, often seated on her father's lap. Kalivaz would tell her stories as he worked, whispering in her ear as the candlelight grew softer and softer, until there was nothing left but the darkness of sleep. She'd felt safe, then, but she no longer saw that strong, comforting presence in her father. Had age made him like this? Or had he always been followed by this shadow, and she'd never noticed it before? *I won't believe it. Something terrible is on his mind, and I will know what it is.*

The man at the desk might as well have been a stranger, a

frantic and paranoid old man, hunched over as he scribbled away with a white-fletched quill. Kasara finally loosened the grip on her sword as she stared at her father's back.

"Well?" Kalivaz demanded without looking up. "You're in here, aren't you? Say what you want to say."

Kasara swallowed. She played nervously with her fingers as she stepped forward, her footsteps echoing quietly through the bedchamber. "What are you doing, Father?" she asked softly.

"Penning yet another letter to the Old King," Kalivaz muttered. "The ninth this moon. All as of yet unanswered. What does he expect me to do if those men rush the gates, aye? Defend Farrenhall with my bare hands?"

Kasara's flesh prickled. There was that unsettling thought again. Why would the men of the Winterwood attack their own liege lord? Even if the Gated Bridge was barred to them, no Vruskman would turn against his own countrymen. It defied every scruple Vrusk had been built upon, a foundation wrought of blood. The Holy Wars had forged a horde of strangers into a single family. They'd endured the God-Emperor's wrath together. They'd built Vrusk together.

"Farrenhall has never been breached, Father," she pointed out, lacing her fingers behind her back as her eyes tried to trace the skittering pen gripped in Kalivaz's hand. Back and forth it went, never lifting from the page for more than an eye's blink. "Our garrison is fifty men strong, and you have another hundred Myrmidons. Even if there was an attack coming, we could hold the Gated Bridge for twenty years."

Kalivaz chuckled dryly as his quill whisked about in front of him. "Farrenhall was never breached because the enemy never made it to the gates. The lords of Vrusk broke the God-Emperor's advance a dozen miles from here, girl. The siege never happened." The quill suddenly stopped. Ink began to bead at its tip, a pool of darkness seeping out beneath it. "Even the Myrmidons couldn't hold this place forever. The Old King was supposed to march five hundred centurions here a week ago."

Are we marshaling an army? It didn't make any sense. Both Havasa and Joromor were allies of Vrusk, and there had been peace across Razzador since the end of the Holy Wars. Nothing she'd heard in rumor or gossip indicated that anything might be ready to change. But even if one of the kingdoms turned against the other, or if some phantom threat rose from across the uncharted lengths of the Blistering Sea, why build an army at Farrenhall? There was nothing east of the Tagalfr but trees and wolves and snow.

"Why did you close the bridge, Father?" she demanded. "Why won't you allow the men of the Winterwood to cross?"

Silence stretched between them. Kasara shifted from one foot to the next. *Skritch, skritch, skritch,* went the pen as it swept from one side of the parchment to the next. The fire in the nearby hearth crackled and snapped, unimpressed by the cold distance now separating father and daughter.

Kasara could've reached out and touched him, but her hands stayed at her side, balled into anxious fists. Just as she opened her mouth to ask again, Kalivaz sighed and set his quill aside. He stood and adjusted the collar of his coat with a stiff shake. He turned, and she crystallized beneath his stare. That wild and frantic eye seized her, tracing her up and down. Even when it lighted on her face, it did not remain fully still, ever flickering. Kalivaz's face was a cold mask, but she could see the panic seeping through its cracks, like he was a viewing a stranger, unsure if she meant him harm.

"I closed the gates of Farrenhall on order of the Old King," Kalivaz finally said. "Word came down from Savisdale almost a month ago, but the matters of a kingdom are slow-moving, even in haste. I wanted to wait until after the harvest, but the Old King was insistent. I could delay no longer." The Lord of Farrenhall's lip curled. "I am a loyal servant to our monarch, as are you. When he commands, we obey."

Kasara folded her arms beneath her breasts, unsatisfied. "You're saying he didn't tell you why?"

"I'm saying you have no right to question," Kalivaz replied. "To defy a king is to invite ruin, and I intend to keep our family in good order until you can produce an heir and take my place."

Kasara was quick to step past that particular conversation. No, better to take a running leap. "You can't tell me you don't know anything, Father. If you're as blind as the rest of us, you'd just say it, aye? You wouldn't be locked in your room day and night, writing endless letters, worrying about an army. An army, Father! And tell me, what man expecting no trouble hires the Myrmidons? What are the Myrmidons here for, if not to spill blood?"

Kalivaz's eye flickered. For a short, terrible moment, their gazes met, and she saw fully how deep his terror ran. "Kasara, you're young yet," his tone was suddenly softer, more familiar. For a moment, it was her father speaking to her again, not that terrified creature that wore his face. "You've got a whole lifespan ahead of you, with a fortress and a fortune ready to take once I pass. It's the same position I was in, when I was your age." A faint smile passed over his face, and with it came a flash of recognition, as if the old man could suddenly see clearly again. "You should be spending your days courting the local gentry, or riding on horses, or even sparring with Berethan, as I've heard you've taken to. Your place isn't here, worrying about matters of war and armies. Leave that to old men, aye? Our days of joy are passing."

The dismissal stung like a hooked barb, and Kasara made no effort to veil her displeasure. "I won't be sent away, Father. I'm not a girl any longer; I'm old enough to wear my sword and use it, should life or name be threatened. I won't let you push me aside and hide whatever this secret of yours is. Tell me *why* the gates are closed."

Her father's solitary eye narrowed, the momentary display of fondness evaporating. "It was not my command that sealed us in here, girl. The Old King—"

"Damn the Old King!" Kasara snarled, taking another step toward her father, who stiffened. "Damn him and his orders. You'd choose him over the counsel of your own daughter? Your own blood? I made a promise to our people, Father. We must let them through. It is their right." Suddenly aware that she was shouting, she cut off and let her arms, now spread wide, drop again. She stood there, panting, fuming, while she awaited his response.

Pallid shock flashed across the Lord of Farrenhall's face, only for it to be crushed by black anger. Kalivaz approached, and she took a wary step back. Her father followed, rushing her until she was backed into a wall. Kalivaz stood over her, nearly nose to nose, as he bellowed, "Remember your place, girl! I am your lord, and you will *not* disrespect me in the house of my fathers. You will not disrespect your king in my presence. You say you are a woman, a sword-swinger, but you act like a spoiled peasant girl denied her after-dinner cream!"

As his voice boomed through the chamber, Kalivaz stumbled back, the redness draining from his face. He stood there for a moment, and Kasara remained pressed against the wall, her heart thrumming with electric fury, but her skin crawling with cold terror.

Kalivaz took a deep breath and loosed it as a soft sigh. The anger did not leave his eye. "The Lord of Farrenhall has given a command, girl. The Gated Bridge will remain shut to all, and will not open again until I receive word from Savisdale. You do not have the right to any more answers, nor any more questions. Do I make myself clear?"

Kasara gritted her teeth, but her head nodded of its own accord, her tongue uttering a begrudging, "Yes, Father."

Kalivaz looked her up and down again, that paranoia still burning in deep pits. What was it he feared she might do? Why didn't he trust her? He finally nodded to himself before turning and shuffling back to his chair. The quill resumed its scrawling. "Perhaps you should spend more time with the Myrimdons," he called back. "Waste your time and shirk your duties to our home even further. At least those are men who understand not to ask questions."

Her face flushing, Kasara turned and fled wordlessly. Sir Joros, the Myrmidon, was still standing in the antechamber, but other than a cursory glance, the man seemed to take her as no more threat than a floating puff of dust. The mercenary slammed the door in her wake the moment she was through the threshold, the solid wood panel slapping her rump and making her stumble. Bjern and the other guardsmen, still at their posts, stared goggle-eyed.

Kasara's furious blush only deepened as she hastened on, not daring a backward glance. With every step she took, with every inch of stone she put between herself and her father, her blood boiled until she thought it might erupt through her skin. Kalivaz wasn't even bothering to lie to her; there was some hidden purpose behind the closing of Farrenhall. He was excluding her, and he wouldn't tell even tell her why. *Doesn't he trust me?* What had she ever done besides his will? She was his only daughter, the heir apparent to Farrenhall and the lands of the Winterwood. This realm, these people, they would be hers, one day. *How can he expect me to succeed him, if he hides from me?* It didn't make any sense to her. It made her furious. There had to be some deeper reason, some logic that was escaping her grasp.

Something terrible is happening. She couldn't shake the thought from her mind, but without knowing what it was, how could she help? She resolved to keep her promise to the folk of the Winterwood. She would get them across Farrenhall, and if she had to do it without her father's permission, so be it.

Chapter Nine
Road's End

The sun slipped from the peak of the sky like an exhausted rider from his saddle, drooping toward a somber horizon. Haza could feel frustration and fear building over the crowd like a thunderstorm. Slowly, it drew strength from the mutters and whispers all around, ever darkening. It was only a matter of time before it loosed itself like a flood across the shores of the Tagalfr.

Haza had no strength left for worry, though. He didn't have anything but the pain. He sat in the Ruthborne family wagon, having hardly stirred since they'd arrived at Farrenhall that morning. He was doubled over, his teeth clenched, breaths coming in shallow rustles as he clenched his fist as hard as he could. He wanted to believe that was helping. It wasn't, but somehow, the act of making an effort felt good. Nothing could ease the terrible, gnawing pain in his stump of a shoulder, but he knew if he abandoned the effort, the agony would drive him mad.

It was like the wolf still had hold of him, its teeth grinding back and forth, tearing his arm away tendon by tendon. There was no difference. No relief. The wound was hot, like a blistering, seething rock cooking beneath the summer sun. But the rest of his body was cold, despite several coats draped over his back. It was not the chill of early winter, but the clammy sort of cold that came with sickness. Pain and cold and fear; that was all he was now.

Keep breathing, Haza told himself, repeating the thought over and over. It was a useless mantra, but it was all he had. *Keep breathing, and you'll be all right. Keep breathing.*

The sun's red eye passed between the twin towers of the Gated Bridge, dipping below the rim of the world. Haza couldn't appreciate its beauty, however. Even through his pain, his thoughts wandered toward other matters, other fears. Fortunately, there hadn't been a single report of walking corpses from the beachhead all day, though there were more than enough stories of harrowing encounters floating on the wind, now. In a story wrought of blood and fear, woven by the refugees fleeing their villages, it was becoming clear that the dead were sweeping westward, devouring the Winterwood step by step. They couldn't be far away, now. What if they reached the shore before Lord Kalivaz opened his gates? What was he waiting for?

Thunder rumbled overhead. A storm was coming from the east, promising more snow. They couldn't fight the dead, not in the dark and cold, not with the Tagalfr to their backs. The Rushing Ice was mighty and terrible, having neither shallow fords nor narrow crossings. From the Blistering Sea, it split Razzador until it poured into the Forgotten Ocean far to the north, beyond the highest mountains of Joromor. There was no going around it, no passing through. Farrenhall was the only way across.

Why would they close the bridge? It made no sense. The harvest was upon Vrusk; all across the kingdom, farms and villages would be gathering the spoils of the season. The Winterwood was no exception, and without the Gated Bridge, there would be no exports for House Varkoth. And with the winter arriving early, those resources would be more valuable than ever.

The crowd that was continuing to gather brought Haza no

comfort, either. It made him sick to picture so many people trapped as they were. Hundreds of strong, powerful men, the blood of Vrusk's founders; all helpless. Their families could do nothing but shiver in the unrelenting cold, with nothing to do but watch as the shadow of the storm slowly crept over them.

Haza seized the front of his coats, trying to take multiple folds with just one hand and pull them closer around him. The wind had picked up, gnawing at his cheeks. Mutters of disquiet rose with it, riding the wind up into the darkening sky. Some Vruskmen shouted and bellowed, their voices ringing like tolling bells. Some wept to themselves, while others argued or just whispered softly to each other as they huddled around campfires.

No matter how they manifested, the point of conversation was always the same—*Why?* He listened to several shout that the Old King had abandoned them. Still more talked loudly of the dead things, the animals of the forest that had turned against the living. Haza endured the gaping eyes of hundreds who passed by, their faces haunted by the sight of his disfigurement. Here, though, he was but one of many. Some walked with limps or sported bandages about their faces and arms. Others, however, just lay in carts and wagons, often shrouded by curtains or blankets as their family members fluttered nervously about them. Those last were the only ones who never raised their voices in question.

His spirits only dropped when a group of children walked silently passed his cart. They stared at him, their young faces paling at the sight of his bloodied stump. Haza gave them a weak smile, but they simply hurried on, their eyes wide and fearful.

And yet, as openly as they questioned the dead, Haza never once heard someone offer an answer. Why? Why did dead animals suddenly deny their own demise? Haza had never read of anything like it, not even in the oldest histories of Havasa or the fables of Joromor. These…creatures, these…monsters, what had given them that shadow of life? What had twisted them against anything with hot blood, driving them to kill without need, to destroy without claiming sustenance or growth? Haza couldn't stop thinking about how mindless the attack against him had been, how the wolf had done little more than stumble when he'd put an arrow through its skull. It had turned on him, not to eat, not to defend itself, but to kill. *That hate. I saw it. Hatred for* me. But why?

"Hungry?"

The question startled Haza out of his troubled thoughts, and, for a moment that passed much too swiftly, his pain. "I…I hadn't even thought of it," he placed a hand against his stomach and frowned. "I suppose I am."

"You should eat, regardless," Tayja remarked. "You need your strength, Haza." Her eyes trailed worriedly past his arm. Then she reached over the side of the cart to procure two steaming bowls of soup, one of which she passed to him.

Haza accepted it gratefully and rested it in his lap before raising his spoon. "Where are Haegar and Makin?" he asked before he took his first sip. The comforting warmth of pumpkin and cinnamon was a welcome balm against the cold.

"With Torvust and the other men," Tayja said, sipping from her own bowl. She lightly ran her dark fingers through Rala's hair, who was snuggled up in her lap. The smile that appeared on her face was sad and wistful. "They're at the gates now, speaking with Varkoth's men. Haegar's confident he can get the man to let us through."

Haza nodded, trying to veil his uncertainty. "Lord Varkoth is a good man," he said shakily. "He's always watched over the Winterwood. Whatever disagreement is between us now, Haegar will see it resolved." As he took another bite, he watched his bloodless-sister carefully, his thoughts stewing just as much as the broth still in the cauldron. "I know that face well enough, Tayja. Something still troubles you."

"Nightfall's soon," she replied, gesturing with her spoon up at the orange and purple sky. "And those dead things are still out there, aye?"

"Yes," Haza agreed, nodding hesitantly. "But...they haven't been sighted all day. The caravan moved fast. If they didn't catch up to us today, I doubt they will tonight. Have faith; our numbers will protect us." There was not a word he spoke that he believed, but if it could bring her any scrape of comfort, he would lie as much as needed.

Tayja kept stroking her daughter's hair, whose eyes were already beginning to drift shut. "I've been thinking a lot, Haza. About you. About what happened to you." He felt his stump flare, but he gritted his teeth and nodded wordlessly as she went on. "I thought about what would happen if...if it happened to one of my children. If they got hurt..."

A fearsome rage descended upon the woman's face. She looked up at him, as if he were the threat encroaching on her slumbering daughter. "I couldn't stand that, Haza. I couldn't stand to lose—" She broke off and averted her gaze.

Haza hesitated a moment, but as she folded into herself, he sighed softly and leaned forward to place his hand against her shoulder. "Nothing is going to happen to our family, Tayja. We will protect your children. All of us are going to get safely over that river. This is just...a minor inconvenience. A delay. Nothing more."

A lull followed as Haza withdrew his hand. Even the rumbling of the crowd hushed, and for a moment, the sound of the nearby river was as loud as a legion of marching feet, a continuous and uninterrupted pulse of thunder. Its roar almost seemed mocking, taunting them with its sheer size, its insurmountable scope.

"Are you certain there's safety on the other side?" she asked quietly.

He watched the water roll past. "There must be."

"How can you know, Haza?"

With eyes closed, he drew a deep breath. "Have I ever told you the story of the man who crossed the Forbidden Ocean?" He cracked one eye to see Tayja slowly shake her head, then closed it again. "Across the deserts of Joromor, beyond the Mountain of the Highest Path, lies the Forbidden Ocean. So terrible and cruel an ocean that its waters run black with the blood of those who've tried to cross. With beasts large enough to swallow ships and great glaciers of dark ice, invisible until one's boat is dashed against them, the ocean is impassible. As the maps would say it, there is no other side."

He breathed in again, eyes peeking open to meet Tayja's questioning expression. "But there must be another side, yes? And, in the days before the Holy Wars were but a whisper in the God-Emperor's mind, four brothers resolved that they would find it. They spent their lives perfecting a boat that could traverse the ocean's treacherous reaches. Hooked and weighted nets and spears for the dreadful beasts below, great hammers to swing from the boat's oars to shatter lurking ice—they were unsinkable. From the northernmost point of Razzador, they launched into the Forbidden Ocean, bound for the other side of the sea.

"Their route was dangerous. Already, the monsters of the deep were in their wake. One of the brothers, frightened by the overwhelming weight of their journey, leapt from the boat not an hour after disembarking, swimming back to the shore. The remaining three brothers pressed on, but after two days, another became frightened by the unending darkness ahead and leapt overboard. The last two pressed on, refusing to surrender. They would cross the ocean, no matter how long or far it took them."

Haza breathed in. Tayja had stopped stroking Rala's hair, eyes rapt with attention. He listened to the river for a moment, stared up at the darkening shape of Farrenhall. "Three years into their journey, they were still entombed in the Forbidden Ocean's embrace. Convinced now that the sea had no end, the third man resolved to swim back the way they'd come. His brother wept and begged him to stay, urging him to realize that no man could swim so far and live. But the man was resolute and soon made the jump. A certain death was preferable than whatever might be waiting for him the darkness. The fourth brother watched until the man was swallowed by the horizon, then continued his northward course."

Haza stopped, leaning back against the side of the cart. Tayja blinked. "Well?" she demanded. "Did he reach the other side of the ocean?"

He nearly shrugged before he caught himself. His shoulder throbbed anyway. "Who can say? All I know is that he never turned back."

"Is that supposed to comfort me?" she demanded. "Should I applaud a man who sailed headlong until his own death?"

"He was wise."

"Wise?" Tayja spat incredulously. "No, he was a fool."

Haza chuckled. "He was both, perhaps. He recognized that the only path to take was the one that lay ahead. There was no turning back, not once they'd gone so far. You could argue he was a fool for putting himself into such a position, perhaps. But, unlike his brothers, his desire for whatever lay beyond the sea was greater than whatever certainties he'd left behind." He smiled to himself, the roar of the river still thundering in his ears. "I do wonder what he might've found, when he reached the other side…"

Tayja sighed. Slowly, she stood, gathering Rala gently into her arms. "You don't really think he did, did you? Sailing an ocean like that all alone?"

"It's just a story," he said. His smile faded, but only a little. "We can imagine stories end whatever way we like."

Tayja's features darkened again as she looked up at the Gated Bridge, her voice quaking with a quiet anger. "Damn Varkoth and his blood for this pain," she growled. "This story can only end one way."

"It'll be all right," Haza muttered. His arm prickled and flared.

As the wind rose over the shore, it carried with it the sudden buzz of voices. Haza looked over his shoulder, toward Farrenhall, and saw a small group making their way back up the shore. "It's Haegar," he said, narrowing his eyes to better peer at the pack of men. Tayja set Rala atop the makeshift bed of blankets in the cart.

Haegar was making his way toward them, at the head of a small group of men all wearing matching, scruffy beards and scowls upon their faces. Makin was riding on his shoulders, and though he did not wear the naked outrage of his father, he still seemed crestfallen. Most of the men Haza didn't recognize—they weren't from Palvast.

"Haza," his brother barked, voice booming across the camp. It startled Rala into wakefulness, and she clambered into her mother's lap.

Haza reluctantly put his half-finished bowl at his feet and climbed painfully, unsteadily, to his feet. The eyes of the strangers immediately found the stump of his arm, and he flushed as they regarded him doubtfully.

"We need you, Haza," Haegar declared as they approached the Ruthborne wagon. He reached up and removed Makin from his shoulders, placing him alongside his sister and mother, to whom he gave a weak, weary smile. His eyes immediately flicked back to Haza.

"Me?" He couldn't help the curl of an eyebrow. "Why? What's happened?"

"Those blood-damned Myrmidons at the gate," Haegar snarled. "They won't let us through. They don't believe anything we say to them. These men with us are elders from other villages," he nodded to the dozen or so men who were clustered behind him. "But even with so many voices united, they won't listen."

"Foreigners," Torvust growled dangerously, which earned him a disapproving glance from Tayja.

"Did...did you say M-Myrmidons?" Haza asked. Frigid unease crept up his back as he stared over their heads at the bridge. "As in, the religious mercenaries? The disciples of the God of the Highest Path?"

Corvil scoffed. "Of course you'd know which god they worship, Haza."

He treated the boy to a scathing look, his anger prickling against pain as they vied for his attention. "The Myrmidons are legendary, Corvil. They came from beyond the mists of the Holy Wars, survivors of the purge of the God-Emperor's hierocracy. They learn three things as children, it is said; to climb, to listen, and to kill. They obey their Cardinals without exception. Without. Exception."

It was a troubling revelation. Infamous stories flashed through his head, each bloodier than the last. The Battle of Dead Man's Slough. The Blood Dawn. The Siege of Fire-River Knoll. In each instance, the Myrmidons had emerged victorious...and alone. Entire armies wiped out, but the Myrmidons still left standing, as if they truly were possessed by some divine influence. After all he'd seen, now, Haza was prepared to lend more credence to their god.

Regardless, holy or not, the Myrmidons were not hired to stand watch over bridges or guard small towns. Their price was exorbitant, and that payment was tripled for every Myrmidon who died in their master's service. This inspired only the truly wealthy, or else the truly desperate, to pursue their services. And, as far as Haza had heard, the Myrmidons were worth every coin they demanded. Entire wars had been lost, armies routed, just because their enemies had procured the allegiance of those who worshiped the God of the Highest Path.

"I couldn't care if they worship god or stone," Haegar growled. "They're turning away all comers, even the sick and old. If they won't believe what we say, then we'll show them what we've seen. We'll show them you, Haza." The other men nodded their agreement. More eyes danced across his mangled stump, each stare like a new blade, pricking him with hot needles.

"You want me to go to the gate?" Haza asked, frowning skyward. It was only growing darker, and the wind was picking up again, whipping them all with a fresh blast of cold. The thunderheads of the snowstorm rolled ever closer. "I'll do it. It's past time we were on the other side of the river."

"Thank you, Haza," Haegar said with a grateful nod, his expression never wavering from that glacial anger. He turned to Tayja and stepped close to her, dropping his voice to a soft whisper. "Take the cart and the children and get closer to the bridge. When the gates open, I mean for you to be among the first to cross, aye?"

Tayja nodded, her face as icy and calm as her husband's. Only her shifting eyes betrayed her fear. "Aye, my love."

Haegar reached out his hand, which Haza took before he

hopped to the ground from the cart. Even the small drop was enough to send jarring pain shooting across his body, like icy slivers driven by the wind into his arm. His mind swam in it, drowning, and for a moment, he thought he might faint.

"Are you well?" Haegar growled, gripping tighter as Haza staggered. The other men looked on in mute concern.

"I'm fine," Haza hissed, quick to pull his hand free. "Or else, I will be once we're through that damned bridge."

Haegar nodded to Torvust. "No sense delaying, aye?"

They left Tayja behind, who began to work on rousing Heartwood and gathering their belongings into the wagon. Makin shouted something after them, but Haegar made no reply; already the group of men were pushing their way back through the crowd.

Fires began to appear across the shore all around them, igniting one by one like the Seventeen Stars on a reverse sky, though there were far more than seventeen in this night. Mutters of somber unease quieted as the people of the Winterwood reluctantly began to accept that they'd be spending another long and cold night on the wrong side of the Rushing Ice.

We will get that bridge open, Haza growled to himself as he hobbled in his brother's wake. *This will not be our fate. We won't be trapped here.*

A sense of strange, unfamiliar pride swept over him as he marched with the other men. For a moment, he felt like a true Vruskman, a part of this group of powerful survivors, all working to protect their homes and families. He was part of something greater than himself, fighting for something greater. *Is this what Haegar feels like every day, whenever he looks over Palvast?*

Farrenhall grew before him, an immense shadow standing stark against the sunset. The thunderous fury of the Tagalfr overpowered the hum of the crowd as they drew nearer. Haza watched its thrashing waves throw themselves against the shore. The dark heart of the river stretched long, and chunks of ice were like the massive beasts from his story, breaching the surface in swelling plumes only to plunge back down into its depths.

In contrast, the Gated Bridge was unmoving, utterly still and careless of the river streaming past beneath. For all the water beating against the stone foundations of the bridge, it did not waver. Haza jumped when a great crash rang through the night, accompanied by a splintering groan, and for a horrible moment, he thought Farrenhall might collapse. But his eyes caught sight of a great slab of ice, bigger than any house in Palvast, as it peeled away from one of the bridge's pillars, split now into crumbling fragments that slipped harmlessly away.

Along the side of the bridge, lights glittered in its windows, promising warmth and safety within. Larger bonfires had been lit along the walls at the front of the bridge as well, lighting a courtyard set between the bridge and their destination— Farrenhall's outermost door, the Copper Gate. The Iron Gate, veiled by the walls, was likely sealed, too, but even one being shut to them would be enough to keep them trapped. He caught sight of figures standing along the wall, spears in hand. He shuddered. Myrmidons. Haegar had to be mistaken, right? What would Myrmidons be doing in a place like this?

Dusk settled across the Winterwood, and the sky turned a deep and unpleasant purple, heralding the arrival of the Seventeen Stars. The moon already hung in the north, its full and unblinking eye staring blankly down at them.

As they approached the indomitable walls of the bridge, Haza watched his breath puff from between his clenched teeth as he walked, trying his best to think of anything but the blinding agony in his arm. His breathing was becoming labored; each step only set him on fire, and the cold wind did nothing to stifle the flames. Conversely, it only seemed to make them hungrier.

"Does it hurt?" Haegar asked softly as they walked.

Haza blew an irritable snort. "Is that even a question? It's not exactly a toothache, Haegar."

His brother narrowed his eyes but nodded in understanding. He didn't ask anything more about the wound, and Haza couldn't blame him. What was there to say? What was there to apologize for? What could be done? Haza would be like this for the rest of his life, now. However long that might be.

"Do you really think men like these will show pity to a cripple?" he asked, casting a worried glance up at the waiting gates of Farrenhall. The Copper Gate met the crest of a large hill, setting it some fifty feet above the Tagalfr. The guardsmen loomed overhead, walking along the narrow stretch of the walls. Their armor was broad and flashed darkly in the light of their bonfires. The wicked heads of spears, set on shafts long enough to stab any man standing on the ground below, glittered too. Haza couldn't even imagine trying to lift a weapon like that. How did they wield them? This sort of strength, did he dare believe it to be divine?

"Religious men, you called them?" asked Torvust, shooting Haza a sideways glance.

"They're zealots," Haza whispered.

Torvust sniffed. One hand fell to the top of his axe. "I wouldn't expect mercy from men like them. How could they believe in a god? Even after the Holy Wars showed us all the truth?"

Haza grimaced. A hundred years of bloodshed, all in the name of faith. And through all the suffering and sacrifice, all the offerings of blood and death, none of the gods had come forth to claim their prize. At the end, there had been nothing but ash.

And the truth. All knew it now. Except, it seemed, the Myrmidons.

The gate now stood before them, a behemoth of iron and wood, sealed in a curved arch of stone. Light gleamed through the cracks around its frame, and shadows briefly disturbed it as men on the other side moved back and forth. Intricate swirls of copper engravings—the source of its name—climbed up and down its face like rusted vines. Haegar cupped his hands and turned his head to the battlements looming overhead. "Hail, Farrenhall," he boomed, his breath streaming from his mouth in a long tail of frost. "You wanted proof of our loss, and we have brought it to you."

Three figures appeared above the gate, leaning out to gaze upon the men now clustered on the road. They carried no torches, leaving their faces shadowed, illuminated only by a backdrop of orange and red. Though their silhouettes were veiled by the coming of night, Haza could recognize their armor readily enough. Myrmidons, for certain. He shifted nervously, feeling their scrutiny pass over him.

"You were instructed not to return, Ruthborne," called the man standing in the middle of the trio. His voice was deep and forceful, a voice that sounded at the end of a much-frayed patience. "Turn and go back to your homes. You will find no passage tonight, nor any other night, so long as Lord Varkoth commands it."

"Have you no pity?" Haegar demanded. He swung his torch close to Haza, and he flinched in surprise. Haegar took him by his good arm and directed him closer to the gate. "Look here. This is my brother, my own flesh and blood—Haza Ruthborne. Do you see what has happened to him? The sickness in his eyes? He is but one of many victims of this terror. If you think any of us are leaving by choice, then you do not realize what kind of men we are. We *must* leave. You *must* let us through."

"Haza Ruthborne," the man said in a curious, soft growl. He seemed to roll the name across his tongue, considering it carefully. "No, that is not the name of the man who paid my Faith Price. We will not be swayed."

"Think of the women," Torvust suddenly snarled, taking a step forward. He still had a hand on the head of his axe. "Think of the children! The wounded and dying! I did not believe it myself, I promise you. I know what it sounds like. But the dead are coming. You must let us through!"

Two of the Myrmidons stirred at Torvust's approach, tipping their spears over the battlements, aiming for his head. The man in the center raised a hand, causing them to retract their weapons again. His shadow-wreathed face remained unchanged. "I think of only the God of the Highest Path."

Haza glanced at Haegar, whose face had twisted into a fearsome scowl. "Haegar," he whispered. "These men are dangerous." His eyes darted between his brother and the spears brandished atop the Gated Bridge. "We should turn back."

"And do what, Haza?" Haegar demanded, rounding on him. "Wait to die? Where else can we go?"

"Anywhere but onto the spears of zealots," he hissed back.

"You, there," Haegar bellowed. He ignored Haza and stepped up alongside Torvust, raising his torch above them. "Man who hides in the shadows. Tell me the name of the one who would turn aside the wounded."

If Haegar's insults bothered the Myrmidon, he made no sign in either motion or tone. "Grand-Crusader Berethan Willamere," he announced. "Valiant Shield of the God of the Highest Path. Sworn by Faith Price to the word of Kalivaz Varkoth, Lord of Farrenhall. What is it to you, Ruthborne?"

"You will let us pass," Haegar growled, jabbing a finger first at the Grand-Crusader, then at the gate. "You will open Farrenhall and let us cross through. You consider yourself a holy man, aye? A man of valiance? For the sake of our wounded and weary, let us pass safely through our own country, or else you will force us to act."

Berethan chuckled dryly. He was not alone, a chorus of grim laughter sweeping back across the assembled Myrmidons. Snow began to fall as he spoke, spinning earthward in fractals of white and silver, dancing in the torchlight. "Act, Ruthborne? Tell me, what do you mean to do? Charge at my defenses with all these wounded men you've gathered? Can your brother still swing a sword with his remaining hand? There are quicker ways to find yourself on the end of a spear, if that is all you desire." The Myrmidon flicked his hand, and the men at his slide spun their spears, readying to strike again. "I recommend you leave this place and push my patience no further."

Haza took a wary step back, his stomach knotting at the sight of those unwavering spears. Either of them could slay Torvust and Haegar with only a single thrust. His brother did not retreat. "Haegar," he growled, "Haegar, this is not the way. Come back, please."

But Haegar did not relent. His eyes were locked on the shadowed forms of the Myrmidons, as unyielding as their steel. "I've heard of your kind before," he snarled. "Zealots, they call you, though I prefer to name madness for what it is. Crazed killers who will die for any cause, serve any purpose, so long as your pockets are lined. Lord Varkoth is an honorable man; he'd never turn aside the wounded and the helpless. If you really serve him, then open the gate and let us pass. It is what he would will, I know it."

Haza frowned at his brother's back. Some of the other men

were murmuring. A coup? Is that what Haegar was insinuating? Could it be that Berethan and his followers had seized the bridge from Lord Varkoth? The thought was terrifying—who could they negotiate with, if not fellow Vruskmen?

"I have been more than reasonable with you, Ruthborne," came Berethan's impassive reply. "It is by your Lord Varkoth's command that this gate remain sealed. I prefer to avoid shedding blood, as it has not been explicitly ordered, but our options are dwindling. Return to your family and thank your lord for his lenience. It is by his will that you still breathe. Turn aside now, or I will perceive you a threat to the security of Farrenhall."

Other than a slight rise in the Myrmidon's voice, there was nothing else to indicate any malice in his words. There was no hate, no anger, not even any relief for the prospect of ridding himself of meddlesome thorns. He could've been discussing the fresh snow falling around them, or the price of rope. Haza found the absence of emotion to be more foreboding than the lowered spears. There was no doubt in his mind that Berethan would do as he warned and do it without a second thought. It was nothing more than duty.

"Haegar," he said again. He stepped up with his brother, grinding his teeth through the pain coursing down his side, to grab his forearm. He did not give Haegar another opportunity to resist, wrenching the taller man away from the gate, and from the dangerous creatures who manned it.

"Curdle my blood!" Haegar snarled. He ripped himself free from Haza's grasp, causing him to stumble, but mercifully he stalked past the group of waiting men and down the hill, back toward the camp.

"Is that it, then?" Corvil demanded, throwing up his arms as he hurried to follow. "Is this the resolve of the Winterwood? Turned aside so easily?"

Haza stumbled in the boy's wake, trying to keep close to his brother. He shot Corvil his most withering stare. "If you'd like to be the first Vruskman to die on a Myrmidon spear, then you're welcome to turn back."

Torvust, a hand still on his axe, cast a baleful stare over one shoulder. "We have to do *something*, Haegar. Better a Myrmidon spear than the teeth of a dead wolf. I'd gladly take a blade if it meant passage."

Haegar glanced at him, his voice sharp as a blade's edge. "And leave Magda without a husband? Her babe without a father?"

"Assuming your death would even accomplish so much, Torvust," Haza added. "What if we throw ourselves against Farrenhall, only to be slaughtered for it? We're no army; we have no weapons, other than a few bows and axes between us. We have no artillery, and certainly no advantage against men with spears and armor. Where would we leave our families then if we're butchered like harvest cattle?"

"We're *not* attacking Farrenhall," Haegar growled. "We must find a way to speak to Lord Varkoth. I can convince him to see reason; this Grand-Crusader must've poisoned his mind with worries from the east."

"Not unfounded worries," Haza muttered.

"Regardless," his brother snapped, "if I can speak with him, I can convince him to let us through Farrenhall. The dead cannot follow us." He looked to Torvust. "We'll set a guard around the edge of the forest tonight. If those things were behind us last night, I doubt we put much distance between us. Tomorrow, we'll try again at the bridge, when things are brighter, and we can make sense of things."

The men made no reply, and Haza took their sullen silence as a mirror to his own reluctant acceptance. What more could they do against fighters as fierce as the Myrmidons? Lord Varkoth needed to see the suffering outside his gates firsthand if his will was to be swayed. And how could he ignore this growing crowd for much longer? It seemed more than half the Winterwood had gathered on the shores of the Tagalfr by now. It was a worsening problem that no man could ignore.

Why the Myrmidons? He couldn't escape the question. They were as terrifying firsthand as the stories had always described. The warrior-zealots would've had to cross nearly the whole breadth of Razzador—five hundred leagues from Joromor—just to come here. They were not the kind of men a sane noble employed. *I wonder...has the sickness that has infected the Winterwood also claimed Farrenhall? Has all of Razzador gone mad?*

As the men dispersed into the camp, Haegar dropped back alongside Haza, who was still hobbling at the rear. "Find Tayja and my children. I told them to make their way here, but I don't see them." He looked over the crowd, brow furrowed, but there wasn't much to see in the glow of the hundreds of campfires but huddled, shadow-cloaked figures. "They need to stay close to the bridge."

Haza nodded. "You're going with the guard?"

"Aye," Haegar frowned up at the sky as a line of shadow crawled across the Seventeen Stars, blotting them out one by one. In their place, flecks of snow were falling. "With any fortune, we'll reach the morning without incident. After that...I'm less hopeful."

Haza could only nod again, mutely, as his brother left him. *I've never felt so helpless before...* With his body in ruins, he felt like an old cripple, trapped in place and powerless to influence the world around him. He couldn't protect his family. He couldn't help his brother. All he could do was wait for whatever blow was coming next.

Chapter Ten
An Ill Night

"You might as well be telling me your attacks before you strike," Berethan intoned, voice as deep as the bells that hung over Farrenhall. With his own practice sword, he flicked Kasara's fallen blade and sent it spinning back across the arena toward her. "You telegraph your movements so plainly."

Kasara spat in her palms as she scooped up her sword. She hated how the wood felt in her hands. It was far too light, but in the same breath too sluggish. Even air could not be cut as smoothly with wood as with steel. She longed to take up a real blade against him, even if propriety might demand he do the same. That made her sweat, but also, secretly, shudder with excitement.

"No excuses?" Berethan asked. He stood before her stripped to the waist, dressed only in plain trousers. His armor and swords were up against the back wall, glinting in the torchlight. She was dressed the same way, though with bandages wrapped tight around her breasts. Even so, she still didn't feel limber enough.

"No anger?" he continued. "You're halfway to correcting yourself, Lordling. You use too much emotion in your swings. A furious blow is one that is swift, reckless. One that is too calculating is slow, predictable."

"Which one was I doing?" Kasara asked, holding her blade before her, eager to step back into the battle.

"If you cannot tell me, then it does not matter." With an arcing swing, the Grand-Crusader brought his sword up. "You must rid yourself of them both."

Kasara ground her teeth, then thought better of herself. With a deep breath, she turned her thoughts to steel. Steel. Hard, cold, unyielding. It never changed, never wavered. She had to be as hard as steel. As relentless. She stepped toward the Myrmidon.

Berethan surprised her by lashing out—he usually let her throw the first blow—and Kasara forgot the attack she'd planned, barely managing to lift her blade in time to parry the downward cleave. The man came at her, then, a storm of blows, each swing like lightning, each crash the thunder of wood on wood.

He spun her through the arena, sand churning beneath their feet, as they engaged in a furious dance. Kasara held him off. Barely. Her mind raced, trying to interpret his every movement, predict his next attack. He was trying to drive her into a wall, so she kept turning to remain in the center of the ring. All the while, she had to watch her feet to not trip over herself, had to move her body in time with her parries, relying on her torso, as much as her sword, to avoid oncoming attacks. And then there was the sheer strength of the man. Forgetting speed, each blow he threw at her hit like a hammer, sending aftershocks up her bones.

Think, think! She had to stay in the fight. *There is no defeat. You fight until the fight is finished.* But she could already see that this bout could only go one way. Had she even thrown a single counterattack? Berethan was wearing her down. Eventually, a blow would get through. She had to do something reckless. Something foolish. If she feinted right, she could-

Kasara blinked. Her head was ringing. The world above her swam, and as she continued to blink at it, she registered a dull pain in her right temple. That pain soon turned to a hot, angry pulse, as through the murk, she could see Berethan towering above her. She'd been sat on her rump again. With a groan, she sagged back in the sand, raising a tentative hand to where she'd been struck.

"Better," Berethan rumbled.

"I still can't beat you," Kasara panted. She rolled onto her stomach and slowly pushed herself upright. Her head was throbbing.

"This is why we practice. You will continue to improve."

Grabbing her sword, Kasara rose onto shaky legs. She felt like she was going to fall again. What did she need? More strength? More speed? "Do you think I could ever beat you?"

The man gave her a frigid look. It was not her, specifically, that he regarded so coldly, she was sure. It was just the way he saw the world. "You could," he said. "In time. There is nothing one cannot accomplish, so long as he climbs the mountain. You must not stop climbing, Lordling."

Kasara trudged past him, one hand still clasped to her temple, to replace her practice sword in the waiting barrel. "I told you I want no part of your Highest Path," she muttered. She couldn't keep fighting even if her head wasn't ringing like a bell. She felt like she'd been flayed, facing defeat no matter which direction she turned. Humiliation from Berethan, humiliation from her father. Why couldn't she win?

The Myrmidon was watching her, giving his own sword a few more experimental swings. He hardly looked winded. If not for the sweat rolling down his broad chest, it might've been impossible to tell he'd been fighting at all. "All men climb, whether they realize it or not," he said. "You must continuously seek improvement."

"Isn't that what I'm doing?"

"Is it?"

She cast him a withering look, then turned and put her back to the wall. She slid down and focused on measuring her breaths. Slowly, the pain in her temple was fading. "Did you talk with the men outside the gates, like I asked?"

Berethan came forward, returning his own sword. Then he sat beside her. When he leaned his head back like that, she could finally see that she *had* made him exert himself. That gave her the smallest prickle of pride. "I spoke with them," he said, "though it was no different than my own men were reporting. They seek passage. They are stubborn."

"But did you ask them why?" she looked up at him. Even sitting as they were, he towered over her. "*Why* have they come?"

"They are fleeing something." Berethan was still staring straight ahead, but his eyes narrowed. "They have wounded with them. Injuries akin to those I have seen on battlefields."

"Wounded?" Kasara jerked upright, drawing the man's eyes. "They're hurt? How? Why?"

The Myrmidon's gaze was blank. "It is not my place to know. In-fighting, perhaps. Where are you going, Lordling?"

Kasara hurried toward the door, grinding her teeth as she snatched her coat and pulled it over herself, doing up the front hastily. Damn the man for never acting outside his orders. Might it have killed him to ask them even a single question? How many were wounded? If there was fighting, where was it? Was this why her father had sealed Farrenhall? If he had learned of troubles, even among the villages, it might have frightened him enough to make him irrational. *More irrational, at any rate.*

"Lordling," Berethan called from behind. "You must help me equip my armor. Our agreement—"

She was already out the door. Let him figure it out for himself. The blood-blighted man was so good at everything else he did, he could manage. Kasara needed answers, and if Berethan wouldn't help her, if her father wouldn't help, then so be it. She would do it herself. Well, mostly herself.

She stopped by her chambers to change, swapping out her coat and wrappings for a fine gray tunic—she considered a brooch depicting the Varkoth crest, but opted against it—along with long trousers and a silver-trimmed overcoat. Last came her belt and her real sword.

Her hunt then began, though it didn't take her long to find Bjern. The young soldier was stationed by himself outside of the galley, slouching against the wall with his spear leaned up against him, his head bowed as he snored gently. She had a trace of pity when she came across him—her father was working the garrison soldiers nearly as hard as the Myrmidons, forcing them to keep watch over empty halls day and night—but it was little more than a passing flicker.

"Bjern," she said as she stepped close, rapping her fist against his helmet.

Bjern started with a yelp. At the sight of her, he scrambled upright, fumbling with his spear. "K-Kasara" he said, blue eyes wide. "I mean, my Lady Varkoth, I—"

"Relax, Bjern," she said. "I'm not here to make sure you're doing your job, for once. I need your help."

"My help?" He blinked rapidly, still fighting the stupor of sleep. He frowned, then seemed to register what she'd said and brightened. "You want *my* help?"

"Don't get your beard knotted," Kasara growled. It was irritating just how much she thought that short, black beard suited him. "I've come to you out of desperation. Not that I really have a choice. I don't have anywhere else to turn." She didn't mean it to sound so cruel. Although, seeing the way that smile melted off his face, maybe she did.

"Why don't you just go to that hulking Myrmidon?" Bjern sneered. He crossed his arms and leaned against the wall. His spearhead clattered against the stone, making him flinch. He readjusted it so that it stood beside him, instead. "Hasn't he been carrying your dress's hem, lately?"

She smirked. "Jealous?"

"No," he said, much too quickly. Then he frowned, looking her up and down. "What do you need me for? Are you…going somewhere?"

"Aye." She turned on one heel, beckoning for him to follow. "I'm going outside."

Frantic bootsteps filled the hall behind her. "Outside?" Bjern blurted as he scrambled up to her. "Boil my blood, Kasara, can't you see there's an army brewing on our doorstep? Go out there and they'll probably hang you from a banner pole!"

"An army?" She cast him a sideways glance. "Hardly. They're our people, Bjern. Moreover, they're my responsibility. My father might be content to ignore them, but I won't. Something's happening in the Winterwood, and I mean to find out what it is."

"I can't let you do this." His hand took her shoulder, spinning her around. "It's too dangerous. We don't know anything about what's going on out there."

She waved his hand away, taking a step back and planting fists on hips. "And that's something I mean to change. Now, will you help me, or *should* I go find a Myrmidon?"

Bjern clenched his teeth, eyes darting anxiously back the way they'd come. "What do you need me to do, Kasara?"

"I'm going to use the Pass," she said. "You'll watch my back. Distract anyone who might come by. I mean to return by dawn the same way." No one would know she'd gone, if she had any luck, but the Myrmidons patrolled the courtyard day and night.

The Pass was built into the leftmost wall; it was a narrow tunnel, barely large enough for even a woman to crawl through. Purportedly, it had been used to smuggle food into Farrenhall during the Holy Wars. She doubted her father even remembered it, else he might've sealed it decades ago. Berethan and his men wouldn't know about it, either.

"And if something happens to you?" Bjern demanded. His face had grown a shade paler with each word she'd spoken. "If you don't return?"

Kasara sighed. She put a hand on his shoulder and squeezed it tight. "Then you'll have to be the one to go to my father and tell him what you helped me do, aye? I'm sure it will go well for the both of us. Now, come on." She dragged him the rest of the way.

They were let out through Farrenhall's Iron Gate and into the courtyard without difficulty, despite the hour—she was still the daughter of Lord Varkoth, after all, and there had been no ban on stepping out into the open air for a walk, provided she remained in the courtyard.

It was an empty, barren little space, no wider than the Gated Bridge itself. It gave Kasara a perspective she rarely thought about when within the winding halls of Farrenhall's interior; just how narrow the old fortress really was. Dark, snow-swept stones sat beneath her feet as she and Bjern stepped into the night. The sky overhead had long since surrendered to shadow, the stars and moon hidden from view, while several bonfires burning on the walls lit the underbelly of low-hanging thunderheads in somber orange and red. The Tagalfr's roar was so loud out here, a consistent, demanding bellow.

Men in heavy armor patrolled the rooftops overhead, silver and red armor only revealed when they drifted past the bonfires like flurries on the wind. None seemed to be looking into the courtyard. None noticed two figures scurry across the darkened yard.

It didn't take long for her boot scraping along the base of the wall to find the narrow gap. Kasara took a deep breath, staring into the darkness. She wouldn't light her torch until she reached the other side, but the tunnel was short and straight. Besides, she'd used it a hundred times before, not that her father had ever known.

Before she could take the first step, Bjern grabbed her arm. Even amongst shadows, she could see the breath rise from his mouth in a long, vaporous trail. "Are you sure you want to do this? We don't know what's out there."

"I'll be lord of this land someday," she said. "They are my responsibility."

Bjern swallowed. "Well, if you don't come back, I just want to say—"

"If you're going to apologize for tonguing that troll from the kitchen, I will vomit on your boots."

It was impossible to tell if Bjern was blushing, but he at least had the decency to hang his head and scratch at the back of his scalp. "I, ah, won't, then. Just...come back, aye? And...maybe then we can talk?"

Kasara sighed. "Maybe." Then she turned and slipped into the passage. In truth, she had no time to think about Bjern or how angry she was at him, or how a part of her still wanted him to tongue *her*. She was a Varkoth, and tonight her people needed her. She would go to them, and she would find out what they were running from, else her blood be damned.

"An ill night to be out like this," muttered Torvust as they trudged through the snow.

Haegar passed his axe from one hand to the next, but it did little to stave off the chill seeping through his gloves. His fingers and toes were constantly stiffening, and the night was only going to grow colder still. The wind howling through the trees had a mocking tone to it, taunting the helpless Vruskmen trapped on the shores of the Rushing Ice, and bringing with it the first true embrace of a dark winter.

"Seems to be nothing but ill nights, of late," Haegar replied bitterly. As he trudged through ankle-deep snow alongside his old friend, Haegar felt betrayed by the Winterwood itself. His home had turned against him, like a serpent rearing over itself to strike its own tail. What was this terrible thing that made corpses walk? What had brought it to the animals of the wood? Was this happening all across Razzador, or just Vrusk? Farrenhall was an ironclad door, and behind it lay all the answers he needed to keep his family safe.

"They'll pass," Torvust grunted. The tree line marched with them, dark and quiet. Bare branches swayed like waving hands, seeming to beckon them forward. The wind was at their backs, sweeping snow earthward in heavy sheets. The camp, with its hundreds of flickering campfires to provide a faint glow, was behind them, too.

Haegar readjusted his coat collar against the frigid blast. "My father's blood would boil to see me now. To see me want to leave the Winterwood. He'd never understand, much less believe it. I can hardly believe it myself." He couldn't stop a grim chuckle and shook his head. He kept his eyes on the trees.

"As would mine," Torvust murmured. He held his axe low in one hand, half-moon blade pointed downward, and kept aloft a torch in the other. It painted the surrounding snow in a pale haze of orange. "But it must be done, Haegar. We cannot waver,

not when we're so close. Once the Tagalfr is between us and…
whatever this is, we'll be safe."

He scoffed. "If only it were that simple." The irony of it fell
over him like a blistering veil, scalding even as it dampened the
cold. "It's funny, isn't it? At any season, at any moment, we
could've left, and nothing would've stopped us. But now, the one
winter we must flee, the way is shut. I could almost believe there
really was a god, punishing us for our faithlessness."

Torvust spat ahead of them. "That's what I think of such a
god. What does he mean to us, aye?"

Haegar spat too. "And what would we mean to him?"

As they patrolled, his thoughts were always on his family.
He saw their faces in an alternating pattern, flashing across his
mind again and again. Tayja, his love, the woman who'd tamed a
wild and solitary man. She was a beacon of light in a blizzard, the
one thing calling him home. He saw Makin and Rala, his
purposes for being. His children meant more to him than he
could summon words to describe, something that had startled
him when he first felt it. He'd never imagined being a father,
never imagined being so devoted to it, until he'd held Makin in
his arms for the first time, seen that tiny, perfect face.

And there was Haza, too. Haza, the enigma. Haza, the
benighted, the brother who'd abandoned his family. Haza, who'd
come back again. These last few nights had redefined everything
Haegar felt for his brother. Gone was any hate, any anger.
Instead, he felt shame for all their petty, useless arguments. All
that mattered now was that they were together. Safe.

And…Haegar wasn't sure Haza was going to survive.

The realization only made him redouble his steps.
Exhaustion sloughed from him, and he pushed ahead. He would
not fail. He would get his family across the river.

He and Torvust nodded to another pair of watchmen, men wrapped in heavy woolen cloaks and carrying bows, who returned the gesture as they headed in the opposite direction, patrolling the whole of the camp's perimeter. Haegar and Torvust had made the trek three times, and he was sure dawn was only a few hours away, now. The snowstorm came and went, leaving the sky clear, the broad light of the moon painted the snow-buried shore pale blue. It promised a refreshing morning.

"The question," Haegar began, pausing to yawn, "is how to draw Lord Varkoth out of hiding. I didn't see any of his sworn men on the wall—only the Myrmidons. He is using them as a shield, and not just a metaphorical one."

Torvust nodded. "Those zealots will turn us away if we try to approach again. They do not care for our cause. They will not negotiate with Lord Varkoth for us."

"So we have to get a man to him," he growled. "Maybe if we're insistent enough, if we make enough noise—without drawing blood—he'll be compelled to respond."

Now, the larger man shook his shaggy head. "I met Lord Varkoth once before. He's a stubborn man. Ill-suited to confrontation. He knows the Winterwood doesn't revere him as much as we did his father, and he resents us for it. He will not come out on his own volition."

"And we can't force him," Haegar muttered. Haza had been right about that—even with twice their number, even with armor and weaponry to match, there was no chance they could breach the Gated Bridge. Farrenhall had been built to withstand the greatest army in all of history. And for all the magnificent cities and fortresses the God-Emperor had claimed in his bloody crusade, Farrenhall had endured. It was the pinnacle of Vrusk's architectural prowess. A group like the Myrmidons could hold such a place for a hundred years, he was sure. And the folk of the Winterwood had a matter of days.

What does that leave us with, then? Haegar frowned at the ground in front of him. Tracks marked the way, the footsteps of men who'd patrolled this length of the wood already. *What path can we take?*

"What if we sent a man inside?"

Haegar glanced up at Torvust, who was looking back at him with fervent eyes. "What do you mean?"

"If Lord Varkoth won't come out," Torvust growled, "then let us send someone in."

He shook his head. "If those Myrmidons won't let a bleeding, dying man through, then they won't let an ambassador, of that much I'm certain."

"Aye, but who said anything about going through the Myrmidons?" For a moment, a grin appeared beneath Torvust's wild, black beard. "Farrenhall is lined with windows, and its walls are weathered stone. If something holds that Grand-Crusader's attention, surely he won't notice one man, aye? There must be one good climber in a lot this big."

Haegar scratched at his own beard. "I suppose… It would be dangerous. If the climber is caught, he risks his own head."

"Only if it's the Myrmidons who find him," Torvust said. "The garrison will take him before Lord Varkoth, I know it. The man *will* hear our pleas if he can be reached."

"And what if he still rejects us?" he asked softly. "What then?"

Torvust nodded toward the forest. "We'll have to make a choice, then. Go home, and risk whatever's waiting for us, or try to breach the gates. A vain effort, aye, but maybe that's better than what's coming for us. You saw that wolf's eyes, same as me."

I did. That horse, too. There could be no pretending, any longer. The forest would kill them, if it got the chance. "We'll need to find someone mad enough to climb."

"Find someone?" Torvust laughed. "Haegar, it's my bloody idea."

Even though Haegar knew it was coming, his heart twisted. "What about your family, Torvust? Magda is with child. She needs you."

"You think there's a single man here that doesn't care about his family, Haegar?" Torvust stopped, forcing Haegar to pause, too. "I'll do it for the same reason I know you would." He reached out and clapped a hand against his shoulder. "We must protect our families, at any cost. I'll do it."

Haegar relented, wilting in his old friend's embrace. "You're a good man, Torvust. Better than—" He cut off abruptly as a sharp, crimson light suddenly illuminated the spindly silhouettes of a hundred trees, glowing through their finger-like branches before fading back into darkness. Something tugged at the weathered threads of his memory. Hadn't he seen that light before? Hadn't it been on…? His thoughts trailed off as a sudden, ghastly smell of sweet-vile rot rushed over him. "They're here," he choked, nearly gagging. It did not stop him from unlooping the axe from his belt.

Torvust spun on his heel as they both faced the edge of the Winterwood. A figure staggered into view, making its haphazard way through the trees. A shadow-wreathed hand caught the trunk of a tree to steady itself, sending a flurry of snow dropping to the ground. Something metallic gleamed in the moonlight.

"Blood of the ancestors," Torvust gasped, "is that…?"

It stumbled beyond the last tree and into a waiting patch of moonlight, which gleefully unveiled the gaunt, lanky figure of a man. The terrible twist to his spine told them how he'd died, but such an injury did nothing to stop the corpse from lurching toward them.

The man wore only rags, and his skin glinted palely, where there was skin at all. Something had taken to his stomach, hollowing it into a black cavern between ribs and exposed hips. The man's hair was long, with a beard to match, and despite the gauntness of his frame, he was clearly a woodsman of Vrusk. A man of the Winterwood. Clutched in his right hand was an axe, its blade dragging through the snow with each lumbering step he took.

"That's a man," Torvust growled, his voice disbelieving. "A bloody man, Haegar. Is he really…?"

There was no sense in denying what was plainly evident. "He's one of them," Haegar whispered. The words sent fingers of ice sliding down his back. *"My mother got back up again…"* Words from the harvest festival, words he'd tried so long to ignore. But the horrid magnitude of it all could no longer be rejected. *All* the dead were rising. Man and beast. Everything that dwelled in the Winterwood. All would be corrupted by this…this madness.

"Blood be burned," Torvust whispered, uttering a vile curse that Haegar had never heard him speak before. Blood was sacred. Blood flowed from man to man, father to son, a lineage that could only be stopped by annihilation. Torvust raised his axe and seemed to steel himself. "Get back to the others," he growled as he took a step forward. The dead man was still staggering toward them, moving as if on an unhurried stroll down the beach. "Sound the bells. Wake the camp."

"And leave you alone?" he bit back. "It's just one corpse. Come, we'll split its skull."

But Torvust's axe came swinging out to bar his path, blade

pointed away. "I'll handle it. There might be more of them, Haegar. Sound the bells. Quickly now." Without another word, Torvust broke into a sprint, rushing the lumbering body.

Haegar hesitated, torn between the camp and the sight of his friend rushing toward a dead man. Torvust bellowed an unearthly roar, the birth of a war cry, as he raised his axe. The corpse didn't acknowledge him. Its shadowed face was downcast, the axe limp at its side.

Haegar wanted to act, but he could only stare, his own axe gripped in a frozen hand. The scalding blue moonlight revealed everything outside the darkened trees, like a hypnotic ray of light drawing his eyes. *This is insanity. This isn't right.*

As he finally brought himself to take his first step, Torvust reached the corpse, and without pause, he brought his axe down in an overhead swing, his cry a triumphant companion to the sickening *crunch* of shattered bone and flesh. The corpse dropped to one knee, utterly silent, as Torvust's axe bit down through its shoulder, sinking all the way into its chest.

Torvust stepped back, tugging on his axe, but he only wrenched the corpse forward a step. Haegar cried out as the corpse brought its weapon up, fast as a striking serpent, and buried itself in Torvust's neck. His blood turned to ice. He watched Torvust jerk, stumbling to one side.

The corpse stalked past as Torvust fell to one knee, hands clutching his neck. The dead man didn't even give him a backward glance as Torvust suddenly fell forward, crumpling in the snow. Haegar drew breath, and it felt like the last breath he'd ever take. It swallowed everything. He couldn't think anymore. Was he dreaming? Had he gone mad?

The corpse was still coming toward him, axe hanging loose in its hand, while the handle of the second weapon wobbled as it protruded from its chest. Torvust lay still in a darkened heap just beyond, and Haegar couldn't bring himself to move, only stare.

And then there was relief, hot and sure, as Torvust stirred again. The man pushed himself upright again, and Haegar knew all would be well. Of course Torvust would get back up again. The man had never fallen before; he would not fall now.

But then his old friend turned around. His head hung at an odd angle, and a dark stain was seeping down the front of his white coat. His mouth hung half-agape, frozen in the final notes of his war cry. He stepped forward, and though he did not stumble as the first corpse did, he moved with that same, unnatural calm. A man possessed by utter carelessness. A man possessed by something that did not live.

The first corpse stopped, wrenching its head back to regard Torvust. Then it reached up and ripped his axe free with a single pull and held it out toward him. Torvust seized it, then let it drop limply in his grasp. Both moon-drenched faces gaped at Haegar, regarding him silently.

He could not have said what finally broke him free from his stupor. Perhaps it was the sight of his friend, now walking toward him with a black-smeared axe in hand. Or perhaps it was the things that began to stir behind him, a score of creatures filtering out of the Winterwood, marching under a curtain of rot so thick that it set his nostrils aflame.

Wolves came creeping out behind Torvust, moving in utter silence. With them came elk and boars, some with twisted necks, others with stripped flesh, and still more without any clear indication of what might've killed them. More men came, too, first alone or in pairs, then in large clusters. Together walked the beasts and the Vruskmen, perfectly silent save for the crunching of snow beneath their sluggish feet.

"The dead!" Haegar screamed, as loud as his lungs could muster. "The dead are here! Ring the bells and gather the weapons! Light fires and drive them back! The dead, the dead!" He'd never screamed so hoarsely, so desperately, in all his life. It was a primal cry, a raw revulsion to the face of death itself, crawling out of the Winterwood that night.

Haegar spun wildly, his nerve deserting him, and he ran for the promise of light. Beneath the moon and the shadow of Farrenhall, the men of the Winterwood slept with their families, unaware of the evil that had come creeping.

"To arms, men of Vrusk!" Haegar bellowed, throwing up snow in his wake as he dashed for the tents and wagons. "To arms and fight! The dead have come for our wives, for our children. We must fight! We must—!" He tripped and fell face-first in the snow. And there, his strength abandoned him. He began to weep, terribly, openly, as loud as he could. His limbs had no strength to rise, his heart no will.

Torvust! Torvust, please... He saw that axe swing up again and again. Each time it collided with Torvust's throat, he watched him die. The sound of crunching bone. The transformation of a shout into a scream. Torvust had a wife. An unborn child. He had a place in Palvast. *There are trees that need chopping before spring. How are we supposed to keep up without you? There's...* he might've laughed at how ridiculous that thought was. It was all gone now. Torvust was gone.

Something seized him from behind, and he braced himself for the impact of an axe. He tried to struggle, to kick and writhe, but he knew it was too late. Tayja would be left without a husband, Makin and Rala without a father.

"Haegar?" someone shouted. "Haegar, what happened?"

He found himself looking up into Corvil's pale, youthful face. The boy's eyes were wide with concern, all traces of brashness banished from his fearful stare. Haegar reached up and seized the boy's collar, and Corvil roughly helped him climb to his feet. "Gather all the men you can," he panted. "They're here."

"You're welcome to wait here until he returns," Haza said, trying to hide his frown as he took another sip of tea. "I told you, my brother is out patrolling. He'll be back when his shift ends. I don't recommend trudging out into the cold to look for him. This wind is only getting stronger." It smelled rank, too. Haza wrinkled his nose and tried to ignore it.

The girl narrowed her eyes at him, causing him to blink. Haza wasn't sure what to make of her. Unable to sleep, he'd risen and stirred the fire back into life, setting a pot to boil. No sooner had he finished than the girl came into view.

He didn't recognize her, and she was dressed in clothes far too fine to be a farmer's daughter—perhaps she was the child of one of the wealthier mayors? With a long face and a broad nose, there was a fox-like cunning to her, and a burning curiosity in her pale gray eyes. Her red hair she wore short, trimmed just above her ears. And, most curiously, was that a real sword at her side? Haza hadn't seen one in years; they simply had little use in the Winterwood.

"I need to speak with him on a matter of some urgency," the girl said. "Unless there is someone else you can direct me to? Some other figure of authority?"

Haza couldn't help his frown. "Ah, we're not the most well-organized troop... You'd do best seeking out one of the mayors, maybe. Or perhaps your father? What did you say his name was, again?"

The girl's lips quirked, teetering on a scowl. "I didn't."

"What is your name, then?"

"Kasara," she said flatly. She was looking past him, eyes sweeping across the camp, as if they might light on some banner that could lead her to whatever it was she was looking for. "Yours?"

"Haza Ruthborne," he said tentatively. Kasara? He was sure he'd heard that name before. Perhaps she was from a village neighboring Palvast. "What did you see?" he found himself asking before he could stop himself. "What made you decide to flee, I mean?"

Her eyes fell on him, a thin red eyebrow rising. "What do you mean?"

"Ah, well, for us it was, ah, my arm." Why did he feel color creeping up his face? As much as pain, shame was a sudden bright fire. *This wasn't my fault. Nothing could've prevented this.* And yet, somehow, he still felt like if only he'd been stronger, faster, he could've protected himself and his family.

Kasara stared at his stump. "Are there many like you? Wounded in this state?" When he nodded, her features paled. "Boil my blood," she whispered. "And who was it that did this to you? Who organized the attack, do you know?"

"Who?" Haza said the word like he'd never spoken it before. "It was the dead."

"The…dead?"

A bell rang out, sharp and frantic. No sooner had their heads whipped in its direction than it was joined by a dozen others, all crying in panicked unison. And, just beyond them, he could hear shouting. "Blood be preserved," he whispered, his heart shriveling in his chest. "I think they're here."

When he looked back at Kasara, the girl was gone.

Haegar pushed Corvil aside, spinning toward the ringing of a bell. Men were shouting, their voices rising in a disjointed cacophony. The warning had been given. Haegar raised his axe and turned back to face the darkened wood. Men began to gather around him, sporting torches to push back the darkness. That smell came over them in rolling waves, so putrid and thick that it was a wonder he could not see foul clouds.

"Form a line!" he heard himself bellow, raising his axe. For some reason, the men obeyed. Why was he surprised? They were Vruskmen, and they would protect their home from any threat. *Even our own dead?* There had to be more than a hundred of them now, with more creeping into the moonlight. His stomach turned at the sight and stench as the figures slunk through the darkness, coming right toward him. How many would it take to overwhelm the camp? *Can we even stop them?* He'd decapitated that wolf, hamstrung that horse, and both had kept coming. *Can the dead die again?*

It didn't matter. Haegar wouldn't let them reach the camp. He couldn't let what happened to Torvust happens to anyone else. *Especially not my family. Please, me before them. Me before anyone.*

"What is this, Haegar?" Corvil asked quietly from beside him. The boy was holding an axe in both hands, its blade visibly trembling. He didn't look like a fledgling man anymore, only a child. Haegar almost commanded him to flee, to hide in the camp, but he bit his tongue. He wouldn't impugn the poor lad like that. Besides…they needed him. They needed everyone who could fight.

"The dead," he growled, and he raised his voice so he could address all the men gathered around him. "Dead men, too. They have axes and teeth and claws. If you fall, you get back up again, as one of them. Keep them away. For the blood of your fathers, don't let them touch you."

The crunch of wood made him start, and he turned to see men from Palvast hewing apart one of the nearby wagons. A man split a wheel in two with his axe and tossed one of the halves to Haegar. "Here," he growled. "Should turn back a fang or two, aye?"

Haegar undid his scarf and hastily wrapped it about wood and flesh, strapping the broken wheel to his hand before taking up his axe again. Men armed themselves similarly, while others pushed carts further up to the line and clambered up onto them, bows in hand. Shouts were coming from somewhere behind, but Haegar ignored them. The ringing of the bells was surely doing its part to drive the women and children closer to the Tagalfr.

There's nowhere to go, he suddenly realized. The Rushing Ice might as well have been a sheer cliff; if the dead caught them here, they could never get away. And when men started to fall, the numbers of the dead would only swell. No one would last until morning. *We have to stop them here. Now. Not one man can die.*

The dead lumbered closer, but they'd yet to cross into the puddles of torchlight now cast ahead of the makeshift battle line. They were coming, though, trudging in silence, animal and man, filtering out from between the trees. Around him, the living stood stiffly, crouched behind overturned wagons and hastily shoveled mounds of snow. The sound of their labored breaths, rising like tendrils of smoke, climbed even over the wind and the crackle of their torches.

Haegar tried to swallow with a dry throat as he stepped up to the edge of the light. He'd never seen armed combat before. That's what this was, wasn't it? Should he order a charge? That's what all the stories seemed to say, but he didn't know them as well as Haza did. Was this how it was supposed to work? Had he assembled a proper battle line? He wished Haza were here to tell him. Haegar lowered himself into a crouch, assuming what he thought to be a proper fighting stance, with his makeshift shield raised over his chest and his axe readied at his side.

He glanced back at his waiting men, watched them shift nervously on their feet as their breaths escaped from between their clenched teeth. There was terror in their eyes as they watched death creep toward them. *No, this isn't going to work.* Haegar had frozen when Torvust fell. If that happened again when the killing started, to all the defenders…

"Let the blood of any man who fails to fight be burned!" he bellowed, the words leaping unbidden to his tongue. He had to act, to shape the men into a focused, fighting militia, by any means he could muster. "Death comes, but it shall not touch us. We're men of the Winterwood, aye? If you fall, this thing will use your corpse against us. You will *not* die this night. I forbid it. You will live to see the other side of the river. You will live to see your families safe, your wives and children in warmth and comfort, but you *must* fight. Burn my blood, but I swear it."

Haegar looked down the line as his words were swept along on the wind. A few raised their voices in a half-hearted cheer, but most didn't give him more than a nervous glance. "Fight and live," he growled. "All of you."

They waited. The wind blew cold and insidious, its creeping whisper light and taunting on his ear. Beyond the light, darkness swam in twisting shadows, blurring what was enemy and what was imagination. How long until the dawn? One hour? Two? At least the light would show them what they were facing. *If we can hold that long.*

"They're in reach of my bow, Haegar," a man shouted from atop one of the carts. "I can hit them."

"Do it, then," Haegar growled. *Why are they waiting on my approval?* "Aim for their legs and shoulders. They can't die like living things, but they can't walk and fight if their tendons are cut, aye? Shoot as if to lame them."

A volley of some fifty arrows split the night with a sharp whistle. They cut through the air, passing from the light and into the shadows beyond. They fell among the unhurried horde, but Haegar couldn't have said if any arrows found their mark, as the sound of faint thuds came without cries of pain or anger.

"Keep going!" he commanded. "Loose until your quivers are empty!"

The archers of the Winterwood nocked arrows to their bows and shot again. This time, Haegar saw three figures fall. One was the man at their head—the one who'd killed Torvust. He collapsed just shy of the light, an arrow pierced through his knee.

Then Torvust stepped out of the shadows. The man's face was pale, his eyes bulging and wide, mouth half-agape. Bright, glistening crimson was still pulsing from the ruin of his throat, and his head hung at a crooked angle. He raised his axe in both hands, and as soon as the light touched his lifeless eyes, broke into a sprint. Haegar's breath caught in his throat, taking a step back in pure revulsion, his skin squirming as if a thousand worms crawled beneath his flesh. Those corpses that came behind Torvust exploded into motion as well. The elk threw themselves forward, long legs churning snow, while wolves and foxes fell into swift, fluid gaits, while the dead men came with their weapons raised.

"Run them down!" Haegar roared. *Bloodied shit. Let it all be damned. I can't do this.* But, somehow, his feet moved. He waved with his half-shield, and a wide-eyed Corvil made to follow, as did the men behind. Another volley went before them, transforming the front ranks of the dead into walking thorn bushes.

A shaft erupted from Torvust's temple, causing the man to

stagger. Haegar rushed him in the same breath, a furious scream of outrage, of terror, ripping from his throat as he swung his axe for his friend's throat. With all his strength, he drove his axe into Torvust's already-hewn neck and severed the man's head.

He did not see it as Torvust anymore—he could not. It was only some twisted stranger wearing his face. And Haegar wouldn't allow that. The defiling would go no further than this. Torvust's head spun through the air and landed in the snow. His body stumbled drunkenly, but Haegar would not repeat Torvust's same mistake. Even before the headless corpse could raise its axe, Haegar had swung low, driving his blade into its knee. The corpse fell, blood spurting across the fresh snow, and Haegar put his boot into its back, shoving it to the ground. It spasmed and thrashed, but could not rise.

Haegar took a step back, his breaths coming in a rattling gasp. He found himself possessed by a strange thrill; his whole body pulsing with an unknown energy. He spun in a slow circle and saw for the first time the combat unfolding around him.

Corvil had charged screaming toward a wolf, which had pounced on the boy like an avalanche given fur and teeth. Corvil staggered back when it struck his shield, but he did not fall, instead using the wolf's own momentum to push it to one side, letting him bring his axe down on the back of its neck. In two blows, he'd severed its head.

Axes flashed through the night, battling gleaming fangs and claws, hacking through flesh that was near hard as ice, struggling against bodies that would not fall. Arrows whizzed overhead, slamming into the back ranks of the dead who'd yet to reach the battle, felling more of them in the darkness.

For a moment, Haegar felt like he could breathe. He could see the dead for what they were; disorganized and disoriented, a shapeless horde without a leader, without coordination. Even an old woodsman like himself could see through their strategy; overwhelm and swallow with an undying rush. But their reckless charge led them heedlessly into the waiting axes and arrows of the Vruskmen. He breathed through his teeth, long and sharp, and turned his heart to steel. They could survive the night.

He flinched when something drenched his face, hot and stinging. He choked, hastily wiping his face, as Corvil dropped in front of him. The boy was screaming. The sound scraped across his bones like glass. Had he not been staring into Corvil's wild, terrified eyes, he never would've believed that such a noise could come from something human.

The boy curled into himself as he wailed, clutching at his ruined stomach. His entrails lay before him, as did his fallen axe. The shaggy, hulking form of a bear lumbered closer, placing its gray forepaw upon Corvil's head, and the boy's own blood trailed from its claws to his cheek. Corvil only screamed louder as the bear pressed its weight upon the boy, until the cry was cut off with a sickening *crunch* of bone and flesh.

Haegar gaped. His knees turned to slush beneath him. Beyond the dead boy, he saw the battle turn. Scenes of madness, nightmares given rotting flesh. He saw Torvust toppling forward again, blood spraying from his neck, dragging one leg behind him. He saw wolves leap up and torches fall to the ground. The wolves came away with throats clutched in their teeth, young men thrashing before them. Elks drove hooves and horns through wooden shields and axe handles, shattering wood and bone beneath.

The men of the Winterwood fell, only to rise just as quickly, the newly dead turning their axes on their still-living brethren. Arrows whizzed down from the carts just beyond the carnage, but few fell beneath their onslaught. Bears and horses became pincushions, sprouting coats of arrows that did nothing to slow them down. One black bear slammed itself into a cart, tossing it onto its side. The three archers cried out as they were dislodged, and the bear was on them before they hit the ground, snatching one by the head. His cry, too, echoed Corvil's until it faded into haunting silence.

The makeshift battle line was buckling. Still more corpses were shambling from the forest, while men whose blood still steamed in the cold were rising from the fallen, some with missing throats, others with crooked necks or twisted backs. Shapes filled the sky, too, swooping out of the darkness. Wide-winged owls and hawks, and tiny swarms of songbirds and sparrows, assailed the archers on their carts, driving some to fall into the chaos below. Others screamed as birds latched onto their faces, refusing to come loose no matter how they were beaten or pulled.

And Haegar had no time to think about any of it. The gray grizzly, its paw still pressed over the ruin of a twitching Corvil's skull, raised its head to regard Haegar, who stood frozen in the light of a fallen torch. He made himself meet its eyes, only to realize to his horror that it had none. Maggots filled sunken sockets, squirming and writhing in a greasy yellow mass. Some fell from its face when it took a step, wriggling all the way to the ground. No breaths came from its gaping mouth. There wasn't a twitch of an ear, a flick of its tongue, to show Haegar that it even knew he was there. But there was no doubting that it was coming for him. Nothing to see but those maggot eyes, and that certain step toward him.

Screams echoed around him and figures darted like flies across his periphery. Whether they were living or dead, fighting or falling, it didn't matter. He had eyes only for the bear, which came at him in a silent rush. A paw, topped with cruel, hooked claws, swung for his throat. With a cry, Haegar threw himself aside, feeling the air from those claws whistle past his neck. He swung his axe into the side of its skull, feeling it bite deep, but the bear was not so much as startled. It threw itself up onto its hind legs, sending Haegar to the ground with a pained gasp.

He scrambled away, axe forgotten, and broke into a run. He didn't have time to think about anything, not his terror, not his shame, not anything but his own survival. He heard the terrible *whoom, whoom* of massive paws and glanced back, only to see a flurry of white and gray as the bear churned snow.

Haegar ran blindly. He saw patches of blood staining the ground at every turn, alongside fallen weapons and overturned wagons, but no bodies. Never any bodies. Men were still screaming, which meant they were still fighting. Only the living made sound. Metal crashed against metal, thumped against wood and flesh, but the shapes around were all shapeless and instinct. He couldn't find a direction to follow, a sound to recognize. The bear thundered behind him, rapidly closing whatever small gap he'd managed to garner.

The scream of a horse caused his head to whip to one side, and he saw a man astride a stallion gallop through a pool of mingled fire and moonlight. There was a spear in his hand, and he charged the bear, which paused its pursuit and reared up to face him.

With a bellow, the man drove his spear straight into the bear's heart. Then he died with confusion on his face when the beast did not flinch, when his spear snapped, and he was carried right into its waiting paws. Haegar watched his would-be rescuer topple from his horse, a dark spray painted across the callous eye of the moon. The horse screamed again as the beast seized its flank, burying its teeth in its haunches. The horse bucked, kicking both back hooves into the monster's head. The bear's neck snapped to one side, and it stumbled. The horse dashed away, still crying madly.

I'm insane, Haegar realized as the bear again turned its attention on him, its head now twisted sharply to the right. *This is what madness looks like.* It felt…hot. So hot. Haegar felt like he was melting, as if Razzador itself was collapsing into a crazed, shapeless stew of noise and pain and fear. He stood there, waiting, weaponless, as the bear approached. *We should've just stayed home.* If they'd locked themselves in their houses, stayed quiet, the walls of Palvast would've protected them. *We all might've lived.* Instead, he'd led his family right into their graves, and he would be the first to be swallowed by the dark. *Burn my worthless blood.*

And then a girl leapt in front of him. For a moment, Haegar could only gape as the red-haired youth slashed at the bear, driving her weapon through its throat. *Is that a sword?* He didn't think he'd ever seen one before, but she was swinging it with clear skill, hacking at the massive beast's head. It swung its paw at her, forcing her back with a sharp curse. Haegar seized the opportunity to dash forward and rip his axe free from the bear's head. He brought it down again, splitting its skull.

"The back legs!" he bellowed, leaping away from its next swing. "Hamstring it!"

The girl raced past him, and as Haegar drew its strikes—a glancing blow on his shield sending shards of wood pinwheeling past his face—she was behind the beast, driving her sword though its back leg. The bear staggered, its next lunge going wide. It spun toward her, dragging its lame leg, and Haegar pounced on its second hind limb. His axe split gray fur and bloodless flesh, and the bear fell heavily. It began to drag itself forward, clawing at the ground, but the girl was easily able to dance out of reach.

Their eyes met. There was fear in her stare. Haegar opened

his mouth, but he didn't know if it was to thank her or berate her for leaping into sure death. That sword, unbloodied despite its victories, caught both the moonlight and his eye.

"We must fall back!" a voice bellowed, sharp and sudden. It was like a blow to his head, ringing it so hard that his thoughts finally cleared. "Fall behind the wagons; we're forming a wall. Do not let them through, Vruskmen!"

Haegar whipped his head in the direction of the voice. Some fifteen paces away, the men of the Winterwood had regrouped. While teams worked hurriedly to drag wagons and carts into a haphazard wall, defenders with poles and axes and shields climbed atop them.

He rushed the barrier, waving his shield frantically over his head to signal he was still a living man. For a harrowing moment, archers with nocked arrows sighted him, but they were quick to swing past him again. The girl was with him, blue eyes still bulging from her head, her sword now slick with black. More survivors abandoned their fights, scrambling away from silent, gaping opponents to answer the call of the unseen man. As they rushed through, more wagons were shoved into the gaps, lengthening the wall, sealing it off.

Only the thunder of feet and hooves told Haegar that the dead still came behind him, but he didn't look back, not for a moment. He dashed toward the wagon, where waiting hands pulled him and his savior up.

"Curdle my blood," grunted a blood-drenched man. It took Haegar a moment to recognize Bofor, a man from a neighboring village, beneath the grime and sweat. The normally jovial woodsman looked like as nightmarish as any corpse, his eyes almost seeming to glow while framed by a spattering of crimson. "I'm glad to see you still alive, Haegar."

"Bloodied shit," cursed the wide-eyed girl. "What are these things? What's happening?"

"They're still coming," Haegar snarled. He raised his voice again. When had it grown so hoarse? "Hold them back! Our wives and children lie behind us! Stop them at any cost!"

Bofor spat in his hand, readying his axe. "Just like cutting down trees. This forest can't last forever, aye?"

"Just keep fighting," Haegar whispered. He looked out across the improvised battlefield, his stomach churning with bitter memories of the soup he'd eaten. Not more than five hours ago, he'd been at his family's campfire, just eating soup… Such a thing seemed like a child's dream, now.

Reality was a battlefield without stillness. The only things on the ground were the twitching forms of bodies wounded beyond the ability to crawl. The dismembered dead would shift and jitter, but they never rose more than that. *Do they really not use their eyes to see? Their ears to hear?* Some animals limped along on three legs, the fourth severed or dragging behind them. Discarded torches and moonlight intermingled in strange, shadowed pools, and the blood sat dark and heavy on the snow. And for every fallen creature Haegar could see, a dozen more were still coming. Were those still more emerging from the Winterwood? *How many corpses can there possibly be?* This…this sickness…it couldn't have slain everything that lived in the forest, right? *If it has, how long would it take us to hack down every animal and man it has taken?* This was not a winnable fight.

There was no time for any further thought. Snow, blood, torches—all was swallowed by a tide of gray surging toward the wagons. Haegar found himself standing at the edge of the cart alongside a line of weary, blood-drenched men. He wasn't sure if he'd gone to the front willingly, or if he'd been pushed. Men jostled and shoved him from behind, and for a moment he wobbled on the edge, certain he'd topple over. Furious and terrified shouts rang around him as men tried to call orders, call for help, call for anything, but it all melted into an indistinct babble. He didn't hear a single cry of pain, though. What time had there been to carry their fallen to safety? Had any wounded made it behind the wagon line? He didn't have to imagine the fate of those left behind, too injured to stand. A deep, echoing remorse for those abandoned stacked upon his already mountainous guilt, but he had to force that aside. There was nothing he could do, except hope, selfishly, that they endured their wounds, and remained alive out there. At least then they wouldn't be forced to turn against their own. And what of the wounded they'd managed to get behind the line? What if they succumbed? There would be dead loose in the camp, an attack growing on both sides. He felt so helpless.

I should've wakened from this nightmare by now.

A sudden explosion of wood and flesh and fur made Haegar jump to one side as a massive buck charged the line and leapt into it, slamming into defenders just a pace from his position. Men screamed as great horns gored them, as vicious hoofs kicked over and over, smashing jaws and crushing ribs. Three men were sent tumbling atop the wagons, where a horde of pigs, all gutted for a butcher's table, swarmed them and began to tear them apart.

The buck was flipped on its side as men pushed back, hacking it with their axes until they'd hewn it to wriggling pieces. Arrows whipped overhead, and Haegar felt the buzz of their passing, where they met swarms of dark shapes winging down from the sky. Some never stopped falling, their wings transfixed, while the rest came upon them like a blizzard's gale. Haegar kept his head low as men staggered back all around him, swatting at crows and sparrows with talons now glistening red. He'd seized a fallen axe, taking it when a howling man dropped it as he tried to peel a white owl from his face. Haegar impaled it upon the half-moon blade, flinging it into the slavering animals below. But the man had already sunk to his knees, blood pumping from his neck, the light in his eyes beginning to fade. Haegar acted by instinct, pushing the dying man over the edge without a second thought. Those eyes seared his soul.

He turned the axe on the dead, hacking at outstretched hands, swiping paws, and kicking feet, all straining to reach him atop the wagon. A wolf came flying out of the half-darkness, barreling into him. Maneuvering in such a cramped space was difficult, and he knew his swing went wide even before the beast hit him, driving him into the men clustered behind.

Haegar slammed his shield into the beast, trying to push it back, and nearly got his hand seized in snapping teeth. The girl was at his side again, driving her blade down its gullet. Haegar planted his axe in its chest, and together, they were able to hurl it off their makeshift wall.

But similar bloody collisions were happening all across the wagon line as the dead threw themselves into waiting flurries of axes and poles, careless for any damage they received, so long as they managed to draw living blood.

A man came upon Haegar, and he almost reached out for the fellow's hand, but instead of a hand there was a swinging axe, rising above wild, lifeless eyes. Haegar brought his half-wheel shield down, catching the blade, which bit deep into the wood. He grunted beneath the force that wracked his arm, but braced himself and did not fall.

The corpse tried to scale the wagon, stepping upon the arrow-riddled pigs which now formed a twisting pile at the base of the wall. How long until there were enough mangled bodies to give the dead an easy slope to climb? With inhuman speed, the dead man threw one foot atop the wagon, launching itself upright. A gloved hand came reaching for his throat, those terrible, dead eyes locked on his. Such *hate*. It was the same as that wolf's stare, a seething rage lurking deep beneath the mask of death. This malice would never yield, not until every living creature on Razzador was swallowed.

The hand wrapped around his throat, fingers squeezing with relentless strength. He couldn't breathe. He tried to wrench himself free, but the corpse was on the wagon now. Those eyes. They lacked life, but somehow he could see the hatred, see the delight, as it throttled his life away. Unable to scream, unable to pull himself away, Haegar swallowed his terror and slammed his own axe down on the man's shoulder. The hand dropped limply away.

Gasping wildly, he threw himself against the body, but it was kept in place now by more dead coming up behind it. Young men in familiar heavy coats. Men who'd been alive not an hour before. The corpse pulled its axe free from his shield, so Haegar drove it into its throat and was rewarded with an audible *crunch*. The body finally fell, only to be trampled by other dead who clambered over it.

Haegar used his shield to shove the next three back, sending them tumbling into the horde. Beside him, the girl was screaming. A boar had her by the leg and was lurching backward with sharp, powerful tugs. A Vruskman had her by the arm, trying to keep her from being pulled away.

For a moment, he saw Haza, his arm hanging from bloody strings. With a roar, he drove his axe through the boar's snout, severing its jaws. The girl came free with a gasp and scrambled back. With all his strength, Haegar pushed himself against the monster, driving the stricken pig up onto its hind legs, then over the side of the wagons, where it fell, still thrashing.

Haegar gritted his teeth, casting a quick glance across the

line. Some men had been pulled away, others were still struggling with their winged attackers, but most of the leaping animals had been repelled, and arrows were harrying the rest. Exhilaration rushed over him, the same kind he felt when a tree finally started to fall. It was the feeling of certainty. They could do this. Here, they could hold.

He fell into a strange rhythm, then. He couldn't have said how much time had passed—there was no time to count seconds between swings of his axe. Despite the ferocity of the dead's attacks, the holes in the line, the men of the Winterwood held their ground atop their makeshift wall.

Haegar found himself working in a manageable rotation. Makeshift spearmen with scythes and long poles would rush forward and drive their blades into the dead, pushing them back. When a corpse broke through the line, Haegar and the other axe men would move forward to disable them, all while archers helped pick off stragglers and outliers who tried to circle around the wall.

The girl fought with him, her sword proving more effective than his axe for killing limbs and severing spines. Despite her injury, despite his exhaustion, they kept fighting. Back and forth, and never once did he recall stopping for a breath or a thought. There was nothing but the fight, the strange synchronization that had come upon the Vruskmen. When he barked orders, the men obeyed. Where the line buckled or crumbled, men rushed to fill the gap. Not one corpse came through. And when a man died, his body was seized by the men behind him. They would swiftly hamstring the newly dead's thighs and forearms before tossing him atop the growing pile of maimed, still-twitching corpses.

It was grim, exhausting, and bone-chilling work, but Haegar did it without question. He stopped flinching when men fell around him. His stomach stopped turning at the sight of blood.

He even stopped wondering if he was going to die. Why wonder when one could see truth in the eyes of the dead? A blade or a claw would find him soon enough.

That was how the world was, now. This was existence, caught in a miserable crunch of men, struggling to stay atop a wobbling cart while a gaping, half-skinned snow leopard jumped at him. But then, just as it seized the rim of the cart, it dropped away again of its own accord. He lowered his shield in astonishment. What had hit it? His eyes widened in disbelief.

The dead slumped quietly to the ground, dropping into piles of snow and blood. Wolves tripped mid-run, while elk and moose and pigs tried to hobble ahead on shaking legs, only to collapse in broken heaps. Even the men, many still with fresh, bleeding wounds, stumbled and sank slowly to their knees.

It was finished. The wind was like a long, whispering breath, finally released after being held for anxious hours.

Haegar looked out upon a battlefield now flooded with corpses. Unmoving corpses. Not one remaining standing. From those who'd been hacked to pieces, to those just emerging from the tree line, all had stopped moving. He looked down upon a body, lying atop the pile that had risen abreast with his wagon, only to see that it was a boy not much older than Makin. His eyes were still open, his mouth slightly agape, and a veil of ashen gentleness upon his face. The peace of death had taken him at last.

It's...over? He panted. *Just like that?* He could hear his confusion echoed by others down the wagon line. Tentatively, men began to descend from their makeshift wall, and he watched them stumble among the dead, turning them over to ensure that they'd finally stilled.

He sank to one knee, gently setting his battered shield in front of him. He sucked in cold air, struggling to process everything he was seeing. Everything he had seen. The grisly reality of their situation took hold as he looked across the battlefield again. Hundreds of corpses lay in huddled shadows, man and beast fallen together. From the edge of the wall, all the way to the Winterwood, they coated the ground in haphazard piles. The men moving among them, searching for survivors, looked like spirits from out of the old stories, souls who'd forgotten their own deaths, ceaselessly wandering in search for a life that had vanished.

"What…happened?" he whispered aloud. Why this mercy? What had made them stop? He turned his eyes skyward, beyond the grasping branches of the Winterwood, and saw a line of crimson burning on the horizon. *Dawn?* It was like the lid of a great, smoldering eye, slowly widening to lance the dark underbelly of the night with lines of purple and orange. Dawn had come—the line had held until morning. Was that the answer?

What twisted magic is at play here? he found himself wondering as he hopped down from the cart. Even such a short fall was enough to make him grunt. His whole body ached. He'd never felt an exhaustion so thorough, so deep before. His mind strayed to that first wolf, and to the horse on the road. Both had come at night. It couldn't be that the dead only walked with the night, could it? Was this a mere respite until the evening shadows returned, or could it already be over?

No. This evil will not release us so easily. They had to get over the river. Today.

"Attention!" he made himself call, ignoring the rasp in his voice. He'd been shouting all night. Eyes turned to face him. He started counting—it didn't take long. Of all the Vruskmen who'd stood with him last night, half of them must've been gone. The thinning was so plain that it speared him with a fresh, cold jab of terror. *We can't survive this again.*

"They must fall with daylight," he said, hoping fervently that his guess was correct. What other explanation could there be? Had sheer coincidence saved them? His men gathered around him in a loose semi-circle, many still on the makeshift wall. Less than three hundred, he was sure. They were all watching him now. Waiting. What is it they expected him to say? *What* can *I say?* "The morning brings us reprieve," he finally managed, haltingly. "Burn the dead. All of them. Reduce them to ash and bones; not even they can move after that." He hoped that was true, too. "After that, we rouse the camp. We're getting everyone across the Tagalfr before nightfall."

No one moved. Haegar could feel himself shrinking. What more were they looking for? He tried to swallow, but his throat was too dry. "We…we have to keep moving. We bought ourselves a day with blood. It must be spent. We haven't the time to lose…" his eyes wandered out toward that silent, waiting field. Among those lifeless shapes, how many names did he know? *Torvust…Corvil… That girl with the sword.* He looked for her quickly among the onlookers, but could not find her. She was out there somewhere, with the dead. How many more?

"We will mourn our brothers," he made himself say, "but first we have to get their families to safety, aye?" A few half-hearted murmurs of agreement followed, and he shook his head. "Let me hear you say it, Vruskmen. They laid down their lives for us, and now we will see their loved ones protected, aye?"

"Aye!" Now it rang like thunder, and suddenly it was a chant, ringing in front of the makeshift wall. "Aye! Aye!"

"Let's get the wounded behind the wall," called Bofor, waving a hand for others to follow. The man was now sporting a bleeding gash on his right arm. "The rest of you, start seeing to the dead. Come on, daylight won't last forever."

As the men scrambled away, Haegar found his eyes locked on Bofor's bleeding wound. "Conyr," he said, and was met with blank stares. "Physicians. Send for the physicians. We need to have the wounded seen to. I won't have any injured man walking around before…" he trailed off, seized by sudden vertigo. "Before…" *Before what?* His thoughts were swimming through the Tagalfr, pulled under by the thick, spinning waters before they could reach him. He turned to one side to vomit, then fell.

Mercifully, the nightmare had ended, but the sun would set again. And he would have his family across that bloodied river, even if he had to tear down Farrenhall stone by stone.

Chapter Eleven
A Lesson

"Kasara!" Bjern shouted as she stumbled into his arms. She felt herself slipping through his grip, so she seized the front of his coat to keep herself from toppling. She groaned through clenched teeth. Her right leg felt aflame, burning bright against the cold morning. Hot blood was sloshing in her boot, and her head was spinning. She'd staggered through the crazed refugee camp, dodging around rumbling carts and screaming villagers, mules bucking against their handlers and dogs racing underfoot. By the time she'd reached Farrenhall's wall, she'd sagged against it and used her hands to find the narrow gap that would lead her back inside the bridge.

Bjern was still waiting for her. Of course he was. Had she really expected anything else? He'd waited for her in the cold, waited all through the night. His face was haggard, his eyes bloodshot, but he held her now as firmly as Farrenhall's foundations kept them aloft. What had she been furious with him about, again?

"What happened out there?" he demanded, still holding her. "Bloodied shit, Kasara, you're bleeding! It sounded like the God-Emperor's hordes had come again, with all that screaming and howling."

Kasara raised her face from the crook of his shoulder, ignoring the fresh tears rolling down her face. She'd thought she'd run out of those hours ago. She looked up at the wall, where Myrmidons in their crimson-silver armor still watched. They hadn't moved through the night, either. *They couldn't have missed the fighting from up there. They watched us die.* Only now did they move, heads turning toward her, drawn by Bjern's shouts.

"Get me inside," she hissed into his coat. There would be no using the Pass in the wall after this—no doubt the Myrmidons would have it sealed within the hour.

"We need to get you to a physician," Bjern said, already moving. He helped her hobble toward the main gates. "Bloodied shit. Bloodied- Who did this to you, Kasara? Your leg…"

"I need to see my father," she said through her teeth. Each step she took struck her with a new, biting agony. A dozen other scrapes and cuts burned across her body too, but it was nothing compared to that gash. She could still feel the boar's tusks scraping against her flesh. If not for that red-bearded man, the one she'd helped fight the bear, she'd be dead. Or…something else? *Did I really see what I think I saw?* Men she'd watched die, some hacked to bloody pieces, rising again, turning against the ones they'd died fighting beside. *This has to be a nightmare. I'm still inside Farrenhall, just dreaming…*

But a cold pit was slowly solidifying in her stomach. The sealed bridge. The Myrmidons. Whatever had come out of the Winterwood last night, she was certain her father had known about it. And he'd done nothing to warn the men of the Winterwood. Nothing to protect them. Neither had Berethan. Why did she find the Myrmidon's apathy so disappointing?

"I heard…screaming," Bjern whispered as he ushered her through the seam in the gates. The warmth of Farrenhall washed over her, but what might've been a soothing balm against the cold served only to redouble her pain. "What happened?" he asked again.

Kasara stumbled, causing him to take her by the arm. Begrudgingly, she leaned against him again. Now that she was back in the familiar, quiet halls of the Gated Bridge, her mind was clearing. Hundreds of images were flashing through her mind—blood and bone, fallen torches and splintered wood, screaming faces begging for mercy. And the eyes. The dead eyes. Such hate. It had burned her flesh to meet their empty stares. *No, not empty at all.* Some*thing* had taken hold of them, had bid them to rise again.

"Kasara?"

"The refugees were attacked."

Bjern missed a step, nearly dragging her down with him. "Attacked? That doesn't make any sense. I mean, the shouting…I tried to get up on the walls, but the Myrmidons blocked the way. No one from inside came out to help investigate, so I just went back to wait for you. But that can't be right. Why would Vruskmen turn on each other?"

"I…" she had to swallow, "It wasn't Vruskmen, Bjern. I don't know what it was."

Bjern turned her down a nearby hall, then helped her hobble up to Farrenhall's third level. But instead of heading for Varkoth's lavish apartments, they went right instead. "What are you doing?" she demanded, turning to pull away from him. "I must speak with my father."

"You're bleeding all across the bridge," Bjern growled. "That wound needs tending, Kasara."

She pulled against him. "Let go! We have no time to waste!" She didn't know why the corpses had suddenly collapsed, ending the battle, but she'd taken it as a sign to retreat. A single glance at the shore had told her the woodsmen had suffered significant losses. If the garrison of Farrenhall didn't mobilize—the Myrmidons too—they would never survive another assault. "I have to help them, Bjern. We have to help them!"

"You can help no one if you bleed out," he snapped, his grip unrelenting.

Though she muttered and snarled under her breath all the way, Kasara let herself be dragged to the infirmary. Bjern hovered like an anxious wood thrush watching her eggs hatch as Kasara let a spindly old woman see to her bleeding calf. She seized Bjern's hand when the stitching began, refusing to scream. And if she whimpered, well, that was hardly the same thing.

Unfortunately, the moment the daughter of Lord Varkoth appeared in the infirmary, any chance she had at surprising her father with a confrontation evaporated. She knew the moment a few of the scullions went scurrying from the chamber that her father would know of her injury long before she could confront him. "Damn my blood," she snarled as the needle delivered its final prick of pain. Would he try to hide from her again? Would he turn her sneaking outside into an excuse to evade her accusations? She wouldn't let him weasel his way free of responsibility. This blood was on his hands.

"I'll fetch you a cane, my lady," said the physician, giving a slight bow as she rose from her work.

"Do I look like some doddering old noblewoman?" Kasara growled, using Bjern's shoulder to brace herself as she stood. However, upon attempting her first step—which rewarded her with pain so heavy the room went black—she quietly accepted the cane.

With as much grace as she could muster, she set her jaw and started hobbling toward the door, with Bjern following like a second fretting shadow. "We'll need to muster the garrison," she growled. "Hundreds died last night." So many. Too many. It was unconscionable. *Did my father know this was going to happen?* She felt sick. Her leg was a pale shadow of what suffering those people on the beach were enduring. "My father must—"

The door swung open when she reached for the handle. She took a step back as Berethan stepped through. The Grand-Crusader wore full plate, broadsword slung across his back, short sword at the waist, and helmet held to one side. His eyes were hooded and sleepless, but his expression was as typically harsh and blank as a cliff's face.

"Lordling," Berethan began. His gray eyes found her leg. What was that flicker on his face? His tone never changed. "What happened to you?"

Maybe it was the sight of his clean, ever-perfect polished plate. Maybe it was his flat, apathetic tone. But rage boiled over fear and pain, drowning them both. "You saw us," she said quietly. "Didn't you, Berethan? You didn't help us." They stared at one another, the Myrmidon still filling the doorway. Bjern fluttered behind her, looking ready to leap out the nearby window and into the Tagalfr below. The physician and her attendants looked on with wide eyes.

"I knew only as much as your father told me, which was to hold the gate at all costs. This attack surprised me as much as you, Lordling." The Myrmidon did not sound surprised. He sounded like he'd just learned his supper would be a few minutes late.

The man's emotionless candor made her fingers clench. "Did you watch it happen?"

Berethan stepped into the room, armor clanking, and closed the door behind him. "You should sit," he said. "You are filthy."

Kasara blinked and looked down at her hands, only now realizing just how caked she was with dirt and dried blood. Her clothes had been soaked through by melting snow, and the earth had been churned to a mingled slurry of mud, blood, and ice, which clung to her like a carapace. "Did you watch?" she asked again.

He stepped toward the window, moving past the empty beds. "I did," he said simply. "They came well after midnight and fell with the dawn." He glanced back at her, a hand on the hilt of his short sword. "Though I suspect you know far more of what happened than I do."

"What are they?" asked Bjern, looking between the two of them. "What do you mean, 'they fell?'"

Kasara ignored him, her eyes on Berethan's back. "You could've saved them, aye?"

The Myrmidon turned back to the window. Under the light of the morning sun, the ice floes glittered as they slid along the Tagalfr's churning surface. "Quite easily. This foe was unorganized and aimless. They came without standards or drums or commanders, as far as I could tell. Even those farmers, once they entrenched themselves, held them back without difficulty."

She stepped toward them, breathing through her teeth. "And you didn't help them, because my father didn't ask it of you?"

"Kasara," Bjern said quietly. "You're shaking. Come, let's sit you back down." His was a gentle, insistent pull on her arm.

She ripped herself free, hobbling toward the giant knight. Her sword was still at her side, but she had to shift her cane to her other side in order to free a hand to draw it. "You're a coward," she growled. "You had the power to save them, but you didn't. It might have been my father's order, but you're still the one who refused to act, Berethan."

"I have my orders, Lordling," Berethan replied, still watching the river. "I do as the God of the Highest Path dictates, and for now, his words come from your father's tongue."

"You are not slave to this god," she bit back. "You are your own man."

"No man knows when his climb will end. You must reach as high as you can."

Kasara wanted to hit him. She wanted to stab him. She just wanted to do *something*. She'd never felt so helpless before, so useless. She'd spent the night battling half-rotted monsters, while the Myrmidons had looked on. They'd *watched*. "If those people are attacked again, they will all be slaughtered. I will not ask you to abandon your post, Berethan, or betray your orders. But those men mean us no harm. They are *our* people." She swallowed. "If…if I ask you to open the gates and let them pass, would you do it? We could have them through before nightfall, then the gates could be sealed again."

A look of annoyance fluttered across the Myrmidon's face, catching her by surprise. She'd never seen such a naked emotion on the man before. "We are conscripted until spring, Lordling," he said. "To replace your father's active Faith Price, you would have to pay us double our usual fare. Are you sitting upon such a fortune?"

Kasara met his stare. *Could the Old King himself afford such a price?* "There is no other way?" she found herself asking pointlessly. "Those people…they are not our enemy."

"None."

"My father knew this was coming," Kasara said, leaning against her cane. She felt like all her energy was gone. Boil her blood, when was the last time she'd slept? It was like she owed a debt to the night, and it was only now coming to collect. Bjern was at her side, helping her stand straight. Her sword, still smeared with black, felt too heavy to hold. She didn't even have the strength to lift it enough to sheathe it again. "This threat is why you are here," she said, eyes still on the Grand-Crusader, "why the gates have been sealed."

"Maybe."

"What is it? Some enemy nation from the east? From beyond the Winterwood? They...they have magic." She felt Bjern stiffen. Even the word alone made her recoil. Magic was a silly word, a baseless thing from the days of the Holy Wars, where the God-Emperor's disgraceful fall gave testament to how much power the concept ever really had. But...why the Winterwood? As far as she knew, as far as anyone knew, there was nothing east of Farrenhall but a wasteland of ice and snow, utterly barren beyond the edge of the forest and forever gripped by a cruel and endless winter. What sort of thing could from there?

For once, the impassive glower that forever lurked on Berethan's face slipped away. His eyes flicked toward her, considering her for a moment. The man set his jaw to one side, and the sudden honesty in his voice took her by surprise. "I've seen many strange things in my crusades, Lordling. Blood and death. Suffering and salvation. I saw last night too...but I saw nothing that warrants the need for my presence here. Nothing that warrants the sealing of the gate. Vrusk's king could've turned aside such an attack with his own armies had he wished it. Instead, he left it to your father, and your father has entrusted it to me. Neither man is willing to fight his own battles. You are noble of heart to desire to protect your people. It is a rare thing, found only in the young and foolish. And brave. Wear that wound of yours proudly, and climb the Highest Path your way, as I must climb it mine."

Kasara closed her mouth. Bjern's sympathetic stare was only stirring her ire. *This can't be coincidence.* Disorganized rabble or not, whatever those things had been, it had to be the source of her father's paranoia. "This has to be it," she finally said.

"Nothing else makes sense. This must be a…a precursor to something greater."

"It matters little," Berethan said. "Your Lord Father will not change his orders. If anything, I expect he will redouble his convictions. The men on the beach must fight for their own survival now, and at least their deaths will show us what to expect from this new enemy."

"You're despicable," she spat. Had she really admired this man? All his strength, his talent with the blade, and he was unwilling to lend it to help those who needed it. Damn him. Was duty any excuse? What of blood? The man was Joromori, not Vrusk, but should that make any difference? "If it had been you and your Myrmidons on the beach last night, I still would've gone."

"I do not doubt it." Berethan turned and walked back to the door. "I am glad to see that you are well. When I heard you'd been injured, I…" he frowned and then shook his head, opening the door to step back into the hall.

"You could defy him," Kasara shouted after him, careless for how her voice rang off the stone around her. "My father couldn't stop you. You could open the gates and save every living person in the Winterwood. But you won't do it. Damn your god…doesn't he wish for the good of all of Razzador? For all men to reach your bloodied peak? Isn't that what gods are supposed to do? Shield us and love us?"

A smile appeared on the man's stony face. "The God of the Highest Path admires fortitude, Lordling. But he does not love. Why should he love what cannot understand him? We are beneath him, and that is why we must climb the mountain. He would appreciate your zeal, but you lack an understanding of the inexorable. Some things are as they are, and they cannot be changed. There is no fighting it."

Kasara watched her knuckles curl around the top of her cane, heard them pop. "Watch me," she snarled. After a quick bathing from the dutiful physician staff, and a change into a fresh, clean gray dress, she buckled her sword-belt—she had no time to clean the blade—and hobbled out of the infirmary as fast as her injured leg would allow. "Come on, Bjern." She snapped, and he walked with her, his arms out as if he expected her to fall at any moment.

They descended into Farrenhall's belly, forging a path through wide-eyed servants and garrison soldiers who hastened out of her way. She could feel their worried eyes on her back, feel their whispers following. Good. Let them talk. Let unease seep through the bridge. The more doubt she could harbor, the more pressure she could levy against her father. She meant to put an end to all this madness before the noonday bell.

Past glittering torches and proud wall tapestries, by suits of polished armor and carvings of marble and precious stone, Kasara could feel her blood boiling with each step she took. Kalivaz had spent his days cramming Farrenhall with tokens of power and wealth. As a girl, she'd thought nothing of them. Last night, wandering among the wagons and often-frayed tents of her people, she'd felt bile rising in her throat long before she'd smelled that terrible stench on the wind. Her father disgusted her even more than those rotting monsters.

Soon, they emerged into one of the great antechambers of the bridge, one, she knew, that was directly above the central road on Farrenhall's lowest level. Here, breakfast was still being served to the denizens of the bridge. Long wooden tables were set up through its length in neat rows, and at the far end were the doors that led into the kitchens. Off-duty soldiers, some still in piecemeal armor, were beginning to file in and take their seats at the tables. The rest of the gathered men and women were the servants of the Varkoth family, the stewards and scribes and scullions who kept the Gated Bridge in order. All looked well fed and happy, a matter of pride for Kasara. She'd heard plenty of grim stories of nobles who treated their servants as worse than peasants. But not the Varkoth family. Here, fellow Vruskmen were respected and cared for. *Even those outside our walls.*

There was a fire blazing in a great hearth on the west side of the room, spilling a bright, crimson light through the chamber, yet it did little to stave off the gnawing chill. Long pillars held the room aloft, and they would've cast longer shadows, if not for the torches hung upon them to keep the darkness at bay. Between them hung long tapestries in silver and green, depicting the crests of Vrusk and House Varkoth respectively. There were no windows here, as nothing surrounded chambers like these except more passageways on all sides, and the Rushing Ice below.

As she swept into the room—or swept as well as a cane would allow—she drew looks of surprise. Some began to mutter, fear and apprehension rising like tendrils of vapor. They couldn't have missed the clamor of the battle last night, and to have the daughter of Lord Varkoth appear before them in such a state could only be an ill omen.

Kasara moved to stand in front of the hearth, her eyes downcast and heedless of the stares she'd garnered. She stared into the flames and the great iron cauldron suspended over it. A rich, brown broth was bubbling in its basin, and the pleasant smell was a warm welcome into the chamber. She wrinkled her nose. That stink of blood and smoke still lingered on her skin.

She put her back to the cauldron and looked across the room. Near a hundred eyes were on her now. Soldiers and workers had all fallen silent, sensing, at least on some level, what she was about to say. She met Bjern's eyes as he lingered by one of the pillars.

"My father," she began, her voice ringing through the

chamber, "has decided the Gated Bridge should remain closed. Last night, an enemy of unknown origin and strength appeared from the Winterwood. Those men trapped on the beach were forced into battle, and they drove this foe away just before dawn. Their victory came at the cost of much blood." With a pained wince, she lifted the hem of her dress to better show the bandages wrapped around her ankle. "As they see to their wounded and dead, they turn their eyes to us in question. For do you know what we did, while our kinsfolk and countrymen were dying?"

No one offered her an answer. The watching eyes were meek, their faces ashen, as they waited for her to tell them what they already knew. "We supped and slept in Farrenhall," she boomed. As she spoke, Berethan slipped into the room. He crossed his arms over his breastplate and leaned against the wall, watching impassively. She ignored him. "While blood was shed, here we huddled in the warmth and safety of the Gated Bridge. Our so-called protectors stood atop our walls and watched death unfold through the night! They kept their vigil over our gates, keeping them sealed against all comers. *All* comers!" Kasara wiped spittle from her lip with her sleeve. She'd never shouted so loudly, so furiously before, and she watched her people crumble beneath her accusations. "When dawn came, brothers and sisters, when those on the beach began to bury their dead, what did we do? What do we *still* do? Eat and feast like craven kings!"

She turned, drew her stained sword, and swung it with all her strength against the chain suspending the cauldron over the flames. It snapped with a sharp *clang*, and the cauldron helplessly overturned its contents into the fire. The hearth hissed like a dying serpent as it was extinguished, and hot steam washed over her face. She spun back and drove her blade into its scabbard. The haunting, hollow eyes of an ashamed crowd stared back at her.

"How dare we?" she demanded. "How dare we sit here and let this happen?" She would not exclude herself from these accusations. She had not gone out last night intending to fight alongside her people; she'd been seized by the surprise of it all, just like them. It should never have happened. She was not exempt. "The blood of all men who did not see this sunrise is on our hands. We did not act. No one came to their aid. Even those who had power to interfere," she glanced at Berethan, but the Grand-Crusader only raised his chin at her and looked on quietly, "they did nothing. The cowardice of Farrenhall will not be forgotten. They will sing dirges of this night for generations to come—and let them! Let them all hear of our failure! Blood does not forget."

Her words echoed through the hall, and she took advantage of the resounding sound to draw a gasping breath. Her heart was pounding in her chest, and her knees wobbled beneath her. Her eyelids were like anchors, trying to drag her into the dark. But she did not let herself fall. She saw shame in the crowd, mirrored expressions of her own guilt. Soldiers stared sullenly into their bowls, while washerwomen nervously whispered, and the stewards shuffled their feet.

We left them to die. This responsibility belongs to us all, not just some foreign mercenaries, and not just my father. Kasara bit her lip until she tasted blood. *But maybe more blame should lay on their shoulders, aye?* Berethan was still watching her. She could hardly bear to look at him. She'd been in the thick of the fighting—she'd seen the horrors of battle firsthand. Those images, those ruined men, would never leave her mind. How could any man watch that unfold and not move to interfere? And how could her father let an atrocity like this befall his own people? It was almost unbelievable, but one couldn't argue against the black smoke rising from the shore of the Tagalfr.

Kasara cleared her throat and straightened, readjusting her cane. "This tale is not yet fully written," she declared. "Farrenhall will suffer this shame, yes, but what we do next will define how we are remembered. We will neglect our brothers of the Winterwood no more. The Gated Bridge will open, today, and we will let the refugees pass through. We will give them food and shelter and medicine, and anything else they may need, and we will remember why House Varkoth is the Eastern Shield of Vrusk. The protector of all her people. Bjern." His head snapped up the moment he was addressed. "Gather as many able-bodied Vruskmen as you can—the garrison and more. You'll arm yourselves and depart from Farrenhall. March ahead of the refugees and watch over the Winterwood. Whatever came last night will come again. I will also require you to appoint men to organize the crowd and begin safely moving them over the bridge." She bit her lip again. "And…you will ensure there is peace, if our brothers do not take last night's betrayal easily."

Bjern's face had turned pale as the Seventeen Stars. "M-me? The garrison's commander is L-Lord—"

"My father has placed the daily management of Farrenhall into my care," she announced. "That includes overseeing the garrison. You will deploy as I have ordered, Captain."

Bjern blinked, then swelled with newfound pride. It deflated again just as quickly. "What about the Gated Bridge, m-my Lady? Who will guard it?"

Her eyes flicked toward Berethan again. The man's face was unreadable, but his eyes had narrowed. She was pushing the limits of her authority, she knew. The garrison would obey her father over her, if it came to that, but at least the Grand-Crusader's men wouldn't interfere. Not unless they were ordered to. *Right?*

"The Myrmidons have been tasked with Farrenhall's

protection this winter," she said. "leave them to the task, since they're so faithfully sworn to it." She met Berethan's eyes, awaiting a challenge. When it didn't come, she went on. "As for the rest of you, you are to gather food, water, and blankets. Place them in wagons and take them behind the garrison; distribute them to the folk on the beach freely. Help the wounded and prioritize those with the gravest injuries; bring them into the bridge first. Remain calm. They will be nervous after last night at best, and panicked at worst. We can't risk them trying to storm the bridge."

Bjern glanced at his fellow soldiers, who stared back at him blankly, awaiting further command. Someone coughed, and the sound of shifting, creaking chairs echoed through the galley. The ruined stew continued to hiss atop the drowning coals of the hearth.

"What are you waiting for?" Kasara snapped. "We've delayed long enough, aye?"

All at once, her people scrambled to rise, some throwing back their seats in their haste to obey. Kasara couldn't help a broad, proud smile. She was making things right. Bjern smiled back at her, then he turned to address his men. But before he could take more than a step, a voice cracked like thunder through the chamber. "Any man who steps foot from this room on order of Kasara Varkoth," Berethan roared, his voice cold and hard as ice, "I will cut his head from his shoulders."

Silence fell. The servants of Farrenhall hesitated, frozen in half-risen positions. They wavered before the Myrmidon, who'd yet to stir from his casual lean beside the central door. His eyes were still locked on Kasara, and they flashed with a dark, certain flame. No one dared to move.

Kasara closed her eyes for a moment. Berethan had not been given any orders to oppose her, she was certain of it. If he wanted to, he could give her this victory and remain in the confines of his oaths. But no. He wouldn't help her, not even in this. *Aren't you supposed to be a man of virtue, Berethan?*

But she couldn't relent. She needed the momentum of fear and shame to drive her people to the aid of the Winterwood, before her father was able to crush what little authority she had. They needed to act now, and she wouldn't let Berethan, or any Myrmidon, stop her.

"And what of me, Grand-Crusader?" she demanded, spreading her arms wide as she stepped purposefully across the hall, leaving her cane behind. "Will you slay me, too?" Her walk was unsteady, but her path was sure, and the pained jolts from her calf only propelled her with more certainty. She already knew that answer. She'd seen it in the eyes of the knight who guarded her father's door, and she'd seen it in the empty way Berethan spoke of the men suffering outside. Name and rank and blood did not matter to them; Kasara would just be another step on their Highest Path.

Berethan watched her approach, motionless, and she did not slow. She kept her arms outstretched, hands away from her sword. Her steps without aid were slow and painful, but she would not stop. "Those men outside are my brothers," she declared. "You might not know any sense of brotherhood in Joromor, Berethan, but here in Vrusk, there is nothing more sacred than blood. I am the daughter of Lord Varkoth and heir to Farrenhall, and I have commanded that we shall go and help our people. So, I ask you again," she stepped up to him. Towering over her, he still did not move, leaving the doorway clear. But Kasara knew the moment she stepped through its threshold, he'd kill her. She set her jaw. "Will you slay me?"

Berethan's stony face twisted, first with frustration, then with fury. The man shifted, finally. He was gathering himself.

For the first time, as the crowd looked on, Kasara beheld hesitation in the holy man.

Then, with a sweeping flourish, Berethan suddenly drew his broadsword from over his back. Kasara flinched, stumbling back on her aching leg, a vicious whistle following the razor blade as it carved the air. Berethan fell into a crouch, his marbled crimson and silver armor flashing in the flickering torchlight. There was a shadow over his face as he stared down his sword at her. "One more step," he said simply, "and I will kill you in the name of your father."

But as she stared into his eyes, she saw a faint uncertainty.

"Blood be damned," spat a voice from behind. Kasara glanced back, then gaped, as Bjern drew his sword and unshouldered an iron buckler. "You've just threatened our lord's heir," he growled, stepping across the chamber with his sword raised. Kasara couldn't believe what she was seeing. Was…was this the same Bjern who used to cry as a boy when she'd shout at him? "Shed one drop of her blood, and we'll kill you." There was a look of determination on his face, and all terror had evaporated from his eyes. "Give us a reason, foreigner. Just one."

The other soldiers drew their swords, too. Nearly forty men and women, all in varying levels of armor, gathered behind Bjern. Despite their lack of complete armaments, each held a sword, and each shared their newfound captain's vigor. Behind them, the scullions and servants quietly withdrew into the kitchens, creeping like mice careful not to disturb hissing cats.

Kasara looked back to Berethan, resting a hand against her own sword. But she did not draw it. "Well?" she asked. "You'll have to kill us all, if you can." Then she lowered her voice. "Please, Berethan, make the right choice. Help me."

The Myrmidon, his back to the wall, broadsword held before him in both hands, did not waver, not for a moment. His eyes finally turned from from hers, to sweep across the guardsmen of Farrenhall who'd approached him. The hesitation returned to his face, and slowly, almost imperceptibly, he shifted from one foot to the other. Kasara drew a deep breath. Even a man like him had to know he couldn't slay forty men single-handled. Yet, she found herself quailing before the determination in his eyes. Maybe Berethan couldn't kill a two-score garrison, but he could try. By the name of his god, by the holy blood in his veins, he *would* try.

"Take one more step, Lordling," he said slowly, "and I will show you how *I* do what is right."

Kasara braced herself. Berethan stared back, and between them, his blade hung. Utter silence descended on the room, and it seemed that every man was holding his breath, waiting for it to shatter.

"What is this?" demanded a voice. From down the hall, a figure hurried into view, his fluorescent red and blue robes swishing about his feet. Two Myrmidons escorted the Lord of Farrenhall into view, their clanking, heavy footfalls echoing across the long hall on the chamber's other side. Unlike Berethan, they wore close-faced helms, their faces invisible behind barred visors. "Stand down!" Kalivaz Varkoth commanded, raising his hands. "Put up your weapons, all of you! That includes you, Grand-Crusader."

The collective exhaled. Bjern hastened a step back, fumbling with his sword and missing its scabbard twice before he managed to slide it into place. The other men followed suit and stared abashedly at their liege lord as he swept through the room. Berethan, with as fluid grace as he'd drawn it, returned his sword to its own holster over his back, and he folded his arms across his breastplate once more.

"Your shouts ring through this keep like bells of madness!"

Kalivaz bellowed, his voice a shrill, echoing cry. He ignored Kasara, rounding instead on Bjern and the garrison when he reached the middle of the room. "Aren't there orders you're currently shirking? Has Farrenhall suddenly found itself without duties to accomplish? If you've left the table, clearly you're finished with your plates, aye?"

"Father," Kasara stepped forward, turning from Berethan. Her heart was fluttering a dreadful beat. Of all possible resolutions, she hadn't expected her father to appear. He'd sealed himself in his chambers for days, refusing to see to any of his own duties, but *now* he decided to show himself? Still, with the reclusive Lord of Farrenhall now coaxed from his chambers, she meant to convince him to act. Further tragedy could be avoided on all fronts. "These men stand on my orders."

Kalivaz ignored her. He looked more haggard than she'd ever seen him, garbed in disheveled robes that ill-fit a frame that had grown thin and worn of late. His single eye was hollow and darting, but there was more than a skittish terror harbored there. What was that malice? It made his tongue sharp, too. "Return to your quarters, all of you," he growled. "Sharpen your swords and polish your armor. Remain there until I tell you otherwise. The Myrmidons will see to our defenses this day."

Bjern looked between Kalivaz and Kasara, his face ashen. "My Lord, Kasara, ah, I mean, My Lady has given us an order. You put her in charge of Farrenhall's garrison yourself. We're to help the folk of the Winterwood pass through the bridge. They have wounded men with them, and women and children. They need immediate aid." He looked to her again, and she smiled.

"Is my daughter the lord of this keep?" Kalivaz roared, his voice thundering through the chamber. "Last I recall, *Kalivaz Varkoth* still reigns in Farrenhall, and over all the Hinterlands and the Winterwood. I will contend with my daughter momentarily, but I suggest you obey *my* command, boy, or I'll station you in the stockade until next winter!"

Cowed, Bjern gave his lord a hasty salute and beckoned for the others to follow. Together, they shuffled out of the dining hall, their stares sullen and downcast. Bjern could not meet her eyes as he passed. She tried to feel anger for him, but only felt helpless instead. Kasara shrank into herself, and the galley chamber seemed to grow as she diminished. She stared helplessly at her father's impassive back, watched him dash any hopes she had of helping the wounded. There was no compassion, no pity, in this man. Who was he? This was not her father. Berethan watched them all pass, his face as blank as ever. What was that small glance he threw her? Pity, from *him*?

When the chamber stood empty, Kalivaz turned, and she was once again confronted with the shadow of what had once been her father and liege lord. The man was nearly unrecognizable, now. His Myrmidons loomed on either side of him, statues of glistening red and silver steel. Kalivaz looked invulnerable, protected behind a wall of monstrous, holy men. But what was he shielding himself from? Her? *Why?*

"Has your blood curdled, girl?" Kalivaz hissed, advancing on her. "Why is it that my servants must come running to my chambers and tell me that my daughter is planning a mutiny in my galley?"

Kasara had to make a conscious effort not to wet her lips. "Father, I…Time is short. Perhaps we should return to your chambers? We should speak, but—"

"You don't speak for me, girl," Kalivaz growled, his face growing red. "You don't act in my stead. Giving my men orders. Going against my commands. I don't know what's crawled into your head, but I mean to drag it out and flay it right here."

She nearly took a step back. Her leg flared painfully, making her grimace. Had he even noticed her wound? She'd never seen such fury in his eye before. For a moment, she felt like a child again, quailing before this strange man's wrath. But she made herself face his gaze. If Berethan couldn't cow her, then neither could he. "This isn't about me," she snapped. "Maybe you didn't see it, sealed in your chambers as you are, but the Winterwood refugees were attacked last night. It…it was a massacre, father." She'd watched a wolf rip out a man's throat. Bloodied shit, had she really *seen* that? The images burned into her mind seemed false, somehow, like nightmares recalled to frightening lucidity. She couldn't banish them, though, not even when she opened her eyes. "We need to help them."

"And invite that which killed them *here*?" Kalivaz seized the bridge of his nose between thumb and forefinger. "Damn my blood, girl, do you even hear yourself when you speak? What sort of keep opens its gates when the enemy is gnawing at its foundations?"

"What enemy might that be, Father?" she demanded. "Perhaps if you told me, I could understand your decisions. No…not even then. I saw them for myself." She couldn't stop seeing them. "And what I see here is a coward hiding behind his walls. We leave our kinsmen to die. Our own sworn subjects die on your order."

As she watched, her father's face began to change. It became a warping kaleidoscope of ill-fitting colors; the red of anger, then the gray and green of fear, before finally settling on a pale hue that she could only call despair. "The Old King's order, not mine," he snarled. His voice was trembling again. He sounded ancient, pushed to the limits of life. "Something terrible beyond the river, he said. A hunger without thought or reason. A malice that cannot be tamed, cannot be bargained with, will not be questioned. If it has already begun, it is imperative that the gates stay shut." His gaze solidified, suddenly, but he was looking to Berethan. "They must not be allowed to cross the river. The gates stay shut."

In turn, the Myrmidon only inclined his head.

Kasara seized a clump of her own hair. She could've torn it out right there. "Hunger? Malice?" She was ready to scream. "I saw the dead, Father!" From the corner of her eye, Berethan frowned. "They tore us apart! I watched the fallen rise again and turn against us. Who is behind this? If the Old King knew it was coming before it happened, why...?" She trailed off, a sudden heavy veil falling over her. If the king *did* know, why hadn't he sent his army? Why had he left Farrenhall to fight alone? Why didn't he give the people of the Winterwood warning? *And my father knew, too...*

It was all too much. She felt like she'd been kicked in the throat, and she fought bitterly against the tears forming in her eyes with frustrated blinks.

Kalivaz had turned pale as ice. He stared blankly at her, then began to wobble unsteadily. He reached out with one hand until he found the nearby table, then he lowered himself onto the bench. His Myrmidons moved with him, flanking him even as he sat. Idly, Kalivaz reached out for a bowl of steaming soup, left untouched. When the old man's eye opened again, it stared into the smoldering hearth, unblinking, as he began to shove spoonfuls of soup into his mouth.

Kasara fumed over her father, rocking back and forth on her one good heel as she stared at him. "Father?" she said after a moment. "Did you hear me? Who is behind this? Did the Old King know?"

The Lord of Farrenhall did not look up at her. He only paused, spoon half-raised to his lips, and whispered, "Pray to all the dead gods we never find out.

Another non-answer. Kasara couldn't stand it anymore. She jabbed an accusing finger at her father, who'd resumed absently feeding himself. "You are unfit to rule this hall, Father. Clearly some malady has stolen your senses. Farrenhall and its people are in danger, and they need someone who can lead them." She hesitated. How could this man be anyone but her father, the man who'd raised her, who'd laughed and sang with her on so many cold and dark nights? This was the man who'd led Farrenhall faithfully and fairly for twenty years, who'd inspired her to be like him some day. How could it ever have come to this? "I'm sorry, Father," she whispered, "but I must do this. I'm opening the gates."

She turned, only to nearly collide with Berethan. The Grand-Crusader seized her by the shoulder. She struggled and thrashed, beating at his breastplate, but he forcibly turned her to face Kalivaz and hugged her tight to his chest. She gasped as his vambraces squeezed her, and though he loosened his grip in response, she still was pinned tight. She could feel the man's steady breaths rustling her hair while her fingers, grasping at empty air, were so far from the hilt of her sword that it may as well have been in a different room.

"Father!" Kasara shouted. Her efforts to pull away from Berethan were hobbled by her injured foot, and when her struggling drove her wound against his armored leg, she had to stop, fresh tears leaping to her eyes. He held her fast. If he willed it, she was sure, he could snap her spine. "Berethan! Release me, please!"

Kalivaz continued to sip at his soup, the firelight flickering off his empty, unblinking eye. Then, slowly, his head turned to regard her. "You are my daughter," he said. "These are terrifying times, I know, but now, in our darkest hour, I cannot tolerate rebellion. A leader must be hard, child, and they must make choices that no one else can. That they cannot understand. The gates *will* stay shut. You will not cross me again, else you'll make me consider another hard choice. Am I understood?"

She could only stare. *This…this man isn't my father.* She saw in the eyes of the Lord of Farrenhall that same zealousness she'd seen in Berethan. Kalivaz was making no weightless threat. *He'd really kill me.* She sagged into the Myrmidon's arms, her strength depleted. Her blood had never felt so cold.

Kalivaz was watching her, eye darting across her face. "Am I understood?" he barked again.

"Yes, Father," she whispered.

Kalivaz's lip twitched. Then he nodded to Berethan. When his grip loosened, she dropped to the ground, her leg burning. She pulled herself upright again, but found herself unable to raise her head and meet either man's eyes. Instead, she stepped as quickly and lightly as she could toward the door and fled the hall.

She could feel the lingering echo of Berethan's eyes scorching her skin. His expression, what she'd glimpsed of it, had been one of passive disapproval. Why did that sting more than her ravaged ankle? Why did a part of her wish he'd be furious? Or that he'd be smug, that he'd revel in her defeat. But Berethan just seemed more a disappointed father, watching his daughter walk away with a valuable lesson. Her real father, she was certain, never looked up.

Kasara kept walking, her pained footsteps ringing hollowly through the depths of the Gated Bridge. She didn't know where she was going. She just knew she couldn't stop.

Chapter Twelve
The Blood Price

Smoke in the sky. It was a strange sight, especially without the usual storm clouds that had been lurking overhead these last few days. Grim, dark columns stood alone, like drifting fingers clawing a naked blue underbelly.

Haza shivered and slumped forward, half from exhaustion, half from agony. He had to shut his eyes for a moment and focus on his breathing. That trick seemed to be growing less effective with each subsequent use. His arm stump was a pulsing mass of pain; every slight movement, every minor adjustment, sent nails through his bones. He could almost feel himself rotting, his flesh festering even as he sat there, creeping further into his body. *Breathe, breathe, breathe. This doesn't matter right now. It can't matter.* He couldn't worry about his arm killing him—the dead were going to take him long before it had the chance.

"We no longer have a choice," growled an unfamiliar voice. "Three hundred men dead, and a hundred more wounded beyond the ability to fight. You think we'll survive another night like that with what we have left?"

"No," said Haegar. "There's another solution, I know it. One that doesn't end with our heads on the top of Myrmidon spears."

"We can't go back," came the grunt from Conyr, Palvast's

elderly physician. The man was sitting beside Haza, slumped forward. Just looking at the huddled man made him feel tired; he'd been seeing to the wounds of near a hundred men all morning. "I...I recognized some of those faces, last night. The ones who walked, who didn't come here with us. Our homes are gone."

"Then we must push through," said the first man.

"Enough, Bofor," snapped another voice. "Three years the God-Emperor held Farrenhall under siege, aye? If he couldn't break it with all his holy magics, then what good will our axes do? We're not getting in."

Haza stirred at that. It was a misconception he'd heard before. The God-Emperor had never reached Farrenhall; Vrusk's final stand against his crusade had been further west, in the Grey Hinterlands. And as for holy magics, well...once, Haza would've dismissed that outright. But how could he banish such stories anymore?

"Haza?" Haegar was looking at him. "You had something to add?" His brother had changed since the battle, returning with the dawn a hesitant and quiet man. There was an ashen pallor to his skin and his long, crimson beard was matted and unkempt. His eyes were constantly darting, and his clenched fist had yet to loosen from the axe that hung at his side.

With a start, Haza realized everyone's eyes had fallen on him. Nearly a hundred Vruskmen, all watching, waiting for him. The desperation in their eyes took him off-guard, but none more so than Haegar. Gone was the usual disdain he'd come to expect from his brother. They were equals now, made more alike by one night than they had been in decades. It pained him that he had no real solution to offer them. "We could...go north?" he suggested tentatively. "It's a long, long walk from here, but the Tagalfr meets the Blistering Sea at Joromor's peak. There's a port city—Ael'vas—with ships that would help us cross. It's better than staying here, right? Or…trying something more drastic."

Bofor gave a derisive snort. "That'd take us months, on foot."

"The dead followed us out of the heart of the forest," said Laklin, a thin, middle-aged fellow with a long braid of red hair hanging down his back. "If they hunted us all the way here, they'd follow us to Joromor. Putting the water between us and them is the only way to escape. The sea is too far."

Slowly, Haegar and Bofor nodded, and looks of faint hope that had risen among the other men faded like smoke from a banished flame. Haza chewed his lip. Was Laklin right? The dead had proven relentless, so far, and even if the burned bodies couldn't rise again, there had to be more in the Winterwood. If Haegar's deduction was correct, that they came to life with the shadows of night, then they had until evening to escape, else what had happened mere hours ago would occur again.

Three hundred men. It was an incomprehensible number, the kind that he struggled to even picture in his head. The dead had come upon them like a winter storm, and most of the guardsmen at the camp's perimeter had been swallowed. Haegar and his men had held the wagon line through the entire night, and though the dead had not passed through, they'd picked away at the defenders for hours. The morning had made the direness of their situation clear. *We're only…what, three thousand in number?* And more than half of them were women, children, the wounded and the old. Half of the Winterwood's able-bodied men were now dead or incapacitated. *Could we hold for another night, at least? Give ourselves that much more time?* He feared that would cost them twice as many as they'd already lost. *Old blood help us…*

Silence settled over the small group as they each quietly contemplated their coming fate. Haza watched the pillars of smoke climb ever higher into the sky. The sun hung frozen on its mid-morning track, but it would not stay there forever. He would blink, and night would come, and by then it would be too late. "Bofor is right," he said, "there's no choice, is there?" He laughed to himself, a panicked sound. "We have to take Farrenhall."

"It's not possible," Laklin said again. "We'd never be able to breach both of those gates. Steel and Winterwood they are. You'll find none stronger in all Razzador."

"Who said we needed to breach both gates, aye?" Haegar said. He looked up, a familiar gleam in his eye.

Laklin frowned. "What are you suggesting?"

"That we take the courtyard," Haegar said. "The walls might be well defended, but we outnumber those Myrmidons. If we can breach the outer gate, we can overwhelm them and claim the courtyard for ourselves. Kill anyone who stands against us. Seal the gates behind us again and use Farrenhall's own walls to shield us from the dead. We'll buy ourselves more time."

Uncertain and grim looks greeted Haegar's proposition, but Haza's heart began to race with sudden inspiration. "If we push the Myrmidons back behind the inner gates, they'll have no way to attack us—the bridge itself is sealed."

"They could attack from the roof," Laklin pointed out, "or from the high windows."

Bofor clapped him on the shoulder. "Better arrows from above than the teeth of the dead, aye? Archers we can attack. Archers we can kill."

The men exchanged uncertain looks. "Even if we can take it, can we fit this whole crowd in that courtyard?" Laklin asked.

Another moment of silence passed. Haegar exhaled slowly. "Let's worry about that once we're through, aye?"

"So, we have time," Conyr grunted, still slumped over on the edge of the wagon. "What then? Will we grow old there, while the Myrmidons pepper us with arrows from above?"

Laklin lightly touched the bright gash that decorated his right cheek, wincing. "Aye, we're not breaching that second gate, Haegar. The courtyard they might surrender easily enough, but the interior…?"

"We won't be assaulting the Iron Gate," he replied. Haza lifted his head to frown at his brother, who met his eyes. "Torvust wanted to climb the bridge," he said quietly. "He thought he could talk Varkoth into letting us through. We send someone up there. Through the upper windows and into the bridge."

Haza tried to swallow the hard lump in his throat. He couldn't. The last he'd seen of Magda, she'd been crying on Tayja's shoulder while Makin and Rala looked on in confusion. Haegar had yet to speak of how his old friend had died, but he knew they'd been patrolling the border together. He wasn't about to push. "You…think we can get him to negotiate?"

"No," Haegar spat in the snow. "That bastard's lost his chance. But the idea is still sound, aye? A weakness in Farrenhall's defenses. I can open the Iron Gate from within. The Myrmidons will be down below, preparing for an assault. By the time they realize what's happening, I'll have infiltrated the gatehouse and opened the way. Then we fight our way through. It's just a straight road on the bottom level, aye?" Several men nodded quietly in confirmation.

"You think you can make that climb?" Haza found himself asking. "What happens if you fall, Haegar? Even if you make it inside, what happens if they catch you before you reach the gatehouse?"

"Then you send someone else." Haegar's stare was ruthless. "Send as many men as you must. We get that gate open at any cost, aye?"

"Aye," the others chorused in a quiet mutter.

Conyr grunted again. "Those Myrmidons are accomplished killers. Isn't that right, Haza? How are we supposed to fight our way through them with only wood axes and broken wagon wheels?"

"Look at what we did last night." Haegar thrust a finger eastward. No one followed it. "How many hundreds of monsters did we cut down last night? Once we're past gates and walls, it'll be no different than felling a grove. We'll kill anyone who stands in our way, soak the halls of the Gated Bridge crimson, if we must, because I will *not* let another man die on this beach. Damn Varkoth and damn his blood for forcing this upon us, but it is the only action we can take."

Nods and rumbles of approval followed, like the first forewarning of a coming avalanche. "Varkoth brought this doom upon himself," growled Bofor, thumbing the side of his axe blade.

"We'll put his head atop the bridge," someone else snarled. Then the shouts began. Some raised their blades. Conyr buried his face in his hands.

"What are we waiting for, aye?" Haegar said, loud enough to cut across the din. He looked out at Farrenhall, and black smoke crawled up behind him, like it was his own grim shadow cast over the sky. "Bofor, gather as many Vruskmen as can still hold an axe or bow. Leave behind only the old and the maimed; we'll have to keep them at our backs, but as long as we're through by nightfall, they'll be safe long before the dead return. Surprise will be our only true advantage against the Myrmidons. We must strike swiftly, and definitively." He met each of their eyes in turn. Haza was almost surprised to be included, but the look his brother gave him was no less meaningful than any of the others.

"We won't get a second chance at this," Haegar finished.

Haza raised a hand to glance dubiously at the sun. Was it

true that the dead only attacked in darkness? He couldn't be sure, and the awful idea of the dead emerging from behind while they besieged Farrenhall plagued his mind. The children, the wounded, the elderly, they'd be butchered while they struggled at the gates of... He blinked, suddenly remembering that he wouldn't be fighting at all. He *was* one of the wounded.

"Three hours," Haegar went on, "that's when we'll attack. I dare not wait any longer than that. Be ready by then for whatever comes next." He unslung his axe and held it before him in one hand, and he nodded to Laklin and Bofor, who both readied their own. One by one, the Vruskmen raised their axes, their battered shields and blood-stained sickles. It was a silent sign, but every man understood. If they did not win, there would be no sunrise for their loved ones. They dispersed then, some toward the greater camp, the rest lead by Haegar back east, toward the battlefield.

Haza staggered to his feet and gave chase, ignoring the fire in his flesh. "Wait, Haegar, where are you going?"

His brother paused, looking over his shoulder. "To cut down a battering ram," he growled. "I'll be back by noon, don't worry. Get Tayja and the children. Keep them close to the front for me, aye?" He glanced away, then lowered his voice. "It's selfish, aye, but I mean to have them through those gates first, once the battle is finished. If there's any chance we can't get everyone in..." he dropped his gaze, crimson flushing his cheeks. Without waiting for a reply, he turned as quickly again.

Haza scrambled to catch up, seizing Haegar's shoulder. "Wait," he panted.

Haegar stopped, and exhaustion crowned his face as he met him with weary eyes. "What is it?" he asked softly. "What is there still to say, Haza?"

"Do you have to be the one to climb?"

"Well, you certainly can't do it," Haegar chuckled. The smirk he gave was half-hearted. It was gone like afternoon snow.

Haza glowered up at him. "What are you laughing for? This doesn't have to be you. What if you don't come back? What will I do then?"

"Torvust was going to do this," Haegar said. His stare solidified, like ice. No, like steel. "He knew the risk. For himself. For his family. *Someone* has to do it, Haza. Someone strong, who won't be cowed by whatever's waiting inside that bridge. Someone who's not afraid to do what might have to be done."

Haza's skin crawled as he met that searing certainty in Haegar's eyes. In just a few hours, his brother would be killing men. Living, breathing men. Taking the courtyard would cost blood on both sides. Foreigners or not, the Myrmidons were still human, and that wasn't even accounting for Farrenhall's regular garrison.

"I know we don't have a choice, Haegar," he admitted, dropping his gaze. Right beneath his boot, a large shard of wood sprouted from the snow. Its jagged edge was smeared with a dark stain, but he looked past it, into nothing. How he wished there was another choice. He'd give his other arm for just one. "But why does it have to be *you*? If you die, where does that leave us? Your children? Tayja? Or...me? You never wanted to do any of this. You didn't even want to leave Palvast."

"You think I don't know that?" Haegar's face was red now, his wild eyes popping from his head. "You think I don't know that you were right all along, Haza? Bloodied shit, I know you were right! Torvust, he—" Haegar shut his mouth. A vein on his neck was bulging. "It has to be me," he said, the anger deflating from his voice. "And I need you to be there for our family. We must all do our part in what's coming, if any of us are going to survive. Take care of our family; they're your blood, as much as you are mine. Promise me you'll do it."

He started to tremble. For once, the pain in his shoulder felt distant and insignificant. "You don't have to do this," he said. "Someone else can—"

"Haza," Haegar growled over him. "Promise me."

He spoke through his teeth. "Yes."

"Good." Slinging his axe back over one shoulder, he turned. "Find them and keep them close behind the fighters. Then, get them behind those walls, if I can't. I'll see you soon, before it all starts." He'd taken no more than three steps before he paused again and glanced back. "Thank you, Haza."

Haza could only bring himself to nod. His brother turned and hurried after the other men, and they were soon swallowed by the Winterwood. He stared blankly at the tree line for a moment, trying to collect his thoughts. Then it seized him. He doubled over and cried out, but the wracking pain did not relent. It was worse than it had been before. Like fire. No, like that wolf's fangs gripping him anew. Tearing, tearing…

Boil my blood, boil my blood! His mind was filled with screaming curses as he sagged to one knee and retched into the snow, expelling the half-bowl of soup he'd managed to eat for breakfast. He knelt there, shaking, staring down at the contents of his stomach through a veil of tears. Vertigo had him swimming, rocking back and forth. Finally, with the agonizing lethargy of melting ice, the pain began to subside to a bearable level.

He drew a shuddering breath. *This needs to stop. I can't stand this any longer.* He'd never felt a pain so sickening before. He could feel it sucking away his life, as if devouring him from within. In his head, he saw the eyes of that wolf again, watching him, waiting for him to succumb. "Just…just kill me…" he panted. "Stop…playing with me."

Those hateful eyes made no reply.

After a moment, he managed to collect his thoughts and pull himself back to his feet. He hastened back into the camp and searched for Conyr, but the old physician seemed to have disappeared, maybe to bed, or more likely to aid the other men.

What he did manage to find was his own family. In the morning, the Ruthborne family had camped near the front, Haegar shamelessly using his own newfound position among the refugees to maneuver his wife and children closer to safety. He couldn't blame him for that; any man would've done the same, but he still felt a pang of guilt as he passed through the camp. No one seemed to stare at him anymore. The elderly sat huddled in their carts around fading campfires, their grandchildren clutched tightly to them and draped in blankets. The wounded lay about like discarded piles of rubble, many sporting crude, red-soaked bandages. With haunted and hollow eyes, they stared at nothing, they said nothing. A mute terror had gripped them all.

Could anyone believe that this was where they were, now? That only days ago, they'd still been in their homes, celebrating another successful harvest? Haza already thought it felt like a lifetime ago, but maybe that was because each passing hour seemed years in length. Time had slowed to prolong their agony, another cruel jest from whatever phantom force was torturing them.

He saw Tayja's head pop up above the huddled crowd, and she frantically waved at him with both hands. No doubt she'd been watching all morning for him or her husband to return. Behind her, down only a short slope of snow, the Tagalfr swept pass, a frothing cauldron where massive floes of ice came to the surface like breaching whales, before being swallowed into the depths once more. It may as well have been a solid wall; one they were now pinned against.

"Haza," she gasped as soon as he was close enough to hear her shouting. "Have you spoken to Haegar? What will he have us do next?"

Haza frowned and hastened to her. The Ruthborne cart was parked right at the edge of the slope. Other families were stacked all along the edge too, positioned close to the road that led up the hill to Farrenhall. Those in the carts perked up when they heard Tayja shouting, their hopeful eyes lighting on him. He grimaced and kept his head down until he reached his family. *I have nothing to offer them. Haegar will tell them what they need to know.*

"Keep your voice down," he hissed. Once he reached the cart, he sagged against it, careful not to disturb his hot, throbbing shoulder. "You'll cause a panic, Tayja."

Tayja was standing in the bed of the cart, her arms clutched to her chest protectively. The wind whipped her black hair about her face, behind which peered wide, red-rimmed eyes. Haza couldn't fault her terror. The weeping of many widowed women had rung through the night, and loudest among them had been Magda, Torvust's pregnant wife. Tayja had spent the night comforting them all as best as she could, and from what he'd heard, she hadn't learned Haegar was still alive until he'd found her well after dawn.

"As if we're not already panicked," she snapped back, but she did listen, dropping her roar to only an indignant growl. "What's happening now, Haza? Where is my husband?"

"He'll be back soon." He struggled to swallow a groan. He let himself slide to the ground, his shoulder reverberating like a disturbed pond. "It's happening at midday," he said through the pain. "The men are going to rush the gates. Once they've been breached, we'll start to move the women and children through. You'll be among the first; Haegar made sure of it."

Tayja stepped down from the wagon and lowered herself onto her knees, smoothing her skirts before gripping her hem tight. "Where will Haegar be? At...at the front?"

He stared at his own hand, coiled into a fist in his lap, and considered waiting to let Haegar tell her himself. What his brother was going to do was brave, but rash. And stupid. With a battle in the courtyard, the defenders of Farrenhall wouldn't treat an interloper well if he was caught. Especially not the Myrmidons. If they did catch him, Haza suspected they'd hang him over the gate, as a warning to the others. *These people trust him.* He'd proven himself before them last night, and if he died, their tenuous resolve would shatter. *And Haegar certainly* will *be caught. Stupid, stupid, brave man.*

"The Iron Gate will be too strong to breach," he finally said. He couldn't hide this from her. She deserved to know, no matter what it might make her do. Not that she could stop him, anyway. "Maybe if we were a real army, with armor and siege weapons, we might take it. We have neither, but still we must try. While the battle unfolds, Haegar will climb along the outside of the Gated Bridge and enter. He'll open the inner gate and let us through."

Tayja's head snapped toward him, her furious eyes aflame. "He's going alone?" she demanded.

"Mama?" came a soft voice before he could reply. "What's happening to Papa?" Rala poked her head over the edge of the wagon, still wrapped in heavy blankets, her little freckled face red from the cold. Her lip quivered as she looked between them. "Is Papa going to die?"

With a strangled sob, Tayja buried her face in her hands. Haza stared blankly up at the little girl, but he felt that same pain in his gut, in his soul. It was a desperate and hopeless feeling. How could one explain the inevitability of death to one so young? How could she possibly be made to understand what was happening? That her father might vanish forever, as so many from the Winterwood already had? Haza weighed the question as he stared at his niece, unable to formulate the answer.

"No," Tayja announced. She stood and scooped Rala into her arms, drawing the girl to her chest. "Your Papa is not going to die. He's going to come back and get us over that river, just like we talked about back home. Over the river for a little while, then home again." She glanced down at him as she stroked her daughter's hair. "He is not going to die," she whispered.

Haza could only nod.

Makin appeared from beneath the blankets too, his eyes haggard. He likely hadn't slept, and Haza could hardly fault the poor lad. The boy yawned, but then grinned when he saw Haza. "Did Papa tell you about the fight?" he asked, eyes alight. "Everyone's talking about it. Did you see the dead men? When they come again, Papa will let me slay them too!"

It was the excitement in the boy's voice that surprised him most. There was a genuine enthusiasm for the spectacle of it all. Looking up at his nephew, he saw just how young the boy really was. *Not a man at all, no matter what Haegar thinks.* "Pray they do not come again," he said. "They *will* hurt you, you or your sister."

"Not me," Makin said, straightening in the cart. He puffed out his chest. "I'll fight them off, just like Papa. They don't scare me."

"You won't be able to fight them, Makin," he replied in a low, toneless voice. "They'll kill you. They'll wash this beach with your blood, as they already have with hundreds of our countrymen."

"Haza!" Tayja snapped, mouth agape in mingled shock and

fury. Rala whimpered and curled tighter against her mother's chest.

He didn't even look at them. His eyes were locked on the boy, who had withered beneath his stare, enthusiasm finally fading. "He has to know, Tayja. He has to understand what this will cost us. This isn't a story, Makin. We're not great warriors, we're not kings and generals like I've told you about. This is different."

Makin frowned uncertainly. "But you were the one who told me those stories, Uncle. You said we could chase away the night, if we fought like Kama'Thrail. I can fight it. I'm not afraid."

"Were you afraid of the wolf?"

The boy's eyes betrayed him, glancing immediately to the stump of Haza's arm before fleeing again. "Papa killed the wolf," he protested softly.

"Yes, but there are more," he said. "Many more. And that's why you're going to stay in this wagon with your mother, no matter what happens. Your Papa has to go away for a while, so someone needs to stay here and protect your family. Can you do that instead, Makin? Stay here and protect your family?"

Makin bobbed his head, eyes downcast. "Aye, Uncle."

"Good." Haza looked up at Tayja, who glowered at him. Let her be angry, then. He wasn't going to risk Makin getting the fool idea to run off and see a real battle up close. He knew how the minds of boys worked; were he as young as Makin, he'd likely have run off himself. "You'll keep them here, won't you?" he asked. "Keep them close?"

Tayja narrowed her eyes at him. "Aye, but where do you plan on being? Are you going to climb with Haegar, too?"

"Hardly," Haza muttered. "I think my rock-climbing days are behind me. I won't be far." *I'll protect them, Haegar,* he quietly promised. *But I'll watch your back, too. For this family until my dying breath. For love, for blood.* Haegar, who despite all that had transpired between them, had let him into his home, had fed him, clothed him. And then saved his life. *Now I can do the same for you, my brother.*

And maybe then, the insurmountable debt between them would finally be settled.

Chapter Thirteen
Payment

The tolling of Farrenhall's bells hastened a dreadful countdown. Every second they spent in the camp, rather than assaulting the gates, only gave the Myrmidons time to shore up the Gated Bridge's defenses. Worse, each passing hour brought the night marching closer. And the dead with it.

They would only have one chance at this. The people of the Winterwood would not survive another night trapped on the Tagalfr's beach. *Just get my family across*, he silently begged, though he wasn't sure where he was directing his pleas. *Give me whatever miserable end you can conjure, but get my family across.*

The afternoon sun turned the snow to gray sludge. Haegar panted as he trudged through it, his bones aching, joints and ligaments protesting his every motion. The exhaustion of the night's battle, coupled with a lack of sleep, only compounded his weariness. He felt ready to collapse with every new step he took, but somehow he found the strength to take the next.

Upon his shoulder rested the heavy burden of a Winterwood tree's broad trunk. Stripped of its branches, the log was one of the four largest they'd found and hewn at the forest's edge. Haegar had been working all morning with Bofor to cut them down and shear them of their limbs. Now, he and seven other men carried the tree upon their shoulders, right through the heart of the refugee camp.

Other teams carried the rest behind them. The logs were awkward and rough-cut, but there was no time to worry about precision, much less perfection. Already, Haegar felt they'd wasted too much time, and they'd yet to truly begin. *It doesn't matter what they look like, so long as they're strong enough to batter down that gate. Let the blood of all Vruskmen run strong this day.*

A path had been cleared through the swollen camp, leaving the cobblestone road that led up the hill to Farrenhall free for travel. Tents and wagons and weary, frightened travelers were still gathered on either side of the road, watching as Haegar and his team moved toward the bridge.

Haegar couldn't keep his eyes off them. He kept scanning their faces for a glimpse of his family, even though he knew they'd be waiting up ahead, closer to Farrenhall. He was desperate to see them, though. The onlookers were mostly the elderly and the children, interspersed with wounded who were able to stand, but not fight. The rest had gone west, called by the sound of the bells to marshal with Laklin, while their families remained behind, silent and waiting. Everyone knew what was coming next. There was nothing any of them could do now but watch.

Despite the ache in his bones, the weight of the tree on his shoulder, and the great terror that had him seized in its jaws, he didn't envy the onlookers. He couldn't imagine how helpless they must feel, to be unable to act, unable to do anything to influence what was about to happen. They could only remain and watch from a distance, left to sit quietly and hope. And if the battle went poorly, if dusk came and they'd yet to be called to cross, they would be the first to face the dead.

The road came to an abrupt end when it met the back of a second crowd. Instead of frightened onlookers sheltering the weak and wounded, this was a horde of frightened men, corralled into a rough ramshackle image of an army by captains who'd been farmers and lumberjacks mere hours before. Haegar could already see the fragility of it, just by coming up the rear.

Hundreds of men, as many with gray hair as bald chins, were cramped into tight rows, made to stand in long lines that spanned the length of the beach. They were little more than five hundred in total, a number that was made to seem quite small when he viewed it all together, but they put on what he thought was a workable impression of a real army. *Should we task the women to fight, too?* It would bolster their numbers, but who would that leave the children with, should they fail? The injured? The infirm? No, this was a man's place. It was a man's purpose to die for the sake of his family, should it be demanded. He could not picture Tayja with an axe. He would not.

As he'd planned with the other men who'd become his captains—*My captains? Am I general now?* It was a staggering thought—had divided their soldiers into two groups, based on their own self-professed talents. Three hundred axe and sickle-bearers outfitted with shields hastily cobbled from scavenged wagons would go first, to escort the battering rams into position. Behind, the remaining platoon would come equipped with bows and all the arrows that could be found in the entire camp. They would put their hunting acumen to work as they came up the rear, hammering the defenders on the wall tops.

The bells had stopped ringing, as had motion in the camp. Haegar raised a hand over his head, scanning the fortifications of the Gated Bridge. Grand-Crusader Berethan had to know they were coming—even a blind man couldn't miss the racket an army made as it marshaled, a mere seven hundred paces from the Copper Gate. They needed to act swiftly. The less time the man who'd turned them aside before the attack and his Myrmidons had to react, the cleaner this would be. And Haegar needed speed more than anything. Speed at any cost. *So long as the bloodied gates open...nothing else matters.*

"Blood of my fathers," Bofor cursed as he stepped up beside Haegar. The logs had been deposited in front of the army, looking up the road that led to Farrenhall. Bofor, however, was looking across the lines of Vruskmen staring back at them. "Is this all we have left?" he asked, running a hand across his scalp.

Haegar clenched his jaw and nodded. The other captains gathered with him, and together they turned to face their hastily assembled army. His heart was pounding in his throat, and it was all he could do to keep from trembling beneath the terrified stares of the woodsmen. "This is it," he muttered quietly. "It has to be enough, or none of us are getting over that river."

A hand fell on his shoulder. "It *will* be enough," Laklin said, an exhausted smile slipping across his pale face. "The blood of old Vrusk is in our veins, as it was in our fathers' before us. It will be enough."

Haegar glanced at the man, someone he hadn't known the night before, and smiled faintly as a stirring of kinship momentarily soothed his fears. What did it matter if they were all strangers? They were Vruskmen. Men of the Winterwood.

And yet...as he looked across them, a rough assemblage of a few hundred Vruskmen, with nothing more than axes and planks of wood, without armor or burnished steel or banners to lead them forward, he doubted. *And yet...we must march forward.* Haegar was no commander. He'd never even thought of himself as a leader, before. But someone had to be the one to give the order, and for some bloodied reason, every eye was on him.

Of all the places I could be standing, how did I come to be here? How has it come to this?

"Kinsmen!" he shouted, raising his voice above the distant

crash of the Tagalfr. It echoed faintly across the beachhead, but every man assembled stirred as they came to attention. "Vruskmen! I don't know all your names, nor all your faces, but I know your blood. When our ancestors settled in the hinterlands, only the bravest dared look beyond the Rushing Ice and imagine what could be found there. Some called them fools, aye, but it didn't stop them from doing what they needed to do. They crossed the river and faced the wilds of the Winterwood, faced its fury and took it for their own. We are the descendants of those brave men." His voice wavered as he suddenly glimpsed a vision of his father standing in the crowd, his arms crossed and a soft smile on his face as his son described their home, his most favorite place. He did not let his speech falter, though. He had to capture the crowd, here and now.

"When I look into your eyes, I do not see strangers. I do not see men and women from distant villages, I do not see travelers from places unknown. I see brothers and sisters. Kinsmen of the Winterwood! But, the fellowship that has united us has been betrayed." His voice rose with that. "Lord Varkoth has abandoned us. The Old King has abandoned us. All of Vrusk has shut its gates and turned its back on us. This is our fate, in their eyes, to be left across the river, left to the claws of the dead!"

An angry voice rose from the crowd. "The Old King promised to protect us!" It was an old man, struggling to hold his axe high with both hands. The man should've been back with the other elderly, but Haegar wouldn't turn a body aside. "He promised it when I was still young, he did!"

Other voices began to rise from the crowd, the first snapping sparks of a flame. "Aye, and what has Varkoth ever done for us?" "His family grew fat and rich on our toil, and this is how he repays us?" "Blood was shed last night; blood of Vrusk! Where are the king's armies to protect us?" "Varkoth should hang, him and his kin!"

Haegar breathed out slowly as he watched fury sweep across the small army like a second, fetid wind. He had no desire to temper their ire, as anger was the only thing that would override the fear of battle. If the men were blind with rage, they would fight. They would die, too. *It has to be done.* Maybe Varkoth really had ordered the gates shut himself, or maybe the Myrmidons had commandeered the bridge. Maybe the Old King didn't know any of this was happening, but it didn't matter. The truth had to be whatever would make his kinsmen rush into death. And if a brutal, blood-frenzied mob killed Varkoth and his servants when the bridge fell, that wouldn't matter either, so long as his family was safe.

He hoped it wouldn't come to that—no doubt the Vruskmen who manned Farrenhall wanted no part of the Myrmidons and their dark business, but the blood of their kinsmen had been shed. His ancestors had built great monuments like Farrenhall to showcase their strength, like a wolf baring its teeth. And when blood was shed, the pack would prove they made no empty threats. The God-Emperor had been the last to taste such terrible wrath, and it had vanished from Vrusk for generations, but Haegar was looking at it now.

Men began to bang axes and sickles against their makeshift shields, their accusations blurring into a wordless bellow of rage. Others drummed on the empty carts that been rolled among their ranks, striking with bows or bare fists. He glanced over his shoulder as the noise rolled over him. Above it all, Farrenhall sat unperturbed. Little did it notice the men who gnashed their teeth at it, their cries of outrage and pain, their call for justice, for passage. For as great a noise as it was, the Gated Bridge did not quail.

"We will not let ourselves be abandoned!" Haegar roared, surprising himself. The crowd fell silent, all eyes on him once more. "If Lord Varkoth cannot remember us, then let us remind him. Let us remind him, and all who bar those gates, that our blood is as strong and old as theirs. Our ancestors fought their way into the Winterwood, and by their blood, we shall fight our way back out!"

A roar followed as men raised their axes toward the sky. And while gray clouds rolled across the afternoon sun, promising the cold touch of winter, a single bell began to toll, a dull and hollow sound, yet loud enough to cut across the turmoil.

Though he couldn't see who rang the bells in the towers of Farrenhall, he knew Varkoth must be watching. *We're out of time.* With his own axe raised, he took the first step toward the Gated Bridge. "Fight not for glory, not for honor, not for land, but for blood! For our families! For blood!" *And for the dead,* he added silently. All he could see when he thought of Torvust was the man's final, twisted expression. It supplanted every memory he had with his old friend, overriding all with its blood-graven image. He let himself drown in that fury.

It began with that first step. Suddenly, he wasn't alone in his charge. The host of the Winterwood spurred itself into motion, commanded by nothing more than his own words. A phantom thrill seized him by the heart, but anger kept him moving forward. He resumed his position aside one of the battering rams alongside half a dozen other men, seizing the groove they'd carved into its length, and together they hefted it onto their shoulders.

In unison, the battering rams rose, and Haegar took the lead. The weight of the log on his shoulder paled before that which fell upon his soul, one that got heavier every time he lifted a foot. *No turning back. Only forward.* The army came marching up behind, their boots like a rolling drum. The wagons trundled, advancing up the road, archers taking up positions in the rear. Farrenhall loomed above them all, framed by the gray face of the sky, a stately and motionless silhouette, its fear betrayed only by the tolling bell.

Had trees always been so heavy? Haegar panted, his shoulder ablaze, as they reached the shallow slope of the hill. Exhaustion was already harrying his heels. He'd never been more acutely aware of how long it had been since he'd last slept, but the sight of movement on the walls ahead kept his eyes snapped open. *And this before the fighting even begins. Let the blood run strong today. Please.* He couldn't falter, not with all who were depending on him, all following him into the unknown. How had this responsibility ever fallen on his shoulders?

The rattling of wheels caused him to glance away from the Gated Bridge, and he watched as teams of men pushed the wagons ahead of the archers. They'd been shoddily outfitted with planks of wood standing erect, like walls on wheels. As the men manipulated the carts ahead of the advancing army, Haegar felt naked. He and the other bearers would make easy targets. *All we have to do is reach the gate,* he told himself. *Just one ram has to make it through. Once the gate is breached, the courtyard is ours. It doesn't matter how strong those bloodied Myrmidons are—there are too few of them to stop us all.*

Despite the bravado that had initiated the charge, it was a slow process. Men panted and groaned beneath the weight of the battering rams, their already-heavy burden encumbered further by the incline. The army was forced to match the pace of the bearers, trundling slowly behind them.

Farrenhall crept closer. His eyes found the Copper Gate, a double-door barrier of solid Winterwood, with iron bars straddling its length. They'd open inward, if they ever opened again. The rams would have to split that seam and throw them back, and the passageway, large enough to admit a steady stream of travelers and merchants, would be more than enough to let the army storm through.

He let himself feel a faint strum of hope. They *could* do this. These gates seemed an obvious flaw in Farrenhall's defenses, especially when compared to the stark, heavy stone that comprised the bridge. It was the Iron Gate, a mechanism of grinding wheels and metal—as Haza described it—that could prove impossible to breach.

As the bell continued to sing its slow, morose melody, figures were gathering atop the wall. Men clustered over the gates, their heavy voices shouting indistinctly. Sunlight peeking through the clouds glinted off red and silver armor.

Time seemed to quicken with each step he took. Suddenly, Farrenhall was before them, and the end of the road was only a hundred paces away. He could see the marbled armor of the Myrmidons, their long crimson capes, their faceless helms with dark, t-shaped slits for visors. As he strained under the weight of the battering ram, he heard Bofor shout for the archers to nock their arrows and draw. Beside him, on the other side of the trunk, Laklin's face was growing red, like the man had forgotten how to breathe.

And in that same breathless instant, the Myrmidons gathered in a straight line above, standing between the staggered crenellations of stone. In perfect unison, they raised longbows with shining, silver arrows drawn, all pointed straight at the ram-bearers. Straight at him.

This is madness. It was at that moment that he finally stumbled. The battering ram lurched, and Haegar had to brace himself against it to keep from falling. "Steady!" Bofor bellowed from behind. Laklin cried out, but as he pushed it back into place,

Haegar was able to return to his proper station. The gate was before them, mere paces away. They were well within range of those arrows. *What are they waiting for?*

He dared not breathe. His eyes were on the Myrmidons perched above, and their arrows tracked with him, almost as if every one was pointed directly at him. And only him. He saw the faces of his family flash before him. Tayja, his truest love. Makin and Rala, his children, his purpose. Haza, his brother.

I didn't say goodbye.

The thought struck him like an ironclad punch. In the chaos of the day, he'd forgotten to go back before joining with the bearers. He hadn't seen them since early that morning, right after dawn. He'd been so consumed by the preparations and planning, by worry for the terrible constraint of time, that they'd slipped his mind. Guilt burned white hot beneath his flesh. What if he never saw them again? Could Haza protect them?

No, I will *see them again.* This was not where Haegar Ruthborne ended, nor would it be for any man of the Winterwood. They were going to win this. They were going to get every man, woman and child across the Tagalfr. Nothing would stop them.

He never saw the arrows land, only heard the sudden, blood-curdling screams. Beside him, Laklin stumbled, his glazed eyes staring at nothing, while three arrows wobbled like red-fletched banners from his chest. Then he dropped.

The battering ram lurched to one side, but Haegar threw himself beneath the tremendous weight of the trunk, screaming as its heavy girth was held aloft by only his back. Then Bofor appeared beside him, taking up the other side, and they were able to keep their overlarge burden from collapsing.

One of the other rams went down with a crash, its heavy front smashing atop the man who had fallen before it, grinding him into the cobblestones. Arrows bristled along the ram's length, and from the near-dozen men who'd fallen with it. None of the other rams fell, but all left a trail of pierced men in their passing. Vruskmen leapt down from behind the shielded carts, which now sported red-fletched shafts like harvest decorations, and hurried to take up the positions of the fallen, giving new strength to the rams.

Yet just as the weight was lifted from Haegar's shoulders, the Myrmidons drew back their bows and loosed again. A swarm of hissing arrows slammed into the front of the charge like black rain, and while the carts took the brunt of the onslaught, the rams and their carriers had no such protection. One seemed to suddenly grow from the wood just beside his hand, a mere hairsbreadth from his flesh.

An answering volley came from the men on the carts, peeking around the barricades to loosen back toward the wall. The counter-volley slammed into the Myrmidons, causing the knights to withdraw behind the battlements. Arrows fell back to the road, having found no target, but it had disrupted the defender's third attack, and the charge was closing quickly on the Copper Gate.

Haegar wanted to shout, to give encouragement, but he could hardly find the strength to breathe. Each man had to find the courage to march on their own. The gate loomed overhead now, great and tall, but he saw it as a weakness in a beast of stone and steel. Old wood, he could see, cracked, rotted, and warped by the harsh winds and snow of the Winterwood. He knew it could be breached. They just had to reach it.

The air stank of salt and frost and something more. Red mist hung in the air, thick as fog. His boots trudged over something, a lump in the road far too large to be a misplaced stone. He watched a boy topple from the nearest cart, his bow flying from his hands, a shaft jutting from his pale throat. Arrows flew like snow on a high wind; it was impossible to tell, now, which was bound for the wall or for his own flesh. He kept his head down, his arms up, and his feet moving.

And then they'd reached it. A half dozen more steps, and their ram connected. Haegar jolted at the sudden impact, the trunk slipping from his grasp as he was suddenly thrust backward. They'd run into a gate that did not break. And even as four more rams drove themselves against it, the first gate of Farrenhall did not yield.

"Again!" Haegar cried, repositioning his feet. Bofor and the others drew back with him, preparing for the next push. "No man retreats until we've breached, or we'll all be dead come nightfall!" He didn't know who was able to hear him over the screams of the wounded, the frightened shouts, and angry hisses of swarming arrows, but it didn't matter. "Again!"

He rushed forward, using all his weight to shove the ram against the wall of wood before him. Though it lacked the same force of the initial charge, an ominous groan followed the ram's heavy crash. He stood with his face nearly pressed against the gate, but he pushed back again, rallying for another charge, while the other rams struck in their place, giving rise to a rhythmic *thoom, thoom, thoom!*

Furious swarms still poisoned the air, like flies descending upon living and dead both, and his skin crawled with every rattle they made. People were screaming behind, above, all around. But he had ears only for the sound of cracking wood. His arms and legs burned as he pushed them further than he ever had before, in unison with the other bearers so that their ram struck the gate like a hammer on a gong, landing over and over.

"Keep going!" he bellowed with a strangled, dry throat. "Keep going. It will fall. We're almost through!"

A heavy *thunk* made him look across the ram. Bofor's sightless eyes stared back at him. The man's head lolled to one side, lips agape as blood bubbled from between clenched teeth. Haegar didn't notice the iron pole that forced the man's head to one side until it was wrenched from his ruined neck, revealing the red-drenched, leaf-shaped blade on its end.

Bofor dropped, one of half a dozen men skewered from above, and the ram went down with them, dragging Haegar and the rest of the bearers to the ground, too. He found himself lying atop the ram, staring up as the pikes withdrew like coiling serpents to the hands of their masters, only to lash out again.

It was a practiced and experienced butchering. Dozens of long spears flew down from the top of the wall, driving into the crowd clustered beneath the shadow of the gates. With perfect precision, the blades would lunge into the mass in a strangely languid fashion, as if it was nothing to gut a man where he stood. They pierced through upraised hands and makeshift shields, goring hearts and throats and heads.

The screams were unlike anything he'd ever before, unmatched even by last night's attack. There, at least, men had fought and died like soldiers. Here, they were cattle. Haegar could only stare up through films of red as the pikes smashed through the wagon barriers, through makeshift spears, to cut down entire lines of men as they tried to rush the fallen rams.

Arrows did nothing to waylay the Myrmidons—even when some men threw down their axes to take up fallen bows, the additional onslaught was rewarded only with the clatter of metal on metal, arrows bouncing harmlessly off Myrmidon armor. The spears were quick to find these lone archers, gutting them from where they stood safely behind Farrenhall's battlements.

The Vruskmen coming behind buckled. With dozens of their own lying dead or bleeding at their feet, terror swept over them like the shadow of the storm overwhelming the sky. Some turned and fled, only to come up against the men trying to push behind them, throwing the ranks into further confusion. And even those who made it out of reach of the spears found arrows in their unprotected backs.

It was while lying there, unable to move, that Haegar learned the importance of armor for the first time. He'd never thought its benefits worth the restrictions to mobility, the dreadful weight it must bring. But here, he watched blades slice through flesh and bone and wood like wool. The Myrmidons used their strength and position to lethal advantage, slamming their pikes into the unprotected men, who could do nothing but send arrows to rattle harmlessly off their iron hides.

One of the rams teetered as five of its men were cut down in unison. Then it dropped entirely as its bearers let it fall, turning to flee. There was only one ram left, now, carried by seven men whose names and faces he did not know. They drove their burden against the Copper Gate again, resulting in a sharp, grinding crack from the other side. The gates did not fall, though. This was finished. This was where they were all going to die.

Then, as the ram withdrew, Haegar saw light spilling through the gate. It had buckled in its middle, spars bent backward by the repeated hammering. Farrenhall was bleeding; they were almost through. But as the ram moved in for its next strike, a pike found a man's shoulder, shoving him off his feet, and the siege weapon began to list.

It can't fall. Seizing energy he didn't know he had, Haegar rose. "It's breaking," he rasped quietly. Then, he gathered his strength and rushed the ram, ducking a thrusting pike. "It's breaking!" He seized the trunk, pushing it back into place. They hurried it forward, striking the gate again. He grunted and caught his breath when they pulled back. "Continue the assault! Don't let them turn us away!" Others were joining him, filling the gaps. Some were bloodied, and one fellow had an arrow growing from his torso, but still they came. They struck a third time.

"Think of your kinsfolk who've died!" He saw faces before him. Torvust. Corvil. Old Sorvak. All the men who'd died on the beach, all who died here, all who'd never made it out of the forest. He was aflame with rage; it consumed all else. "Think of those who yet live, waiting for us to break through! Think of-!"

He never got to finish. He never had to. With frantic cries, a group of bleeding men threw themselves from one of the ruined carts and sent it careening into the gate, while others rushed it and began to hack through with their axes, chopping away large splinters with every blow. The men behind him pushed forward, and the battering ram collided with the Copper Gate one final time.

And the gates of Farrenhall gave a heaving groan and split asunder.

He was the first one through, propelled by the force of his crew as they suddenly found themselves without a wall in their path. He dropped the ram immediately, hands rushing to the handle of his axe, as he hurried across deep green flagstones, dusted lightly with snow. He couldn't help but stare for a moment, his eyes following fragments of wood that were still rolling across the ground before him like heralds. *We...we really did it?* Time seemed to slow, the screams of the dying, the fighting, all fading away, as he saw the path forward, the continuation of a road for so long blocked to him. The path to safety, to freedom.

But that path barely made it more than two hundred paces before it came to yet another end. Farrenhall's Iron Gate was twice the height of the first, and rather than old, warped wood, it was a masterwork of burnished steel, inscribed with iron-clad figures with swords in hand, and over them coiled the scaled serpent of Vrusk, its wide mouth splayed in a defiant grimace.

And even that road was not without its treachery, for though the courtyard was barren save for high walls and weathered cobblestones, it was not empty. Twoscore men in shining armor, marbled silver and crimson like blood spilled across steel, gathered before him in twin lines. They'd shed their capes behind them, leaving them draped across the courtyard like a crimson carpet.

Forty men. More on the walls. He didn't look, but he knew they were turning their bows inward. Vruskmen would continue to hound them from outside, but they wouldn't hold their attention. Not entirely. *Only forty…we outnumber them beyond count. Archers or no, we can't lose.* And yet, as Haegar took his first steady, purposeful step into Farrenhall, he hesitated. The Myrmidons, with their faceless, slit-visor helms, their burnished armor, did not falter as the first gate was thrown inward. They stood their ground, having abandoned their spears for swords and kite-shaped shields marked by the sigil of a gaping eye. There were still cries from behind, too. He could feel the arrows trained on the back of his neck like the razor stingers of hunting wasps, hovering just inches above his skin.

There was no time for hesitation. "Forward, Vrusk!" he bellowed. "Forward, old blood!" Before the last word could leave his tongue, the Myrmidons rushed him. And though he was the first to charge to meet them, he was not the only.

The men of the Winterwood went fearlessly to their deaths, their axes raised high, their voices rebounding through the courtyard. Boots crunched on stones laden with snow, while above, dark clouds loomed over Farrenhall, yet the air remained barren and cold. Even the biting wind had gone still, leaving the fury of winter to be carried by the men rushing the fortress.

As he ran, he felt something slam into his shield, causing him to lurch to one side. He couldn't spare more than a half glance at the razor arrowhead now poking through the backside of his shield, just inches below where his hand gripped a fistful of straps. More arrows fell among them, and the screams of death were renewed with haunting fervor.

The Myrmidon archers had abandoned the front wall, now rushing along either side of the courtyard, continuing to loose shafts upon the Vruskmen spilling through the gates. Unchallenged, scores of arrows harried their charge, one volley after the next. The cart that had been pushed through, now riddled with enough arrows to serve an army twice their size, continued to roll, and huntsmen were able to loose back at the men on the walls from behind its splintering cover.

He had eyes only for the enemy ahead. The phalanx of Myrmidons came on, and he braced himself for the impact. Twenty paces. The armored knights split ranks, allowing those behind to come forward. These wielded gargantuan, double-handed swords, with blades near wide as a tree trunk. He'd never seen anything like them. Fifteen paces.

Haegar was at the head of the charge, shield still raised against oncoming arrows. Men all around him were screaming, bleeding, dying. And all from arrows alone. The mercenaries standing in their way seemed a wall even more solid than the one they'd just breached. *Their armor is too thick, their shields too strong. We'll never breach them.* Ten. The Myrmidons would effortlessly cut through his ragtag mob, butchering them here just as easily as they had at the gate. Without armor and organization to protect them, how could the Vruskmen expect to win? Five paces.

He refused to close his eyes. Refused to slow. If even one man balked, the others would falter, their fighting spirit would collapse. There was nothing to do but rush into death and accept it when it came. *Let my blood join with the old. Let it-*

Impact was the soft whistle of air splitting before the swing of a blade. The sword ripped past him, but he didn't have time to notice the gash it had opened on his cheek, nor the bellow of the stricken man behind him. Instead, he brought his axe down with a wordless cry, channeling all his strength and fury into a single blow. It crashed into the Myrmidon's shield, piercing the crimson eye and denting the metal. In the same instant, all around him, the Vruskmen made contact, slamming axes, shields, and spears into the wall of steel, trying to push it back.

The next swing came for his throat. Haegar danced back, but the sword caught the top of his shield, shearing away a quarter of its length. The Myrmidon came at him again, this time with an overhead swipe, his shield raised before his faceless helm. Haegar tried to block, his retreat foiled by the men coming behind, who thrust him forward. Haegar suddenly found himself crushed up against an unyielding barrier, knights who refused to be moved by the charge.

The crush saved Haegar's life, throwing him past the swing of the Myrmidon's sword—but left it threatened again when he found himself pinned against the man's chest. An insufferable, agonizing weight ground him into the metal, flattening flesh and bone. Curdled blood, he couldn't breathe! He tried to shove back, but more men collided with him, driven by the men coming behind *them.*

How did the Myrmidons still stand unbroken? How could they resist the power of a hundred Vruskmen? The Winterwood itself would sooner fall against such an onslaught.

Back and forth the line seemed to go, throbbing to the phantom tune of dying screams. Myrmidon swords swept all around him, cleaving through limbs and necks like bothersome branches. Haegar kept low, and though dying men let him step back, it was never for more than a few paces before he was pushed back into reach of those swords. The Myrmidons with the shields and shorter blades held the line, while their companions with the broadswords stepped between to lash out, only to swiftly withdraw behind their protection. The Vruskmen were throwing themselves into a thresher, and no matter how Haegar battered with his axe, he could not break the deadly machine.

He'd never seen such reckless valor before. Through air that was thick with crimson, his kinsmen kept coming. For every man who fell, three more stepped in to fill the gap. Though they could not push the Myrmidons back, neither could their charge be broken. He saw two men seize a knight's shield and wrench it free, yet a sword swiftly appeared through the breach, running a young, blonde Vruskman through his chest. His fellows poured in behind him, using the Myrmidon's own shield to block his attacks, but still made no ground.

We have to get through. Bravery would not win them this battle. Blood could grant no strength while spilled on the ground. *If we all die here, our families will die on that beach. I know it.* He looked up at the Myrmidon before him, the same man he'd first been forced up against. The man had lost his shield and had abandoned the short sword for the larger broadsword that had hung from his back. His expression was unreadable behind the darkness of his helm, but Haegar could see his shoulders rise and fall with labored breath, see the way that his blood-soaked blade wobbled in his hands.

He rushed the man. The Myrmidon swung low, but he caught the blade with his axe, driving it back up. His next swing raked across the man's chest, but only succeeded in sending a shower of sparks flying through the air. The Myrmidon's sword was already up again. Haegar didn't need to look at the mangled remnants of his shield to know it wouldn't block another strike. So, instead, he dropped it and threw himself at the man, shoulder up.

Sharp pain shot through his shoulder, but he was rewarded with an audible grunt from his opponent as the Myrmidon stumbled. Haegar spun around the man, his axe seized in both hands, and swung for the back of the Myrmidon's knee. The blade bit through unprotected flesh. The Myrmidon screamed, his leg dropping beneath him. But even as he fell to one knee, that massive sword came around.

Haegar ripped his axe free and danced back, only for the blade to lop his weapon in half. He fumbled for the axehead and managed to catch it before it fell and looked up to see the Myrmidon pulling himself to his feet. Blood was gushing down his right leg, but still he was going to stand. Without thinking, Haegar launched himself at the man, slamming into his chest, and they fell together.

For a moment, he lay atop the Myrmidon, panting. He found himself staring into a baleful emerald eye, leering at him from beneath that protective visor. The knight drove his gauntleted fist into Haegar's side. He buckled with a gasp, nearly falling from his perch, but he grappled with the man, using one knee to try and pin his other shoulder to the ground. The Myrmidon still had hold of his sword-hilt—if he wrestled free, Haegar was dead.

The man hit him again, but he sucked air through his teeth and rammed the handle of his axe like a club into the Myrmidon's face. The helmet rebounded the blow with a dull *thunk,* but the man beneath it jolted, his head bouncing off the ground. For a heartbeat, his struggling waned. Abandoning the handle, Haegar seized his axehead with both hands, shoving the blade down into the Myrmidon's face.

An armored hand shot up, catching what remained of the haft. Haegar threw his weight against it, pushing the half-moon down into the t-shaped visor, the only weakness he could see in the armor. Beneath him, the Myrmidon writhed like a worm, his iron fortress transformed into a prison. Bracing himself with one knee against the man's chest, he was able to keep him pinned. The man was forced to abandon his own blade, adding his second hand to try and waylay the axe's slow descent.

The struggle stretched on, and they were reduced to nothing but their struggling breaths, their strengths deadlocked. Figures thrashed all around them, but the sounds of the battle seemed distant to Haegar. He could feel sweat rolling down his back, feel the blood soaking through his shirt from his gashed cheek. The broken axehead hovered inches from the Myrmidon's face as the two men pushed against each other, keeping it suspended in place. Haegar's arms started to wobble, his elbows seizing as he pushed himself to his limit. How long had they been stuck like this? It felt like hours.

There was no way to abandon this attack. The Myrmidon would kill him the moment he recovered his sword. He could do nothing but stare down into those unwavering emerald eyes. Neither of them blinked, and for a moment, Haegar understood his opponent's resolve. Neither of them could surrender.

He considered that eye as he pushed. It struck him how dissimilar it was to the eyes of that wolf, or the horse from the forest. There was anger in it, certainly, but also determination, a will to fight and endure. Absent was that utter malice he'd glimpsed in the dead, that radiant and overwhelming hatred. This, though, this was something true. The eyes of a beating heart. The eyes of a man. A man he was about to kill.

What am I doing? The thought was only a flicker, but his grip flickered too. The Myrmidon's hand shot up, wrapping iron fingers about his throat. His eyes bulged as the man began to crush his throat, fingers squeezed so tight he felt caught between a bear's jaws.

Panicked, Haegar tried to pull away, but the Myrmidon's grip was as unyielding in attack as defense. He couldn't draw so much as a trickle of air, not enough to even gasp in pain. The knight was trying to pull him closer, wrap him in a crushing embrace. Vainly, he writhed, attempting to roll away, but there was nothing he could do. His vision was swimming, darkness cloying at its corners. The man's other hand was still holding the axe blade at bay. *Only one hand.*

Haegar gave into the Myrmidon's pull and threw his full weight against the axehead. And he finally found give. The man beneath him jerked, then the hand fell away. Haegar threw his head back, sucking in gulps of cold air, though each felt like fire down his bruised throat. Beneath him, the axehead grew from the Myrmidon's own face, having split right through his visor. Those emerald eyes held nothing anymore but a cold and distant stare.

I killed a man. The thought didn't frighten him as much as he thought it would. Instead, he felt…numb. He staggered to his feet, transfixed by the corpse laid out beneath him. He was no stranger to ending life, to watching the light vanish from his prey as they faded from Razzador. But he'd only ever killed to eat. *And killed the dead?* Was that the same? *No, I didn't kill them. They couldn't die.* To feel the Myrmidon struggle against him, to see him fight so hard for his life, only to watch it vanish like spring snow… The numbness spread up his gut, and there it stayed until something jostled him from behind.

Two Vruskmen nearly shoved him back to the ground as they struggled with another Myrmidon. They both held axes, and they'd managed to hack away pieces of their opponent's armor, revealing bruised and bloodied flesh beneath. The knight held them at bay with a sword in each hand, but by the way he staggered, his fall would come soon.

Haegar had forgotten the battle in his deathly struggle, but it all came rushing over him like the Tagalfr itself. Shouts and screams, the clatter of metal on metal, metal on wood. The deadly thrum of arrows. Ducking beneath the battling men, Haegar snatched the dead Myrmidon's shortsword, leaving his broken axe where it had been planted. The sword was lighter than he'd anticipated, and far less unwieldy than his axe. He found himself gaping for half a heart's beat as he swung it about himself. Little wonder the Myrmidons had so effortlessly cut through them.

Have to keep moving. Have to kill them. Anger made his blood boil. One of the Vruskmen went down, a sword slashing through his neck. *Have to kill them all.* As the Myrmidon turned his twin blades on his last opponent, Haegar rushed him from the side. The knight turned at the last moment, pivoting to parry his blade, but it let the other Vruskman bury his axe in the man's shoulder. The Myrmidon bellowed, jerked down to one knee by the blow, and Haegar lashed out with his own sword, running it through his throat. The second knight toppled face-forward to join his fellow.

He found himself fighting alongside the man, turning upon the next Myrmidon. Another Vruskman joined them. Then half a dozen. Together, they bowled the knight over and began to hack at him, only stopping when his armor had turned completely crimson. They moved on after that, seeking opponent after opponent. One by one, they surrounded them and brought them down. The Myrmidon swords flashed through the afternoon, sending limbs and heads flying, but they were always outflanked and dragged down.

It was only then, driving his sword up through the seam

between shoulder and chest, that he realized what was happening. The Myrmidon line had finally shattered, split apart by overwhelming numbers. The arrows had stopped flying, too; he caught sight of Vruskmen rushing up onto the walls, forcing the Myrmidons to abandon their bows in favor of blades.

The Vruskmen fought in packs, splitting the knights apart and forcing them down with overwhelming might. But just as the men of the Winterwood began to claim advantage, the Myrmidons abandoned their established formations entirely. They split into pairs or small groups, fighting back-to-back, their long swords flashing across the battlefield. Men fell like a grove before them, parted with graceful swings that hesitated not for flesh or bone.

Bile burned in his throat, but it was overpowered by his hatred. His feet trod on uneven ground, but he dared not to look at what the Myrmidons had paved the courtyard with. He pushed alongside his kinsmen, hacking and swiping at the armored monsters, trying to pick under their defenses. He watched two heads fall from their owners' shoulders in perfect unison. He watched hands pinwheel free, still gripping their axes. He saw a white-haired man drop to his knees, clutching at his own innards as they spilled from his belly.

The Myrmidons fought on, untouchable. Haegar and three others tried to rush one from behind, but he spun, ripping his broadsword through the boy trying to draw his attention, then turned calmly to meet them. Haegar threw himself to one side. Something hot ripped past his arm—a narrow miss? Two men fell at the knight's feet, and the Myrmidon stepped over them, unblemished.

As he traded blows with the knight, Haegar heard a sound from far away, the groan of metal far louder than any clashing blades. He glanced behind the Myrmidon and saw the Iron Gate of Farrenhall slide open. His heart raced. Lord Varkoth had changed his mind. He was opening the way. He was going to save-

Myrmidons marched from out the dark gullet of the Gated Bridge, their armor gleaming. How many? He couldn't count. The knight in front of him was swinging again. He raised his sword to block the blow, but the heavy strike sent it flying from his hands. He danced back, letting another man with an axe rush in to fill his place. The Myrmidon didn't even seem to look at him, lopping off his head like he were snuffing out a candle, eyes still locked on Haegar. What was this warmth running down his right arm? He didn't remember being struck. He could still see the Myrmidons spilling out the gate. They were charging now, a line of unbreakable steel. The first knight took another step forward, blade raised again.

This was where he was going to die. Balling his fists, Haegar stepped forward to meet it.

Chapter Fourteen
A Step on the Highest Path

Sleep did not come for Kasara, much as she desired it. Between the pain gnawing through her ankle, and the boiling fury gnawing at her heart, she feared she would not find rest for the remainder of her days. After an hour spent fitfully turning on her bed, she rose again and stalked through the Gated Bridge, fast as her limp would allow.

Exhaustion was like a weighted blanket over her shoulders, its suffocating veil growing heavier with each step she took. But she couldn't stop. There was no time for rest. It wasn't right, not while her people were still trapped outside. They might not know it, but they were counting on her. By word or by steel, she had to get Farrenhall open.

But the path forward had no direction, and not knowing where else to go, Kasara found herself in the training arena. Isolated by thick, dark stone, with a single window overlooking the churning mist of the Tagalfr, Kasara fetched a practice sword.

She set her feet in the hard-packed clay and, ignoring both her tiredness and the pain, she began to work through her Ka'lori stances, as Berethan had taught her. The wooden sword whooshed stiffly through the air, too light and ephemeral compared to actual steel. It seemed fitting, though, a mirror of her own impotence. She could not open the gates herself, nor could she sway her father's will, or enact any real change herself. She was a child who'd thought mistakenly that she was a woman grown. *There's nothing I can do.*

Crushing as the thought was, it made her redouble her swings, push her wounded ankle harder. After working through the Ka'lori, she started again, faster this time, cutting through invisible opponents. Dark and twisted images flashed through her mind, of bared, bloody teeth, of lifeless, furious eyes. She could feel the tug of meat and bone as she hacked them down, but the dead kept coming for her, reaching for her.

It was an unwinnable fight. The dead were relentless, and as more spilled across the battlefield, even those that went down came up again, unbreakable. Kasara was so tired. So, so tired.

Maybe she should surrender to it. Would it have been better for her to die out there on the beach, lain to rest alongside her own countrymen? She wouldn't have had to face her father's betrayal. Wouldn't feel so helpless. Her life would've meant something. Except...the dead were rising. There was no denying it, anymore. Impossible though it sounded, terrible as it was to imagine, it was real. If she'd died, she would've turned against her own people. *My father does that, and he still lives...*

No. She couldn't stop. She couldn't give in. With her teeth bared, she slashed the air, her sword snaking back and forth. She would not die here. She would not stop fighting. *Surrender is death.*

"You should be resting," said a voice.

Upon seeing Berethan standing in the doorway, encased in full plate armor, his broadsword's hilt rising like a tower over one shoulder, she nearly threw her sword at him. Instead, she turned her back and restarted her practice. "You care, suddenly?" she asked.

"You have had a foolish day, Lordling," the Myrmidon said in his usual toneless voice, made especially hollow by the echo of his helm. "You risked your life without need."

Kasara picked up her pace, pushing through the piercing agony of her ankle. She would not yield to pain. "Who else will fight for my people? Not you. Certainly not my father."

"You openly defied him," Berethan replied. "He seemed close to ordering your death."

Kasara's swings suddenly slowed before a wave of sorrow. She was trying not to think about it. She'd never seen such murderous wrath in her father's eye before, never could've imagined he was capable of such a thing. Killing his own daughter. And why? Because she wanted to protect the people he was sworn to protect himself?

"And you would've done it?" she asked quietly. The Myrmidon's answering silence was enough to stir the coals of anger again. "You are a coward."

"I am devout."

She blew out a long, suffering breath. "I see no difference."

The clank of armor announced the Myrmidon's entry into the arena. "I admire your dedication, Lordling, but it is clear to me that you have yet to understand my first lesson. The only way to win some battles is to not fight at all."

"I've already started it," Kasara replied, swinging her blade low, pointedly keeping her view forward as Berethan stepped into the corner of her vision. "I'm not turning back."

A soft sight came rattling through the Grand Crusader's helm. "I know. That lesson of the sword, at least, I'm sure you know. So, you've drawn steel in battle. Was it everything you'd dreamed of?"

Sensing the faint smirk in his voice, Kasara finally lowered her sword and turned to face him. "You told me once that you betrayed your Faith Price. You chose what I firmly believe was the right thing to do. What made you decide to disobey?"

For a moment, the man regarded her, his gaze cold behind silver-crimson armor. "I made a mistake," he finally said. "And I paid for it. The Grey Cardinals, they who govern us, they found me. I did my best to hide from them, when I left the Path. I went as far as I could, to a place where I was sure God's eye could not find."

Kasara, startled by the man's sudden honesty, slowly lowered herself to the ground, the pain of her ankle winning out. She gritted her teeth as she crossed her legs, before laying her sword across her lap and staring up at the towering Joromori. "You left the Path…? You mean, you stopped being a Myrmidon?" Berethan's answer was a stiff nod, so she asked, "What made you go back?"

"I was…relieved of my distractions." The Myrmidon's gauntleted hand curled into a fist.

Kasara lowered her gaze. Berethan had not just betrayed his Faith Price, whatever it had been at the time, but had left the Highest Path entirely. She never would've thought it possible. What could have drawn the man away from something he was so clearly now devoted to? And could his mind be changed again?

"You remind me of her, I think," Berethan suddenly said, unprompted. "You have her tenacity."

She blinked at him. "Of who?"

But the Myrmidon shook his head. "It seems your skill with the sword has improved. You are a quick learner. But you are not ready for the task you wish to undertake. Even a hundred years of training cannot prepare you for what a battlefield is truly like. When the lines of combat dissolve, when the crowd crushes in around you, and when the enemy becomes a faceless mass of thrashing, stabbing flesh, no training will keep you alive. It must be experienced to be understood. Lived. Endured."

Kasara looked at the ground. Once, she might've argued with him. She'd read countless books about the Holy Wars, about the great Battle of the Bone Fields, of the Siege of Thrainhold. The heroics of ancient heroes, the toll of terrible conflicts. None of it could capture what she'd witnessed last night. The terror of it, the smell, the sight of those who died around her climbing back to their feet. "I know this," she said.

"Because you snuck away to join some skirmish?"

"It was no skirmish, Berethan!" Curdle her blood, but how many times did she have to say it? Sometimes it felt like the man wasn't listening to her, as if he only spoke to himself. "I saw hundreds die. I saw the dead walk. I fought alongside my people, I…I tried to save them, but I…" So many dead. They'd trusted her, as much as her father, to protect them. The Varkoth family was supposed to be the Winterwood's shield, as it had been when the God-Emperor had come so long ago.

"You still refuse to understand," Berethan noted.

Kasara rose unsteadily to her feet, waving away the helping hand he offered. "You told me to keep fighting until I have no strength left. That's what I intend to do."

"No," came the man's flat reply. "Recognize that there are battles you cannot win. Do not throw what you love away."

Kasara spat in the sand. "That's not the only way you taught me. You told me to fight for victory, always. To fight like I am going to win because I *am* going to win."

Berethan's impatience bled through his steely exterior. "That *is* the only way, once a fight has begun. But there is another path, too. And that is to not fight at all. No steps are gained on the Highest Path through useless death. There is nothing noble about fighting for a cause already lost."

She watched him through narrowed eyes. "I am not like you. I am not afraid. Not of my father, and not of you."

Gray eyes watched her ponderously. "You must hate me," he finally said. "You wanted me to turn on your father, didn't you? To betray my oaths and all I have ever known, for the sake of a girl I've known little more than a month? For peasants I'll never meet?"

"I don't hate you," she snapped quickly. He just made her so angry, was all. So frustrated and powerless. "You were following my father's orders, aye? You didn't have a choice."

The Grand-Crusader shook his head. "But you don't believe that, do you, Lordling?"

"You're better than this, Berethan," she said, unable to meet his eyes.

"Am I?"

Before she could find another frustrated reply, she heard it.

She cocked her head to one side, frowning at the roof overhead as the phantom sound grew louder, ringing stoically through the halls of the bridge. A tolling bell. "It already rang for noon, didn't it?"

"Yes," Berethan said, his eyes on the roof, too. "This is something else."

She didn't wait. Seizing her coat and her real sword from where they leaned against the wall, she hurried from the chamber, leaving the Grand-Crusader behind. Berethan made no attempt to call after her, not that it would've mattered. She hobbled through Farrenhall, following the sound of the bell even though she already knew where it would lead. Likewise, she had no need to search for a guardsman or ask a servant where the trouble was. *Have the dead returned already?* Her ankle burned with her every step, but she didn't slow.

The passages of Farrenhall began to fill with milling,

confused people, drawn from their quarters by the tolling. Kasara brushed by her father's noble courtiers and shoved her way past swarms of servants and guardsmen. Shouts followed her through the halls, and she once had to wait as a column of gray-armored guardsmen rushed past in tight ranks, the sound of their boots ringing in odd unison with that bell.

She soon found herself in the gatehouse. Past pillars and walls decorated with silken banners, past the chain-wrapped wheel that operated Farrenhall's innermost gates, she raced to the broad window that looked out over the Winterwood below, facing a sky now choked by gray storm clouds. Streaks of black still marred the uniformity of the sky, staining it with memories of a night of death.

What she saw brought a matching chill to her bones far deeper than the cold air that clogged the chamber. Her breath fogged the glass as she pressed herself further up against it, peering desperately down at a grisly sight, silently praying it was anything but what she knew it was.

A mass of men, lacking any uniforms or banners or spears or swords, were swarming into the outer courtyard. With a wheeled cart at their front, they met a line of armored Myrmidons, and there they broke like water smashing on rocks. Like flies on carrion, she could see their bodies building in dark piles, clogging the wreckage of the Copper Gate, strewn back down the hill. But still, the Vruskmen came on.

From so far above, men seemed to die soundlessly. They fell in droves, dissolving before the unflinching Myrmidons, whose blades gleamed red as they went about their ruthless toil. Kasara screamed and drove her fist against the window, which rattled in warning. She didn't care.

Holes appeared in the Myrmidon's line, individuals pulled away from their fellows and brought down, but it only made those still standing redouble their efforts. Vruskmen fell before their sweeping blades. No doubt they'd soon be scattered and routed, leaving only the dead in their wake.

She did not feel the terror she'd always imagined she would at seeing her home besieged. This was a more desperate, helpless siege than anything her mind could've conjured. And these people did not fight with the intention to pillage and destroy. They fought to live. The dead still had to be out there in the forest, if they were so willing to face a certain—but perhaps cleaner—death before the gates of Farrenhall.

Why didn't I see the truth sooner? Surely there must've been some warning or whisper of what was happening deeper in the forest, some clue that her father meant to leave the Winterwood to its fate. She should've been able to see through her father's paranoia and done whatever was necessary to remove him from power. *Why didn't he stop this? We could've saved them all. Damn my blood, but we could've saved them.* Her eyes wandered to the gatehouse wheel, but even that glance told her what she needed to know about her chances of opening it alone. Those men were going to die, all because she wasn't strong enough.

Her hands balled into fists. *No. This is not my doing. I did all I could.* The blame for this misery fell on the shoulders of only one man, a man she'd once regarded with endless respect and admiration. Kalivaz Varkoth, Lord of Farrenhall; the blood of the Winterwood was on his hands this day, him and his burnt-blood mercenaries.

And there was nothing she could do about it. She clutched at her own heart, longing for claws with which she might rip it out. *I would save you. I am duty-bound as heir to this wretched place. I would die to see you through. But I can't. I am worthless. Worthless!* Hot tears cut their way down her cheeks as she watched the massacre unfold. What could she do against her father? Against the Myrmidons? All she could do was stand by and watch what she had failed to stop. At least that way, maybe, these men would be remembered. Maybe, once the grave had taken them all, the people of western Vrusk would begin to wonder what had happened to their kin over the river. Maybe then, justice for the Winterwood could be met.

"Step aside, Lordling," came the Grand-Crusader's voice. She spun on her heel to see Berethan stride into the room, armor clanking. She watched wide-eyed as he approached the wheel and seized the handles on its sides with one hand. Behind him came four more Myrmidons, their capes sweeping behind them like crimson rivers.

"What are you doing?" she asked. Her answer came with the groan of wood and the grinding of metal. "You're opening the gates?"

He made no answer, only continued to turn the wheel, a vein in his head bulging as his jaw seized with the tremendous effort. Slowly, he wrested the gates from their perch. Feeling a thrill, Kasara rushed back to the window. Finally, the man had found a heart. Finally, he'd- Her breath escaped her in a shallow gasp.

Through the open gates of Farrenhall, the whole of the Myrmidons emptied themselves into the courtyard, spears and broadswords bristling to hammer back any meager progress the Vruskmen had obtained. It would end right here. Any pitiable chance the invaders might've had evaporated in that moment. She spun back on Berethan, but the fury now clawing up her throat would let nothing pass. It was hotter, deadlier, than anything she'd ever felt before.

Her sword—her real sword—came sliding from its scabbard with a deadly hiss.

Berethan took only a single step back from the wheel, drawing his broadsword from over his shoulder, holding it before him in both hands. In perfect unison, his followers bared their own steel, moving to join the Grand-Crusader in forming a half-circle around her. "Kasara," he said sharply, "don't make me do something I do not wish to do."

"Damn you," she snarled. "Damn you and whatever you and your bloodied god wants! How can you do this to them?" She thrust her sword at the window, then brought it swinging back around at the Myrmidon again. "How can you look at this and not help them?"

"I do only as your father commands, and it took me long enough to convince him to let me open the gates and deploy any reinforce—"

"Stop it!" She thundered, advancing on him. "I don't want to hear it anymore, Berethan. I'm tired of hearing you try to justify it. Just give the courtesy of an honest thought, aye? Tell me you don't care. Tell me what I know I see in those lifeless eyes of yours." Another step. "Tell me!"

The Myrmidon retreated again. Through the slits in his helm, his pale eyes had never seemed so cold. "What are you going to do?" he asked.

She hesitated, glancing down at her sword. She hadn't thought about it. What time was there to think? She knew what would happen if she tried to fight Berethan. Even while training, when he did not use his armor or his broadsword, she couldn't touch him. *But those people down there…they know they can't win either, aye?* And yet they fought. They died. *So be it.*

"Kasara," Berethan growled.

"You don't have to make me do this," she said quietly. There was that flicker in the knight's face again. What was making him hesitate? A single rush of blows, and she'd be dead. His duty would be fulfilled. And yet… "There's another way."

"I will not let them through," he growled.

Kasara's heart raced. The man had to have an opening, some gap in the armor of his philosophy. She had to find it and strike. "You don't have to, Berethan. Spare their lives. Call your men back inside." She took a step back, leaving the gate wheel clear. "You can close the Iron Gate behind them. A horde of farmers isn't getting through that, aye? This doesn't have to end in blood." She looked down at her sword and saw her own pale gray eye staring back. "For any of us."

"I will not go against my Faith Price."

"But you did it before," Kasara said. "You betrayed the orders you were given, didn't you?" To her surprise, the man's eyes dropped. Shame? She pressed her advantage as if with a plunging sword. "Did my father order you to send those men out there now?"

The moment of weakness passed. His eyes were on hers again, cast iron. "He has commanded me to defend Farrenhall."

"Which you can do from behind the gates, aye?" She had to keep pushing. If there was some fiber of advantage here, she had to seize it. "The Gated Bridge is not lost if we give up one courtyard. The attack took us by surprise. Pull back to regroup. It's a sound tactical solution, aye?" *Please, Berethan. Please.*

But the Myrmidon was unmoving. His followers had turned their heads, their eyes now locked upon their commander. "I cannot disobey my orders. You know this."

"I am not asking you to do that," she said back. Her every nerve felt ablaze, her muscles tensed. This would be the place she died, if he did not relent. She wouldn't back down. She couldn't. "This is a compromise, nothing more." Still, Berethan said nothing. Below them, men were dying. She was running out of time. "I know you don't want to kill me," she said softly, lowering her gaze. "I saw it, in the galley. This isn't what you want." She looked up again and met his eyes. "Please, Berethan. A compromise."

"A compromise," he repeated slowly. "Sir Joros, go to the gate and order the retreat. We withdraw behind the Iron Gate."

One of the other Myrmidons stepped forward. "Grand-Crusader," he began, notes of surprise in his icy voice, "we can't—"

"I have given you an order, Sir Joros," Berethan thundered, his voice loud enough to rattle the window. He seemed to grow before the other knights, a living tower of steel. "Carry it out."

Sir Joros gave his companions a wary look, and for a breathless moment, Kasara feared a confrontation would erupt between the zealots. But then the man turned and hurried from the room. The remaining three shifted restlessly, but said nothing.

Kasara hastened back to the window, where she waited nervously as the battle continued to rage. But then she heard the wail of a horn, and she watched in near disbelief as the Myrmidons broke away from their fight. With their backs to the gate, they slowly retreated the way they'd come. The Vruskmen followed them at a distance, hesitant to attack. Behind her, the wheel began to groan again, and as the Myrmidons were swallowed by Farrenhall, the Iron Gate sealed behind them, leaving the courtyard to her people.

Kasara exhaled, and a puff of fog briefly obscured the scene below. She leaned her head against the windowpane, finally letting exhaustion wrap its dark hands about her. "Thank you, Berethan," she whispered. When she turned back again, the Grand-Crusader was gone.

Chapter Fifteen
Ascension

The sky had turned a worrying shade of amber. Haegar walked along a line of exhausted men, trying not to show his own exhaustion lurking just beneath his flesh. Of the five hundred Vruskmen who had charged the gates of Farrenhall, three hundred now occupied the courtyard. Another thirty had been wounded beyond the ability to fight. The women, children and the elderly would come soon, then the Copper gate would be set back in place before nightfall. With any fortune, it would hold when the dead came again.

It will *hold*, Haegar thought as he walked. The price paid for the mere opportunity had been too high. An acrid stench made his stomach turn. He had experienced the smell of burning human flesh more than any man should. Another two hundred kinsmen denied the dignity of a proper burial—even if he had the hands, or the time, to tend to them, he couldn't risk what might crawl out of a shallow grave come nightfall. The bonfires now blazing beyond the courtyard were the only way.

And of those bodies now burning on the Tagalfr's shores, only eleven had been Myrmidons. *Only eleven.* It was almost incredible. Such a monumental effort to claim the courtyard, such a high price to pay, and they'd only killed eleven men. *How much blood will it cost us to cross the breadth of the bridge?* He had to get the inner gates open before he could worry about that. He looked up at Farrenhall's impassive stone face, looming over him, taller than any tree, tall as the sky, tall as—he made himself look down before vertigo made him collapse.

"We have bought ourselves time," he said loudly, his voice booming off the walls of the courtyard. His small army, even cramped as it was in tight ranks, filled nearly half of the space they'd won. The refugees beginning to pour through the breach would swiftly take up what remained. "At nightfall, we seal the Copper Gate. It will hold until morning." Or, he hoped it would. There was no guarantee. He had no time to spare. They'd have no choice but to close it, when the darkness came. Anyone still on the outside, anyone who couldn't fit... He took a breath, pushing the bleakness of it all from his mind.

"Tonight," he continued, "I will climb the face of Farrenhall and open the way. Rest, but stay alert. When the gate opens, we cross through, and we'll be on the other side before dawn. You won a great victory today. You have saved the lives of your families, your brethren. But we must not let ourselves be idle. When the Iron Gate opens, they will be waiting for us. And we will defeat them again." He looked across their bedraggled faces. All eyes were on him, fixated and desperate. He didn't recognize a single one of them; not any of the men who'd helped him organize yesterday, not anyone from Palvast. *Are they really all gone?* He couldn't let himself think about it. He had to keep them moving. "If the gate does not open, assume I am dead. Send someone else to climb. After that, assume the Myrmidons will have all entry points barred. You'll have to attempt to breach the gates."

"You." He pointed at a scrawny, older woman with her gray hair tied back in a bun. Despite her diminutive stature and wrinkled face, the exhaustion on her face did not reach those auburn eyes. The axe hanging from the loop of her belt was still smeared with blood. She must've snuck away from the refugees, joined the fighting ranks. "What's your name?"

The woman met his stare levelly. "Maega," she said softly.

"You're promoted," he said. "Gather as many men as you need and name them captains. See to it our people are brought inside before nightfall, and make whatever preparations are necessary before morning."

"Me?" Maega blinked. She met him with searching eyes, but he had no advice or specifics to offer her. He knew just as little about this as she did. He looked across the crowd. So many brave men. They didn't know his name—he didn't know theirs—and yet, they had fought for each other. Died for each other. "Why me, sir?"

He gave her a weary smile. "Because I see you have a strength about you. And that is what our people need." In truth, he'd chosen her because hers were the first eyes he'd met. What other metrics did he have to judge these people? He'd stay with them, if he could, but he'd never ask them to do what he was about to do, either.

He could feel the eyes of the Gated Bridge on his back as he made his way in the opposite direction, toward the battered outer gates. The Myrmidons had yet to attack them, as he'd feared they might, with arrows from the high windows. Were they waiting for something? Their retreat had been so sudden, too. Lord Varkoth must've called off their attack. He did not want to think about what might've happened had he not intervened. *The courtyard…its shelter is the smallest mercy he could offer us.* He still did not intend to show the man any mercy.

As woodsmen cut new spars to seal the Copper Gate, a steady stream of people was flowing through, watched over by archers who stood on the remains of the carts lining either side of the gates, providing a funnel through which the Vruskmen came through.

For a while, Haegar stood there, watching the people filter past to fill the courtyard, but he saw precious little, as his mind wandered aimlessly through the maze of strife and worry his thoughts had become. He could still feel that Myrmidon die beneath him, feel his axe bite through bone and flesh. He couldn't wrap his head around the pain he felt, smothering veils of shame that piled ever higher atop him the more he gave them thought. *I'm a killer.*

The man had brought his fate upon himself. Haegar had warned them all. He'd tried to bargain, to plead. He'd have done anything Varkoth wanted to avoid bloodshed, so long as his family made it through. *He probably never wanted this,* a quiet part of him whispered, speaking of the man he'd killed. *No more than a boy, really. He only stood in our way because he was made to. He didn't ask for this.* Haegar looked down at his axe, still hanging from his belt. The blade was clean; he'd wiped it free of blood before even tending to the gash on his cheek. He hadn't been able to stand the sight of it.

He made his fist close around the blade, biting as deep as he dared short of drawing blood. *Torvust didn't ask for this, either,* he told that voice. *Nor did Corvil. Or Garvim. Or Laklin.* They'd all been thrown into this, their lives uprooted, forced to flee or join those who hunted them. This was all Varkoth's fault. He had to remember that, even as he killed Myrmidons or Vruskmen on that bridge, or anyone else who stood in his way. And when he found Varkoth, when his hands squeezed around the old man's throat until he could feel his bones pop beneath his fingers, he would remember the dead.

His eyes finally found what he'd been subconsciously

looking for, and he jerked to attention with a sharp pull of air. In nearly the same instant, Tayja's eyes found him too. He threw himself into the crowd, fording through the people like a neck-high stream. Tayja cut her way toward him, Haza beside her, both leading the children along by their hands.

They met in the broad shadow of Farrenhall's bell tower far above, stretched across the length of the courtyard. He threw his arms around Tayja, unable to contain the sob of relief that escaped his lips. Her arms entwined around his back, and she squeezed him hard enough to make him gasp. Behind her, Haza smiled at him. Boil his blood, but when had the man become so frail? He looked gray as a late-winter salmon. Haegar felt twin thumps against his legs and pulled away from his wife to smile down at his children. He scooped them both up, one in each arm, and held them at his waist, grinning broadly.

Tayja flicked his nose. Haza's eyes widened.

"What did you do that for?" Makin demanded, only a half second ahead of Haegar himself.

"Because your father," came Tayja's stiff reply, "threw himself into a bloodied battle without so much as a *word* of goodbye, and I think it would be a touch unfair to slap him while he's holding you." She took a step toward him, and Haegar was suddenly explicitly aware of the fury burning in her pale eyes. "Have you gone mad?" she snarled. "How could you do that to me? To us?"

He tried to meet her gaze but could stand it no more than he could his hand on a burning pan. He looked to Haza instead, but that was only worse, somehow. There was no condemnation in his brother's stare, only a quiet understanding. Yes, quite worse.

"I'm sorry," he said. He kissed Rala's cheek. She snuggled up against him, one hand gripping his beard. He was painfully aware of the dried blood in his hair, so close to her little fingers. "I'm sorry," he said again.

"Did you kill them all?" Makin demanded, squinting up at Farrenhall. The sun had veiled half its face behind the tower of stone.

Haegar looked into his son's eyes. They were colder than he remembered. "Not yet," he said softly. Then he placed his children on the ground beside their mother, and looked to her and Haza. "Tomorrow, the way will be open. There will be another fight. You two stay with the children, no matter what, aye? But be near the front, and if the gates are open, get them through. Do you understand me? Get them through."

"You sound like you don't mean to be with us," Haza said slowly.

Haegar made himself nod. "There's no time to wait. I still have strength yet." Sleep felt like a distant memory, and before the battle it had felt like exhaustion would never leave him. Now, though, he just felt numb.

"And where," Tayja growled, "precisely, do you think you're going?"

"Up there." Without looking, he pointed toward Farrenhall. "The inner gates won't be breached. Not in time, anyway. I'll sneak inside and open them from within. Then we will cross through Farrenhall, no matter what it costs."

"There must be another way," Haza said softly, his eyes bulging as he traced the scope of the Gated Bridge.

"I'll come with you," Makin blurted.

"No," Tayja snatched the boy and his sister from his grip, dropping low and hugging them to her chest. She stared up at him. Why were her eyes so accusing? "That's enough, Haegar. Haven't you risked your life enough for one day? For one lifetime? Your place is here. With us."

He knelt with her and put a hand on her shoulder, another on Makin's. He pulled all three close. "I'm sorry," he whispered. "I must do this. For you."

"It doesn't have to be you," Tayja said.

"It has to be someone."

"It doesn't have to be *you*, Haegar!" She stared at him, teeth bared defiantly. Cradled between their arms, Rala started to cry.

His heart twisted. It turned to dust in his chest. She was right. He didn't have to do this. His place was here, with them. Why should he have to risk himself again? Why should he have to be the one to make the sacrifice? He hadn't wanted any of this. He hadn't asked for it. Burn his blood, but he'd wanted to just stay home!

And then he saw Torvust's face. The man was smiling at him. *"This is the right choice,"* he heard him whisper. Haegar understood. "I'm doing this for those who can't," he finally said. "They might've gone in my place, but now they can't. It is owed in blood."

"Damn your blood," Tayja snarled. Now both children were crying. "Don't go, Haegar."

There was a crushing weight where his heart had once been. Bloodied shit. When had it become so hard to look into her eyes? He kissed both his children tenderly, then placed his hand aside his wife's face, running a thumb lightly across her cheek to catch the tear that was falling. "I'll come back," he said. "I promise. Makin, be brave for me." The boy didn't look up at him, his face pinched and red as he buried it further in the crook of his mother's arm. "Rala, be strong." She nodded, her lip quivering, and she threw herself around his neck. Gently, he untangled her and placed her back into her mother's waiting hands. "Tayja. My love. I'll come back."

Tears flowed unhindered down her face now, but she still

managed to scowl at him. "Aye, sure as spring you will. Else I'll follow you into your grave and drag you back to Razzador screaming all the while." A smile appeared briefly through the anger, but it was quick to fade. "Do you hear me, Haegar Ruthborne?"

"Aye." He straightened, then looked to Haza. He hadn't even noticed the cane his brother had fashioned for himself. Even leaning against it, he still seemed to sway like a Winterwood sapling. "Haza, you remember what I asked of you?"

"I'll protect them," Haza said. His voice did not share the shakiness of his body. His eyes, haggard though they were, were steel. "You just do what needs doing. We'll be here waiting when you get back."

Haegar made himself nod. He found himself staring at his brother as if recognizing him for the first time. No, that wasn't quite it. He was seeing a man, not a brother. A man he hadn't known existed. "Just get them across that bridge, Haza. Do that, and…"

"And?"

He struggled to find the words. He knew he had to say something, something to undo the years of animosity that had lurked between the two of them. But a meager apology wouldn't be sufficient. There was no excuse he could make, no justification he could offer. But it *had* to be said, else he might not get another-

"Haegar." His brother's voice cut across his jumbled thoughts. Haza was looking at him, his face somewhere between bemusement and understanding. "You don't have to say anything more. I'll see you in the morning, yes?"

It was like a weight had been lifted from his shoulders. He exhaled gratefully and pulled Haza into an embrace, careful not to jostle his wound. "Aye," he said softly. "You will."

He let go, then, and looked at his family. Damn his blood, but he wanted to stay here. He wanted to be with them forever. But the light was fading, and Farrenhall called. "Don't let them watch," he said to Tayja, and then he made his way back into the crowd.

He knew their eyes followed him, though, all the way to the base of the Gated Bridge. He examined the face of the bridge with a worried frown, tracing its broad, sheer scale up toward the setting sun. He'd climbed more than enough rocks as a boy to be familiar with the sport. His father had never been able to follow him up some of those old quarry cliffs, much to his chagrin. Haza had never wanted to come, of course. And he was usually the one who ran to Father to tell the old man what Haegar was doing.

But this was nothing like those quarries. Farrenhall was immense, like a mountain tamed by man, wrought into shape. And he would have no rope to aid him, no companions in his climb. Only his own two hands, and an axe. The one he'd carried with him for so long, that he'd used to fell many a Winterwood, was gone, and the new one at his waist felt like an imposter. He was in no position to be picky, though.

He stood beside the inner gate now, feeling the ancient stonework with his fingertips. He gave an experimental leg-up, testing his footing on an outcropping of stone. There were plenty of handholds and uneven grips, at the least. It was just the sheer height that made his heart drop into his stomach.

There was no time to think about it.

He took a deep breath, then took his first step upwards. He quickly fell into a familiar rhythm. First one hand, then his opposite leg, and switch. It was a comfortable cycle, and Farrenhall proved to be an easier climb than he'd originally feared. Every step was surrendered freely to him, and he made a decent pace up the bridge's face.

There were hundreds of eyes on his back, but he dared not look back. The wind whipped all around him, cold and high, its influence seeming to grow with every inch he claimed. He clung to the stone like an insect caught in the Tagalfr's surf, helpless but to endure its wrath. *And to think those dark clouds ended up blowing away.* He ground his teeth and reached up for the next handhold. He'd hate to make such a climb in a storm.

He was able to swallow his apprehension, ignore the ache in his ankles and his fingers, and focus only on his destination above. He could see it, a broad window near the bridge's pinnacle. It had a narrow sill; he wasn't sure if he'd be able to stand on it. There was only one way to find out.

Slowly, inch by freezing, cramping inch, he gained ground. How long had it been? He didn't look down—he couldn't—but that window was creeping closer. Prying his hands free from their grips was a greater struggle than fighting that Myrmidon. Every time he raised a limb, he was sure it would be his last before he slipped free. His wife and children would watch him plummet to the ground, and with him would die any hope his people yet clung to. How many others would dare to follow him after he fell? If he couldn't make it, who could? He couldn't stop. Bloodied shit. He just couldn't.

And then, almost without realizing it, he found himself just beneath the sill of the window. He was parallel with the setting sun, and for a moment, he scowled at it. A part of him couldn't believe he was still alive, a distant, resonant pride. But another part was furious. *Too long. I'm taking too long. It's almost nightfall again.* Had they managed to reseal the Copper Gate? Were the dead already advancing? How many had made it inside?

Resisting the urge to seize the windowsill, he instead shuffled to one side and climbed up beside it, then tentatively reached out with a leg. While it felt marvelous to have one foot on level ground again, it was clear the sill was too narrow to perch on, especially as the glass would offer him nothing to hold onto.

So, with another gulp of air—curdled blood, but he hadn't realized how fast he was breathing—he braced his feet and leaned into his left hand, while the other came free and reached for his axe. It wobbled in his hand as he awkwardly wrested it free from its loop. His heart thrummed with panic; if he dropped it, he was finished. Somehow, he held on, even as he swung it out over the abyss below. When he brought it back, it pierced through the window, sending a spiderweb of cracks crawling across its surface. He winced at the sound and wrenched his axe free, jerking precariously with the exertion. Without hesitation, he swung again, and this time the window shattered inward in an explosion of glittering shards. He threw himself through the gap, landing heavily on his shoulder, yelping at the feel of broken glass beneath his flesh.

He scrambled upright, axe in hand, and had no time to relish the relief he felt to still be alive as he surveyed his surroundings. Were the walls of Farrenhall made of green stone? He'd never noticed it before, but as his eyes darted across columns decorated with colorful tapestries depicting unfamiliar scenes, the streams of gold and purple light pouring in behind him painted the room in a new light. It was oddly tranquil, and he could've stood there for an eternity, just breathing in the cold, life-giving air that filled the old keep.

Hope was redoubled when his eyes immediately fell on the gate wheel, standing right in front of him. It was little more than twin wheels flanking a spool of chain. He was relieved to see its simplicity; a part of him had feared it might take more than one man to use. But he could do this himself, he was now sure of it. Confidence was then flattened by the sound of rushing boots echoing from beyond the closed door at the end of the room, growing steadily louder.

With a quiet curse, his eyes leapt frantically across the room, searching for refuge. All he could see were the pillars, three on either side of the room. He scrambled for the closest one and ducked behind, just as the door was slammed open, bringing the sound of boots far too close.

Haegar kept low, his axe raised. Though it had been cleaned, memories of dried blood made his skin crawl. He wanted nothing more than to cast it aside and never lift it again. How many men were coming into the room? Three? Four? Too many.

"Another attack?" said a heavy voice. The all-too familiar clank of the Myrmidon's armor was now plain, rebounding off the walls. Through the sunlight, Haegar counted the shadows passing on the walls behind him, swallowed only when they passed by a pillar.

"They'd have to fling a projectile quite far to hit this window," came a second, rasping voice. "I'd wager a red mark that there's not a half-decent archer in the whole of that mangy rabble."

"Don't let zealotry blind you," said a third. This one Haegar recognized. The man who'd turned Haza away from the gates, Berethan, the one they called Grand-Crusader. He was the man who led the Myrmidons, who had put so many fine Vruskmen to the sword just hours ago. His blood began to boil. "That 'mangy rabble,' as you so delicately put it, Sir Joros," continued Berethan, "just routed our entire division." The man's broad shadow passed the edge of Haegar's pillar, vanishing for a moment, then appearing out the other side. Boots crunched on glass. "We must not underestimate them."

"Rout is an interesting word, Grand-Crusader," said the

other man, who Haegar thought must be Joros, "for a retreat you ordered."

The Myrmidons were silent for a moment. Haegar tried to shrink against the pillar, hoping he might melt into the stone. He couldn't take three men at once, especially armored as they were. *Bloodied shit.* He had to relax. He had no need to leave this room; he'd stay here until they left, then open the gate. As long as he stayed quiet, as long as those men didn't look around his pillar... *It was an arrow. Nothing more. Damn you, Berethan, it was nothing more!*

"I see no arrow," Berethan said, his deep voice making the pillar rumble. "No stone. No projectile of any kind."

"Perhaps it fell back?" suggested Joros.

"Perhaps." Armor clanked again. Berethan's shadow reemerged on the other side of Haegar's pillar, facing those of the other two men. "Someone has entered Farrenhall."

Boots shuffled on stone as the pair of shadows stirred. "You're certain, Grand-Crusader? That's quite a climb, even for a woodsman."

"Nothing for a desperate man," Berethan said coldly. "I should've stationed a watch here. This is my mistake. Sir Raegal, Sir Joros, fetch Sir Barrick and rouse the division. Alert the garrison, as well. I want the halls of this place scoured."

One of the shadows retreated without a word, and the door slammed shut again. Neither of the others moved. "And you, Grand Crusader?"

"Did I not give you an order, Sir Joros?"

"Is a knight no longer permitted a question?"

Haegar could hear his own blood pumping in the long silence that followed, before Berethan finally broke it. "I'll remain. Can you think of any likelier target for our enemies than the gates? It is fortunate we were nearby to hear the assault; the intruder can't be far. To your duty, now."

Haegar, breathing slowly through his teeth, let himself relax, if only a little. One man. He could kill one man. Berethan would turn his back to him, eventually. *I can kill just one more man.*

The shadow of Sir Joros stirred. "If you'll pardon a loose tongue, it seems you make many mistakes of late, Grand Crusader."

Berethan, however, was motionless. "You have something to say to me, Sir Joros? As they say, loose tongues lead to loose steps on the Highest Path."

"This rout," Joros said, his voice dropping to a low hush. "That's not how I saw it." He paused, but when no response came, continued. "As I see it, we were routing *them* when you ordered us to retreat. We could've finished this nonsense today. You let that girl tease you."

"The battle was finished," Berethan replied tonelessly. "That will be all, Sir Joros. Go about your assigned task."

But Joros did not retreat. Instead, he took a step forward. "We were *winning*, Sir Berethan. And now you let them sit in a stolen courtyard and pick at our gate like crows. You do not let us attack them. You do not let us push them back. Why? Because of you, the blood of our brothers lies in this foreign dirt unanswered."

"Blood is only lost by unbelievers." Now the Grand-Crusader sounded stern, a teacher launching into a tired and familiar lecture. "And where they die in thrashing darkness, our blood salts the mountain, our souls pave the eternal climb. Each death is a step toward our true destination, another stone offered to the God of—"

"Don't lecture *me*, Berethan," the other man snarled. He took another step forward. Was that the sound of a sword being drawn? Haegar could hear his blood thundering in his ears. If these two men killed each other, all the better, right? The winner would be weakened. Blood help him, all he had to do was endure until morning. *Please.*

"The God of the Highest Paths does not require blood sacrifices any longer," Joros went on, his anger ringing nakedly through the chamber. "You boast of wasted flesh. Eleven of our brothers are dead, and you denied us the opportunity to avenge them. This is worse than defeat, Grand-Crusader. You breached the Faith Price, and I mean for the Cardinals to hear—"

"It was commanded." Berethan's voice was like the crack of a whip. The man still hadn't seemed to move, but it was like his shadow grew, swelling to fill the room, seeping into every crack and nook until the light was swallowed.

Joros hesitated. "Lord Varkoth…?"

"He gave me the order before you arrived. The Lordling had nothing to do with it."

Another stretch of silence. Even as his heart pounded, Haegar's treacherous eyelids fell heavily over his eyes. How long had it been since he'd slept? Not since arriving on the beachhead. The silence was like a crooning lullaby. But he had to stay awake. He could sleep when he was dead.

"I apologize, Grand-Crusader," Joros said, inclining his head. "I spoke out of turn. Surely her groveling was just for your pleasure, then? I did not realize you had such a…cruel disposition." The heat of danger lingered on his tongue.

"You are forgiven," the other Myrmidon rumbled. "And dismissed."

With a second nod, the shadow of the shorter man stepped back, then turned and melted away, the door slamming in his wake. Haegar roused himself, hands sweating around the handle of his axe, eyes on the now solitary shadow of Berethan. One man. Just one man. *I can kill just one more man.* And this was the same zealot who'd turned Haza away from the gate. *Razzador will be better off without a monster like him walking her soil.* Why was he even trying to justify it? If killing him was the only way to set his family free, then he'd do it. Blood be damned, but he would.

Then he hesitated. What if he couldn't kill him? What if the sound of his ambush drew more Myrmidons? Besides, Berethan couldn't mean to guard the wheel himself—he would send for another of his underlings. Yes, the Grand-Crusader was too important for a task like this. He would step out of the room. Let the Myrmidons scour Farrenhall and find no intruder. Perhaps their guard would fall lax. Then he could open the gate without contest.

Yes, he should wait. But as Haegar lowered himself into a crouch, he had to shove a fist in his mouth to stop a yawn. There was still light coming through the window, but it was the last fitful sputters of a day extinguished. How many hours until dawn? He didn't dare close his eyes, not with Berethan separated from him by only a pillar of stone. He just had to wait. And he had to be strong.

It was fully dark when the clank of armor startled him. He wobbled on his aching knees, only then realizing that he'd been half dozing. The chamber was filled with torchlight now, harsher than the setting sun and nebulous, constantly flickering. Berethan's shadow, in contrast, was steady, yet now it moved, stalking across the chamber. Haegar glanced at the darkened window, where the emptiness of the night sky was visible beyond, clear and vacant, not one of the Seventeen Stars present. He couldn't hear anything from below. The dead had no doubt returned, but the Copper Gate should hold them. They'd managed to seal it properly, hadn't they? He wouldn't know until he was able to move.

His heart took up a frantic beat again when the chamber door opened and shut. Berethan's shadow was gone—he was alone, finally. After waiting several moments and hearing nothing from beyond the chamber, Haegar crept out from behind the pillar.

It felt good to be on his own legs again—he'd been crouching for hours now. Slowly, he padded across the room and made his way to the gate wheel. He didn't dare try to pull it; the sound would be heard even by the dead. But he did look it over, reassuring himself that he could have the gates open in a matter of minutes. He'd wait just a bit longer, to buy himself enough time to open the gates before resistance could arrive. Then, he'd already decided, he would remain here. The Myrmidons would surely rush to close them before all the refugees pass through. He had to hold the room for as long as he could, to ensure as many of them could make it into Farrenhall as possible. If he was strong enough, all of them would.

He already knew he wouldn't be rejoining his family below. This wouldn't be the kind of fight a man walked away from.

Don't you cry. You're too tired to cry. With his back to the closed door, Haegar seized the twin wheels in both hands and leaned his head forward, for a moment allowing the weight of exhaustion and pain, sorrow and anger, to crush him. The window was before him, a black door that seemed to draw in the torchlight. All men had to pass through such a door, in the end. There was no other side. No light to be found at its end. Just a final step. Haegar was ready, but he feared when he opened the Iron Gate, all his family would find was that same blackness. *I should've made more time for them.* He found himself going over every moment he'd spent in the Winterwood, hacking at trees or hunting game, or even just walking alone beneath the white-cloaked canopy. He should've been back home, instead. What did his work matter if all it meant now was that he'd lost time? *I'm so sorry. I should've seen this coming. I should've...*

There was nothing he could've done, of course, but he didn't let that stop his mind from devouring itself. Somehow, deep down, he knew this was all his fault. *And if I must die for it, maybe that's fair.* He shook his head. *No. I choose to die here.* It was a right denied to so many of his friends since this madness had begun. That wasn't so bad a fate, right? He was dying for his family, not for any nameless sins. For his family.

He put his strength against the wheel, and the Iron Gate's chains groaned as they began to turn.

"Hey!" The shout made him jump. "You. Vruskman. What are you doing?"

Haegar spun around, hand leaping to his axe. He hadn't heard the door open. Bloodied shit, but he hadn't heard it! He'd unhooked his weapon by the time he'd fully turned, except he didn't find himself staring up at a Myrmidon. A girl stood in the doorway. She stepped into the chamber, a look of annoyance on her face, but froze the moment she saw his axe. Or maybe it was the intensity she saw in his eyes. Her own widened. Why did she look like she was seeing a corpse?

It was then he realized he recognized her, too. Stout and pale, with short-cropped red hair and a dusting of freckles across her long, ruddy face, she looked like any girl from Palvast. And that's what he'd mistaken her for, even though she'd wielded a sword more fiercely than any man. That bloodied sword. He should've realized it then, what he realized now. In her fine gray dress worn beneath a shawl studded with patterns of swirling silver and flecks of moonstone, it was impossible to see her as anything but a noblewoman. Even the dark, gold-ornamented scabbard in which her sword hung was regal.

They stared at each other, Haegar with his axe half-raised, the girl with her gray eyes wide. They'd fought alongside each other. He could see bandages wrapped about her injured ankle, highlighted with blotches of crimson. But she was of the bridge. Whatever she'd done last night, he couldn't risk trusting her. And he couldn't wait any longer.

I'm sorry.

He rushed her, swinging his axe above his head. He'd at least make it quick. He reached her before she could turn and flee, his boots thundering off the marble floor tiles. But when he brought his blade down, it crashed against steel instead of flesh. The girl had not fled. She was still staring up at him with horrified eyes, but she'd drawn her sword in time to turn aside his axe.

He swung again. This time she retreated, leaping back with a sharp cry, her bandaged foot buckling beneath her. Haegar pressed his advantage, ignoring the furious tears in his eyes as he hacked at her. She blocked his swing again, but this time he sent her sword spinning from her grasp. His next blow cleaved only empty air, but now he'd backed her out into the hall, and she struck the opposite wall with a grunt. *I'm sorry.*

The axe struck steel again. Haegar cursed, leaping back. This time, the sword was not held by the girl, but had leapt out of the darkness of the hall. Berethan was there, his face like stone, his armor warping the torchlight into strange, glowing pools. The broadsword was nearly as tall as him.

Haegar backed into the gatehouse chamber, leaving the girl where she was against the wall. The Myrmidon followed him, sword still raised. His mind raced. His breaths came in panicked, frightened gulps. He was found. He had to get the gate open now. And to do that, he first had to kill the Myrmidon.

With a bellow, he threw himself at the man, axe raised. Instead of bringing his own sword up to block, Berethan dropped into a crouch, and before Haegar could react, he brought the blade back up in an arcing sweep, lopping the axe in half. Haegar was still following through with his swing, staring stupidly at the severed haft of wood in his hands, when something hard and heavy collided with his face.

He found himself on the ground, spitting blood on the tiles beneath him. The wooden handle went rolling away. A boot fell in front of him; the Myrmidon's shadow draped across him like a burial shroud. *No. Not yet.* The gate wasn't open. *The gate! I have to get to the gate!*

"Stop!" The girl's cry rang through the chamber. Other boots clambered all around her, and Haegar could see the armored feet of more Myrmidons flooding into the room, filing in alongside their leader. "You will not kill him," the girl snarled.

Berethan did not step away. Haegar tried to pull himself up, but his head was pounding. Why was his vision so groggy? *I have to reach the gate.* "This man tried to kill you, Lordling," the Myrmidon said. "That axe would've split your skull."

"You've relieved him of it, aye?" said the girl. "I will not have you strike down an unarmed man in Farrenhall."

"You ask much of me this day," Berethan growled softly.

"Think logically," she snapped back. "Shouldn't we question him about today's rebellion?"

Through the haze, Haegar looked up to see Berethan's brow slowly furrow. "What is there to ask? He is the man who breached the window, clearly. He is here to sabotage our defenses. I wouldn't have thought it possible to make such a climb, but you Vruskmen often surprise me with your...tenacity."

The girl stepped toward Berethan, seemingly fearless of the gigantic knight looming above her. "Well, you might be confident you've accounted for everything, but need I remind you that this man got past your defenses? There may be more. I want him questioned."

"It is better to kill him, Lordling."

"Did my father give you that order?"

Now Berethan's face darkened. "He did not."

"Then you won't do it." The girl folded her arms beneath her breasts. "Farrenhall has a stockades for just such a purpose, you know. Take him there."

"As you say, Lordling."

Haegar tried to crawl away, but something seized him beneath the shoulder and began to pull. He groaned and twisted about, but that just made his head spin. The last thing he saw before darkness took him was the girl's worried frown. The last thing he felt was naked terror.

The gate...

Chapter Sixteen
A Night Passes

With the evening came clouds, dark and full and heavy, and like great, grasping claws, they clambered over the deep orange sky, smothering it in shadow. The wind howled in whistling fury, driving sweeping blasts of cold across the shores of the Tagalfr, which thundered in ceaseless torment. Beyond that came the crackling of flames, billowing from the twin bonfires that stood just north of the road to Farrenhall, where the Vruskmen had piled the dead, both their own and the Myrmidons they'd slain. None who'd fallen in the battle would be rising tonight, but Haza feared their efforts to deny their enemy reinforcements would prove little more than a symbolic defiance. There was no knowing how many were still hidden behind the trees. They'd find out soon enough.

Standing on the wall, Haza could see everything. The shadowed trees. The frothing waters illuminated by the rising flames. Torches, sparkling like a thousand stars, revealed the great swathe of people who'd yet to pass through the gates of Farrenhall. There had to still be a thousand out there, all striving to reach the gap, pressing themselves up against the walls below. Behind him, the courtyard was a churning cauldron of noise, vicious and desperate, as men and women jostled each other and shouted, fighting to hold their coveted positions in the shelter of stone. The courtyard was packed to bursting, with people flooding up onto the parapets just to find room to stand. And yet more were still trying to come through.

As he stared on mutely, the already-weary fighters used their shields and makeshift siege engines to keep the crowd in order, barking angrily at anyone who tried to step out of line. He'd watched their consternation boil into fury as the hours darkened. Shouts had turned to shoving. Shoves had turned to blows with clubs and axe-handles. And still the crowd pushed. What choice did they have? Night had come to the Winterwood once more.

A fresh wave of cold blasted him, and he clamped his teeth together to keep them from chattering. The involuntary motion sent spasms of pain through his phantom arm. The wound itself just pulsed. Steady, yet faint, like a weakening heartbeat. He hadn't been able to find Conyr, or any other physicians. Besides, there were so many wounded now that any aid to be spared would be given to those who could still fight. It frightened him, but there was nothing to be done. No point in worrying about rot when he might not live long enough to die of it, right?

Where is he? He looked up at the dark face of Farrenhall again as snow began to fall, sudden and heavy in swirling flurries of white, sweeping past the wall and into the waiting, rumbling crowd. Farrenhall itself was lit along its sides by three lines of glowing windows, but they looked as distant as the Seventeen Stars. Haegar had vanished into the darkness long ago. He hadn't fallen; of that, Haza could be sure. He'd breached the Gated Bridge. But Haza had little hope that he was still alive, else the gate would already be open. What had happened to him? Was there even still a way inside? Urged by such fears, two other men had followed him, but both had fallen, one shattering his arm,

ANDREW WOOD

the other his neck. None had gone after them; the wind was too strong, the cliff too sheer.

Of course, there was little point in worrying about that, either. He might not live long enough to know Haegar's fate. *I would've gone in his place. I wouldn't have made him do such a climb. He should be here with his family.* It was his arm. His bloodied arm. That wolf had reduced him to a useless mouth. He had nothing to offer the world anymore, no way to protect his family. He watched the crowd, watched their torches flicker uncertainly, and shivered in despair. Hot tears rolled down his cheeks, but the kiss of the wind turned them into flashes of frost as he silently wept at his own uselessness.

Someone jostled him from behind. Like a leaping beast, pain was upon him. Haza cried out, doubling over, his fingers racing toward the stub of his shoulder, but stopping just short. He stood there, screaming, and the people around him backed away, some shouting at him, but the noise was all indistinct. The wave of agony did not pass. He sank to his knees, breathing raggedly as he suffered beneath that stabbing blade of pain. *Stop it, please! Please, make it stop!* He begged and wept and gnashed his teeth, but it did not show mercy.

Finally, ebbing away in furious pulses, the agony receded. Puffing his cheeks as he exhaled, he pulled himself back onto shaking feet, gripping the crenelations to keep from toppling over. It had not been the first time that day a bout of paralyzing pain had seized him. They were coming almost every hour now, and he could feel them steadily growing worse.

As gingerly as he dared, Haza reached over and gently lifted the corner of the dry bandage wrapped around the stump of his arm. The wind blasted a rank odor into his face as he saw bubbles of white pus rising from between stitches that crossed through flesh marbled red and black. His stomach turned as sickly streams of yellow began to ooze from the boils. Lightly, he let the bandage fall back into place, hiding the decay from view. *Neither of us are getting across that river, eh, brother?*

"Haza?" It was Tayja. She carried a small basket of food. From what he'd heard, there was plenty to go around, now that there were so many fewer mouths to feed. Rala clung to her hip, cradled between the crook of her elbow and her breast. Makin was at her side, his face despondent.

"Is something wrong?" she asked. She seemed to realize it was a foolish thing to ask the moment it left her lips, but he was still grateful for it. Behind her, Farrenhall loomed over them like a hideous gravestone, its black towers pointing toward the storm above. Her hair whipped about her dark face, unleashed by the wind, and the tear stains on her cheeks glinted plainly in the torchlight. Snow and embers danced together in the sky. Makin reached out his hands for a glowing speck, but it slipped between his fingers and was carried over the side of the wall.

"I'll be all right," he made himself say, smiling at his niece and nephew. Rala stared back at him with wide, dubious eyes. Makin just nodded stoically. "By this time tomorrow, we'll be safely on the other side of the river."

"You sound so certain," Tayja said, moving up beside him to the edge of the wall. She set Rala down and then began to distribute heels of bread from her basket. Her movements were gentle, but her eyes were sharp as steel, pinning him back against the battlements. "Why?"

Haza did his best not to glance down at the children. "Ah… Tayja, we must have faith in Haegar. He brought us safely this far, didn't he? He will see us through the morning." He felt like a hypocrite, but what else could he say? Gentle lies were what Haegar would want.

"No." The word, so soft, cut across the babbling all around

them like an axe. Tayja's face contorted before his eyes, collapsing in on itself. He'd never seen such a sudden, thorough birth of despair. "He's not coming back. We're not getting through."

He chewed his lip, then made himself chew his bread instead. He swallowed. Men had been driving their axes and rams into the Iron Gate all evening, working in short shifts to conserve their energy. Yet for all their battering, the gates had not so much as shuddered. It would not crack, not in one day. There was no getting through. *You promised him you'd protect them.*

"We'll just have to buy ourselves more time," he told her quietly. Beside her, Makin and Rala chewed fitfully, but Tayja's own bread sat untouched in her lap. Her hands were on their shoulders instead, gripped so tight that Rala whimpered. "Captain Maega has this all sorted. The Copper Gate will hold, when it's closed. We'll last until Haegar opens the way for us. He'll be waiting when we cross through. He *will* be, Tayja." And if not? He turned a shudder into a deep breath. If not, they'd have another day to decide what to do.

"We're not going to last until morning," Tayja suddenly bellowed, her voice like a strike to his face. Makin flinched while Rala started to cry. She went on, unhindered. "We barely endured the first night, and how many men have we lost since then? It's finished, Haza! Can't you see that? These walls won't protect anyone. Neither will our king, or our liege lord. We've been abandoned. And Haegar's dead. You let him go on that fool's errand, and now he's lost. We're all lost!" With that final scream, she sank into herself, back bent so far her head was in her lap, and began to sob. The Vruskmen on the wall stared. Some worried onlookers began to edge away, while others began to voice their own despair, a grim and self-indulgent dirge.

Beside her, her children hesitated. Makin, looking lost, slowly reached out a hand and placed it on her shoulder. Rala was still whimpering. "Where's Papa?" she asked, clinging to her mother's skirts. "When will Papa come back?"

Before he could form words of his own, Tayja's head snapped back up, her face a mask of ice, her eyes wide with a feverish light as if seized by sudden inspiration. "Haza, you have to think of something. You're our blood, aye? Protect us."

"I...I..." He felt about himself, as if he might find the solution in one of his coat pockets. He felt his pipe, bought so long ago in a place far from here. *If only I had stayed.* He felt one of his books, *Legends of Kama'Thrail,* the one he always tried to keep on him. It was his favorite, found in a rundown shop in the far west of Havasa. What use were all those stories he loved now? What could they do to help him here?

As he fumbled for an answer, Tayja's face twisted again. "Useless," she snarled. "I should've let Haegar throw you out the day you came crawling back into his life. You've ever been the lead stone drowning this family as it tries to swim!" She blinked, and the moment passed. Regret fermented in her eyes, but it was too late. Her children were staring, waiting.

"Ah," he said softly. "It finally comes to the surface, then." It had always been there, he knew. Only his father had welcomed him back, though Haza still did not understand why. The ache he felt in his heart, was it from what she'd said, or because, deep down, he agreed?

"Haza, I'm sorry," she blurted. She reached out a hand for his knee. "I spoke out of turn. I...I forgot myself. I'm sorry, I—"

"It's all right," he said. He scooted back from her seeking fingers, then stared up at the black sky overhead. Snow was still falling, crowning him in a swirling veil of white. "I've never had anything to offer you." *I should not have come back.* It wasn't just for the sake of his own life. If he had not returned, then maybe the last years of his family's lives would've been happy.

Unless the Lord of Farrenhall showed them mercy, there would be no escape. The folk of the Winterwood had been abandoned by their own, damned to perish on the shores of the Tagalfr, separated from safety by only a single bridge.

"We could swim across the river," he suggested in a half-hearted whisper. It would mean their deaths, most likely. Even if the ice floes didn't crush them, the disorienting current, the freezing waters would finish what was left. *It's not that wide of a river, is it?* The thought made him laugh. It was ridiculous. But the more he thought about it, the more reasonable it seemed to become. At the least, it was more passable than solid stone, right? Tayja was strong. The children were young. Maybe they could make it. Maybe it would be an easier way to die than in the jaws of a wolf. He shut his eyes, biting away tears, as he struggled to banish the image of Makin or Rala seized in those fangs. *Yes, it has to be easier.* He shook himself of such mad thoughts.

"Drown in the river?" Tayja demanded. Her anger had not been buried far, it seemed. "That's your plan?"

"I don't know what to do."

"Neither did Haegar," she said without looking up. "At least he did *something*."

"I'm not meant for this, Tayja." He could feel himself choking. He couldn't stop it. His arm burned. "I…I'm not s-strong enough. Not like him." He wouldn't be able to keep his promise. He couldn't be like his brother, like his father, or like any Ruthborne man who'd come before him. He was no protector, no fighter. He was just…Haza. Haza, the renegade. The runaway. The sniveling coward who'd abandoned his family to see the world, then come crawling back when he needed them. "He should be here, not me."

Tayja's silence was more agreement than any words could muster.

"Uncle," Makin said slowly. The boy had stood. His eyes glinted in the torchlight. "Is that them?" He pointed with one chubby finger, and as if beckoned by his words, screams began to rise from beyond the wall.

Haza struggled to his feet, gasping as the sudden movement greeted him with fresh stabs of agony. That was soon forgotten as he looked out across the battlements, past the restless crowd waiting to cross through the gates, and at the shadowed line where the Winterwood met the Tagalfr's shore. A line that was now starting to roil.

It was every nightmare he'd ever had, given shape. From between the trees they came, only their sheer shadow visible in the darkness as it caused the silhouette of the forest to change form. Hundreds of figures poured out of the Winterwood in a dark, silent mass, without the need of paths or torches to guide their way. Whatever phantom had bid them rise now drove them forward again, its banishment by daylight ended. With all its hungering fury, it stirred the dead to seek the living once more.

And the screaming. It curdled his blood. It turned his flesh to ice. The approach of the dead was inaudible beneath the dreadful choir of a thousand Vruskmen, who were only now beginning to grasp the reality of their fate. Mostly the elderly and the children, the wounded and the sick, now rose in a concerted mass. Abandoning animals and possessions, they rushed the gate. There was nothing standing between them and the dead save for an empty beach, one that was rapidly vanishing beneath that dark shape.

So fast, Haza thought, to his terror. Safe in his family's cart last night, he hadn't seen so much as a glimpse of the dead, only heard the fighting distantly on the edge of the camp. He'd never seen something so large move so quickly. With no defenders to bar their path, the dead had already crossed half the distance between the forest and the trapped Vruskmen.

He reached out for Tayja, ignoring her cry, and pulled her close. How he longed for his other hand to seize Makin and Rala, but he had to trust that to her. "Stay up here!" he bellowed. Voices all around them were shouting now, struggling to avoid being swallowed by the screams. "Don't leave the wall! There isn't enough room in the courtyard, and people are going to start pushing their way up here. We can't let them shove us over!"

Tayja looked down at the staggered crenelations, standing little more than waist high, and recognized just how perilously close to the edge they were. "What do we do, Haza?" she screamed. But he didn't wait to give her reply. He dashed past them, and her scream followed him as he cut through the crowd. He didn't look back.

He fought against a flood of people streaming past as he made for the stairs. Three times, he was jostled in the arm, but he ground his teeth and kept moving. As frantic shouts and cries reached a new fervor, he cast a glance into the courtyard below, and his heart twisted.

What had been an already overcrowded mob had transformed into a boiling sea of limbs. Screaming Vruskmen forced their way forward, pushing deeper into the courtyard. Aimless shapes shoved their way through and over anyone in their way. He watched people stumble and fall, or else be dragged down, where they vanished into the deep. Others were driven up against the walls, crushed by those forced up behind them, where they thrashed against the stone, helpless to get free again. At the gates, it was worse. Hundreds of people had rushed it, and they became entangled in its narrow confines. He had to stop near the top of the stairs, helpless but to watch in horror as they writhed and screamed, straining desperately to wriggle free. Some managed to climb over the mass and leap into the courtyard but others just became stuck, and the horrific pile of twisted limbs climbed ever higher.

Behind the mass, the rest of the crowd bunched up against itself, wedged between Farrenhall and those behind. Piercing howls rang through the night, but they were swallowed by the concerted uproar in the courtyard. The dead had reached the back of the crowd, Haza was sure of it. The Copper Gate still wasn't closed.

He made himself move. When he reached the bottom of the walls, a few dozen men had claimed the leftmost corner of the courtyard, using their wagons and axes to warn away the unarmed women and children who threatened to spill into them.

He couldn't believe what he was seeing. *What are we doing?* "Hey!" He made himself shout, straining to be heard over the cacophony. He waved with his remaining hand. "Hey!" To his surprise, through the chaos, the eyes of men found him, and he saw momentary relief dawn upon their faces. His missing arm made him recognizable as Haegar's brother; they were looking to him for authority. *I can't do this.* "Why are you holding them back? We need the space! We need to reach the Copper Gate and help them through!" He continued to shout as he ran into their midst, waving to be followed. Bodies bumped and jostled his stump. He could barely speak through his own screams. "Hurry! Clear the crowd and drive through. The rear flank *must* be protected!" They had to get outside, to hold back the dead long enough that the Copper Gate could close. It would mean their deaths, but the women and children would be safe.

Despite his determination, he could see what came next. It was already too late. *We were too slow, the courtyard too small.* The dead were hacking into their people as he spoke, and with every

Vruskman that fell, their grim army grew. *I made a promise.* He had to fight.

To his relief, and surprise, the armed men followed him, and they battered their axes against their shields, finally restoring a modicum of order to the swarming mob as men and women shied away from their blades. It was a slow march, and each timid step made his terror grow. His anger, too. Every second cost them lives. Every inch they took was matched by the dead outside of Farrenhall.

Somehow, finally, they reached the Copper Gate, where a mass of bodies was still entangled. Standing before it, he felt his blood evaporate, leaving veins cold and empty, as he watched fingers snap at flesh, eyes bulge and mouths gasp. It was a twisted, heaving pile of human flesh, wedged in the narrow confines of the gate's mouth. No matter how it writhed, it could not free itself, and any man who got too close was pulled into it by hands trying to claw for freedom.

How can we possibly get through that? Haza found himself breathing so fast he felt dizzy. How many of those crushed bodies were still living people? If they didn't get outside, they could never form a line against the dead. How else could they stop them from seizing Farrenhall? "We must..." he started. *We must...* But he couldn't even think of a solution, just stare at the bulging flesh, listen to the piercing screams.

The groan of wood made him jump. He turned to see his men rushing the gates, which a team had spent the better part of the day repairing for tonight. They'd seized the twin doors and were pushing them inward, to seal the opening.

"What are you doing?" Haza demanded, his voice a high shriek. He grabbed at one of the people at the door, hauling her back. It was Maega, the woman Haegar had put in command.

"You can't close it! We have to get outside! We have to push the dead back, and help everyone get inside!"

The woman just stared at him with wide, terrified eyes. "You think we're getting through *that*? You're looking at corpses, Haza. We have to close the gate, or they'll come for us next." She turned back to her men, who were now struggling to push the Copper Gate against those pinned within its mouth. "Close them off! Hurry, seal it, or we'll be next!"

His whole body went numb. Even pain was forgotten as he staggered back a pace, watching Maega lead more men and women from the watching crowd to rush the gates. From out of that tangled mass, hands reached out to push them back. For the onlookers in the courtyard, a hush finally descended as all eyes turned to watch. Outside, the screaming only intensified. Men bellowed and howled, while women wept and pleaded for someone to take their children. Cries from further out were less distinct and were growing steadily quieter as the dead came closer.

I have to do something. I have to stop this! But Haza just stood there. He just watched.

The force of Maega's crowd proved too strong, and the snarl of people could not hold them back. They screamed and cursed as those who'd so bravely defended them the night before now slammed the gate shut, shoving them back and barring them from sight. The moment the doors were closed, men came forward with dozens of planks of wood to brace it. The lock that had once been used to seal them had been shattered by their own attack earlier that day, so they'd cut new ones from the battering rams and hurried to get them in place. The gate groaned and shook as the trapped people beat against it, but their own kin held them at bay.

Haza turned slowly, putting his back to the screaming. He

looked out at a courtyard that was filled with people, many wedged shoulder-to-shoulder, leaving only a small place for the soldiers to operate with the gates. On the walls, some stared at the carnage beyond. Others stared right at him. What did Tayja think of him now? Makin and Rala? He began to laugh. *They're safe, Haegar. Damn by blood, but they're safe.*

Between giggles and hiccups, he slowly lowered himself down and sat cross-legged before the gate and watched its doors rattle. They continued to shake long after the screaming had stopped. And there he sat until dawn returned, bringing with it, at last, a heavy and matchless stillness. *Damn us all.*

Chapter Seventeen
Salvation

Haegar did not want to open his eyes. He wanted to stay where he was, swaddled in darkness until the end of his days. Maybe he was already dead. Or maybe he was just sleeping. Either way, he'd gladly run back into its embrace. It had to be better than whatever was waiting for him when he opened his eyes.

He groaned and rolled onto his back. The light seeping through his eyelids was too much, even when he squinted. His head was pounding, and felt stuffed with a thick, groggy cloud. He draped an arm over his face to try and banish the light, but his head made the quest to return to unconsciousness a vain one. For a moment, he didn't consider where he was or why. There was just that endless pounding.

What happened to…? The thought didn't need to finish. Haegar sat up with a startled, horrified gasp. He immediately regretted his overzealous movement as the pain in his head was redoubled, but he couldn't care. It all came flooding back to him. The battle in the courtyard. His perilous climb. The Myrmidons, and the girl who'd fought by his side in the snow. The girl he'd tried to kill. *The girl who spared my life. Why?*

There was no time to dwell on it. His family, his people,

stood on the edge of a cliff as night's deadly hours crept past. How long had he been sleeping?

He bolted to his feet, swinging his legs out over an unfamiliar cot, only to find himself facing a set of iron bars blocking the way forward. He was in a cell, encased by damp, dark green stone, with nothing but a cot and a wooden bucket tucked into one corner. There was a barred window behind him, overlooking the Tagalfr below, which glinted in the golden light of the rising sun. *Dawn?*

Panic seized him by the throat. How could it be dawn already? What had happened on the beachhead? Had the repaired gate managed to hold? Had they sent more climbers? If those had failed, too, then he'd ordered them to begin their assault on the Iron Gate, but he knew they'd never get through. He had to escape. He had to get back to the gatehouse. Haegar threw himself to his feet with a curse, but he made it no more than a single pace before he saw the figure seated on a chair outside his barred cell.

"Finally awake?" the girl asked. It was her, the girl with the sword. Who he'd tried to kill. She was regarding him with hooded eyes, her face marred by a grimace. She was undeniably Vrusk, from her sharp gray eyes, crimson hair, and skin white as the blanketed Winterwood, but the familiar features one might find in Palvast were distorted somewhat by her emerald fineries; a coat trimmed in silver, boots of elk-skin leather, and that sword sheathed at her side. "You're a heavy sleeper," she remarked.

Haegar tried to take another step, but the abrupt motion sent his head spinning, and he was forced to seat himself again, groaning as he did.

"Careful," the girl said, pursing her lips. "You took a nasty blow to the head. The Grand-Crusader can be a touch…

overzealous. Forgive me if I'm not entirely apologetic; you *were* trying to kill me."

He met her eyes. He felt no need to offer excuses, and he suspected she was not looking for one, anyway. He glanced at her right boot, where the top of her bandages were barely visible against her skin. "Are you badly injured?"

"I'll be well," came her soft reply. "It's nothing."

"Who are you?" he found himself asking. Even as he did, his body itched. He was wasting time. "I need you to let me out. I need you to tell me what's happening outside."

"Your people survived the night." Her eyes flickered, dropping away for a moment. "They are safe within the courtyard, for now. Those who were able to get inside, at least."

His heart sank. "The dead came again?" There had been some feeble hope that he'd been wrong, that the dead hadn't simply retreated with the dawn, but rather had all been destroyed that first night. *My family was already inside the courtyard. I made sure of it. They're safe.* They had to be. And they'd bought themselves another day to make it across the river. When he realized the girl had not replied to his first question, he took a deep breath and asked, "Who are you?"

She looked up at him. "I am Lady Kasara Varkoth. Though I insist you call me Kasara. We are past the formalities of—"

"You're the daughter of Lord Varkoth?" Haegar was on his feet again, his bellow shaking the hall. "You abandoned us!" Wrath unlike anything he'd ever known, that had been lurking unseen in his blood, boiled over. Everything else was forgotten. There was only his desire to wrap his fingers around this bitch's treacherous throat. "Why would you seal the gates? Why would you deny us passage? The blood of my people—*our* people— stains your hands, girl! You and your blood-damned father!"

Kasara only stared at him, her expression hollow. Her hands

were in her lap, fingers washing themselves ceaselessly. "I know it," she said quietly, her eyes locked on his. "And for my part, I am sorry. Words cannot express my sorrow. As for my father, I... I fear he's gone mad with terror. Something has been gnawing at his mind, forcing his hand into irrationality."

Haegar stood beside the bars now, longing for them to vanish so that he might wring her neck. He'd never felt such hatred for one person before. Here was the heir to Farrenhall, the one who could've ordered the gates to open at any time, the one who had stood aside and let death take the Winterwood. "You could've stopped him," he snarled.

"Maybe," she whispered. "Maybe I could've tried harder. Acted sooner. The Myrmidons are his enforcers, now, and he holds Farrenhall at the edge of their blade. My guardsmen deserted me. I cannot open the gates alone."

"I got all the way to the gatehouse," he growled. "I had to climb a cliff to reach it, but you could've walked right in. No one would've stopped you. My people were butchered like animals! We fought our own dead, girl! While our own kinsmen sat here, protected behind your walls, and turned away blind eyes as we died!" His voice resounded through the cramped cell, but as the world shook, the girl just sat there, refusing to look away.

"I did watch you die," Kasara said. "I was there. I didn't know what was going to happen. I left Farrenhall without my father's knowledge to speak with you. I didn't know if we were facing rebellion, or if you were fleeing from something. Before I even understood what was happening, I was caught up in the fighting." She shifted her bandaged leg, a spark of pain flashing across her youthful face. "I didn't leave until the battle was won. In truth, I was surprised to still be alive." She let out a single, dry chuckle. A frightened sound. "I fled back to Farrenhall, to my father, to tell him what had happened. I was sure that once he learned what we faced, he would let you pass. That he would realize his mistake. I was so certain." Her hands clenched into fists. "But…he knew. Damn my blood, but he already knew. He told me he would kill me if I intervened again. My own father…"

He knew? Even as Haegar stared down at her from behind the bars, burning in a river of fury, he felt the cold wind of shock. "What do you mean, 'he knew?' He knew what? That we were under attack? That the dead themselves walked our wood?"

"I think he knew everything," the girl whispered. "Even before winter came, I…I think he knew. Why else would he bring the Myrmidons here? The Old King…he must've ordered it. Whatever this is…whatever causes the dead to walk. They both knew of it. They both decided to let you die, rather than risk whatever it is crossing the river." Another shock as tears rolled down her face. Even her pale, pink lip quivered. "I think they meant to sacrifice you."

Haegar ran a hand through his hair as he stepped back. Curdle his blood, but Kasara was really little more than a girl. Sitting there in front of him, shaking softly, she looked no larger than Rala. What could a child be expected to do against a horde of Myrmidons? Against the Gated Bridge's garrison? Against her own lord father?

"I didn't know of it," the girl said, rising to her feet, her voice rising with her. "You have to believe me. I didn't know what he planned. I would've acted sooner. On my blood, I swear it."

He lowered himself back onto the cot as her voice rang around him. He buried his face in his hands. "I believe you," he murmured.

The girl's voice became a soft gasp. "Aye?"

"Aye." He lifted his head and spat to the side. "Damn my blood, but I do. You fought by our side." He nodded toward her leg. "It was your father who hid behind these walls, not you."

Maybe she could've done more. *But then, couldn't I?* Was Torvust dead because he'd failed to protect him, or because Kasara hadn't stopped her father, or because Varkoth had ordered the gates sealed? Or was it the Old King, for ordering him to do it? The dead, for rising at all? He was so tired of chasing blame, of seeking vengeance. He could feel that Myrmidon dying beneath his hands again, watch the light fade from his eyes. *He'd been no older than this girl.* "I…I just want to see my family to safety."

Kasara nodded blankly, still pulling and pushing on her fingers.

"Let me out," he said. "I'll go open the gate. We'll do whatever we must to get across. You won't have to do anything else, then. You'll be absolved."

"I…" she swallowed, "I can't do that. Even if I could trust you not to wrap your fingers around my throat, Master, ah…?"

"Haegar Ruthborne," he grunted, his temper starting to thrum again.

"Master Ruthborne," she continued hastily. "My father will skin us both alive if we cross him. Berethan has the gatehouse sealed. The Myrmidons will not let you through."

"Order them aside," he growled. "You're a Varkoth, aren't you? Get them to stand aside for just a moment, and I'll do the rest."

"Clearly you've never met a Myrmidon personally," the girl said, a strangely disappointed frown spanning her face, "if you think something as trivial as a name could sway them."

He shook his head. "This is all a waste of time. You have to let me go. What time is it now? How far past daybreak are we?"

"Daybreak?" Kasara's eyes widened slightly. "Haegar, we're well past afternoon. The sun is setting again, and…"

He rushed the iron bars and slammed his shoulder into the door. He rebounded with a heavy *thunk*, causing her to stumble to her feet, overturning her chair in her haste. The door did not budge. "Let me out!" He roared, beating his fist against the iron bars again. "Blood-damned bastard! Let me go. I have to get out!"

Kasara had a hand over her heart, her fist shaking uncertainly as she peered up at him. "Haegar, you have to understand. My father will kill us both. The Myrmidons, they—"

"I understand just fine," he snarled, throwing his weight against the door again. It stood unyielding. "You're a coward. My family is down there, trapped in that bloodied courtyard. The dead come at night, Kasara. That gate might not hold to see another dawn. They can't stay in there forever."

Kasara leaned over and righted her chair. Slowly, she sat back down in it. "I can't do anything more to help your family, and I'm sorry for it. Truly, I am." Tears slid down her cheeks, but her face remained ice. "The sin of House Varkoth will follow me the rest of my days. We will be known as deserters and cowards. Too afraid—or else too weak—to do anything but abandon our kinsfolk to their deaths."

He drew back, surprised by her lucidity. She *did* understand, he realized, exactly what was being done to the folk of the Winterwood. But a touch of pity on the face of a noble girl was little comfort. Haegar sagged back, his heart racing. If he'd really been unconscious for the whole day, then it was too late. Clearly, his men had failed to breach the Iron Gate, and with nightfall came another chance for the dead to penetrate the courtyard. And then it would be over. His family would die; hacked to pieces in the shadow of salvation. Likely, they thought him dead already. *Or maybe they think I abandoned them.* The thought crept up on him like a wave of nausea, and he felt the crushing weight of his failure redouble. They would never know what became of him, only that he'd failed. Beneath this deluge of thought, he sank back onto his cot, his anger fast deserting him.

Kasara continued to appraise him carefully. "But…while I have you here," she said, "I'd like to ask you some questions. You don't have to answer them, but everywhere else I've turned, I've found walls in my way. What you know might help save the rest of Vrusk. Help prevent what's happened here from happening anywhere else."

Why should I help them? The thought was bitter. He swallowed it. There was an intense curiosity in the girl's eyes. But if it was just curiosity he saw, morbid or otherwise, he never would've spoken again. It was something else that loosened his tongue, a spark of resolve, of fortitude. There was an unwavering intensity to Kasara Varkoth. *She knows what her father has done is wrong…and she wants to fix it. All by herself, if she must.* If the blood she'd shed on the shores of the Tagalfr weren't enough, he knew then that this girl was his ally. "What is it you want to know?"

"What gives rise to the dead?" she asked, scooting her chair forward. "Have you heard anything? Any whisper at all? I cannot wrap my head around it. They cannot rise from their graves on their own. Death is eternal. Permanent."

He grimaced. "Not anymore, it would seem." To hear Kasara try to rationalize it was like an itch on his psyche. Not once since the battle on the beachhead had he heard anyone from the Winterwood try to justify it, to give it reason. Even the whispers and rumors from the heart of the forest had vanished.

"Dark magic?" Kasara muttered to herself. "Once, I never would've believed it. But…I've seen them, of course, same as you. And I know men who believe in such things. Berethan, he—"

"The Myrmidon?" Haegar asked, arching an eyebrow.

"This could be the work of some forgotten god, perhaps,"

she went on. "They say magic used to be everywhere, once, long ago. They built cities in the skies, wrote books without need for quill or parchment, and wove new stars into the night at will. The light of the Helm-King, and the Holy Empire built upon his ancient precepts." She scratched her chin and frowned. "But the *dead*? I've never read about anything like it before. It's foul. Unholy."

Haegar watched the girl mutely. She seemed to notice and looked up sharply. "Surely there's someone behind this?" she pressed. "A sorcerer of old? Some priest of the God-Emperor? I wonder what he could want. To conquer the ancient lands of his kin? Vengeance, perhaps?"

"What does it matter?"

The girl frowned. "What do you mean? Why wouldn't it matter?"

He took a breath, but he couldn't keep his voice from quivering as emotion and fatigue reverberated from his heart. "Our people are dying," he said softly. "This thing...it kills everything it comes across. I've seen its eyes. Its hunger. I don't care what it wants. I don't care why it came. There's no bargaining with it, and there's no stopping it. That's why we have to get across the river."

"Don't you want to know the name of your persecutor?" Kasara demanded. "Why it's doing any of this? Understanding your enemies is the only way to defeat them, aye? I want to know everything I can to best prepare for it."

Haegar didn't bother to suppress his forceful snort. "You don't understand, do you? It doesn't matter. Knowing why this is happening won't change anything." He didn't know why, but that truth broke him. The tears came fast and heavy now. They could be gone, and he wouldn't know it. Tayja, Makin, Rala, Haza. All his friends, his family, his lineage. Dead. Gone. There one day, vanished in the next, destroyed without purpose, without reason. "What point is there in asking questions no one can answer, aye? We'll all be dead soon enough, once those monsters breach Farrenhall. Then I suppose we'll march with them, to wherever they're going. That's one way to get your answers, Kasara, but what good will they do you, once your name has been wiped out? Once there's nothing left of any of us?"

The girl paled beneath his tirade. Her glistening eyes fell. "Haegar, I understand this must be hard for you, but I must ask you to think. Is there anything you can recall that might help—?"

"No!" His voice was sharp as a thundercrack, causing her to start. "I've already told you; it doesn't matter! We're dead men already. It's here, at the gates of this wretched place, ravenous for more blood. My children might be *dead*, and you dare hold me here? You dare interrogate me as if I'm some scholar on the subject?" He rose to his feet as he shouted, unleashing all his fury, all his hate, into one stone-rattling rant. "I'm just another dead man, Lady Varkoth. It's what you'll be, too. All dead, all because the Old King and your blood-damned coward of a father abandoned us. Go ask him why we're dying and leave me to mourn my family in peace."

As his voice echoed into morose silence, he stood there, his body shaking. Tears trailed darkly down the front of his blood-stained coat, and he breathed hoarsely through his clenched, bared teeth. His fists, balled at his side, squeezed so tight he could hear his fingers crack.

Kasara was staring at him, still wide-eyed. Then, slowly, she stood and began to walk down the hall. Haegar drew a sharp, fearful breath. "Wait!" The girl looked back at him. He rushed to the bars again, seizing them, as if hoping he might pass through. He could barely form words through his sobs. "Please... Please,

Kasara… My family. Just bring them through…please find them. Nothing else m-matters. Please…"

The girl put a hand on the hilt of her sword, staring transfixed at its iron pommel as if it glowered back at her. "I will do what I can, Haegar Ruthborne," she said quietly. "I promise." The young lord turned again and was gone, swallowed by the darkness of Farrenhall.

Through the window, the sky was darkening. The torch upon the wall flickered, its faint crackle the only noise, other than his own quiet sobs. There was nothing left now. He'd failed. He'd never see his family again. He'd languish here, trapped in this cold, dark cell, until the gates of Farrenhall finally fell. The dead would find him again.

Maybe then he'd be reunited with his family once more.

It would be the longest night of his life, Haza already knew. There had been no burning today. The Winterwood survivors had remained sealed within Farrenhall's outer courtyard, switching between attempts to hammer down the indomitable Iron Gate and shoring up Copper with what remained of their carts and wagons. He hadn't brought himself to look over the wall. He already knew what he would see. They'd screamed and pounded on the gates, begging for entrance, for salvation, only for their voices to finally grow silent. The pounding, however, had not stopped. Only the rising sun had brought an end to it. The dead had grown quiet again, trapped just outside the Gated Bridge, this time locked out by their own kinsmen.

He hated himself for the slaughter. He hated himself for not stopping it. He hated himself for feeling such hatred for his kinsmen. They'd done what they needed to do to reach another day. Only that day was now fading into night, once more. The dead would come again, soon.

All around him, chaos had made its berth within the walls of the courtyard. The remnants of the camp had divided itself in two; the armed men who'd settled around the Iron Gate—some still worked in small teams with axes and hammers to try and batter through the steel—and all the rest. The unarmed, the wounded, the old, the mothers and children, were crowded between the walls and the Copper Gate. They were a silent group, most just sitting where they were, watching the soldiers work, knowing that if entry into Farrenhall was not achieved, they would be the first to die.

Though it was an unspoken rule, a general understanding had settled over the two groups that one would not trespass against the other. The armed men had claimed that piece of the courtyard that was farthest from harm, putting as many bodies between themselves and the coming horde as possible. It was a vain, petulant advantage. The Iron Gate was not going to fall. But what could the others do? Maega's men had axes and sickles. The rest had blankets and bandages.

Haza, however, a wounded, one-armed excuse for a Vruskman, found himself able to pass freely between the two parties. He wasn't entirely sure why. They all regarded him strangely, almost reverently. He was a Ruthborne, he heard them whisper. Haegar's brother. And the man who'd organized last night's resistance, saving those now sealed in the courtyard. The man who'd damned everyone still outside, though no one seemed to be talking about that. He hadn't given the order, in fact, he'd wanted to save them, but it still gnawed at him, like his stump gnawed at him, eroding his sanity second by second.

"We're not doing enough to shore up the Copper Gate," he found himself saying, and not for the first time. He'd been saying it since sun up, but the frequency of his requests to work harder and faster had only increased as the sun began its slow, final descent. Haza's anxieties were like nettles just beneath his skin.

"Do you think we have time to fight a losing battle?" Maega growled. The woman wore her graying hair in a tail behind her head. Sweat trickled down her forehead and soaked through the thin shirt she wore, despite the cold. Her coat was tied around her waist, tucked beneath her axehead. "You think those gates are going to last the night whatever we do, Haza?" She didn't bother lowering her voice. Frightened eyes from both parties watched them. "The only hope is forward. That's where I'll direct our strength."

He didn't bother glancing over his shoulder, to where the Copper Gate sat crooked and disheveled in its frame. Following the initial charge that had breached them, and an entire night enduring the pounding of both the living and the dead, the doors had been left splintered and cracked. Maega was right; they *wouldn't* endure tonight.

"We have to try," he growled. "We can't just leave our flank undefended."

"We?" Maega shook her head and walked away, moving back toward the inner gates. "What 'we' is there, Haza? Or do you mean to take up an axe yourself? The only way we're surviving tonight is if we get into Farrenhall. Put your shoulder up against that wreck and stand there all night, if you're so certain it will do any good."

He stalked after her, each step making his heart pound louder in his ears. "And what if we manage to break through? What then? The Myrmidons will be waiting for us on the other side. Do you really think you're getting past them?" He was speaking a bitter fear, but one he was becoming more convinced was an inevitable truth.

Maega paused, spinning back on him. "What would you have me do?" Now her voice dropped, a low and dangerous hiss. "Don't you think I know what's going to happen? We either push through and hope, or we sit here and die."

"Or we secure our rear," Haza countered. "We endure and hold out for Haegar. With more time, more rest, we can cut a path through Farrenhall to the other side."

"Haegar?" Maega frowned. For a moment, if only a moment, there was a flicker of sympathy on her face. "Your brother is dead, Ruthborne. I must do what I can for as many of our people as I can. If I could do more, I would." She turned again, and this time he did not follow. He stood there for a moment, watched as she joined a fresh team taking up position at the Iron Gate, relieving a ragged group with tired eyes. The ringing of metal on metal resumed.

He cast a glance upward. The sky overhead was pink, but its edges were slowly deepening into shadow. *Not much time left now. Do what I can for the people that I can.* Haza took one last look out across the courtyard, at the hundreds of eyes staring hopelessly back at him and bowed his head in shame. Then he hurried for the stairs leading up to the walls. If nothing else, he would protect his family. For Haegar.

The moment he reached the battlements, the pounding began. Screams followed just as quickly as the trapped refugees rushed to the outer gates, which had begun to shiver and moan as the onslaught from outside resumed. He dared not look over the wall himself. He did not need to see to know what was about to happen. He had to find his family.

But the crowd was a wall of its own. There were too many people atop them, all packed too tightly. He found himself struggling to push through a kicking, undulating throng, like he was trying to ford a river's current. People kept jostling him, sending lightning bolts of pain stabbing through his shoulder. He ground his teeth and kept moving forward. He had to find Tayja and the children.

That phantom pounding continued, rising above confused and frightened shouts. They'd never last until morning. Daylight would bring relief, an end to the attack, but he knew they'd never make it. The already-battered defenses of Farrenhall wouldn't stand.

Has any people faced death as certainly as us? He found himself panicking as he pushed on, his stump burning as he struggled. Then, as he was shoved toward the edge of the wall, he found himself looking out across the Tagalfr. Moonlight played on its frothing surface, and the Seventeen Stars glittered in the black sky. The rushing of the water, the ice floes grinding across its surface, it all seemed serene, somehow. A Razzador at peace.

It struck him that few were ever granted such a clear vision of their own deaths. Most went unknowingly, ripped from the face of Razzador before they even realized they'd reached the end. But not him. Not the men of the Winterwood. No, their deaths would come after hours of suffering. They had been fated to witness their deaths in full. They would lack no understanding when it finally came, save perhaps for one question. *Why?*

Haza bit the inside of his cheek, but it did nothing to stifle his tears. He let them fall without care, for he wasn't the only Vruskman weeping atop the wall. Shouts and screams rang through the night, while the dead beat on the gates as if they were war drums, sounding them forward.

Maybe in ten years, men would look back on the ruin of the Winterwood and nod their heads as they quietly discussed the tragedy of it all. Maybe they'd know why the dead had risen, and they'd know how to keep it from happening again. Or maybe

Farrenhall would be nothing more than the first warning for a soon-to-be-common enemy.

Will our sacrifice be worth it?

He watched the water. Clouds of shapeless mist chased each other across its churning surface. The reflection of the moon was an unstable one, constantly in flux, only coalescing for a heartbeat when a block of ice cruised across it. His fingers tightened on hard, craggy stone. This was too soon. He hadn't done all he'd wanted to do. He'd seen less than half of all he'd wanted to see. *I don't want to die.*

Crack! The sound of splintering timber rang sharply through the night. Haza whirled about, his stare dropping back into the courtyard. Screams and frightened shouts rose before him as the outermost gates wobbled. The central bar, replaced last night by the Vruskmen fighters, had split in two. The gate slid inward, only to be stopped by the carts and wagons—all with wheels stripped from them—that had been braced against it. People rushed forward, pressing up against the doors, pushing them back into place. Yet the dead on the other side came relentlessly, and the gate groaned as it was passed between the two forces, both equally desperate to gain control.

How long had it been since nightfall? An hour? They'd never last. *I* don't *want to die.* He turned back to watch the water, putting the screams from his mind. There was only the water below. The opposite shore was barely visible. Or perhaps that was only a line of distant fog. But it had to be empty of the terror shrieking below. The night was serene. Gentle. The waves were calling to him. Had they ever really been fearsome? A man could swim that distance, right? It was hardly long at all. And covered in coats as he was, what could the cold even do to him? Even a one-armed man could make that swim. Even a one-armed man. *Just a nice swim, and all else goes away…*

Something tugged at his tunic, but he swept it away. Nothing else mattered now. He would keep to himself and stay out of the crowd as much as he could. He'd witnessed just last night how easy it was to be crushed by a mob. He'd seen it before, too, in the riots he'd been unfortunate enough to be caught in as he'd traveled through the cities of Havasa, likely the same ones that had sent Tayja and so many others like her fleeing east. *I wonder if Joromor has crowds like this, too. How I'd love to finally see those mountains...*

The tugging persisted, so he turned to swat the offender, but froze when he saw Makin staring up at him. It was Haegar's face he saw, minus the beard and the perpetual sneer. His nephew had those same sky-blue eyes, the same fiery, crimson hair, and that same sturdiness that always promised stability. Safety. But the illusion of his brother was dashed by the terror stamped onto the young boy's face. "Uncle!" he cried breathlessly.

"Makin!" Heedless of the pain it caused him, Haza swept down and scooped his nephew into his remaining arm. Makin threw his arms about his neck and held tight. "Where is your mother?" Haza demanded. "Your sister?"

"I don't know!" Makin's wail made his heart wrench. "We... we got pulled apart! Everyone's shouting and screaming... Uncle, are we going to die?"

How he longed for a second arm to wrap around his nephew's back. Instead, he held the boy as tight as he could to his chest and blinked away his own tears. In the corner of his eye, the black waters of the Tagalfr thundered past. He drew a steadying breath. "Of course not. I promised to protect you, don't you remember? That's what I told you. Your father would skin me alive if I didn't do as I said."

Makin nodded in the crook of Haza's shoulder, where his face was buried. "I remember, Uncle."

"Good lad," Haza said. He turned, searching the crowded, bristling parapet again. The icy wind whipped at his back. Tayja had to be close by. She had to be. "Where did you last see your mother? Can you tell me? Is Rala still with her?"

Again, the boy nodded. "Over the gate, I think... Rala was crying. I tried to hold her hand, but...we were pushed apart. I couldn't see where they went. Uncle, I'm so scared..."

"I know," he soothed, but his whisper was nearly swallowed by the surrounding din. "I know," louder this time. "But it'll be well. Your father will be back soon, yes? Once that gate opens," he had to swallow, "then- then we'll be safe." *Over the gate... Where?* He couldn't see her, but even beneath the torches wielded by the crowd, they all seemed a shapeless mass. Below, the dead were still hammering their ceaseless dirge.

A great cheer suddenly swept through the crowd, a rising wind sweeping back from the inner gates. He spun in the direction of the commotion, and his breath froze in his chest. He was unable to move, clutching to his trembling nephew as if the boy were an anchor.

The Iron Gate of Farrenhall were swinging inward. Men began to rush for the opening, and that ragged, weary cheer became a roar of jubilation. Haza stared into the dark, widening mouth of the Gated Bridge, his own sagging in disbelief.

Did he do it? Did Haegar get them open? He couldn't believe it. After all this time, his brother was still alive. But why now? What had taken him so long? It didn't matter.

It was over. Salvation was at hand.

The crowd was like a single, surging beast. Before the gates had even fully opened, men were leaping through the gap, crawling and clambering over each other in their haste to escape into its maw. The people on the walls stirred too, their cries lighting up all around him, as they shifted and shuffled. With no swift way down, they were funneled in one direction, moving in a shambling line. Those bracing the outer gates down below abandoned their posts to flee, and the pounding of the dead suddenly grew louder, the groan of wood more pronounced.

"Hold on to me," Haza whispered in Makin's ear as he joined the slow-winding line. "We'll find your mother and your sister once we're inside. It's not far. Just hold on." It was half to himself he meant the words of comfort. His stump was a molten heart, thrumming thrice as fast as his other. *Hold on.* The Iron Gate was fully open now, and the cheering of the bedraggled survivors gave his heart a lightness he had not felt in an age.

Something silver flashed within the mouth of the opening. Haza stopped short, clutching his nephew tighter, as the first men of the Winterwood carried their torches through the gate, and illuminated what lay in wait within the darkness of Farrenhall.

Relief died as swiftly as it had come, as swiftly as the first hopeful survivors died upon the shining blades of the Myrmidons. As the first three heads pirouetted through the clear, dark sky, any trace of order disappeared.

The Myrmidons drove themselves into the crowd like a plunging spear, their armor and swords flashing in the torchlight as they began to cut a ruthless, bloody path through the startled Vruskmen. Those who still had their axes and shields tried to bring them to bear, but they were shoved forward by the women and men behind them, many of whom had yet to realize what was happening. Haza watched Maega as she was cut down, a plume like a crimson rainbow rising from her throat.

Unlike the Vruskmen's defense, the Myrmidons did not crumble before the rush of bodies, but instead put their broadswords to deadly, immaculate work. It was impossible to miss in such an ocean of flesh.

Those atop the walls went silent, watching helplessly as the massacre unfolded. Haza couldn't even breathe. He could only stare in stupefied, mute silence as the Myrmidons reaped a crimson harvest. Their counter charge plunged deep into the crowd of refugees, before fanning out to cut off any survivors from slipping around their rush. In the narrow confines of Farrenhall's throat, murder was done easily and efficiently, and the Myrmidons were soon to emerge into the courtyard, leaving fallen torches in their wake. Heads were lopped from shoulders, upraised arms were cloven from shouting men, and legs were cut out from beneath screaming women. And from behind the Myrmidons, that carpet of lifeless forms began to stir.

Men died gored on heavy blades. Some beat uselessly on armor now showered crimson, but the shining knights turned and cut them down without pause. Gradually, the screams of fear and terror began to wane, for there were too few throats remaining to continue the chorus.

Haza stared on. He couldn't feel anything anymore, not even his stump. He watched women hold their babies aloft, screaming and begging for those atop the walls to seize them. But no one could reach, and he felt nothing, anyway. He had no more fear to express, no more hope to lose. They were all going to die here together, the Vruskmen and the Myrmidons, all prey for the dead.

Before he could summon his next thought—whether it chased some vain hope or despair, he'd never be able to say—Farrenhall's Copper Gate began to groan. It changed sharply to a death rattle, a *crack!* that split the night. A wagon skidded backward and tipped over, spilling hay and barrels across the snow-dusted cobblestones. Through a large seam in the gates, which remained hampered only by the carts still jammed against it, he could see dark figures moving back and forth. Hands shot through the breach, grasping and clawing.

Haza turned his back to the slaughter, still gripping a silent, motionless Makin, but that could not shield him from the screaming, the wailing. The turbulent waters of the Tagalfr faced him again. Glaciers of ice cut through the rippling waves, while the wind made snow and mist dance in mad rivulets. Standing there, listening to the screams, staring down into the darkness, he felt…warm.

I will not let my nephew die on a Myrmidon's sword. It was a fierce thought, so fierce it startled himself. But he set his jaw and looked to the far side of the Rushing Ice. *Is the shore really so far away? That's it over there, isn't it?* A line of white, kissed by the moon and its seventeen companions. Empty. Safe. Surely he could reach it, if he let the current carry him in that direction? *I will not let him die in a wolf's jaw.* This would not be their end.

A dark shape rushing past him made him recoil, but the stranger threw himself over the side of the wall. He was not alone. One by one, Haza watched them drop. They fell for a breathtaking moment, suspended in the darkness between the hungry river and the bridge of death. Plumes of mist rose like smoke over where they vanished into the water, like lonely banners to watch their passing. He never saw them surface—the river's current was too fast was all. *They must've resurfaced on the other side of the bridge.* Yes, that was it.

With screams and cracking wood in his ears, he inched closer to the edge. His heart crashed against his ribs with such force it was a wonder it didn't break through. His stump burned with gnawing pain, but he hardly noticed it. Makin stirred in his grasp, face still nestled in the cradle of Haza's shoulder.

"Makin," he whispered, "it's going to be all right. We're going to swim to the other side. It's not so far. You don't have to do anything. Just hold on. Promise me you'll hold on, and we'll see our family on the other side, all right?"

"I don't want to go, Uncle," the boy whimpered.

"I know." *I should never have come back home.* Haza stepped onto the lowest part of the staggered crenelations. *Forgive me.* A breath. A step. Then terror. This was a mistake. A mistake! The wind became a roaring tempest around him, but he held to Makin. *The water, or the fangs of a wolf?* The boy was all that mattered. He could not let him suffer such a death. The water was better. In the water, at least, he could swim. He could see him safely to the shore. He only had to-

Razzador vanished.

He was spinning, he thought, but the world was black. The pain. Not pain from his arm, no, he'd been hit by something. A wall of ice? The pain was deep. The ice was inside of him, freezing slivers driven all the way to his marrow. Deeper and deeper he sank as he kicked and thrashed, struggling for traction, for ground, for anything.

The cold was spreading. Nothing else mattered to him, not the cold, not the dark, not the burning sensation now rising in his lungs. Which way was up? Why couldn't he find it? He was kicking, he was swimming, he- he wasn't holding Makin. Panic drove away all pain. Makin! He reached out. The boy had to be close. His eyes snapped open, but he saw nothing. The cold bit his eyes.

And then he broke the surface. Haza swallowed air with a gasping bellow. The stinging wind on his flesh only served to further blind him as he was spun about. He couldn't force himself to turn one way or the other, he was caught by the Tagalfr, tumbling like a snowflake on the wind. "Makin!" he screamed. "Makin, where are you?" All he could see were crashing waves, rising around him like swelling beasts that never managed to breach the water. For an instant, he saw a shape in the sky, decorated with shining lights. Farrenhall? How was it already so far away?

"Swim, Makin!" he bellowed. Surely the boy could hear him, could follow. "Listen to my voice! I'll lead you to the shore! Swim!"

Haza struck out, paddling with his legs, throwing out his remaining arm, but his head kept bobbing back beneath the water, as if something were drawing him downward. That pain in his chest; it was spreading. Had he broken something? Instinctively, he reached out with his missing hand, only to be rolled to one side. "Makin-!" he gasped through a mouthful of water. "Makin! Where are you?" He choked again. "Keep swimming, Makin! Keep swim—"

The Tagalfr pulled him down again. Haza fought with it, wrestling with the current, all while he was propelled helplessly through the dark. He might've considered that he could be dashed against a glacier at any moment, or worry that he might never draw another breath. He might've wondered why Makin didn't call back to him, or if he was still heading toward the right shore. But his mind no longer processed such thoughts. There was only one singular directive—swim.

And so, Haza swam, into darkness, into the cold, and away from the certain death that awaited him at Farrenhall. Wherever he was going now, it had to be better than there.

Chapter Eighteen
The Fruits of Faith

Framed against a shadowed sky and lit from beneath by the torchlight far below, Grand-Crusader Berethan looked like a god from one of the old stories, a figure of shadow and light, like the Helm-King or the God-Emperor himself. Shouts and strangled screams were rising in the night like smoke, a grim accompaniment to a god's bloody harvest. He carried his helmet under one hand, and the other lay draped across his sword. The moonlight glinted off spaulders of coiling red and silver.

Kasara was certain it was not fear she felt as she stepped up onto the roof of Farrenhall, facing the narrow path that led through the bell tower and out the other side, right to the bridge's precipice. It was not fear. Anything but that. But it *was* something, and she couldn't find the strength to name it.

At the end of that path, at the eclipse of stone and empty air, the Grand-Crusader stood. Why had he come here, of all places? She'd been certain she'd find him at the gatehouse, when she'd learned the Myrmidons were attacking yet again, but she'd only found the sour-faced Joros there, instead. Why the roof? No one ever came up here but the bellringers.

The serene, silent figure of Berethan was stained by the screams from below. They were dying, down there. Crushed between the sword and the shield. The dead would drive the living straight into the waiting blades of the Myrmidons. Every shriek, every cry that suddenly went silent, were razors on her soul. She might've been sick, had she not steeled her nerves long before braving the ladder up to the roof, where Joros had told her the lone knight would be waiting.

Steel's whisper was soft as a lover's kiss as she drew it from her sheathe. At its call, Berethan stirred. He cocked his head to one side but did not look away from the carnage below. "Lordling," he rasped. "You and I...we go in circles. I cannot continue to play games with you."

She didn't give him the chance to say anything else, nor to reach for either the blade hanging from his waist or the broadsword strapped to his back. In a blink, she'd crossed beneath the belltower and leveled her sword at the back of his neck, her labored breaths streaming from her mouth like pale clouds against the naked night. "Call off your Myrmidons," she commanded. "Do it. Or I'll kill you here and now."

"You don't believe you can." Tilted as his head was, only one of his eyes was on her, glimmering with a pale, almost eager flame.

She stepped closer, pressing the tip of her sword against his chainmail. This close, even with her ankle throbbing like it were aflame, she could kill him before he drew his blade. He had to know that, didn't he? He had to.

"Killing a man from behind is dishonorable," the man said in his usual, toneless rumble.

"You think I give a bloodied shit about honor?" she growled. Her breathing, light as it was, still caused the tip of her blade to clink against his armor. Every second she wasted cost more lives. *They trusted me.* The memory of Haegar's eyes bored into her, augers of fury cutting straight to the soul. "You accuse me of going in circles? We've been here before. I told you to call off your knights; killing these refugees was not ordered by my father."

Berethan finally turned, and she steadied herself, keeping the point of her blade at his throat. One of his hands still held his helm at his waist, and the other hung loose. She watched it from her peripheral like it were a viper. "New orders, Lordling," he said. "Not half an hour past, your father gave the command. The refugees are to be purged. I care little if these trespassers squat on Farrenhall's doorstep until the winter snows melt, but it seems that saboteur we captured has put Lord Varkoth's mind to terror. I...allowed myself to circumvent an exception in my previous orders to do as you wished. There can be no other interpretation of a command this direct." For a moment, he stared at her, his face marred by a sudden, unfamiliar frown. "I...am sorry. It is good to see a leader care for her people. In brighter days, they will be fortunate to have you."

Kasara turned her head and spat into the wind. "My father's blood can boil away. *You* still gave your men the order, Berethan. They butcher the helpless by *your* will, no matter how you might wish to cower behind my father's name. His hands might be red, but you are drenched in it. This is your choice." She paused, waiting for a reaction, for any flicker of guilt. She'd seen something in this man once. Something that might've been recognizable as compassion. It eluded her in the emptiness of his face, so she pressed her blade into his neck. "I'm going to give you something you've denied my people—a choice. Call off the attack or die."

Berethan glanced down the tip of her blade. A thin line of crimson was running down its length, leaking between the chainmail links, and though its sight revulsed her, she dared not pull it away. She would do it, if he forced her to. "Your hand does not tremble," he said. Then he met her eyes. "What will you do after you kill me? My knights will not listen to you, and you cannot persuade them all by the point of your blade. Do you think your father will allow you to rebel again?"

"My father is mad." How it seared her heart to say it, but she could no longer deny that the creature who wore Kalivaz Varkoth's face was not her father. That thing was as dead inside as any of the monsters on the shore. "After tonight, he will no longer rule as the Lord of Farrenhall. Your pact will rest in my hands, then."

"But you cannot kill him," Berethan replied, "else you would've done it before coming to me. The Faith Price would be nullified with his demise."

"Listen to me," Kasara snarled. With her bluff called, panic was swelling inside her, so she took a step forward, pressing on her sword. The Myrmidon was forced to step back, lest he be skewered, and now he teetered on the edge of Farrenhall, his back to the steep plummet. "You think I want to do this?" she demanded. She ignored the tears that stung her cheeks. The wind was a blistering whip, but she welcomed the lashing. She deserved pain on a night like this, where her people died and she would spill her own blood. *Not father. There has to be another way. There has to be a solution I'm not thinking of. Please, find another way. Please!* The screams of the dying made it easy to banish those thoughts. *"A leader must be hard."* It was her father's own words. *"They must make choices no one else can."*

She blinked away her tears. "I do not want to kill you." *Don't make me do this. Please.* She respected the man, and not just for the skill of his sword. He had a strength to him, and a faith she had never before witnessed. They could work together, if Berethan wanted. They could save her people together.

Staring up at him, meeting those cold, blank eyes, she could feel her resolve fracturing. Her ankle groaned beneath her weight, a pain that was nearly blinding. Her sword began to tremble. This man was going to kill her. Bjern was waiting for her, back below, him and a few more loyal garrison fighters, but they would fare no better than she would. *But I knew that was going to happen. I am…well with this, aren't I?* If nothing else, at least the people she'd failed would have their vengeance before this night was over. Her death would be just, for her failings. She would see how far this man's devotion could be pushed. And if that thing she'd thought she'd seen in him…if it weren't real, if Berethan did what she hoped he wouldn't, then she would know, in her last living second, at least. *Let your wretched God of the Highest Path entomb you so high on that bloodied mountain that no one will ever find you again.*

"Why haven't you killed your father?" Berethan asked.

"What?"

"You heard me," he said. "If you kill him, all resistance toward you evaporates. I will no longer be under obligation to stand in your way. While he lives, convincing me is the only chance you have to save your people, and you must know it to be no chance at all. So why haven't you killed him?"

Kasara wavered at the end of her sword, the leatherbound hilt slick in her grasp. *Why haven't you killed him?* Was it because his corpse might rise, another victim of the curse befouling the Winterwood? Was it because she was too scared? *No…*

"I can't," she managed to whisper.

"Why?"

"I…I love him."

"More than your own people?"

She blinked away hot tears. Damn Berethan. Damn her father, too. Damn them all for forcing this upon her. She hadn't asked for this responsibility. She'd been born into it. It wasn't fair.

None of this was fair. Why should she have to make such a terrible, terrible choice?

"I can't do it," she finally sobbed. "I...I just can't. I don't want to. I don't want to kill anyone. I want you to make the right choice, Berethan. Please."

And as she searched his eyes, she saw it. Hesitation. Not fear, though. This man was never afraid, she suspected. Berethan didn't blink, didn't so much as stir an inch of flesh, but she could see the flicker in his eyes. *How can I make you understand? Your faith has its limit, you told me yourself.* He had to see that this was wrong.

"Call off the attack," she said breathlessly. Did she have him? Was he going to help her? She'd been more than prepared to die. Maybe her corpse could've accomplished what she could not. "The gates will open and the survivors will be brought inside. Seal the entrance behind them, before the dead can follow."

"The dead?" Berethan asked incredulously. "You've said that before, and I am not certain I can bring myself to believe such a thing."

"What does it matter if you believe it?" she spat back. "My people will be slaughtered, regardless." Whether or not the Myrmidons accepted the truth didn't matter. She still had to save her people. She let her anger take her tongue. "And what a hypocrite you are, a zealot, of all people, to doubt something from beyond the creation of men?"

Berethan's eyes narrowed, but only slightly. "It does not matter. The refugees will not cooperate with us. Not after what happened today."

The man was wasting time. "You don't need to escort them in arm-in-arm," she growled. "Just stand aside and let them pass. My men and I will do the rest."

For a moment, a look of icy steel solidified on the man's face, and she was certain he would waver again. "I knew a girl, once," he said. "Ainara. She was like you. Fierce of will. Unflinching. I think...I think she would say to me the same things you have said." He closed his eyes.

"Is she why you broke your Faith Price?"

"No." The ghost of a frown tugged at the Myrmidon's face, vanishing as quickly as it came. "But she came to exist because I did. I will call off the attack. I..." he choked off, then took a deep breath. "Damn me..."

Kasara grimaced, and after considering only for a moment that the man might be tricking her, decided to find some faith of her own. She lowered her sword to one side. "Thank you," she said stiffly, unable to meet his eyes, suddenly. She could feel it, the Faith Price crumbling around her. She'd made him break something inside of himself, something that would never be fixed.

Yet time was still wasting. "After you bring the refugees inside, go and fetch my father. Bring him to the thoroughfare. I'll tell him his fate, then." She hesitated, her sword hanging at her side, as Berethan's hand rested on his hilt. Then he stepped past her, his crimson cape stretched out behind him like a banner. "Thank you, Berethan," she said again, quietly as he passed. Once more, he had chosen to listen to her over his own scruples. *Ainara. Who was she to you, Berethan? Why sacrifice your Faith Price for her? And for me?* She was grateful for it, of course, more grateful than she'd ever been. But she didn't think she'd ever understand it, fully.

"Your love for your father," Berethan said, his voice a low whisper, "it goes unnoticed. A tragedy." Then he vanished through the bell tower and across the roof, to the trapdoor that would take him back into the Gated Bridge. Kasara let herself breathe again, and she sheathed her sword. Gingerly, she edged herself toward the overlook, where embers danced in the sky like backward snow. She waited until the madness of it all ended. It was hard to follow in the dark and distance, but eventually the horns stopped blaring and the torches disappeared, and the Iron Grate protested as it was pulled shut. After that, she saw nothing distinct, only shifting shadows in the muddied light of the courtyard. At least some were still alive. *I should've done this sooner. I should've been stronger.*

The Myrmidons had withdrawn, she was sure, but there was no telling how many of her countrymen had survived. The courtyard was empty save for dozens of scattered, lifeless figures, but a shadow stretched back beyond the walls, past the beach and back into the Winterwood like a shroud, burying all.

She lingered still at the precipice, listening to the wind as its howl filled the void the battle had left, tugging at her cloak and hair. She watched dark clouds swallow the northernmost of the Seventeen Stars, promising another storm. She listened to the Tagalfr as it rumbled past. And then another sound, sharp and sudden; the cry of wood as the Copper Gate finally gave way with a splintering snap. She held her breath.

The dead came with nothing. No torches to light their way, no banners to mark their name or lines of battle to lay siege. She could almost believe they were survivors, staggering slowly toward the Iron Gate. They shambled through the courtyard, moving amongst the dead, who lay still in large swathes, slain because of her weakness. Why hadn't they risen yet? She'd seen men she'd battled with rise almost the moment they died, turning on their brothers before they even hit the ground. But not these. What was different What—?

She saw it then, high above the trees of the Winterwood, a large, floating ember drifting across leafless branches. But no ember had such a blood-red hue. Three flashes, *flicker, flicker, flicker,* and it vanished from the air. Then the dead stood up.

It happened soundlessly, all at once. In perfect unison, they rose, and the few invaders became many. Quietly, motionless, they now stood, once more filling the courtyard near its limit. The night was undisturbed by their rising; the water still churned, the wind still sang, and the dead did not breathe.

They looked up as one.

Kasara exhaled sharply, leaping back from the edge. The dead vanished from view. Her heart shuddered like the bells of Farrenhall, tolling terror. She could *feel* them all staring up at her. Not at Farrenhall, at *her.* Like searing heat, their stares had cut to the bone. In that stare, she felt their hatred. A hatred for all living things. Senseless. Meaningless. Terrifying.

They will do murder in this place tonight, she realized. It no longer felt like a possibility. They were *going* to get through. In that moment, she understood why her father had sealed the gates of Farrenhall. And she hated him all the more for it. *There must've been another way, Father. There had to be.*

She banished all thoughts of strange magic and unanswered questions. The dead would have to wait. Before she could see to the defense of Farrenhall, she had to unmake that which would destroy it from within. Maybe then she could see some of her people to the end of winter.

Though she was brimming with manic energy, equally restless and terrified to confront her father, she made herself walk with slow, measured steps, which her ankle thanked her for. Climbing down the ladder back into the bridge proper was a particular agony she didn't want to experience ever again.

"Bloodied shit," said Bjern as she reached the bottom. She turned to face him and half a dozen other members of the garrison, all in full armor, with swords at their waists and spears on their backs. "I thought we'd be burying you tonight, Kasara." He tried to smile confidently, but the way he ran his fingers through his hair betrayed his anxiety. "You're brave enough for the garrison in Savisdale."

Kasara hoped her own smile wasn't half so pusillanimous. "That went better than I dared hope. We must move quickly, now. Berethan recalled the Myrmidons, but he and his men are still free to roam our halls as they wish. There's no telling how my father will react to what we've done here tonight." She hoped fear of retribution would keep Berethan from revealing his own treachery, but she didn't dare try to correctly predict that man again. "The refugees are our first priority. I will secure my father. Bjern, relieve the Myrmidons of their escort of the men they were just butchering. Bring them to the great hall, and gather the garrison. Wait there for me; I will have need of your swords."

"Aye, my Lady." The guardsmen bobbed their heads and scattered down the hall. Except for Bjern, who lingered in the doorway, his fingers drumming an uncertain beat on the hilt of his sword. "Kasara?" he asked quietly. "A moment?"

"You have it," she said without hesitation.

He stepped closer to her. "What we're about to do tonight… are you certain?"

"We have to do it," she said with a nod. Curdle her blood, but it had to be done.

"That's not what I meant." Bjern scratched the bottom of his chin, where dark stubble clung on doggedly. He really was a handsome man. Not that she'd ever say it where he could hear, of course. "Is it what *you* want to do? There will be no going back from it. Perhaps, if there's another way…?"

She sighed softly. He was right, though she'd asked herself that same question far too many times. When the sun rose tomorrow, either Kalivaz Varkoth would no longer reign in

Farrenhall, or else she and everyone else who'd followed her would be at the bottom of the Tagalfr. "I have to thank you," she found herself saying, "for trusting me this far. I've asked much of you." If Berethan had killed her up on the roof, Bjern would have seen that he wouldn't have made it out of this room alive. Seven men against one, it would've been too much even for a Myrmidon. But she had no doubt Berethan would've taken some of them to that wretched mountain of his as he went.

Bjern said nothing. He didn't need to.

"Your loyalty tonight means a lot to me…" she said slowly, her eyes on the floor. Bloodied shit, a simple conversation like this should've been the easiest part of her night. Why did she still feel so much dread?

"Kasara, you have to know how sorry I am. I didn't know how you felt. I never meant to. Not just for…for kissing that girl. But the galley, too, when your father threatened your life. I should've protected you. I should've—"

"Hush." Her finger was on his lips, suddenly. His eyes widened, and so did hers. *Damn my blood. Why now, of all times?* "It doesn't matter anymore. Thank you, for helping me." She wouldn't blame him for standing down against Berethan, nor any of the other soldiers, not when she'd been forced to back down herself.

"Can I kiss you?" he asked sheepishly.

Kasara lowered her finger, then pulled him into an embrace. They held to each other, and for a moment, she could forget everything else. She could let herself remember petty jealousy, and petty love. It would be the last such moment. "When dawn breaks," she said softly as she pulled back, "come and find me. Maybe we'll see what happens then, aye?"

Bjern nodded stoically. "Aye."

She lowered her eyes, and all vestiges of warmth evaporated

in the cold air. "I have something to ask of you." This was the moment she'd been dreading. The question she could barely bring herself to ask. "It has to be done, like you said. But it can't be me." The tears came then, her words catching in her throat. "It can't. I'm sorry, I—"

"I'll do it," he said simply. "I'll kill him for you, if it comes to it." And it was at that moment she knew that he loved her. And she thought she might love him, too.

Kasara hastened through the darkened halls of the Gated Bridge, ignoring the sharp prickles of agony that came with every step of her injured foot. The armor she now wore did little to ease her passage, clanking loudly off the surrounding stone and weighing down tired shoulders and knees. She felt stronger in her armor, though. Taller, somehow. Prouder. The crest of Varkoth—a silver fish with long, flowing fins—was engraved over her left breast. The image also decorated the pommel of her sword.

The corridors ahead of her were steeped in shadow, despite the torches that flickered on the walls every few paces. She'd always thought Farrenhall was dark, especially as a little girl. The only windows were on the outermost hallways that overlooked the Tagalfr, leaving the rest of the bridge more like a cave than a true fortress. She could remember her father coming into her room at night, torch in hand, to chase away the shadows that lurked in its corners. They'd always come back, of course, but she'd slept soundly knowing he'd come and banish them again, if she called. That image in her mind almost seemed like a different man.

That is how I must think of him now. A different man. For her own sanity, she had to, no matter how it might bleed her soul.

It *was* a different man she sought now, and the dark,

twisting passages eventually led her to the abrupt end of a hallway, where a single window overlooked the night. Most of the cells that lined the walls were empty, black pits where no life ever dwelled, but one flickering torch hung by the window, shedding light on Farrenhall's lonely prisoner.

Haegar Ruthborne was the perfect picture of what came to mind when she thought of men of the Winterwood. All Vruskmen were strong and stocky, but there was a fierceness to the Winterwood's folk that the men of the bridge and greater Vrusk lacked. It was that same tenacity, that determination, that brought these hardened survivors into Farrenhall. Lesser men and women would've been swallowed long ago.

Though shadows surrounded him, Haegar sat upright in his cot, a hulking giant of a man with a long red beard and a mane of long, untamed hair. Gone were the tears she'd witnessed hours before. Proud, strong, unyielding—the Vruskman was all these things, even locked in a cell. Murder flashed in his sapphire eyes when he looked up at her footsteps.

"Is it time?" he rasped hoarsely. No doubt his weeping had left him raw. "Has your bastard of a father asked for my head already? Does he want to parade me about for his Myrmidon dogs before he gives me to the dead?"

She stepped up to his cell quietly. She couldn't imagine the grief he must feel. When she'd lost her mother, it had nearly broken her. It *had* broken her father. But losing one's entire family? His home, everything he'd ever known? She could not understand. She dared not. *Was I quick enough to save them?*

"It's done," she found herself saying. The nervous flutter in her voice made her pause to swallow.

"What's done?" the Vruskman growled.

"Kalivaz Varkoth has been deposed." Her words echoed starkly through the vacant hall. "Well, mostly." She had to swallow again. *Boil my blood, hold yourself together.* "There's still a few, ah, final arrangements to be made. But within the hour, I will be Lord of Farrenhall. The garrison is loyal to me; the Myrmidons will not be required to enforce my father's madness."

Haegar stared at her, his eyes weighing her words. The man was like a beast whose cage had just vanished. She knew he could be coaxed back into the light. But would he still bite? "Did you put that bastard's head on a spear?"

She shuddered at that. "No...but I've opened the gates of Farrenhall. There was ferocious fighting, but it's over now. Your people are inside. They're safe." *Only what's left of them,* said a small voice. *You weren't fast enough. The blood of his family may be on your hands.*

Haegar studied her with suspicious eyes, his frown thin and disbelieving. But then, slowly, a light began to flicker, one she thought might've been absent for a long time. Hope. Taut as a drawn bowstring, the man slowly rose from his cot. "You...you're not trying to trick me, aye?"

She flushed angrily at the notion but kept her voice calm. "Your people are safe now, I promise you. There will be no more innocent blood shed tonight, nor any other night. You have my word."

"My family?" the man demanded, stalking toward the bars of his cell. "You saw them? Did they come through?"

"I...I don't know your family," she admitted. "I cannot say. Nor will I. All I can promise you is that the survivors are through, and I mean to escort them to the other side of the river. You'll be welcome to join them, of course. To...see for yourself." She took a calming breath. "I'm going to let you out now, Haegar. You've done nothing to make yourself an enemy of the Gated Bridge. We failed you."

She produced the key, but as she raised it toward the lock,

panic flashed through her mind, the shape of an axe falling toward her face. This man was still dangerous. He blamed her for what had happened to the Winterwood, and no matter how justified that might be, she couldn't do anything more for them if he killed her right here. But as she met his tired, grief-burdened eyes, she no longer saw that burning fury. The hope was still there, no matter how vain. She thrust the key into the door and turned the lock, swinging it outward before extending her hand to let him step out into the hall.

The hulking Vruskman emerged quietly from his cell. Kasara refused to brace herself. He turned his head and met her eyes. "My people. Where are they?"

"The thoroughfare," she replied, turning to face the dark length of the hall. "It leads right through the heart of the bridge. It passes the great hall, where the Lord of Farrenhall sits in times of mediation or trouble. I've summoned my father there; he will see the faces of those he abandoned. If your family lives, that is where they'll be. Come."

She stepped ahead of the man, but he was quick to fall into place alongside her. Though he matched her stride, she could feel his apprehension like jellied air, his ache to race ahead and find his family. She tried to hasten her own steps, but her ankle's angry flashes kept her hobbled.

Haegar remained silent as she led him through the gullet of the Gated Bridge, his eyes straight ahead, gaping into the beyond. She wasn't certain what he was going to do, whether he found his family or not. How many refugees were still alive? Enough to take the bridge, if they wished it? There was the matter of the dead, too. They'd reached the Iron Gate, but those had withheld the armies of the God-Emperor himself in days long past. They could hold against anything. *But that wasn't true, was it? The God-Emperor never reached Farrenhall.*

She could trust the gates to hold a while longer, though. She was sure of that. Pushing aside that problem for now, she focused on what she was rushing toward. Her father. How would he respond to her coup? The Myrmidons would still follow his orders, whatever he decided to do. That was why she needed to gather as many people for this confrontation as she could, smother any chance he might see violence as an escape.

Kasara chewed her lip. Once, she might've been able to guess what Kalivaz Varkoth might do. But the stranger who wore his face was beyond her understanding. She didn't know what would happen next, but she was finished with hiding. She was finished with failure.

After tonight, everything would be well. By word or sword, it would be well.

A gentle flurry of snow was sent rising from the flagstones as Malice settled upon the ground. Their eyelids were heavy—it would've been a wonder to let them slide shut, to stay closed forever. To rest. But there was no rest for Malice. No rest until it was done. Daylight would come soon. Then they would be forced away again, forced away by its burning eye.

But there still time yet. Still so much work to do. Malice leaned against their cane, panting for breath. Silent eyes were on their back, thousands of eyes. Man, beast, bird and insect, all gathered in perfect silence. They paid them no mind, of course. After all, they were their own eyes.

Malice bent forward, using one hand to keep themselves aloft, the other to cover their mouth as they gave a wracking cough. They stared into their palm when they were done, frowning at the black blood that now stained bone-white flesh. *So much time has passed.* Their overlong nails spilled from them in yellow spirals, trailing lightly across the ground. "No rest," they reminded themselves in a rasping voice. No rest until their long-awaited vengeance was finally satisfied.

With effort, they raised their head and found themselves staring up at a pair of iron doors. The figures of men adorned them, clad in armor, faceless. Men. Rage was a crimson storm in their chest. It pulsed beneath their flesh, sent their bones quivering. Rage was all they knew. All they remembered. That, and their unending hate.

They were compelled to march on, compelled by magics so ancient they did not recall their names. But now that they'd been awakened, called from beyond the night by a power they could no longer name, they would turn their wrath upon the living. Extinction. That was all mankind deserved.

Stone and steel would not stop them, no more than flesh and bone. Malice raised their hand before the gate, and as a blinding red light split the night before them, they resumed their inevitable march.

Chapter Nineteen
The Crossing

Haegar's thoughts were like a plume of whirling snow, caught and spinning on endless winds. He couldn't have rightly put a name to his emotions as he followed Kasara through winding, unfamiliar halls. It wasn't precisely guilt, nor was it relief. Not terror. Not doubt. But, somehow, a mingling that stirred into something nameless and foreign. It wouldn't coalesce until he reached the thoroughfare. Not until he knew whether his family still lived.

I must not surrender to despair. Not now. One way or another, this nightmare was finally over. It was the only thing he could know for certain, assuming this girl spoke the truth. *And…I believe I trust her.* He made his steps more certain, eager, but Kasara was limping lightly on her wounded leg, so he measured himself and focused on his breaths instead. Calm. Deep. The gates of Farrenhall had finally opened, and not too late. The survivors had come through.

Survivors. That word tolled like a hollow bell. *How many did I fail to save? Who?* He saw Torvust and Corvil. Bofor and Laklin. Conyr, Sorvak, Garvim, Magda… So many. Nearly every soul he'd ever known. Hundreds of strangers, all following him into the grave.

Who else? Who was next? How many more would be taken from him?

For a moment, he could see it. He saw the gates of the courtyard, breached yet again. The dead clawing their way inward, swarming across his brothers and sisters, devouring them where they stood. Tayja took the children and tried to run, but there was nowhere left to go. Haza would die first, weakened as he was, dragged down so the dead could finish what the wolf had started. And when the dead cornered them, Tayja would put herself between them and her children. But it wouldn't matter. He could see Makin and Rala, their faces blue masks of death, shambling alongside everyone else who'd been butchered by this relentless evil. He saw them reach stiffened hands out toward him, their eyes now home to a blazing malice. They seized him, and–

Stop. The command was so forceful it made him stumble.

Kasara stopped too, looking back at him with a worried frown. "What's wrong? The thoroughfare is just ahead."

Haegar was panting, his hands on his knees. Bloodied shit, his head was swimming. "Just…a moment," he managed to rasp. He gulped air as if he'd just swum the length of the Tagalfr. Try as he might, though, he couldn't banish those thoughts. His children, his wife and brother, slaughtered, then twisted into a foul mockery of the people they'd once been, puppeted by something he feared no man was able to understand. *After all this…will I be the only one from Palvast to survive?* He could see himself now, standing alone on the other side of the shore, far from home, bereft of friend or family. It was a fate worse than any death.

It was there, bent over double and nearly gasping, that he somberly realized that if his family had not entered Farrenhall safely, he would not be living through the night.

"I can take you to see the physician, if you need?" Kasara asked. She was dancing anxiously from one foot to the next and casting glances down the hall ahead.

He made himself straighten. His epiphany had brought him a strange, quiet clarity. "Just take me to my people." *Then we'll see what happens next.*

Kasara eyed him again, but their journey resumed. They soon came to a stairway descending into darkness, but he did not hesitate again while stepping into the unknown. He kept his thoughts clear, focused on the stones in front of him. By keeping his eyes ahead, forcing them to take note of every crack in the ancient stonework, every seam beneath his feet, he staved off darker thoughts.

Just breathe. Keep going. A few more steps, and it will all be over. One way or another, there will be rest. Boil his blood, but he was so tired.

The stairway then gave out, opening into a long, vast cavern. He was quick to recognize the large cobblestones that composed the surface of the bridge, forming Farrenhall's lowest floor. For the first time since he'd met Tayja, a lifetime ago, he looked upon the heart of the Gated Bridge, the road that joined the two halves of Vrusk together. Come spring, it would be packed with wagons and bleating livestock and chattering Vruskmen again. They would crowd the road to overflowing, transforming it into a river of people that passed from one end of Vrusk to the next. Everything would be as it should.

But now, the road was empty. Pairs of stone pillars marched up and down its length, holding aloft a stone roof some twenty feet overhead. At their pinnacles hung bowls of flame, caged by bronze bars. These were inefficient to light the road, and he imagined torches carried by hundreds of merchants were needed to banish the broad swathes of empty shadow that lurked between the pillars. Their footsteps echoed sharply up and down and then back again as they stepped onto it.

"Quite dreary, I've always thought," Kasara murmured. Though her voice was soft, the echo of the cavern made it rebound. "I wish there were windows, but there are tunnels and rooms all along its length, as you'll soon see. And there's nothing below but the Rushing Ice."

Before he could ask her to hurry, the sound of echoing footsteps suddenly struck him as far too many to be spawned by just the two of them. Glancing over his shoulder, he saw torches bobbing in the darkness. A dozen men and women filtered out of the shadows, all clad in gray, unornamented armor and armed with swords and spears. The garrison?

"We've swept the upper levels," said one of the soldiers, a boy with long blonde hair and the makings of a beard clinging to the underside of his chin. "The staff has been ordered to evacuate. All who are going to leave are gone."

"None were willing to fight?" Kasara asked, that stern look on her face wavering just a hair.

The boy just shook his head. "The rest are still ahead, with the refugees, just like you ordered. Lord Vark—Ah, your father has yet to arrive, my Lady. The Myrmidons are bringing him."

"Evacuate?" Haegar asked. "You're abandoning Farrenhall?"

She nodded, clenching her jaw. "The Iron Gate might stand for now, but this place has been cursed. I cannot bear it another minute. We will seal the western gates in our wake, and return with armies strong enough to purge the Winterwood of the dead."

Kasara frowned at her feet for a moment, her features contorted by uncertainty. Then she started forward again. Haegar moved with her, not missing a step, while the guardsmen scrambled to fall into line behind her.

"I do not know what my father will do," she said, her voice bouncing loudly off the walls. "The Myrmidons will follow his command, so long as he lives, but I think I can convince Berethan to step aside. If not…" she paused, and the only sounds were their own echoing footsteps. "Once the Lord of Farrenhall is gone, the Myrmidons will no longer have reason to fight."

"We will follow you, My Lady," said the boy. "Whatever comes next. To the last."

"You'll wait for my signal, Bjern," she said. "I…I want to talk to him first. I want to be certain. You won't do anything unless I command it."

The young soldier nodded. "Your command, My Lady."

Haegar found himself regarding Kasara Varkoth in a different light. He knew she was brave, but to be willing to kill her own father? He wouldn't have been able to do such a thing, no matter his father's sins. But Kasara seemed determined to correct what had gone so terribly wrong in Farrenhall, heavy price or no. His hand itched for his axe. He'd help her if he could. Maybe he could spare her from having to pay that price herself.

He feared war was brewing between the Myrmidons and the garrison. When the line was drawn, how many men would side with Lord Varkoth over his daughter? So many men had stood by as Vruskmen were slaughtered on their doorstep. None of the guardsmen were looking at him. That boy close to Kasara even ducked his head away when he tried to meet his eye. Why should Haegar believe they would stand for him now? Because one girl dared defy her father?

None of it mattered, he supposed, so long as his family wasn't caught in the middle of the conflict. *They're still alive, blood be damned. I won't believe anything else.* He just had to get them and move forward. This road would lead him all the way to the other side of the Tagalfr, and into safety beyond. They just had to reach its end.

The marching of men, the echo of footsteps, all seemed to vanish when lights appeared ahead in the gloom, soon revealing the shape of a group clustered on the thoroughfare. At first, he didn't recognize it. He had to stop, and this time, Kasara and her men didn't wait with him. But he couldn't move. A numb horror had frozen his marrow. The crowd was small, much too small. *This…this is all who survived?* There couldn't be more than a hundred left.

How could this have happened? How could this be all that remained? When he'd left, even after all the fighting, there'd been so many. His climb had amounted to nothing. Kasara had been too late. They'd all failed the people of the Winterwood.

And of the thousands who'd fled to Farrenhall in search of salvation, what chance was there that his family still endured?

He forced himself to move again, spurred by that vain, selfish hope that his family had been granted the fortune that so many others had been denied. There were more soldiers in the regalia of Farrenhall waiting for Kasara, their numbers equaling the survivors who huddled in their shadow. His people looked more like prisoners, surrounded as they were by men with spears and swords.

The irregular brightness on his right finally caught his eye, and he saw that a vast chamber was carved into the side of the already immense thoroughfare. It opened before the roadway as if it were a stage, the road just an auditorium to gaze upon its spectacle. And maybe it was a stage, for at its heart, fixed between two great braziers that belched smoke into tunnels up above, sat an empty throne of swirling gold, like flashes of sunlight frozen in place. Gathered about it, their silver-crimson armor gleaming in the stark pools of firelight, stood the Myrmidons.

The two groups faced off in silence, the guards never stepping foot off the road, the Myrmidons never straying from the light. Heads turned toward Kasara as she approached, first slowly, one by one, and then in a great, sweeping mass.

Haegar outstripped his escort, racing past Kasara as he made straight for the survivors. His eyes swept the small crowd, darting from one unfamiliar face to the next. None stood out to him. They all had the same hollow eyes, the same broken, exhausted expressions. They blended, bloodied rags and bruised flesh, their faces stubborn masks of disbelief, refusing to accept that refuge had come at last. He could've believed that they were already dead.

And then, as he wandered among them, he saw a flash of dark hair, like a raven's feather adrift over fresh snow. The kind of hair that could never be found in the wilds of Vrusk. "Tayja!" The shout was instinctive, half desperate cry, half gasp of shock.

She was weeping when he reached her. Rala was crying, too. Tayja clutched their daughter to her bosom, and Rala had buried herself in her mother's neck, but he threw his arms around them both. All three of them cried together, then, their sobs cutting through the bitter emptiness that clung to Farrenhall.

He pulled back. Tayja met his eyes. They were hollow. "Makin?" he asked softly. That quiver in his own voice turned his blood to ice. The tears were already flowing. "H-Haza?"

Tayja sank to her knees, where she continued to sob quietly, still clinging to Rala.

Haegar stumbled back, a blade in his heart. *No.* He'd just seen them. Yesterday. Hadn't it been yesterday? *No.* That blade bit deeper, pushing and pushing until it burst through him. *No.* Makin, his son, his firstborn. His greatest treasure. Haza, his brother, who'd once made him laugh as they huddled together in the darkness of their room, mimicking the voices of their parents while they watched them argue from a distance. Haza, a light and warmth in his life, even through the coldest of winters, one he had failed to recognize for so long. His blood. His everything. *No!*

Gone.

He stared down at his wife, at his daughter, but he had no words for them. He had nothing. No comfort, no questions, no answers. His son was dead. He tried to think, tried to reason with himself. It couldn't be real. It couldn't be happening. Not *his* Makin. Beautiful, stubborn boy, so full of life, of laughter. He couldn't be dead.

He screamed. He threw back his head, as everything he'd ever been shattered. Into his wife's arms he fell, and they screamed together. Soon, even strength enough for that vanished. "It should've been me," he whispered as they rocked together. The pain was blinding. "It should've been me. It should've been me."

"I only turned around for a moment," Tayja kept repeating. "He was right there. I swear it, Haegar. On my blood, I swear it. I didn't want to leave him. But the gates opened. I had to get Rala through. I killed our son, Haegar. Damn me, I killed him."

He wasn't sure how long it took, but slow as the thawing Tagalfr, something seized him, something that buried all else. It was anger, he realized. A freezing fury that jolted him to his feet. Tayja reached out for him, his name on her lips, but he didn't have eyes for her anymore. They were fixed now to the throne of Farrenhall, and the man who'd emerged from the darkness beyond it to lower himself onto its purple, cushioned seat.

He'd never seen Kalivaz Varkoth before, but even at a glance, he looked like the sort of man he'd always imagined the Lord of Farrenhall to be—a tall figure dressed in flowing, silken robes, woven layers of resplendent gold and red and silver. At the heart of that finery was a thin, ashen man, his years long spent, his youth vanished. His face was framed by wisps of gray hair, and a crooked nose protruded from a sallow face. The Myrmidons encircled him, standing with their hands draped meaningfully across the hilts of their swords. All but one wore their heavy helms, obscuring their faces from view.

That exception was the Grand-Crusader himself. Berethan Willamere, Valiant Shield of whatever god he proclaimed to follow, looked more statue than man. His pale eyes were empty, emotionless. He watched the crowd but did not seem to really see them. Or, at least, he did not see them as people. They passed over Haegar without recognition, landing on Kasara. And finally, there was a flicker of life as they narrowed.

Kasara moved, her own stare locked on her father. A half dozen men went with her, but the blonde-haired boy hung back, a bow and a loose arrow in his hand. Haegar made himself approach too, ignoring his wife's pleas. Her voice couldn't pierce the glacier of frigid hate that had buried his mind. He had only one goal now. One purpose.

Lord Varkoth stared imperiously down from his throne, a sneer of distaste tickling the corners of his mouth. No doubt he thought himself safe on that throne, surrounded by armored zealots. But Haegar's rage would not be denied. He ached for his axe, but his hands would have to do. He'd throttle the old man, and he'd laugh as he choked his life away. Even as the Myrmidons drove their swords through his back, he would not let go, not until the Lord of Farrenhall had breathed his last, not until he'd joined those he'd betrayed.

"It's finished, father," Kasara said, and her voice boomed through the hall, raised for all the assembly to hear. Guards and refugees alike held their breath, their anxious shuffles audible in the following hush. Only the Myrmidons were unmoved. "It doesn't have to come to bloodshed," she continued. Yet, she drew her sword as she approached, as did the men at her side. She paused with a grimace. "*Further* bloodshed."

"Look at how my daughter humiliates me," came the soft, sneering reply. The quiet that came in its wake seemed far louder than his words, banished only when Varkoth spoke again. "After all I've done for this wretch, after so many years of teaching her the proper path, this is how I am repaid. Mutiny and sabotage. Defiance and treachery."

"The only traitor here is you, Father," Kasara growled, taking another step forward. She stood on the precipice between the road and the chamber, just inches from the firelight. "There is no escaping this justice. I will set things right."

But as she spoke, the Myrmidons suddenly closed ranks, forming a wall of marbled steel between her and her father. They drew their broadswords in a single, startling motion, their faces dark and leering from behind their helms. Veiled by a shield of steel and living flesh, the gnarled man leaned forward from his throne, his eyes burning. "So brazen, girl. You tried this once before, aye? Remind me how it ended."

Haegar came forward, pushing aside a guardsman as he stepped up beside Kasara. Someone tried to grab him, but he shrugged from their grip. "I killed a Myrmidon," he shouted. His voice cracked like thunder. Soldiers rushed to take him by the arms, but as they began to drag him back, the girl shook her head. They released him, and he gave her a grateful nod before he focused again on the Lord of Farrenhall. "I split his skull with my axe. I watched the light leave his eyes. Your men are not immortal. You want to speak of treachery? I will show you the wrath of the Winterwood."

Varkoth sat back on his throne, and for a moment, his nerve wavered. He shrank into his robes, his solitary eye wide and unblinking. But then it narrowed. That scathing heat lashed his words. "Treachery? I wouldn't expect you to understand, farmer. I preserved Vrusk from your rapacious horde. Look at what you've done to my doorstep. Murder and defilement."

An avalanche of hatred slid slowly forward, and Haegar had to seize himself to keep from stepping forward. There were nearly fifty blades between him and the nobleman, and his hand was still empty. "We arrived well before the dead, and you know it, old bastard. You're the protector of the Winterwood, aye? Our liege lord? You left us to be butchered. You did nothing."

Whispers of concern and confusion rose in a hushed flurry as his words floated through the chamber. They came only from the garrison, though. His own people were silent. They had no need to prove what had befallen them. And everyone would know about the dead soon enough, one way or another. Kasara, standing beside him, had turned a shade of deathly white.

But this time, Varkoth didn't waver. Instead, his eyes flicked to his daughter. "Who is this farmer you're letting speak for you? Can't you insult my name with your own tongue, girl?"

"He is Haegar Ruthborne," came the calm, somber voice of Berethan. The Grand-Crusader stepped forward, his eyes, still lacking light or recognition, were locked on him. Lifeless though that face was, he did not hide his fury well. His hand was clamped to the hilt of his sword, and his jaw was stiff as an anvil.

Haegar spat. "So you do remember me, aye?"

The Myrmidon's stare was still flat as his voice. "This man is responsible for the siege on your bridge, my Lord. He is the saboteur that breached the gatehouse. It is true what he said—the blood of my faithful is on his hands."

"A pale shade compared to the crimson that drenches your hands, zealot." Haegar ground his teeth. He could almost feel them cracking. His words came out in a choking gasp. "My…my son is dead. My brother alongside him."

Silence fell over the hall again. Varkoth fidgeted on his throne, but Berethan's expression did not change. Kasara took advantage of the quiet to speak again. "This is what you have done, Father. What *we* have done. Thousands of our own people came to us, seeking aid and asylum from a new enemy. And what did we do? We shut our doors. We turned our backs as they perished. You sent your lapdogs to slaughter them while they battled for their own survival. Thousands came, and how many do you see before you, aye?" She swept a hand back behind her, toward the pitiable huddle of survivors dwelling quietly in the gloom of the thoroughfare.

A swell of excitement rose within Haegar like a gathering wind, mirror to the quiet shifting of the garrison men, and of his own people. They began to stir, their anger mounting. Sparks floating on the wind, and the girl was about to strike them to flame. He saw only crimson. Red flames, red armor, red blood.

Varkoth's face twisted, his fury finally boiling over. He slammed a fist against his throne. "You will not take Farrenhall from me!" he snarled. "I've spent my life protecting this river, and this bloodied wood! You might see me as a monster, but you have not seen what is coming! The Old King…his warning came too late. They… I called the Myrmidons, but…" the man began to deflate again, his rage evaporating as impotently as it had come. "You don't understand. None of you have seen it yet. I know what's coming for us. I have to stop it somehow. Can't let it get across the river."

"I *have* seen it, Father," Kasara said. Another step forward, now into the light, but her sword was lowered, one hand slightly outstretched, as if she might reach through the wall of steel and take the old man's hand. "I fought them. What did the Old King tell you? Maybe there's still time to help our people. Please, Father. What did he say? Who are we facing?"

Varkoth stared down at his daughter, his chest now heaving. "I… the Old King…he said…" But then he seemed to remember himself. He stood and thrust a finger down at her. "I did what was right for Farrenhall. For all of Vrusk!"

"You sacrificed us," Haegar snarled.

"It's all right to be afraid, Father," Kasara pressed, "but what was done here these last few nights cannot be forgiven. We turned our backs on our people, and many are dead because of it. Because of you. Do what is right; abdicate your position and call off the Myrmidons."

Varkoth's face contorted again, and as Haegar watched, he could see the man couldn't be changed. The Lord of Farrenhall was immutable, as remorseless as the river he ruled over. He could see no wrong in his actions, and he would not be convinced of it. Haegar had no pity for the old man. He'd break his neck and cast him into the Tagalfr and enjoy watching him sink.

"Abdicate?" Varkoth scoffed. "Abandon my throne? My position? Girl, I've ruled these lands for forty years. Should I give it to you?"

"Aye, and why not?" asked the blonde guardsmen. The boy was paler than Kasara, but he had his bow raised, his arrow half-nocked. Though his voice shook, his hands were steady. Rather than shrink under all the eyes now on him, he seemed to swell. "What good have you done for us, aye? You've sat there and supped 'off the teat of this land from winter 'till spring all your life. The Winterwood never asked for anything in return. Until today. Look at what you've made us a part of."

Kasara glanced back at the boy, giving him a determined nod. "We do not need to kill each other. The dead are at our doorstep even as we speak. That's why we must—"

"The dead?" Varkoth suddenly shrieked, his manic voice ringing harsh as steel against steel. "What dead? It's all lies! None of it is real!" The man pressed himself back into his throne, hands gripping white-knuckled as if trying to push himself right through the metal.

"Our fallen," Haegar shouted. "The animals, the people, of the Winterwood. They march to the will of something terrible. But you know about it, aye? You left us to face it alone. The dead are here for all of us. Our dead." The survivors behind him gave rise to a concerted mutter. Many began to weep, but others shouted of the horrors they'd witnessed. The guardsmen quailed to hear them, and even some of the Myrmidons exchanged hesitant glances. Berethan only narrowed his eyes.

"It can't be real!" Varkoth's eye was popping from his head. He stared at something above, something veiled by the darkness of the chimneys. "It's not real." A hand shot forward, a gnarled finger thrust like a spear at Haegar. "This man speaks nonsense! He's a backwater peasant, the dregs of an otherwise proud people. Worms from a forgotten land, aye? The dead have not come to Farrenhall."

"Liar!" someone from the crowd screamed. The survivors were roiling now, their angry shouts ringing down the thoroughfare, growing louder and louder with each echo. A sound rose above it all, like the slow rumble of distant thunder, as if the Gated Bridge itself joined in the protest. Something tugged at Haegar's vision, from deep down the thoroughfare. A flash of red light. *Where have I seen…?*

"Berethan!" Kasara's voice cut through the madness. "Put an end to this. Please. Can't you see he's succumbed to insanity? Don't let this go any further."

"I am bound to my Faith Price," Berethan replied. "I serve—"

"Curdle all that!" Kasara roared. "I need you to do this for me. You already betrayed it once; just one more time, Berethan. Please, help me!"

Haegar expected to see nothing from the Grand Crusader. Instead, he saw naked fear. Berethan took a slight, hesitant step back. The other Myrmidons stared at him like wolves suddenly relieved of their leashes. Kasara's own face was expectant. Almost proud, somehow. Haegar didn't understand.

Steel hissed in deadly warning as Berethan drew his sword. He planted his helm upon his head, and his face was swallowed by shadow. The Myrmidons already had swords bared, but they turned on their commander now, their steps slow, hungry.

"Oathbreaker," one of the knights hissed—he recognized Joros' voice. "Twice you forced us to retreat from certain victory. Will you still deny it? Here, before your entire command? Tell us, Lord Varkoth, was it you who ordered us back? Who told us to allow these peasants inside?"

"I gave no such order," snarled Varkoth.

"The Cardinals will have your head, Berethan," Joros spat, stepping toward the Grand-Crusader. "Your skin will fashion banners for the summit of the Highest Path."

Berethan turned calmly toward the throne. "I am no Oathbreaker," he said quietly. "By your command, Lord Varkoth, and yours only. Give the order, and we will purge these heathens from your halls." His head turned toward the man shrunken on his throne.

Kasara staggered. "Berethan…?" it was a hopeless whisper.

The Lord of Farrenhall stepped down from his throne, coming up beside Berethan. He seemed more himself, suddenly, a wild tempest in his eyes, a thrashing, grinding fury that cut through the fog of madness. "You call me murderer, daughter, yet you bring violence and death to my own gates? Filling my

head with these wretched stories? You are not my daughter."
Spittle flew from his mouth and his hands clutched at nothing,
as if seeking to lunge forward and seize her, but he remained
behind his steel wall. "You pin your woes on me, but the only
troublemaker I see is you. Tell me, where are the dead you speak
of? I only see death in your eyes. Your mother would throw
herself into the Tagalfr to see the wretched, craven bitch you've
become."

Silence followed. Haegar pushed his way past Kasara. But
before he could take another step, Berethan moved, putting
himself between Haegar and the maddened old man. Varkoth
lingered just behind, his hollow eyes still burning. The
Myrmidon's silver and crimson armor flashed in the torchlight.
No one seemed to breathe.

And then, through the quiet, came a soft sound. A steady
echo, resonating along the road from the way he and Kasra had
come. Slowly, heads began to turn, and he made himself look
away from his foe, toward the sound of shuffling steps.

A single man approached, slipping between the broad pools
of firelight shining from the pillars. Haegar knew what it was, but
he could not bring himself to look away. The man dragged one
foot behind him, twisted about the wrong way. An arm had been
severed at the elbow; the stump marked by the clean precision of
a sword's blade. Haunted, unblinking eyes leered out of a pale,
emotionless face. Yet, still as that face was, he felt a familiar heat
in that stare. A thinking, silent malice. A hatred for all living
things.

The dead had come to Farrenhall.

A sharp *snap* sundered the stillness of it all. Haegar flinched
as the arrow made impact. But the shambling corpse did not fall,
nor did it even stumble. In truth, he realized, it hadn't been hit at
all. Then came a gurgle of frothing spit and blood, and the Lord

of Farrenhall sank to his knees. The Myrmidons stepped aside, finally rattled, as Varkoth teetered back, showing all the arrow now sprouting from his ribs. A crimson pool seeped around the shaft, and Varkoth's back arched so far that he fell, propped only by his elbows. And there he froze, facing the roof, the fire in his eye extinguished.

"Bjern!" Kasara screamed. She rushed her father, dropping to her knees alongside him. Behind her, the long-haired boy slowly lowered his bow, a look of shock staining his sweat-slick face.

"The Faith Price is broken!" came the booming roar of Berethan. "The words of Kalivaz Varkoth are hollowed. Avenge our fallen blood; kill the faithless and claim a step on the Highest Path for every head that rolls!"

The Myrmidons needed no further encouragement. Like a pack of wolves, they lunged into the garrison ranks. Haegar, who was staring blankly at Varkoth's corpse, finally blinked. The glaciers of hatred he'd been carrying melted in a flash. In their place were deep, empty pits. And terror for his family. *I have to get them out!* He spun about and ran as the Myrmidons ruthlessly began to butcher the men closest to them.

But not all turned to the task of vengeance. Joros threw himself at Berethan, and the Grand-Crusader brought up his broadsword to parry the man's overhead swing. Two more Myrmidons came at their commander from his sides, swinging for his flanks.

Haegar gave no further thought to whatever an Oathbreaker or his fate was, drawn instead to the Myrmidons assailing the garrison. They were like rabid hounds; hounds whose leashes had been cut. The garrison tried to meet them with a charge, spears lowered, swords raised, but flashing broadswords swept through them like fine axes. The grove seemed to fall in just one swoop.

Through the unfolding chaos, he caught sight of Kasara, standing over the body of her father. She had her sword drawn as a Myrmidon advanced on her.

He did not remain to see the result of the onslaught. He sprinted through the crowd, butting past Bjern and other archers who were loosening shafts over his head. He did not fear them, though, nor did he fear the bite of a sword on his heels. He was failing again. He gave himself to only one thought, one purpose—find his family. Get them to safety.

They were so close. The road ahead led only one direction; westward, to the other side of the river, and the safety of the hinterlands of Vrusk. They could escape and leave the Myrmidons, the dead, the Winterwood, all far behind. All they had to do was run.

"Tayja!" he screamed, but his voice was one of a hundred screaming voices. The ringing of steel against steel echoed harshly through the chamber. He pushed aside frightened faces and ignored hands that clutched at him as he passed.

Then he noticed the dead men. One had become many. Those the Myrmidons had slaughtered were now coming at them from behind, and the knights suddenly found themselves hemmed on both sides by the living and the dead. He could no longer see Kasara. He ground his teeth and left them all to their fates. There was nothing he could do. And in some small way, he felt a measure of satisfaction. Garrison or Myrmidon, they'd brought this on themselves.

"Haegar!" The sound of his own name made him whip about, and he saw Tayja. Relief seared his mind as he raced to her. Seizing her and Rala made him understand the true horror of what was unfolding around him. Every guard and refugee the Myrmidons cut down, every one of their own that fell, only bloated the foes they were facing. *This is insanity. This cannot be where my family dies.*

Everywhere he looked, he saw lifeless, burning eyes, dead hands seizing other refugees, dragging them down in screaming heaps. The wretched, terrifying song of battle played through Farrenhall. He thought he'd go mad with it. Everything was falling apart. But there was Tayja, his beautiful Tayja, sweat soaked through her shirt, her eyes terrified. And Rala, his daughter, his world, huddled in her arms. A single eye stared back at him, veiled by the crook of her mother's arm, questioning and frightened.

He knew what that eye asked. All the horrid questions that had piled upon his soul since the night the wolf came to Palvast. He didn't think he could ever answer them. *I'm sorry, Makin. I'm sorry, brother. I...*

"Run," he said, pulling his wife by her arm. He didn't wait, he just dragged her until she started running. "Keep going. Get away from the fighting."

"Where are we going?" Tayja screamed, throwing a wild glance over her shoulder. Her eyes only widened.

"It's not far," he panted. Together, they pushed through the crowd. He felt like he was trying to fight a river, one that was dragging him back into the carnage. "The end of the bridge. Vrusk is on the other side. We're almost there."

They broke out the other side of the crowd, but he had to strike a Vruskman, sending the boy sprawling. He felt no remorse, only checked to see if Rala was still clutched safely in her mother's arms.

Others rushed ahead of him, running into the waiting darkness. Three Myrmidons leapt upon them, cutting them down as fled. *We have no choice but to run.* He waited for a moment, watching until the slain began to stir, then pulled Tayja forward again. Just as the dead leapt upon their killers, they rushed by.

A man stumbled ahead of them, wearing gray garrison armor. A sword was impaled through his chest, and yet he still stood. Hollow, hateful eyes met Haegar's. He held out his hand to hold Tayja back and balled his other fist. How long until dawn? Only the sunrise would stop the dead. There wouldn't be a single living creature in Farrenhall, soon enough, and he had no weapons to fight them.

A flash of silver. A toppling head. The unliving man collapsed in a twitching heap as a towering Myrmidon came past. There was another Myrmidon too, his own sword working in wide, terrible sweeps. The knights were…still battling? It was Berethan, then, him and Joros, pushing each other deeper down the hall, careless of the madness spawning around them. The Grand-Crusader's blade was red, Joros' still clean. *None of this matters.*

Quietly, quickly, he seized his wife again, and they hurried down the roadway, rushing into its long, empty throat. He looked back, but the Myrmidons had not followed them, nor, it seemed, had any of the dead.

He didn't look over his shoulder again. Instead, he ran. He ran as if the dead were right behind him in a snarling, snapping pack. Yet for all the clamor the echoing battle commanded, it soon faded into silence, and they were swallowed by the long and heavy darkness of the roadway.

Eventually, there was nothing but crackling torches for company, along with their own heavy footsteps. He did not let them slow, and in turn, Tayja did not loose her grip on their daughter. The pillars of Farrenhall rose high and quiet around them, holding the world aloft.

He braced himself for something to appear ahead of them.

Corpses slinking out of the dark, a Myrmidon to appear out of the many unseen tunnels he knew were winding their way around them. But there was nothing. The road was empty. There wasn't anyone following behind them, not even other refugees.

Were we the only ones to get through? It was a nauseating thought, but he could imagine how easy it might've been to be caught in that twisting, fighting mass. As Myrmidons and guardsmen slew each other, their victims merely rose to rejoin the onslaught. Such an overwhelming enemy could not be fought. Both sides would be destroyed by this nameless hatred. How could men adapt to an unkillable, ever-replenishing foe? The Gated Bridge would fall tonight.

In holding back whatever knowledge he had of this calamity, Kalivaz Varkoth had damned both his followers and enemies—and even his own daughter—to a grim death.

"Stop thinking about it," he growled to himself. He had to keep his eyes on the road ahead, and the safety on the other side.

"I can't," Tayja hiccupped. Her strangled sob bounced off the stones around them. "I'm sorry, Haegar. I tried to find them. Please, believe me. I looked. I lost them, Haegar. I… you should leave me, Haegar. I lost them…"

He pushed their faces from his mind. He wanted to tell her it wasn't her fault, that he loved her. He wanted to fall and weep wordlessly. But he couldn't do any of those things. His tongue had swollen his mouth shut, and only his intense focus kept his feet moving. If he wavered for even a moment, they'd all stop. And he wasn't sure they'd be able to start again. He had no reply for her.

Just how long was this bloodied bridge? Their rush seemed to last hours. Everything looked the same—walls and arches of endless green stone after endless green stone. The pillars were unchanging, as were the flickering braziers mounted upon them, and the rhythmic echoes of their footsteps was a steady beat that never wavered.

At last, a different sort of light appeared ahead of them, gray and distant. It was faint, near imperceptible, but his heart skipped. It could only be Farrenhall's western gates, standing open to unveil the moonlight on a night without snow, a night that lay upon the safety of the hinterlands.

"Not much further," he whispered. "Not much further." Tayja stared ahead, stone-faced. Rala cried softly.

Haegar paused only when a new shape appeared ahead of them. A figure, standing beside a length of chain. That chain ran upward to where a portcullis stood raised above the hallway, its bars like iron teeth, waiting to snap shut. The soldier turned on them, her limp evident as she stepped forward, holding aloft a familiar crest-marked sword.

"Kasara," he rasped, struggling to compose himself as he and his family approached the young girl. "How did you…?" Had she run ahead? When? "Please…" Her sword was held to the single chain holding the portcullis aloft, like a knife to a throat. "I don't want to hurt you. We just want to get through."

The young lord's face was drenched in blood, her eyes shining through like pale gray stars. Her chest flared with heavy, rapid breaths, and her knuckles were white around her sword. Blood marred the crested-fish seal adorning her breastplate.

"We didn't start this war," he growled, watching that sword warily as he inched his family closer to the iron maw of the portcullis. "We didn't want any of this." He didn't want to kill her. He didn't want to see another drop of blood spilled. *I'm so, so tired.* "Please…we just want to go by…"

Kasara met his eyes. Her expression beneath that crimson sheen was focused. "Hurry on, then," she said quietly. "I'm not here to stop you."

"What... What are you doing here, then?"

The girl nodded back the way they'd come. "I came to make sure no one else follows you. You're a good man, Haegar Ruthborne. I'm glad to see your family made it into Farrenhall." She smiled softly at Tayja and Rala. "Perhaps, if I had acted sooner, you might still..." Abashed eyes fell away. "The actions of Farrenhall cannot be forgiven."

Anger flared again, but only for a moment. Then, he found himself regarding the girl with pity. She was so young. Could he have acted any better in her stead? "Aye, maybe not," he muttered. "But you stood up and fought back. We're alive right now because of you, Kasara. We owe you a debt of blood."

Kasara shook her head. "You owe me nothing, except, maybe a promise? When you get to the other side, go to Savisdale. Tell Vrusk what's happened here. Go to Havasa and Joromor, if you must. This cannot happen again. And spit in the Old King's eye for me."

He fumbled for a response. The burden of another responsibility now hung heavy across his neck. Her words left no space for interpretation; no one else would be leaving Farrenhall. "Why don't you come with us? We can travel together. We'll make quick pace. Besides, the nobles would be much quicker to trust the word of a Varkoth than a Ruthborne, aye?"

The girl turned away. "Aye, well, they'll have to listen to a Ruthborne, because you're all they have. I won't be coming with you. I can already hear them."

"Hear them...?" Haegar trailed off when he realized he could hear it, too. From down the dark reaches of the thoroughfare came a clanging echo, the sound of metal sabatons coming steadily closer.

"Hurry," Kasara hissed. "Get through, quickly!"

Haegar swept his family beneath the barred teeth of the

portcullis and into the growing light on the other side. The western courtyard awaited, and then the shore. Kasara turned and loosened a flurry of blows against the chain. They rang out sharply and Rala screamed in protest, but Kasara did not relent her assault.

In time with the seventh blow, a single Myrmidon emerged into the torchlight. The giant seemed easily twice the monster as any of the unliving. His marbled silver-red armor flashed and danced in the torchlight, the shining steel of his bared broadsword smeared the same colors. The man walked with a limp, and Haegar could see a bite in his left leg where sword or spear had carved away armor. Three arrows jutted from his breastplate, too, but they didn't seem to have pierced flesh. His long, flowing red cape still trailed across the ground behind him.

Haegar felt locked in time, like the world around him had turned to ice, Razzador holding its breath as all things dared not to move…except for the Myrmidon. He came closer, sword raised before him, dragging his wounded leg. Behind that dark helmet, fury flared in his eyes.

Kasara's attack never slowed. Her sword rang again and again as she threw her weight against the chain. The Myrmidon limped closer, but there was a sudden, sharp *snap*, and Haegar exhaled. The portcullis fell with a mournful groan, and thick, grated bars now stood between his family and Kasara.

The girl straightened, panting. She stared first at the severed chain now dangling above her, then at the twisted, mangled sword still gripped in her hand. The Myrmidon's labored steps echoed all around them. She looked up, her expression still serene. "Run," she said. "Don't look back."

Haegar seized his family and obeyed. They dashed toward that growing light, and he obeyed her final command. He had to put his hope ahead of them, in the promised safety of the other side, and in that a lone girl and a single portcullis would hold for long enough.

They had to hold.

Chapter Twenty
The Summit

Oathbreaker. The word rang clearly through Berethan's mind like the Bells of the Precepts singing through the Mountain of the Highest Path. Only this was no pious call to worship. This was the last word of a dying man, spat out in a haze of blood. An accusation, whipping him every time it echoed through his skull.

Oathbreaker. The greatest of shames. The unforgivable sin. Of all the Highest God's teachings, only one came without question—a Myrmidon must obey. And now he'd broken a Faith Price twice. He was a fool. He remembered too well how his first lapse of faith had ended. He'd thought he'd be safe in the wild southern jungles of Havasa, as far from the Grey Cardinals as one could go save leaping into the sea. But they'd found him. And then they'd taken from him what they called, "His fount of weakness."

How could he have done it again? Why was he so weak?

Berethan stumbled down the long, empty road of the Gated Bridge, the sound of his own panting bouncing all around him alongside the rhythmic chant of *Oathbreaker, Oathbreaker* in his mind. His sword, coated with both the blood of the unholy and the venerated, he carried at his side. His leg, where Joros' blade had bit him, dragged behind him.

The pain was manageable. He'd tasted worse nearly fifteen years ago, when he'd taken an arrow in the throat at the Siege of Fire-River Knoll. Then, it had felt like he was drowning. Drowning in fire. This was nothing more than a throbbing inconvenience, which he yanked along behind him. There wasn't time enough to worry about it.

"Oathbreaker," Joros damned him again. Berethan had known his knights already suspected him of heresy. The day of the attack in the courtyard, when he'd first ordered the Myrmidons to retreat into Farrenhall, he'd known they would start to whisper. But he hadn't broken his oath in that moment. *I didn't. I...I only worked around it.*

But tonight...on the rooftop, there was no denying it. He'd broken the Faith Price. He'd looked into Kasara's eyes and seen another girl's instead. *Ainara...my flower of the mountains...I thought I could try again, didn't I? I thought I could make it right. Save her, this time.* He really was a fool. He'd broken his first Faith Price to marry the woman he'd loved, and he'd broken his second for a girl who bore a passing resemblance to his daughter. *Weak fool.* By sparing the lives of those wretched woodsmen, allowing them into Farrenhall, he'd betrayed his oaths. The laws of the Highest Path had only one answer for such a crime—desecration. Death was too soft a punishment for such failed men. They would, as the Cardinals put it, be relieved of their weakness.

When he closed his eyes, he saw the cabin he'd built reduced to a charred ruin. Their bodies had still been aside. The Cardinals had been waiting for him to return from his hunting, them and a hundred Myrmidons, eager to reveal that he'd been absolved of his distractions. Joros had been brash, turning to the sword instead of the justice of the Highest Path. But maybe he'd realized Berethan had no intention of facing such punishment again.

Joros was dead now. His entire command was dead. More fatal sins on his soul. He was damned, now. Oathbreakers were buried beneath the roots of the Highest Peak, as far from the Path as any man could fall.

Yet...

The Faith Price was shattered. Kalivaz Varkoth was dead, and the bindings that held the Myrmidons died with him. That was the holy law, without exception, passed down to the Grey Cardinals by the Highest God himself. Under normal circumstances, Berethan would return his command to Joromor, where he'd be reported for heresy, his title passed on to someone more worthy, and his men sent to fulfill a new Faith Price. It was only then that the God of the Highest Path would be made aware of his crimes, and he would answer for them when they met on the Mountain.

Except all the other Myrmidons were dead. Those... monsters. They'd overwhelmed the bridge fighters, both his own knights and Varkoth's own garrison. He'd rarely witnessed a butchery so thorough. What remnants were still fighting in the halls behind him would soon be swallowed. He hadn't believed it when Kasara spoke of the dead. He still wasn't sure he did. But with no witnesses to his breach of oath, with the holder of his Faith Price dead, he could simply...ignore his sins, couldn't he? No one would tell the Cardinals. No one would tell the Highest God. Berethan could take his second failure into the grave and continue to climb the Path.

Yes, that was what he would do. Once he was free of the bridge, he would ride with all haste to the Mountain and inform them of the tragedy that had unfolded. If anyone ever came south to question it, they would find no one who could deny his story. *I am faithful,* he assured himself. *This was a momentary lapse in judgment. I climb the Highest Path. I am a Myrmidon.*

I buried them beside the river. Ainara always loved the river. Mella and I would hold to each other as we watched her swim. We… Stop.

He was not that man anymore. He had never been that man. Kasara's unflinching love for her people had blinded him to his purpose. He would not allow himself to be hurt.

Then he saw Kasara before him, and his heart stopped in his chest. Her eyes widened and she redoubled her assault on a chain holding aloft a great portcullis, which spanned the breadth of the tunnel. His gaze passed beyond her, settling on a Vruskman, and the woman beside him clutching a small child. His grip tightened about the hilt of his sword as he recognized Haegar Ruthborne.

Heathen. Blasphemer. Berethan's blood boiled at the sight. That infidel was the source of all this trouble. If he had not come to Farrenhall, if he had not stirred that rabble to madness, then none of this would've passed. *I could've been a father again. I could've made it right, this time.* But these worthless forest folk had taken his chance from him. There could be no fate for them but death, and their bones would lie as foundation for the Mountain, their flesh salt for the vales. Their souls would be chained within the Mountain's heart, beyond the scope of the pinnacle and lost in darkness forever.

The chain gave way with a sudden snap, and the portcullis fell, closing off the roadway. Berethan paused, seized by lashes of fear. His prey was lost. Haegar and his family were on the wrong side of the gate. Would they run to the Cardinals? Reveal his sin? It was why he'd ordered the Myrmidons to attack, even after the Faith Price had dissolved. He would leave no witnesses to his sin. But now they would escape if he didn't catch them. He had to get past the gate and…Kasara. She was still on his side of the portcullis. Had she meant to do that?

"Run," Kasara said to Ruthborne. "Don't look back."

As she turned, Berethan stopped, lowering his sword. *She means to fight me?* Haegar turned and took his family, and they swiftly vanished down the hall. He narrowed his eyes. *No matter.* They could not get far, not in the snow, in the dark. He was ready to be finished with this grisly business, he realized. It would be well to return to the mountains for a time… He could reflect on the Highest Path, perhaps pursue quiet, private atonement.

All he had to do was bury one final sin.

"Why did you do it?" the girl demanded, her voice heavy and breathless. "You'd already sided with me, Berethan. Why can't you help me? Why can't you do what's right?"

Berethan stared down at her. *Stake my soul, she looks just like Ainara.* That determination, that indomitable spirit, it was all just as he remembered. *I can't do this again.* He had to finish this. Then he'd be free. "What does it matter?" he asked.

"Corpses are inside the walls," Kasara hissed. "*Walking* corpses. They mean to kill us all."

"It is not my war," he said. He wasn't entirely sure what he'd witnessed in the great hall. This new, nameless foe was formidable, but it wasn't well to dwell on the origins of such things. The eldritch magics were a forbidden subject, something even the most sacred Writings spoke of little. "The troubles of this land mean nothing to the followers of the Highest Path. The Mountain will protect us."

Kasara stepped forward, her face darkening with rage. "You're not in Joromor, are you? Damn you. My people are still dying. My father is dead, and you can't speak to me as a person. You're a bloodied Myrmidon, nothing else."

It was what he'd been telling himself, but hearing it from her was like a knife in his heart. *Why? Why couldn't I be weaker, for her?* "We're finished here, Lordling. Let me pass."

For a moment, Kasara's mouth worked. The rage vanished

from her face, and in its place was something that put another arrow in his throat. Disappointment. "I don't understand you," she said. "Twice, you've helped me. You helped me preserve some remnant of my people. But when I needed you most, when we were right at the end of it all, you betrayed me. My father is dead. My garrison, my…m-my friends… All you had to do was stand aside. I would've done the rest, Berethan. That's all you had to do."

Berethan found himself swallowing. "It would've been pointless," he said. "The other Myrmidons… You do not understand what is done to Oathbreakers. They would not have betrayed their Faith Price, just because I commanded it. Even after your father was dead, they had the right to claim vengeance for their slain brethren. The outcome would've been the same, only I'd be dead alongside your father."

"You think that absolves you?" she demanded. "You think that makes it right? You still have a responsibility to choose what is right, no matter what it costs you. Do you think I wanted to do any of this? I could've let those people die out there, and I…I'd still have everyone I love!" Her voice shook the stones. Tears painted streaks down her bloodied face. "How dare you, Berethan. I trusted you."

Berethan let his rage rise. He needed it to burn away his shame. Only hate. That's all he could let himself feel. *Oathbreaker. Coward.* No! He was the Grand-Crusader of the Myrmidons. He was unimpeachable. "You mistake a holy man for a fool in need of a sermon. I should not have broken my oath for an infidel like you, Lordling. I was bound to serve your father. You cannot understand that because you have no true virtue. No faith. You are nothing to me."

"You're lying," she whispered. "Do you love me, the same way you loved your daughter?"

He gaped at her. Guilt was a twisting arrow. Two graves by the river. A woman who'd convinced him to abandon the Highest Path. A love unlike anything he'd ever felt before. And a little girl with wild, determined eyes. He used to hold her in his arms, hold her so tight that nothing could ever hurt her. The smell of burning corpses.

Men did not leave the Highest Path. The Grey Cardinals had found him. *"Destroy the fount of weakness,"* he heard them say, *"and a man will find his faith again."* Berethan had come too late to save his wife, his daughter. What choice had he had but to go back? To take up a Myrmidon's sword again, try to absolve himself of his sins? They'd convinced him of the truth. He'd betrayed ten years of faith for a woman's smile. Then he'd spent another twenty in the service of her killers.

"Say it," Kasara demanded.

"I did it again." Berethan laughed mirthlessly. He really was a fool. "I'm sorry. My weakness brought this upon you."

The girl shook her head, tears still flowing. "I...I don't understand you."

"I'm sorry." *Oathbreaker.* It had to stop. Once this girl was gone, the whispers would vanish, wouldn't they? The secret would die here. "I must pass."

"I won't let you kill any more of them," Kasara snarled. "The bloodshed ends here. With us."

"You're a fool if you believe that." *It never stops. It never would.* He reached down and drew his shortsword, then turned it about to proffer it to her. "You don't have to fight me," he said. "We know how this battle goes. Remember my first lesson. But... if you mean to fight, I would have you do it with a proper blade."

Kasara hesitated, staring at the weapon.

"Take it," he said. "If you mean to die, die with honor."

The girl met his eyes again, searching for something.

Whatever it was, she didn't find it. She tossed aside her ruined blade and took his sword. She stepped back a pace, out of his reach, but she had precious few steps left before she'd be forced against the portcullis. Kasara breathed out slowly, raising her new sword and falling into a fighting stance, just as he'd taught her. Her eyes were furious.

This is all my fault. "Kasara. Let this grim business be finished. When you see the Highest God, tell him of your faith." He suspected it was greater than any he'd ever known.

"Tell him of your love, instead," she spat. Then her eyes flicked to one side, glancing behind him. Her features paled, and he took it as the look of a man who saw certain death. There was a sound, something like thunder, but he thought it must be the hammering of his own heart, urging him forward. He took the first step.

She rushed him, slashing with her blade. Berethan danced back, preventing the girl from slipping past him. Even with his wounded leg, he was quick, and he parried the blow. Catching her second swing, he forced her back again.

Kasara bared her teeth in a wordless snarl. She came again, swinging for his wounded leg. Berethan spun his broadsword with both hands, bringing it up with a harsh *clang* as it wrenched her blade aside. Kasara didn't falter, melting into her next, lightning-fast swing. Berethan swung for her head, instead, but cleaved only empty air. She stumbled back against the portcullis.

He drove for her middle, but she dropped away, dodging a blow that struck the gate with an echoing shudder. Kasara ducked under his arm, seeing her avenue of escape, but he spun with her and lashed out again with a wide, rending swipe. Blood spattered the wall. Her body slid to the floor.

Berethan took a single, quiet breath. He could hardly bring himself to look down at the girl at his feet, who was gasping softly, her eyes wide and bulging. Kasara clutched at the ruin of her chest, where blood was bubbling up through the rent metal of her breastplate. He kept watch, all while thunder played like a phantom, building drum, as the girl's spasms grew slower and slower. When they finally stilled, Berethan sheathed his sword and bowed his head.

Oathbreaker. The guilt did not disappear. Berethan's eyes snapped open, startled by its continued existence. He stared down at the girl, the source of all his faithlessness, and felt...nothing different. Fear still seized him, and in truth, it came upon him now stronger than ever before. It gripped him, choked him, made him tremble in his armor even as he stood victorious.

It was never going to leave, he realized. The guilt, the terror, the very eye of the God of the Highest Path, all fell against him now. Berethan sank to his knees. He wanted to hold her, like he'd once held Ainara. He wanted to scream, to beg her to speak. Why? Why had this happened again?

Oathbreaker. Traitor. Coward. Faithless. An endless cascade of thunder.

Berethan pulled himself to his feet, struggling for air. He had to think. There had to be a solution. He had to- he paused mid-thought and glanced down. His armor was vibrating against his skin. That thunder wasn't just in his head.

He whirled about and saw the vast horde that now clogged the road. A shambling army was surging down the hall, bearing down on him. He saw familiar faces. Guardsmen, refugees, even Myrmidons in gleaming silver and red, all rushing his way, their blood-soaked blades bare. A new terror suddenly supplanted the first, ending a reign that had endured only seconds. *This* was true fear, etched into unholy eyes. Gaping, unblinking eyes. Eyes of smoldering malice and hunger, all fixed upon him.

There was no time to fight. He had to run. Berethan turned

again, rushing the portcullis. He could lift it and hurry through. He could- he stumbled with a yelp, nearly falling, and glanced back to see a hand around his ankle. The eyes of his daughter, staring up at him, held nothing but hate. They saw him for what he really was, what he'd always been.

Oathbreaker. The justice of the Highest Path has found me, at last.

Berethan wrenched his sword from its sheathe and cut the hand away, but the sea of bodies crashed into him. He grunted as he was thrown against the iron gate. His sword was pulled from his grasp, so he began to lash out, kicking and hitting at the hands now grabbing at him. He drove ironclad fists into the squirming mass, and each blow crushed bone and sprayed blood. But they kept coming, pulling at his armor. He could feel them digging deeper and deeper, ripping it away piece by piece. He begged the portcullis to fall, but it did not give way, no matter how hard the horde shoved him against it. He thrashed and struck and killed wherever he could, but the writhing fingers only pushed on.

And when they finally found flesh, he began to scream.

The gates of Farrenhall stood open. The crashing and churning of the Tagalfr, the smell of fresh snow, the sight of a sky tinged pink and umber—all greeted Haegar as he stumbled out into the open, tugging Tayja and Rala along with him.

His heart was hammering, and his knees wobbled with a worrying fluidity. But he held his family close. He kept them moving. They emerged into a sight that was eerily familiar; Farrenhall's western side had a courtyard much like the one they'd first come to, only this one was empty of wreckage and blood. No ruined carts and makeshift battering rams, no frightened men with pleading eyes, no Myrmidons in shining armor.

There were only dark stones, making up silent and empty walls laden with piles of snow. Haegar stared up at the sky, disbelieving, as he led his family slowly forward. The bite of the cold was strangely welcome, as were the twinkling faces of the Seventeen Stars above as they began to fade. For a time, he had been sure he'd never see them again.

Tayja held onto him, and when Rala whimpered softly, she began to hum quietly. Haegar found his breathing slowed as he listened to his wife. Ahead of him, he saw two shadows come past, one with an excited leap, the other with his head buried in a book. Those shadows moved in time to the tune until they passed through the final set of gates, then vanished.

Once they were through the courtyard, the wind whipped up around them, and Haegar extended his cloak around Tayja and Rala. Ahead of them, half buried in the snow, was a straight, cobblestone road cutting its way up and over a series of huddled hills and into the darkness of the world beyond. There wasn't a single tree to be seen. He felt a wordless sorrow, but he never slowed. He wouldn't stop again.

Behind them, the Tagalfr rumbled ceaselessly, and Farrenhall sat dark and quiet over it, forever watchful. Beyond them both, cresting above the Winterwood, the first rays of sunlight cut their way westward, and the road ahead became clear.

THE END

More From Dreamsphere Books

Realms of Valeron
Alison Cybe

When Roka joined the Realms of Valeron, he was a fledgling elven cleric with only a minor healing spell and a dingy brown robe to his name. But that was just fine, since it was the hottest fantasy MMORPG, with over a million players, and Roka could not resist the allure of this rich, bright fantasy world, eccentric NPCs, and ravenous monsters.

And best of all, he met his friends—a wild and eccentric band of misfits who would change his life forever!

Join Roka and his newfound guild as they face devastating Razor-Squirrels, confront the Labyrinths of Ancient Storylines, and rush to max level in order to take part in end-game content (while probably not reading any of the quest text as they go!). But the real treasure that they find isn't the Bejewelled Anklets of Monster-Commanding or even the mythical Pointy Stick—it's the friendship they make along the way.

Enter the Realms of Valeron, a tale of high humor and eager adventuring like nothing before!

Available in paperback and ebook

More From Dreamsphere Books

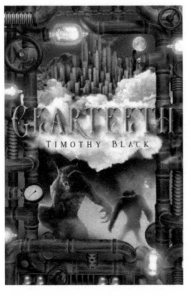

Gearteeth
Timothy Black

On the brink of humanity's extinction, Nikola Tesla and a mysterious order of scientists known as the Tellurians revealed a bold plan to save a world ravaged by a disease that turned sane men into ravenous werewolves: the uninfected would abandon the Earth's surface by rising up in floating salvation cities, iron and steel metropolises that carried tens of thousands of refugees above the savage apocalypse.

Twenty years later, only one salvation city remains aloft, while the beasts still rule the world below. Time has taken its toll on the miraculous machinery of the city, and soon the last of the survivors will plummet to their doom. But when Elijah Kelly, a brakeman aboard the largest of the city's Thunder Trains, is infected by the werewolf virus, he discovers a secret world of lies and horrific experiments that hide the disturbing truth about the Tellurians.

When the beast in his blood surges forth, Elijah must choose between the lives of those he loves, and the city that is humanity's last hope of survival.

Available in paperback and ebook